Falling for London

Falling for London

LJ. Diva

★ Royal Star Publishing ★

R.S.P
Royal Star Publishing

Dedications

To those who inspired the characters in the book, the music I sang, and the actors I used, you know who you are because I mentioned you…thank you for the inspiration you gave me.

Prologue

How do you stop the pain?

How do you recover from death?

Someone tell me because I don't know.

How do you stop the pain of death?

How do you survive death?

Good? Well? Badly?

Death is unsurvivable. Unrecoverable. The pain. The fear. The nightmares. Jack Hammer going off in your head twenty-four seven. You become insane. Living on that island called Insanity. Is there a manual on how to survive death? Does it tell you how to be happy after it? How to ignore the pain and heartache? I wish someone would tell me coz I don't know how to survive death. There's no book. No brochure. No manual.

No. No fucking manual on how to deal with surviving death.

No. No fucking manual at all.

Chapter 1

Here's to another day as a starving writer.

Well…okay, not starving. In fact, I eat quite well. And I was making a bit of a joke. Guess it fell flat! Flat like my publishing career which seems to be going nowhere. But let me get back to the point I was making.

Another day as a *struggling* writer.

Okay, we'll try that one. Sitting here, staring at the laptop for hours each day. Trolling through as many web pages as possible, trying to find another publisher or agent to send my new manuscript to. Deleting emails from those who have said no, crossing them off my list, and seeing that list grow smaller and smaller, wondering if all the months and years I've been doing this is worth it.

Bring bringgg. Bring bringgg.

My hands absentmindedly reached for the remote to turn down Karl on *Today* and pick up the phone at the same time. "Hello."

"Hello… Ms Diva… I'm Bob Sampson from UK Publishing. I want to publish your book."

I stared at my laptop screen, suddenly seeing nothing. "Say what?" I frowned at the computer.

"I want to publish your book. I've read your manuscript and loved it. I want to publish it for next year, get it out as soon as possible."

I forcefully tapped a few keys, trying to get back the web page that had disappeared into the internet's nether regions. Then I realised what he'd just said and thrust myself into a standing position. "Wait...you what?" I yelled, not believing what I'd just heard.

"I want to publish your book, Ms Diva, next year, but in the meantime, how would you like to come to London?"

I...surely...had not heard...him correctly... He wanted to publish my book. *My* book. My little old book that little old me had written. And what was that about London? "Ah, wait a minute, what did you say?" I heard his laughter down the line all the way from London. The *other* side of the world.

"I want to publish your book, and want you to come to London so we can meet and you can sign your contract."

"Bloody hell," I murmured, slamming back down onto my seat. I stared blankly at the screen, my mind going a million miles a second.

"How soon can you come to London?" I heard. "I can put you in a nice hotel for ten days, it's right around the corner from my office. We can talk about the book's cover and promotion while you're here."

"Ah," I muttered. "Ah, ah, I, ah, don't know. Ah." I was trying not to panic, trying to quell the feelings inside of me that were threatening to overload and overwhelm me. "Um, ah, need a passport, and ah, visa, I, uh think." For some reason I was spinning around in my tiny lounge room, moving my head from side to side as if my eyes were looking for answers to my ever increasing anxiety and delusions of grandeur.

"Okay, well how about you get those in order and I'll email you all the details, then you just let me know when you can come," he said, expecting a reply I assumed.

"Ah, okay, um, have you got my email address." Like hello! Of course he did. Just like he had my phone number.

"Of course I do. I'll be in contact soon, I can't wait to meet you, Ms Diva. I've seen your website and have a feeling this is going to be a hoot."

"Um, yeah, ah, okay," I managed and heard the line go dead. "Bloody hell!" exploded out of me. "Bloody hell! Bloody hell! Bloody hell!" I sat there shaking, my muscles clenched around every bone in my body. I got up and walked around. They want my book. He *really* wants my book. *They* want to publish *my* book. Bloody hell! I suddenly realised what it all meant and started jumping up and down as I squealed, "He's publishing my novel. He's publishing my novel. Woohoo!"

I threw myself onto my couch. "Oh, my God! Oh, my God! Oh, my God! Okay, get yourself together, there are things you need to do." I got up and sat in front of my computer, which seemed to have stopped throwing its tantrum. "Okay. I need a passport and maybe a visa," I murmured, tapping into the Australia Post website for passport details. I didn't have one, so was going to need one. After finding the closest store that did passport applications, I shut down the laptop, quickly changed, grabbed my keys and ran for my car, arriving in record time.

Standing at the counter, I asked for a passport application and got my photo taken. It took all of half an hour, but then there was a problem. I needed someone I wasn't related to or living with to fill out part of the form to prove who I was. Bugger! Who was I going to pick? I thought about it, then headed off to see the person in question, breezing into the store and striding up to the counter in front of Maureen. "Hey ho, I need your help with my passport application."

She looked up from the counter to stare quizzically at me. "Why are you getting a passport?" She went back to squinting at the price tags in her hand.

"I, ah, I need to go to London." I hadn't told anyone I'd written a book, so I wasn't ready to mention I'd been picked up by a publisher.

Her head shot up in surprise. "Oh, goodness. Really? Did you win a holiday or something?"

"Um, yeah, or something." I twitched nervously. "Anyway, I need a part of my passport filled out by someone who knows I am who I say I am. If I don't have one, I can't go."

"Of course, dear," she said and turned to look for Susie, the assistant. "Can you take over for me, dear? I'll just be out the back for a few minutes."

"Okay," bubble-headed Susie replied as Maureen

and I headed for the back room.

I handed her the application to fill out, and after reading that she needed her passport or electoral role details, she dug into her bag and pulled out her passport. "Mmm." She read the questions. "Mmm." She filled them in. "Mmm, yes it's her." She signed the back of one of the photos. "Mmm." She wrote her name. "Yes, it's me. Today's date. My signature." With a flourish, she whipped her pen across the line. "There you go." She handed me the form. "How long will you be gone for?"

"Um, not sure. Ten to twelve days or so," I said, safely tucking the papers into my folder. "Well, gotta go, thanks for this." I raced out the door and back to my car. Without breaking any laws, I sped back to the Post Office and ran inside.

OH. MY. GOD! The line is so long!

"Ugh," I mumbled under my breath and through gritted teeth, throwing my head back and staring at the ceiling. Oh, God, please make this go quickly. I dared not mumble anything else as the person behind me was mumbling herself about how long the line was.

Slowly the line moved towards the counter. It also snaked out the door. I looked at my watch for the millionth time.

Bah! Only two minutes from the last time I looked.

After what seemed like an eternity, I finally reached the counter and handed over my papers.

"Okay," said the clerk, pushing my application back at me. "You need to go stand over there." She pointed to a spot five people down the counter. "And someone will be with you shortly."

I stared at her dumbfounded. After waiting for what seemed like hours in a line that was still out the door, I now needed to wait again. But it was all for a good cause. I hung my head in defeat and dragged my feet to where I was supposed to wait.

I stood on the spot and scratched my head. I looked around. I studied my nails and straightened my clothes. I moved my papers from my left hand to my right hand. I looked at the ten people who went up to the counter and got served. I watched the hands on the clock tick over.

FOR FIFTEEN MINUTES!

God-all-bloody-mighty the place is going to shut before I get out of here.

"Next."

Ah…finally!

I stepped up to the counter and shoved my application at the woman. I just wanted to sit down and rest my weary legs, but *nooo*, she kept me waiting *another* five minutes before calling me into a small room off to the side for the interview. I collapsed into the chair and heaved a sigh.

"Is that your name?" she shot at me.

"Yes."

"Your address?"

"Yes."

"Your signature?"

"Yes."

"Mmm." She held the photo up and stared at me. "Is that you?"

I so desperately wanted to roll my eyes, but wearily fought back the urge. "Yes."

She signed off on the application. "Could take anywhere up to two weeks, but you'll know when you get it."

Well, duh! "Thanks," I mumbled and stood up. Walking out of the Post Office and to my car, I felt the excitement building. I was going to London. The *other* side of the world. London, England. A place I'd never been before. Hell, I'd never been outside of Australia before.

OH. MY. GOD!

I shook myself back into reality and drove home to plan the trip, 'cause there were lots of things I was going to need.

*****

The next day, I emailed the publisher, letting them know my passport was on its way and asking them all sorts of questions. What was the weather like? What kinda clothes did I need? Did I need any legal documents for the contract?

Since it was going to be awhile till I got a reply, I headed for my blog where I wrote a post letting everyone know what was going on, and if any of my UK followers were interested, we could get together for lunch or something.

Thanks to my blog being connected to my Twitter and Facebook pages, everyone would find out. What a way to publicise! After logging off, I headed for my bedroom. A half hour later I stopped to see I'd made quite a mess. Clothes were strewn over the entire bed, and my suitcase lay on its back on the floor, with shoes falling out of it and tumbling across the carpet. I sighed and rubbed my eyes.

None of this is worth taking. Certainly not the suitcase. But can I afford new stuff?

Mmm, I scratched my head. *I could buy new stuff. But can I afford it?* My finger shoved itself into my mouth, and my teeth clamped down on its nail. *Mmm, I could if I got an advance on the book. But what if I don't?*

I sighed again and glanced at my clothes. "Well, there's some stuff here I could take," I said in a small voice. "But I definitely need a new suitcase." The moth-eaten red case sat depressed and lonely. "Let's just wait till the reply from Bob, and then I'll see what I need." So with that, I set to work writing list after list of what I would need and what I would take.

*****

I had a pretty good list the next morning and a pile of nice clothes to go with it. I'd been so excited I'd worked until midnight when I'd fallen into bed exhausted. Now, I'd woken up to good lists, good piles and congratulations from my followers.

'Oh, my God! I can't believe you're getting published.'

'Hey, I can't believe you're coming to London. We'll have to catch up.'

'Oh, my God! Congratulations. Make sure I get an autographed copy.'

I checked my emails and printed off the one from Bob Sampson. Knowing I had work to do, I sent a quick thank you post out on my blog, then logged off and walked into the bedroom reading my printout over.

"Weather's cool to cold, ten to fifteen degrees. Need warm clothes, jeans, jumpers, coats. Bring a few party outfits for dining out. Don't forget camcorder and camera for recording the big event."

Oh, crap!

I don't have a camcorder. I'd been looking, but being the stingy person I am, didn't want to pay too much for it. And I needed that on top of a new suitcase *and* new clothes.

Oh, bugger!

I pulled out the phone book and scoured for video cameras and luggage. If I paid cash, I might be able to get them cheaper. I scoured for ages, even jumping back online and completely forgetting about lunch. Finally, around five, I stopped and gathered my papers. I was going to need to go shopping for more than clothes and luggage.

God!

All for ten days.

*****

Until my passport came through, the only thing I could do was shop and blog. For three days I drove around going to as many shopping centres in my area as I possibly could. And while I was bone weary, worn out, exhausted, tired, falling apart – you get the point – I had acquired a brand-new blue camcorder which I got for two hundred, and a three-piece luggage set consisting of two suitcases and a cabin bag for two hundred and fifty. All in bright turquoise blue.

I also managed to grab myself more jeans, jumpers, tops, a few party pieces, and not to forget some decent underwear. After all, you never know who I was going to meet.

Mr Right, maybe?

*****

I jumped online that evening and headed for my blog, ripping out a quick post, letting everyone know what was happening. I popped over to Twitter and brought up another window for Facebook.

'*Hey, everyone,*' I tweeted. '*My passport should be coming any day now. Done a load of shopping too.*' I hit the tweet button and switched to Facebook.

I saw about twenty-five personal messages, clicked on the tab and started reading.

'*Come see me when you get here.*'

'*Hey bitch, how 'bout a fuck when you get here?*' I hit the delete button on that one. "Stupid prick!" I muttered.

'*When is your book going to be in stores?*'

They were all pretty much the same, so I got through them quickly and then checked out the replies on my profile page.

'*Oh, my God! Oh, my God! Oh, my God! Jewelsie's getting published! About time too. Don't forget me when it's out, and can you autograph my copy?*'

"Yes, Cyn, I can," I murmured and flicked back to Twitter seeing a few replies there. Congrats coming from my tweeps and people I watch. Authors, celebs, ordinary folk who think I'm funny enough to follow.

'*What did you buy? Tell me everything.*'

'*Well,*' I tweeted. '*Got a flash new blue camcorder, luggage set, and some fancy clothes.*'

A few seconds later. '*You'll have to take pics and post them so we can see you in them.*'

'*I will. Can't wait for my passport. Not long now peeps, then I'm off. And I'm off now. Been a long week and a long day, see y'all tomorrow.*' I logged off and headed for bed.

*****

Four days later I held my passport in my hand.

I could *not believe* I had it. That I was *holding* it.

With my photo and name on the inside. That new passport smell wafted up and into my nostrils. I took a deep breath.

God!

It was time!

Time to go to London!

I sent an email off to Bob letting him know, and then set about packing my stuff. "Neatly pack jumpers here." I picked up my new jeans. "These go there. Tops tucked in here, underwear…coats…shoes... boots…t-shirts."

I don't know how long it took, all day I expect, because when I finally put my head up, it was almost seven p.m. "Shit. Better flick the TV on and grab something to eat." I ran into the lounge and turned on the TV to catch the rest of *The Project*. Whipping up a plate of food, I flicked through the channels during an ad break. A half hour later, I was back to packing, and finally slamming the lid shut, I checked the clock. Nine p.m. I don't know how many times I'd packed and repacked, not to mention packing my blue laptop bag with all its goodies I was going to need while I was over there.

Nintendo, digital recorder, camera, iPad, iPod, iPhone and charger, camcorder and battery, laptop, power cords, mouse and pad, notebooks, pens, pencils, sharpies for signing autographs, containers, bags, other stationery. It wasn't just me I was taking. It was my life as well.

*****

The next morning, I checked my emails and found one from Bob. He'd already paid for my ticket over, and it would be waiting at the counter in two days.

TWO! DAYS!

Bugger!

I panicked!

How could I not?

In two days, I was headed for London. The *other side* of the world. London, England. A place I'd never been before…

Wait…

Haven't we had this conversation?

Anyhoo, I set my plan into motion!

Jumping online I let everyone know I was heading for London in two days and would be staying for ten.

'*Oh, my God! Oh, my God! Oh, my God!*' I tweeted. '*I'm coming to London. I'm coming to London.*'

Cynthia replied via Facebook. '*It's a pity I can't come see you, but you know I'm nowhere near London!*' Cyn lives in Canada.

'*Yeah well, next time I write a book I'll try and get it picked up by a Canadian publisher so I can come and see you.*'

'*You're on!*'

*****

After making sure my house would be looked after while I was gone, I was ready when the day finally arrived. Having locked my cases and bags for the last time, I checked to make sure the house was in order.

Windows locked?

Check!

Doors bolted?

Check!

Gas off?

Check!

Electricals unplugged except for the fridge?

Check!

There was a honk outside, and I saw the taxi waiting. I gathered up my coat, cases and bags, locked the door, and rolled down the path to the car. After loading up and heading off, it took forty-five minutes to get to the airport. I didn't mind. It gave my nerves time to calm down. The problem was, as the airport came into view, they stirred up again.

Planes flew overhead. Cars drove past. People milled around or stood in lines. I alighted and thanked the cabbie for the ride. Taking my bags as best I could, I found the check in counter, got my ticket, business class no less, sent my cases off on the conveyor belt, went through security, and found a seat in the waiting area of the international section.

International!

International section!

I was going international!

I straightened my clothes and glanced out the window.

SHIT!

The plane was massively huge, and I was insanely small.

BLOODY HELL!

I was going international all right!

All the way in a massive white bird!

Chapter 2

The flight was uneventful with a perfectly smooth landing, so with a quick *thank you, God* and a small mental fist pump, I stood to disembark.

Walking into Heathrow Airport was overwhelming. The noise, the people, the static electricity in the air making my arm hairs stand on end. I glanced around while waiting in the immigration line.

Bright lights. People rushing. Signs telling you where to go.

Thankfully, when I got to the desk, I went through quickly, and after getting my cases from the baggage claim area, I breezed through customs and into the airport.

Wandering into the crowd, I stopped and looked around. In the email Bob had said someone would be there to pick me up.

I scanned the faces and found a blonde woman holding a sign with my name on it. I walked over to her with a huge grin on my face. "Hi, I'm Jewels."

She lowered the sign. "Hi. I'm Megan Mortimer." She reached out her hand to shake mine. "I'm your editor, tour guide, assistant, and anything else you need me for while you're here." We laughed.

I took in her perfect features, shoulder length blonde hair, and pale pink jumper. "As long as you can get me to where I need to be, and when I need to be there, I'll be fine. Are we heading off to the hotel now?"

"Oh, of course," she gushed, grabbing one of my case/bag combinations and leading me through the airport and into the cool evening air. "Since it's getting late we can stop somewhere for food," she said, popping my case into the car's boot.

"Oh, look," I said. "Just a quick drive-through cheeseburger and fries will do." I got into the sedan. With Australia being a part of the Monarchy, it meant the driver's seat was on the same side of the car, and they drove on the same side of the road.

"Are you sure?" she asked, expertly manoeuvring through the traffic. "I'm not sure the hotel is still serving, but we could stop somewhere nice if you want a quick meal." We headed for the middle of town.

"No, it's okay." I stared out the window. "You have drive-throughs don't you?" I glanced at her.

She chuckled. "We can stop and run in. It won't take long." And she was right. We stopped at the local burger shop and ran in and out in minutes.

I munched on my burger as she drove to my hotel, and had swallowed the last mouthful when she pulled up out front of a quaint old style five storey building. "Wow." I sipped my Pepsi Max. "This is nice."

"Bob thought you might like it." Megan popped the

boot, and we got out.

I looked up at the old stonework, ornate detail and red curtained windows. "Nice," I said with a nod. "Really nice."

She stopped beside me with my luggage. "Let's get you settled then."

We walked in and I gasped.

Inside were rich blue carpet, velvet wallpaper, delicate wall lights, and a chandelier twinkling from the ceiling sending shards of colour all around the lobby.

I was gaping so long Megan was already standing at the lift. "Are you ready?" she called.

"What?" My eyes focussed on her. "Oh, right, sorry." I walked over, and the doors silently whooshed open.

"Wow," I said, stepping into the lift. "This is nice too." It was decorated the same as the lobby. "Huh." I almost chuckled. "It even has a chandelier. Since when do lifts have chandeliers?" I looked at Megan.

"Since it's merry old England." She grinned as the doors opened. "Second floor, room eleven," she said. "Bob managed to get the one you wanted. Something to do with lucky numbers." She led me down the hallway to my left and stopped.

"Yeah," I muttered. "Figured I'd need as much luck as possible."

She opened the door and we rolled the cases in.

"Oh," I breathed. "Gorgeous."

The room was similar to the lobby. Rich red curtains framed the window that faced the road. A huge four-poster bed with thick bedding, TV on the wall, small table and chairs, small fridge and a two-seater couch all fitted perfectly into the room.

"I love it." I turned around, taking it all in.

"Great!" Megan exclaimed. "I'll call Bob and let him know you've settled in, and I'm supposed to pick you up at ten tomorrow. But if you need extra time to sleep in or something, then you've got his number. Oh." She reached into her bag and pulled out a small portfolio. "And here's *my* number, the publishing house address, a map, and some touristy bits and pieces so you can brush up on the neighbourhood and London."

I took the folder and glanced through it. "Fantastic. This is exactly what I need." I noticed the wall clock. "I also need a hot shower, to get unpacked, and to get to bed."

"Okay," she said, heading for the door. "If you need anything just call one of us, otherwise I'll be here at ten sharp tomorrow."

"Great, see you then." I turned to look out the window as the door shut and stood gazing across the view. I was on the outskirts of town, but still quite central, and still somewhat busy with cars rolling by. Bright neon lights on shops advertised fancy clothes and accessories. Big Ben and the London Eye sat in the distance.

An idea came to mind, and I quickly dug around in my computer bag for my phone. Back at the window, I snapped a pic. When I saw it turned out all right, I flicked through my apps to the one for Twitter, uploaded the photo, and left a message.

'*Oh, my bloody God, peeps! I'm here! I'm really here! Here in London, England. Bloody Hell!*' I clicked tweet, and within seconds it joined the other hundred million tweets going out around the world that very night. Or day, depending on where they were coming from.

I looked through my Twitter and Facebook pages to see what everyone had thought of my other photos. Me outside the airport in Aus. The plane. Taking off and landing. I was going to document my whole adventure with photos and blogs, which would be going out to millions every day.

Nice!

I closed the curtains, quickly unpacked, then stepped under a steaming hot shower. It felt *sooo* good. Washing my hair, I scrubbed the grimy flight feeling from my skin, then let the hot water flow over me. After towelling down and throwing on a nightie, I pulled out a notebook to document the day's events, so I didn't have to rely on memory alone when I blogged.

Finally putting my pen down, I set my travel alarm to London time and slid down under the thick rose red quilt.

*****

I heard buzzing somewhere in the distance, and morning started nudging me to wake up. Not wanting to surrender just yet, I snuggled down further, but the clock kept buzzing.

"Arghhh." I rolled over and grabbed it, turning off the incessant buzzing, and then wearily opened my eyes to the grey November morning. With a sigh, I hauled myself out of bed, flicked on the TV with the remote, and flung open the curtains. It was eight a.m., and the street was already alive with people.

"Ugh," I whined, wiping the sleep from my eyes. "Arghhh."

I know, I don't say much first thing after waking up. But do most people? I ordered an omelette from room service, then jumped in the shower, managing to dress and log online before my breakfast came.

Shovelling a forkful of chicken egg into my mouth, I read a few tweets and messages. The TV droned in the background, but I had a blog to roll out, so I turned it down then decided to flick through the channels.

Nope!

Nope!

Nope!

"Ah, bugger!" I turned it off instead. I pulled up the dashboard of my blog, clicked on new post, and grabbed my notebook. I laid it out on the table so I could copy it onto the pc.

Well, peeps, as you know from my Twitter pics, I'm here in London.

That's London, England for those who don't know. And if you still don't know, check a map. I'm going to be journaling my ten day adventure here in merry old London, letting you know about my publishing deal, the places I go, the things I see, the men I do...oops, I mean, the things I do. I'll reprimand my bad self later. In the meantime, I'll post the pics I've uploaded on Twitter just so you can see them all again and I can brag.

Oh, look, there's the airport at home.

The plane that's going to, no, make that, did fly me over.

Heathrow.

And the view outside my window.

I'm not sure if I'll be blogging in the morning or night. All depends on the sights I'm seeing, the places I'm being and the men I'll be doing…oops, there's my dirty mind again.

So, until tomorrow peeps, can someone tell me where actor Dominic Power is?

Jewels xxoo

I bolded, arialed and blackened the text, put in a title – **My Adventures in Merry Old England: November 4th, 2011.** I put in some tags and previewed my first London post, checking everything was in order, and the spelling was correct before I hit the publish button. And out to the big wide world, my words went.

Pottering around on Twitter and Facebook for awhile, I lost track of time until there was a knock at the door. I glanced up and frowned, then looked at the wall clock.

Bugger!

I jumped up to open it and saw bright, perky Megan standing there.

"Ready to go?"

"Ah, yeah. I'll just log off and finish getting ready." Quickly running around, I was ready in five minutes, and we were on our way to *UK Publishing.*

"Bob and Linda are really nice," Megan gushed. "In fact, we all are."

I smiled at her and gazed out the window. The view was all around and gone too quickly as we arrived at the offices of my new publishing home.

Megan led me upstairs to a door with the nameplate that read: Bob Sampson. Publisher in Charge. She knocked.

"Come in," a big gruff voice called.

She opened the door, and we walked into the spacious, airy office with the floor-to-ceiling windows which framed one hell of a view of London.

"I'm Bob Sampson." An average, slightly balding well-built man walked around his desk and over to us, grabbing my hand and shaking it vigorously. "You must be Jewels of course you are Megan brought you here and you've got red hair."

My arm was pumping up and down, my hand encaged in his.

"Oh, for goodness sake Bob, let her hand go." A beautiful blonde woman came over to us. "I'm Linda, Bob's wife. It's so good to finally meet you." She took my hand from her husband's and shook it.

"You too," I said, glancing from one to another, not sure what to say next. I was glad when Bob took over.

"So Jewels how do you like your hotel was the plane flight okay are you getting everything you need please sit down do you want something to drink what do you think of the view spectacular isn't it."

"Oh, for goodness sake Bob, take a breath." Linda laughed. "Don't mind him, that's the way he always talks, at least in the office. You'll get used to it. Please sit down." She led me to a seat and we all sat.

Bob plonked down behind his desk. "So Jewels here's your contract you don't have to sign it now you can look over it and read it and if you don't understand it then we can get one of the lawyers here to take you through it sure you don't want a drink?"

"Bob," Linda admonished. "Slow down before you make the poor girl deaf."

Everything had finally sunk in and I laughed. "No, I'm fine. I'll read the papers and let you know if I need a lawyer."

"Okay fantastic here they are do you want us to step out of the room?"

"No, I don't. I'm fine." I smiled and took the papers he handed to me. Reading through them, I found most of it made sense and finished quickly, looking up to see Megan had gone, Linda was writing something, and Bob was staring intently at a manuscript. I couldn't help myself. The change was so opposite from minutes ago that I laughed.

"What's so funny is everything all right the contract's not meant to be hilarious do you want something to drink now?"

I laughed even harder, not being able to help myself. Tears rolled down my cheeks.

Linda and Bob glanced curiously at each other then back to me.

"I'm sorry," I gasped, wiping my face. "I think I'm a

bit delirious." More tears rolled, and I sucked in some air. "You were like this steamroller when I walked in, then bang you went quiet, then bang you started again." I laughed some more. "Sorry, the effect was quite outstanding."

Linda had a huge grin on her face, but Bob looked like he didn't get it.

"Yes," she said. "He can be that way sometimes. All loud and boisterous one minute, then quiet as a church mouse the next. It's quite a strange thing to see."

"I'll say," I muttered, waving the papers. "There are a few things I don't understand, so if you can get that lawyer, I can get these signed."

Still with a confused look on his face, Bob picked up the phone. "Hardy get in here what do you mean you aren't Hardy who are you then well if you're not Hardy where is she never mind just get her in here now."

Linda and I looked at each other and burst out laughing.

"What?" he complained. "I called her she's on her way and she'll explain it to you in no time are you hungry do you want something to eat are you thirsty do you want that drink now?"

"Bob, Bob, Bob," I admonished, putting my hands up. "You need to learn to slow down and talk at the normal pace humans talk, not the high frequency only animals can hear." I laughed.

"Oh." He looked sheepish. "Right. I talk fast when I'm excited and it's really good to meet you and I think this book will be a blockbuster bestseller." The door flew open, and he didn't even stop. "Hardy where have you been?"

"What?" A tall, willowy red-haired woman flung back. "I've been here all the time." She strode over to me in her expensively well-tailored pantsuit and, pulling her right hand from her pants pocket, thrust it toward me. "You must be Jewels. I'm Frances. Good to meet another redhead; we need to stick together you know. Now, what can I help you with?"

This woman was definitely a walking force field, and I could tell that if I ever needed help while I was there, she'd get me out of any situation.

I shook her hand. "There's just a few things I don't understand. So, if you can explain them?"

"Of course, of course, here sit down." She sat me down at Bob's desk, and with him hovering over us, and Linda quietly telling him to stop, Frances informed me in short easy English what it all meant. "Bob, stop hovering and go get that champagne," she said as I signed on the dotted line.

He sighed in relief at my signature. "Of course it's time to celebrate." After he barked a few orders on the phone, the champagne arrived quickly, and between glasses and stories of other authors, I managed to get some photos snapped, sending them out on Twitter in the process.

After a few too many, Bob took Linda, Megan and me to a local restaurant to celebrate. He talked on and on, enthralling me with his life as a publisher, the people he'd met, the parties he'd been to, and the stories he'd been told, all the while trying to pry details about me from between my lips.

"Oh, no, Bobby boy. You're not getting away with that one. Jewels will remain a mystery. That's all part of my story."

Bob and Linda took me on a tour of the city, pointing out Big Ben, the Eye, Tower Bridge, Albert Hall, Westminster, and Kensington Palace, and after dining at another fancy restaurant, they dropped me off at my hotel.

"Now Jewelsh," Bob slurred as he flung an arm around my shoulder. "Megan'sh going be your tour guide sho I'm shure she'll be 'ere brigh 'n early tooomorrow…but don' f'get you'll need to do shum ed-it-ing of your book sho don' have toooo mush fun."

"No, Bob," I said, getting out of the car with a giggle. "I won't. Goodnight."

"Nigh."

I walked up the stairs to my room hoping the exercise would help burn off all the food I'd eaten. Ugh, I feel sick. And fat. And sick. And bloated. Ugh. I unlocked my door, switched on the light, and after taking out my notebook which I'd been making notes in all day, I turned on my laptop.

My Adventures in Merry Old England: November 4th, 2011

Hey there, peeps!
It's been a long day, but here's what went down.
I got to meet my publisher and his wife, and I signed

my book contract. See the happy snaps of us. Yes, that's me looking slightly dazed and confused!

Then we went to a great restaurant for lunch. Yes, that's me stuffing my face and Bob drinking his second bottle of champagne. And look at all the places I got to see on my trip around town.

Anyhoo, it's been a long day, and I'm logging off now. I'll let you all know tomorrow what frivolity I get up to. By the way, has anyone found Dominic Power yet?

Jewels xxoo

Chapter 3

My Adventures in Merry Old England: November 5th, 2011

It's been another long day here in London peeps. This time I was with Megan. She's going to be my tour-guide and chauffeur when she's not being my editor and slave driver. But I told her the week is for working and the ends are for playing. And I plan on playing big time peeps.

BIG. TIME!!!!!

She drove us to the London Eye and tried to get me on it, but I refused. Of course I did. I hate heights!!!!!

And I mean, I HATE HEIGHTS!!!!!

She even started begging, telling me I wouldn't be a "proper tourist" if I didn't go on it.

I laughed at her. "Are you kidding me," I said. "That's bullshit, and I'm not going to believe it."

So, upon realising she couldn't scare the bejesus out of me, she took me shopping along the river in a nice part of London. I bought a few bits and pieces, and we lunched at Fifteen, Jamie Oliver's restaurant.

I'm now back at the hotel for a few hours before we go out again. Megan wants to get me to a club. And I was hard to convince but decided why not. So, now I'm supposed to be resting, in which case I'd better go. Here are my pics from today and I'll see you all tomorrow.

Jewels xxoo

****

My Adventures in Merry Old England: November 6th, 2011

OH!!!!!

MY!!!!!

FUCKING!!!!!

GOD!!!!!

What the hell did I do last night?????

Went to a club, that's what!!!!!

No…wait…

Make that…SEVERAL clubs!!!!!

We started early and ended late. The noise rattled my eardrums so badly they're still going, and it's seven!!!!!

AT NIGHT!!!!!

Ugh!!!!!

All I remember is, running into a few celebs, but you know that coz I tweeted pics. Had a few Pepsi Maxes, got to see all the fireworks of Guy Fawkes Day and the London nightlife, all strong hard manly inches of him. Who? Fucked if I know! It was clearly too much for my psyche because I slept in then wandered around the neighbourhood for awhile, watched a bit of TV, slept some more, and now I'm online.

And now I'm off. See ya tomorrow, peeps.

Jewels xxoo

*****

My Adventures in Merry Old England: November 7th, 2011

I edited all morning then had lunch out. Megan's hilarious. I can't believe she recovered so well from Saturday night. I still feel like shit. She looks a million bucks. I asked her what her secret was.

"I'm twenty-five," she said.

Fuck you! I thought.

She took me to the Sherlock Holmes Museum for a few hours and now I'm ready for bed. Tomorrow's going to be busy so I may not blog until Wednesday or Thursday.

See you then, peeps.

Jewels xxoo

*****

My Adventures in Merry Old England: November 9th, 2011

See, I told you I may not blog until now, coz I was right.

Yesterday was BUSY!!!!!

I spent all day at UK Publishing looking over possible covers, having my say on it, coming up with promotional stuff like what kind of posters do we want to advertise the book? Did we want any other kind of stuff? Bookmarks, key rings, etc. We're keeping it simple, just posters and bookmarks.

As for today, there was more editing and more promotional. Hope you all enjoyed the pics I tweeted. Here they are again for those who didn't see them the first time.

Jewels xxoo

*****

My Adventures in Merry Old England: November 10th, 2011

Got to go to the London Tower and Madame Tussauds today peeps. The Royal jewels are un-freakin-believable. I leaned so close at one stage I nearly fell into the case. The guard didn't like that. He took a few steps toward me and gave me a scowl.

I threw one back!

Sigh. If only I could take them home. I saw one piece that would look fabulous on me, dahlings!

See, take a look at these!

Nice! Right?

Yes, well, from one royal jewels to another, I'm nearly done editing my book and we've chosen a cover. It's all happening so quickly.

I can't believe it's already a week since I flew into this country, and tomorrow's a full week of me being here.

Before I go, I've organised a meeting with some followers on Saturday. We'll take some pics to tweet so you'll be part of the get-together.

Until then, peeps.

Jewels xxoo

*****

Friday morning dawned cool but very sunny, and as I stood staring out the window, I felt sad. I'd be going home in a few days, and there was still so much I wanted to do. To see. To go. I turned from the view to finish getting dressed, switching off the TV just as there was a knock on the door. "Hi there," I said as I opened it.

"Hey, Jewels," Megan said. "Are you ready for our day out?"

"Absolutely!" I grabbed my bag and glanced at her. I felt a bit dowdy and plain in my pale pink shirt, black jeans, and boots. She'd dressed in a gorgeous silk blouse, the highest stilettos, and the latest blue jeans. I noticed the brand on her arse. God, they must have cost a fortune!

"So, I have it all planned. Nothing too full on. Shopping, having lunch at an old style pub, and maybe getting a video of you down by the river. Then you can let everyone see the sights and know you've had a glorious time when you post it on YouTube."

"You want me to do a vlog," I groaned, climbing into her car. "I know I've been taking photos, but to do a vlog." I looked down. "In these clothes? They're so plain. *So not Jewels at all,*" I admonished, with a wave of my finger.

She laughed and pulled into the traffic. "Bob suggested it. Not that you have to do it. He asked me if you've done one, and that it might help with publicity."

I sighed. Normally when I did vlogs, I dressed up and wore glasses to add to the mystery of Jewels Diva. But I had none of that today. "Look, we'll see. Let's get some shopping done first." I guess I could do one. Just as well I always carry my camera and camcorder.

*****

We shopped till we dropped. Money that is! In nearly every store we went in. Well, Megan did anyway. I watched my pounds and tried to get as much on sale as possible, which is why we did a few op shops and second-hand stores. Megan also took me to an amazing vintage store that had rack upon rack, and shelf upon shelf absolutely packed from floor-to-ceiling with goodies.

"Nice," I said, giving the thumbs up at an old style fifties dress Megan was holding in front of her. "The pink hue will look good on you."

She rushed off to try it on, and I kept filing through the rack. My eyes seem to have trained themselves to pick up only on blue and pink which is why I automatically stopped at the blue and pink blazers I came across. They looked old-fashioned. "Made of silk maybe," I murmured, fingering the fabric. "Delicate."

I checked the size tag and sighed. Old-fashioned sizing. I'd have to try them on.

I pulled the blue one off the hanger and slid my left arm into the sleeve. Silky lining slid over my arm, and I gently pushed my right arm in as well. Straightening the collar, I looked for a mirror.

"Oh," I heard. "That's lovely."

I turned around to see Megan standing in her frock. "So is that," I said.

The old style dress fitted her tiny waist perfectly and flared out to her knees. With a sweetheart neckline, a white petticoat, and an array of pink shades, the dress brought out the blush in her cheeks.

"Thanks. I'm definitely getting it. What about the coat? Are you having it?"

I turned back to the mirror and adjusted the waist. The gorgeous turquoise blue silk looked stunning on me, and even though I couldn't quite button it up thanks to my curvy figure, it didn't matter. I wanted it! I quickly tried the pink one on. Same material, different style. Shiny fuchsia pink. I slid it off and checked the price tags.

Fifty pounds each! Yikes!

I tried to do a mental conversion and grimaced. "Oh, bugger," I said. "I'm taking them."

"Fantastic," Megan said. "Let's keep looking."

After an hour, I'd found some gorgeous old-fashioned sequin tops, a royal blue flared skirt, a couple of shawls, an encrusted clutch purse and a sparkly studded belt.

The final tally was a bit high, but because Megan

was buying just as much and we'd come on a Friday, we got fifty percent off.

Fan-freakin-tastic!

We lugged our bags out to the car and piled them into the boot.

"Oh, my God, I'm hungry," I groaned.

"It's all the shopping," Megan replied. "It works up an appetite. Just as well I'm taking you to a pub for lunch. We'll get a good hearty meal to keep us going for the rest of the day."

"Great," I said, getting in the car. "Let's go!"

Five minutes later, we pulled up outside of an old English pub. Well, duh! Of course it's English, I'm in England. What did you expect it to be? An old Belgian pub? An old Turkish pub? An old American pub?

Okay, already, I get my point!

Now, about that meal.

We walked inside and stopped beside the sign that read *wait here until seated,* but within seconds we were escorted to a small booth and given menus.

"This is great," I enthused, looking around. The carpet was red with small coats of arms. The wood was dark and thick. A jukebox and pool table sat on the far side, and the bar had an English soccer team flag hanging over it.

Don't ask which team; I don't know.

"I knew you'd like it," Megan gushed, reading her menu. "And the food is basic and hardy. Should fill you up in no time."

"What about a game of pool after?" I suggested.

"Sure. I'm not very good, though." She glanced at

the waitress who was beside our booth. "The old style fish and chips, thank you," she said with a smile, handing back her menu.

"I'll have the chicken schnitzel and chips, thanks." I gave her my menu as well.

"Anything to drink?"

"Um, Pepsi Max, large, a little bit of ice," I said, indicating with my fingers how much.

"Lemon Lime mineral water," Megan added.

"Okay, girls, that's about twenty minutes," the waitress said, walking away.

"Mmm, twenty minutes," I murmured, gazing at the pool table. "How 'bout that game now?" I pointed toward the other side of the pub.

She glanced around, then perused the rest of the place. "Well, there's no one here, so our bags should be safe. Okay, let's do it."

While Megan walked over to the table to rack up the balls, I popped some coins into the old-fashioned neon lighted jukebox. Picking a few decent songs, I grabbed a cue and let Megan play first. The game was over pretty quick, so we racked them up again.

I cracked the first ball and walked around the table. Bending over to line up a shot I became distracted by the group who walked through the door.

"Hey, Rosie. We'll have the usual thanks."

"Is our table ready?"

"Hey, there Bob. How are you? How's the gallstones?"

I straightened and stared.

Bloody hell!!!!!!!

The boys from Sun Hill!

I know, you're confused. And technically Sun Hill doesn't exist anymore because the TV show it existed on, *The Bill,* is no longer, and hasn't been for ages. But they would always be *The Bill* boys to those who watched the show.

"You're staring," Megan whispered in my ear. "And it's your turn."

I pulled my eyes away from Sam, Alex, Chris, Christopher, Andrew and Ben long enough to glance at Megan. "Right." I looked back and OH, MY BLOODY GOD there he was...

Dominic Power!

Be still my madly, insanely, crazily beating heart!

I quickly glanced back at Megan so they wouldn't notice me staring and out of the corner of my eye watched them sit at the table next to us. OH! MY! BLOODY! GOD! I squealed on the inside. *Okay, Jewels. Get your shit together. They're only men.* ON. LY. MEN! But fucking hot men!

Dominic Power!

Dreamy sigh!

I heaved a sigh and lined up a shot, cracking it into the corner. I stood and gave myself a self-satisfied smug grin.

"Nice shot!"

I looked up to see Christopher Fox looking at me.

OH. MY. BLOODY. GOD!

"Thanks," I managed and kept going. Sinking the rest of the shots I left Megan standing there looking dazed. "Poor baby," I murmured. "I'll let you win next time."

"How many have you played?"

I glanced to my left. Christopher was still watching me. "Games? Only two. And I've won both." I did a smug little dance.

"It's only because I'm not good at pool," Megan said.

"Well, how about playing with me then," he invited.

The others were watching me, and my nerves went nuts. I cocked my left eyebrow and tilted my head slightly. "Sweetie," I crooned seductively. "Play with you? You're not my type…oh…" My brows went up. "You meant *pool.*"

The boys snorted with laughter, but Christopher didn't get the joke. "Of course I meant pool what do you think I…oh…" His tongue clicked, and he pointed at me. "Redheads aren't my type, but give me attitude, and I might be interested."

"Oh, oh, oh," I muttered with a guttural sound and a shake of my head. "Just as well I'm not a real redhead then in'it," I shot back.

"Ohhhhh," the boys chorused.

"Well, that's even better," he added.

"Not in your lifetime," I retorted. I heard Elvis Presley's *Can't Help Falling in Love* start on the jukebox.

He put his hands up in defeat. "A man's gotta try."

"Who said you're a man." I gave him a smart arse look, and a few of the boys clapped. "Real men look like Sam." I waved my finger in his direction, and he went beet red as he got teased for it. "Not you."

"Come on, darlin', of course I'm a man. We come in different shapes and sizes like you girls do, we don't all look Sam, you know."

I scoffed and looked away. And that's when I saw him.

He walked through that door like he owned the place.

I Can't Help…Falling in Love…

That's when my heart raced. That's when the world stopped. That's when I fell millions of miles into eyes so blue I was drowning in a warm ocean of liquid soft rolling waves.

HE. WAS. GORGEOUS!

And I *MEAN* gorgeous!

Movie Star Gorgeous!

Rock Star Gorgeous!

Son of God Gorgeous!

I Can't Help…Falling in Love…

He strode up to the bar and leaned in to flirt with the barmaid.

I had no idea of the world around me. No idea I was staring. No idea my mouth was hanging open. No idea my arms had fallen down beside me, or I hadn't dropped my cue.

The barmaid nodded in my direction, and the Son of God glanced around, a slight smile on his face. He gave me a small nod and turned back.

I have no idea how, but I suddenly had the nerve to move. And not just move in any way, shape, or form, but move toward him. Boldly walking over, my cue trailing behind me, I stopped beside him to stare ever so happily up into those royal blue eyes. And a long way up they were. He towered above me. Well over six feet. He could have easily rested his square chin on my head.

"Hi," I said breathlessly. "I'm Jewels. Who are you?" I couldn't move. I couldn't breathe. I couldn't do.

"Callum." His voice was deep and arousing making me tingly, and not in my stomach.

"Now, now officer," I breathed seductively. "Full name and rank."

His lips turned into a sly grin. "Stone. Sergeant Callum Stone."

"Get out. You *are* not," exploded out of me. "Show me."

He looked stunned and quizzical and moved his coat aside to show me his name tag.

"Get out. You are not," I repeated. "That. Is. Crazy!" My cheeks were hurting from grinning so hard.

"Why's it crazy," his voice rumbled.

"Well, because, Sam Callis, who played Sergeant Callum Stone in *The Bill,* is sitting over there." I glanced to where I was pointing my finger and noticed the boys watching us.

He glanced around then back at me. "So he is," he muttered.

"You're gorgeous," I told him, noticing short brown hair under his hat.

He got a little embarrassed and lightly blushed. "Well…what does one say to that?"

"Are you married?" I looked down at his hand for a ring. "Girlfriend? Partner? Date? Casually dating? Seriously dating? Friend with benefit? Anyone in your life in any way, shape, or form? You are straight, aren't you? I'm single. Very single. And free. Free and single. That's me."

His eyes bored into mine, and I felt like an idiot for not being able to shut my mouth. "Straight! Single! No one in my life! And none of your business!"

"Here you go, darlin'." The barmaid handed a bag of food to him.

He reached out and took it. "Thank you, Marilyn. I know we'll enjoy it." He turned back to me. "Jewels," he said with a nod. "It's been…interesting."

"Same here," I gushed. "And I can't wait to see you again."

He gave me a strange look and started walking away. "That's *if* we see each other again."

"Oh, we'll definitely be seeing each other," I called. "I'll make sure of it." He glanced back. "Not that I'm a stalker or anything." I watched the Son of God walk out the door and out of my life. But only for now.

"Darlin', you need to breathe," I heard. Glancing at Marilyn, I sucked in a huge mouthful of air.

"Oh, my fucking, God!" I ran back to Megan. "Did you see that? Did you see him and guess what his name is?" I turned to look at the boys. "*Sergeant Callum Stone.* I know, get out!" I watched their expressions.

"Really?" Sam asked, intrigue on his face.

"Really," I replied. "Bloody hell!"

"So, then," Christopher piped up. "What's so good about him then, hey?" His face was full of displeasure.

"Hello!" I admonished. "Did you *see* him? Gor. Ge. Ous! Everything I want in a man. He's a tall, broad, muscular, masculine, manly man." My hands were making gestures with each syllable, each word.

Megan sighed. "He certainly was that."

"Uh, yeah!" I said, all animated.

"So what!" Christopher said with a wave of his hand. "That doesn't mean much."

"Well," I added, gazing at the door. "He's also hot, stunning, sexable, nuzzable, extremely fuckable." I was wistful, gazing at the door when I heard the guffaws.

"Whoa!" I heard Megan say.

"What the hell's wrong with you?" Christopher asked. "Get a real man like me!"

"Pfft," I said and walked around the table, so my back was to them. "I already told you, Christopher, you're *not* a real man. *Real* men have balls." I glanced down at the coloured ones before me.

"What? An' I don't?"

I picked up two coloured spheres. "You need something. Let me give you a present." Evil sneaked through my veins and I turned to face him. "Here," I extended my hand. "You need some balls. Have these."

The others laughed, and he stared coldly at me. "No, thanks, love. I already have a pair of my own."

"Really?" My eyes widened in mock surprise. "Where? In a jar on your mother's bedside table?"

The boys roared with laughter, and a look came over his face I couldn't quite name.

"Yeah." I smirked. "Thought so." I placed the balls on the table in front of him then walked toward the rack on the wall. Placing my cue away, I turned to Megan. "Let's go eat. I'm starving."

It didn't take long for us to scarf down our meal, and just as we finished, Chris Simmons came over. He pulled out a business card from his back pocket.

"Here are my details. I want you to appear on my comedy show. Would you like that? I loved the way you dealt with Chris."

"Hello!" I gushed. "Yes."

He laughed at my exuberance. "Well, great."

"Oh, wait." The realisation hit me, and I felt depressed. "I can't. I'm leaving in a couple of days."

Disappointment rained down over his face. "That's not good. But maybe we can film something before you go. Do you have a number?"

"Yeah, let me get it." I dug around in my bag and handed him one of the business cards Bob had had specially made. "Here. Maybe we can do something tomorrow?"

He grinned at me then read my details. "Sure. Otherwise, I'll contact you on one of these."

"Okay." I did a little dance in my seat as he walked away.

"Oh, my God," Megan said. "You might be on TV."

"I know," I squealed then calmed down long enough to glance at my watch. "Oops, better go."

"Absolutely," she agreed. "You've got a vlog to do." I groaned. "Don't get all upset. It will be good preparation for your TV debut." We giggled and headed for the door, and ended up on a river bank somewhere a half hour later.

"Okay, how's my hair? Have I got enough lipstick on? Should I wear sunglasses?"

"Stop fussing," Megan chastised, getting my camcorder ready.

"Is it too cloudy? Should we do it here or move? Is

the picture good?"

"Will you stop it," she cried. "Everything is oops."

I turned to look in the direction she was staring.

The Son of God was walking toward us.

OH. MY. GOD!

"Ladies," he rumbled. "Do you have a permit to film?" He noticed me, and a strange fleeting look passed through his eyes. He tipped his hat. "Miss Jewels."

"Sergeant," I gushed. "See, I told you we'd be seeing each other again. I just didn't expect it to be so soon." I tried desperately to control my excitement.

I failed!

"Mmm," he muttered, inspecting the permit Megan handed him. "So you did." He handed it back. "Well, this seems to be in order. Good day, ladies." He and his partner walked off down the river.

"Oh, my God! Oh, my God! Oh, my God!" I squealed.

"All right," Megan said with a laugh. "Calm down. Let's get this done and then we can go. Okay, now stand here so I can get all the landmarks in." She shoved me onto the spot and backed up.

I looked around at the scenery. The filthy stinking river. The street. The people. I heard the buzzing of life and felt a little sad to be leaving.

"Okay. Here we go. Are you ready?"

"Yes."

"Okay. In five, four, three, two, one." She waved her finger at me.

"Hello, peeps and welcome to…" I looked at the overcast sky. "I was going to say sunny old England, but as you can see, it's dreary old England today. As you know, if you've read my blogs, tweets and messages that is, I've been here in London for the last week. All paid for by my glorious new publisher. That's right. *I* have a publisher. Yes," I hissed and did a double fist pump. "A publisher here in the UK wanted my book so badly that he flew me all the way to the other side of the world just to personally see me sign the contract. It's been quite a whirlwind. Tours of the city, shopping sprees, a bit of editing, and you should see the photo shoot we did for publicity shots." I put both hands up and gushed. "All absolutely fabulous."

"This is going to be the only vlog I do here in dreary old England, so obviously my editor, who's holding the camera, had to get as many touristy things in the background as possible. And apparently, I'm supposed to do this." I put my left hand up. "Is that right? Is it working?" I got the thumbs up. "Yes, peeps, the usual typically corny *leaning against a landmark shot* and it's nothing but an optical illusion." I shook my head in dismay. "Well, I hope you've all enjoyed my blogs and tweets and photos that I've posted. I've had one hell of a time. And," I leaned toward the camera putting my hand up to partially cover my mouth, "I've met a bloody gorgeous cop called Sgt Callum Stone," I whispered before my voice turned into a squeal. "I know, just like in *The Bill.*" I leaned back. "So, that's it from me. I'll post pics of my trip home, and maybe some of the goodies I've bought. Until next time peeps, I'm Jewels Diva. Stay safe and have fun. But not too much fun. And *not* with a really gorgeous guy that I don't know about."

Megan gave me the thumbs up and then indicated I was supposed to now be funny. So, while she moved around filming me, I flitted here and there acting stupid for the camera. Off in the distance, I notice Sgt Stone had turned around and was walking back toward us. I stopped and watched him. Megan stood between us about fifteen feet away.

The sights. The sounds. They all disappeared. I was just content to stare at the gorgeous man walking toward me until I noticed an expression of horror come over Megan's face.

She had turned her head slightly to the left, my right, and was looking at something. Her left arm reached out, and she pointed.

I turned my head and saw a blue sedan barrelling at me, a determined expression on the driver's face. Suddenly the world started again, but all I heard was Megan screaming, car brakes squealing, and my bones crunching as I went flying over the car and into the air while the sedan sailed beneath me. It flew out into the river and landed with an almighty splash. I went falling face first onto the concrete edge of the river wall.

My face smashed…

All I heard was screaming…

All I saw was stars…

Then nothing…

Chapter 4

I tried opening my eyes. I tried gasping for air. I tried to figure out what was happening as cold liquid flowed around me. What…I…happened…where…shit…in the river. My instincts wanted me to open my mouth. To breathe. But instead, I forced my arms and legs against the flow of water that was dragging me down, down, down into the murky depths of the Thames.

I thrashed my arms and kicked my legs trying to propel myself up. Panic threatened to surrender me to the current, but I fought against it and thrust myself upwards. Up toward the world of light. I broke the surface and sucked as much air as possible into my lungs. There was screaming and sirens and yelling and a pounding in my head as I took breath after breath. I wiped my eyes, but the murkiness remained. So did the blood on my left hand, which I looked at before noticing the car beyond it, half in half out of the water, possibly impaled on something lurking in the dark depths.

A child was screaming. So was Megan. I looked up at her staring down at me still holding the camera. I vaguely pointed to the car and tried to dog paddle toward it. Regardless of my pain, there was a woman and child who needed saving.

I saw Sgt Stone stripping off his clothes to race down a set of stairs to the dock and jump into the water toward me. With two strokes he was by my side scooping me into his arms. "Jewels. You're hurt. I'll get you to the dock." He touched my head.

"No," I gasped, indicating the car. "They need help." I pushed his hand away and managed to swim out to the car.

"Get a rope. Get some tools," he yelled.

There was a child who looked to be about two years of age in the back. The mother seemed unconscious.

"We need something to smash it with," Stone said, starting to swim back to the dock.

"Wait." I dug around in my pocket and pulled out my Swiss Army knife. I'd put it on a chain and attached it to my belt loop so I wouldn't lose it. I opened it and started stabbing at the glass. When a spider web crack appeared one punch smashed it. I wiped the blade around the window frame to get rid of excess glass then leaned into the back seat.

"It's okay, sweetie," I crooned. "I'll get you out in no time."

The boy was screaming with ear piercing definition, but it didn't blank out the screaming in my head. I unlocked his safety belt and pulled him toward me, then inched backwards out of the car. I slid through the window clutching him to my chest. "Here," I told Stone. "Take him. I'll get the mother."

Stone took him into his arms, and that's when I saw a rope tied around him. His partner had the other end and was pulling him toward the dock. I noticed all the people standing on the wharf watching. My teeth chattered, and I turned to the driver's window, breaking it the same way as the other one. I cleared away the glass and checked the woman for a pulse.

"Ugh," she groaned, moving her head slightly. Her hand reached up to touch it.

"No, don't move. I'm going to get you out." I reached for the seatbelt button, but it wouldn't release.

"No," she muttered. "Leave me." Her hands feebly tried pushing me away.

"I'll have you out in a minute," I said.

There was a loud groan from the car, and it shifted.

I pushed the shoulder section of the seatbelt over her head, so she was partly free, and thrust my torso into the window. Grabbing my knife, I found the lap belt and started sawing.

"Jewels. Get out of there." Stone raced to my side.

"I'm almost done," I said, sawing like a mad woman.

"No, no, let me go. I want to die." She tried hitting and pushing me, becoming hysterical. "Where's my baby? I want to die. Let me die."

I was almost done. But so was the car.

With a loud groan, it started sinking, water flowed in, and we had almost no space to breathe.

"No, no, no," she screamed.

"Stop it," I screamed back. It stopped her. "Take a deep breath and hold it," I said. "One, two, three." We both took a breath as the water surrounded us.

Down, down, down we went. I don't know how deep, but I'd finished cutting through the belt and was struggling to pull her through. A man appeared by my side. Stone, I assumed, and he helped drag her out.

I vaguely saw him point to the surface and nodded. He pushed off, taking the woman with him. I followed.

Or at least I thought I did.

I couldn't move.

I couldn't see.

I couldn't breathe.

I couldn't move.

I was trapped.

Trying not to panic, although I knew the rolling waves of fear were getting faster and more powerful with every second, my hands flew around my body. Looking, or should I say feeling, for whatever was holding me under.

I couldn't find anything.

No, no, no this can't be happening. This just can't be, can't be, can't be, can't be happening. My lungs were screaming louder than my head, which was being pounded by the excessively loud nuclear bombs going off against my left temple.

I felt around again. My hands found nothing.

"Jewels."

What?

Wait. Was someone talking to me?

"Just let go. Let go, Jewels. Let go to see what the world will bring you."

The bombs stopped going off and my lungs no longer hurt. I closed my eyes.

"Just let go, Jewels. Just let go."

Calm overcame me. A sense of serenity and peace. Then black.

A strong hand grabbed mine. Strong arms wound around my waist. Strong legs thrust me toward the surface.

I saw Stone holding me. His partner pulling us in to the dock. "Jewels," he yelled. "Wake up." He felt my neck. "Jewels."

We reached the dock, and several other officers hauled us up. I was laid out on my back. Stone felt for a pulse, then put his ear to my chest. "Damn it. CPR now!"

I watched him do chest compressions and then blow into my mouth. Nice! He's kissing me. I grinned. Ay, wait…if he's kissing me…how come I'm seeing it? I glanced around. What the fuck! Oh, my God! Oh, my holy fucking God! Why am I? How am I? Oh, my fucking God!

I was floating over the water.

But I can't be! How can I?

"It's all right, Jewels," I heard. "You're going to be just fine." It was a woman's voice, I knew *that*, but I couldn't see her. I twisted around, looking.

"You can't see me, but I need you to listen to me."

"What the fuck is going on?" I screamed looking from the water below to my body on the dock to the people above watching. Panic rolled over me in waves. "What the hell is going on? Am I dead? How the fuck am I dead? How can I be dead?"

"Calm down, Jewels," she said with authority. "Calm

down."

I didn't. Yet somehow I did. Certainly not through my own doing. The serenity I felt underwater came over me again. "Hey, this is nice. It feels warm and fuzzy. Hey, I'm warm and fuzzy," I told the woman I couldn't see.

"Listen to me, Jewels. There's something you need to know and see."

"Am I going to stay dead?" I asked, gazing at Stone trying to bring me back.

"No, you're not. But there are things I need to show you."

Suddenly we weren't in England anymore. Or at least I thought so. Instead, I was standing in a large spacious lounge room holding a two year old girl. "Hey, Rosie," I cooed. "How's my precious baby girl?"

The golden-haired child giggled and clapped her hands.

"There are my two precious girls," a man's voice rumbled.

I was kissed by Callum. "You want anything to drink?" He walked into the kitchen.

The place was open planned, with the kitchen, dining and lounge all on one side of the house I was standing in.

My left hand smoothed down the girl's hair, and I noticed the rings on my wedding finger. I also noticed my slightly bulging belly.

"This is your future," the voice said. "You and Callum are destined for each other in this lifetime. You have had several before. Long lost love. Unrequited. But in this lifetime you are to be together. And you will bring two children into the world. You will do many things and live a long life."

"Where are we?" I gazed around the living room.

"I cannot say. But you will know the house when you find it. It is in Australia. I can tell you that. Callum is a good man, Jewels. He *is* and *will be* everything you want and need. You will have a long happy life together."

I watched us play happy families, then the image was gone, and I was back floating above the murky Thames watching Callum still trying to resuscitate me.

"There's one last thing before you go," she said. "You need to remember these numbers. 5, 9, 18, 27, 32, 42. On the Saturday you leave the hospital, go to the cafeteria and buy yourself a lottery ticket. It will be fortuitous. Remember those numbers. And don't let him carry you up those stairs. Otherwise, you will both go in, and it will all be over."

I repeated the numbers over and over as I watched my body.

I rolled over and vomited river water, coughing and gasping, sucking in air like I'd never stop. I heard the crowd cheering.

"Jewels." Callum rolled me onto my back. "You're going to be okay. There's an ambulance here. We'll get you up top, and you'll be on your way."

I gazed up into his eyes, so tired, so exhausted, so worn out.

"You'll be okay," he murmured, his hand reaching for my head.

"Don't touch her head," I heard Megan scream.

He glanced over his right shoulder at her. I saw her standing, recording the whole thing. He looked back at me and gently touched my wound. He also noticed I didn't have real hair.

"It's a wig," I whispered. "Leave it."

"We can't get a backboard down here; there's not enough room," a voice said. "We might have to get her on the riverboat."

Callum caught a blanket that was thrown at him, and he laid it over my shivering body.

"No," I croaked. "I'll walk."

"You can't walk," he said. "You could have injuries or internal bleeding." His concerned gaze warmed my heart, and I wearily smiled.

"I need to walk." I slowly rolled onto my right side and pushed myself up.

"Easy," he said, trying to help me.

"I'm okay. I'm okay," came through chattering teeth as I stood on unsteady feet.

"It's okay, I've got you. I'll carry you." His strong manly arms slid around me.

"No," I protested. "If you carry me, we'll slip, and both go back in. Let me walk." I reached for the handrail bolted into the wall.

With Callum on my left holding me up, we slowly ascended the stairs. They were slippery, and we took our time, my hand going white from the strain of hanging onto the rail. There was no way I wanted to go back into that river again. "How's the mother and child?" I asked quietly.

"They're okay," he replied, wrapping the blanket around me. "Child's fine. Mother's angry she was saved."

"Yeah," I muttered. "She told me to let her die." I saw a big red patch on the blanket. My left hand reached up to my face.

Blood!

Crap!

We reached the top step, and I saw hundreds of people gathered around just watching. *The Bill* boys were standing behind police tape and gave me a small wave.

"Jewels, Jewels, over here." Megan indicated the gurney I needed to be strapped onto, and Callum helped me over.

"Ugh," I gasped as I sat on it. My body was aching. Every muscle, every bone, every pulsating bit and bob that's packed into the human body was complaining.

Callum lifted my feet, and the ambos covered me in blankets and strapped me in, giving me oxygen and attaching a blood pressure clip to my finger.

I reached for Megan. "Come with me."

"Of course," she said.

My bed was pushed into the back of the ambulance, and she climbed in beside me. I saw Callum standing at my feet.

"I'll be at the hospital after I go back and change. I want to check up on you and the mother and child. I'll see you soon." He looked concerned, and the doors closed on his gorgeous face.

Speeding toward the hospital, I remembered some

of the things I'd been told. I looked at Megan. "Did you film the whole thing?"

She looked at the camcorder. "It's still going."

"Here, film this." She lifted the camera. "5, 9, 18, 27, 35, 42. Saturday I leave the hospital…the cafeteria." I touched my forehead. "My hair." I looked at Megan. "My hair."

She turned to the attendant. "Do you have one of those hat things that doctors and patients wear?" He nodded and found one, handed it to her, and she gave it to me.

"Leave the camera on, but don't film this." I put the hat over the front of my head and slowly slid my wig off backwards while keeping the hat in place with my left hand. It took a bit of manoeuvring, but I managed to hide my real hair from the ambo. I held the wig up, and water dripped from it. "Do you have a Ziploc bag or something?" I asked. He handed me one, and I dropped my hair in. "Here," I handed it to Megan. "Keep it safe."

We arrived at St Hugh's, and I was wheeled into emergency.

"I'll call Bob and Linda," Megan said. "To let them know what's happened."

I only vaguely heard her. I was so tired. My bones ached. My eyelids drooped. I couldn't move. I just wanted to sleep for days. People in hospital garb hovered over me.

"She has a face wound, we'll need x-rays."

"We should do x-rays of her whole body."

"How long was she in the water for?"

I drifted off.

"Jewels. Can you hear me? We need you to stay awake."

My eyelids opened a little. "I just want to sleep."

"What did she say?"

"We should get a head CT so we can see what damage has been done."

I drifted off.

"Jewels, wake up," someone yelled.

My eyes flew open, and I saw doctors hovering. "What?" I mumbled.

"You need to stay awake."

"How is she?" I heard a familiar voice ask. It was Bob. Seems he and Linda have arrived. "Is she okay? What happened? Were you filming the whole thing?" After that, it was low mutterings I couldn't hear.

I heard a radio crackle.

"No, Sarge. She's hanging in there. The doctors are working on her now. All right. I'll let her know." An officer ducked his head into the affray. "Miss, Sgt Stone is on his way. He wanted you to know."

"Ugh. Ah. Oh. Ah," I mumbled, thinking I'd said what I had been thinking. It had made sense to me, but not to the doctors, and now they looked concerned. I gazed into the bright light above my head.

"What did she say?" one face asked.

"I don't know," another said. "We'd better get those scans."

"Arrrgghhhh," I screamed, my body jerking upward.

Then I stopped.

Again!

"What the hell is going on," a doctor yelled.

"It could be the head wound. Blood clot, aneurysm. I don't know."

"Find out now," another demanded.

I stood in the hallway, watching the doctors frantically fight over my body. The officer was to my right, Bob, Linda and Megan to my left. She was holding the camera filming every single second.

"It's a blood clot," one yelled. "Get her head open."

I heard a buzzing sound and saw, while I was being thumped to get my heart started, I was getting a huge slice of hair shaved off from my left temple, over my ear and down the back of my head.

"Oh, God," I said. "How am I going to wear that?"

"Clear," someone yelled, and my heart got 360 volts.

Bip, bip, bip, bip, bip, bip, bip went the heart monitor.

"Get her head open."

A knife sliced down the middle of my bald streak.

"Oh, God did they have to," I groaned.

"Where is she?" a voice rumbled to my right.

I turned and saw Callum barrelling toward me. I smiled. I couldn't help it. The officer pointed at my body, and Callum stopped short, his eyes widening at the sight of my head being drilled. "No." He shook his head, his hand flew to his mouth, and he looked sick. "No."

"Jewels."

"Mmm?"

"There's something else you need to see."

It was that invisible woman again.

I sighed. "Am I coming back? I thought this was over before?"

"You'll be back, but there's something you need to see because there will be something you need to do as part of the plan."

"Plan? What plan? And what am *I* getting out of this? Death so far. And look at my head. I'm getting a big fat scar and a shaved head." I saw blood pouring through a tube extending from my brain.

"This won't take long. But you need to see it so you can do something about it."

We were gone and back before I knew it, and everything was still the same. My chest was being electrocuted. Bob, Linda and Megan were crying. Callum was pursing his lips.

"So, what do I get out of this?" I asked again.

"What do you want?"

"The ability to sing," I replied. "To belt the guts out of a song and sound good doing it. I've always wanted to sing," I added wistfully.

"All right. You can sing."

"Thanks." I looked at Callum. "It's all right, my love. I'll be back soon." I reached up and touched his cheek. His hand flew up, touching mine, or at least where mine sort of was.

"Charge again."

I looked at my body.

The doctors were working hard. I saw a wall clock. How long had it been now? I don't know. But this was the second time I'd died, and I was tired of it.

"Charge again."

The voltage rocked through my weary body.
Beep…beep…beep…
My heartbeat was back.
And I was gone.

Chapter 5

"Ugh." My eyelids fluttered.

"Agh." My fingers moved.

"Ah." My head rolled to the left.

"Jewels Jewels can you hear me it's me Bob Jewels you're in the hospital you're okay Jewels can you hear me why isn't she hearing me?"

God, Bob, shut up. I tried to pry my eyes open again and heard sounds of people rushing and machines beeping.

"Jewels. Jewels. I'm Doctor Martin. Can you open your eyes for me? You're in the hospital and hooked up to machines. You're going to be okay, but I need you to open your eyes and wake up."

"Ugh," I moaned again. My left hand slowly came up to my face. It was hard and fat. I opened my eyes a slit and saw blurred versions of the doctor, Bob, Linda and Megan.

"Open your eyes for me. That's it," the doctor repeated.

"Agh." I forced my eyes open, but only my right one obeyed. "Agh." I touched my left eye and felt fatness.

"Your left eye, along with the left side of your face, is swollen," the doctor said. "It's going to take some time to heal, so you won't be able to see out of it. Let me check your right one."

A light flicked back and forth across my face, and my hand explored some more. It found a bandage on my head. "Ugh." It trailed across to the right side of my face. "Agh." My right hand flew to my left shoulder. Pain started it throbbing.

"It's okay. You sprained your left shoulder in the fall. Nothing's broken, but you pulled a few muscles and ligaments. That will take time to heal as well."

"Ah." My arms slid down.

"You're going to be here for at least a week. It's already Sunday. We've kept you sedated for the last two days so your body could get some healing done."

"Ugh."

"There's been some major damage done to your face. Your eye socket and cheekbone have a spider web fracture, but that should heal. You had a blood clot from the injury, so we shaved your head, cut you open and drilled a hole to drain it. We also needed to resuscitate you so your chest will hurt for awhile."

"Agh." I stared at him through my one good eye. "Callum," I garbled.

"What was that?" He leaned in.

"Ah." I felt myself slipping back into oblivion.

"We'll keep her sedated until tomorrow…"

*****

I shifted. I heard rustling. I licked my lips and moved again. "Ugh." I took a deep breath and woke up. "Agh." My right eye opened. My left one remained tightly welded. "Ah." My tongue tried to wet my lips, but it felt like sandpaper. "Water," I managed to croak.

A nurse came rushing in. "What's that, dear?"

"Water," I croaked again.

"Of course. Let me get you some."

I blearily saw her dash out the door and sighing, I looked around. Tried to move. Tried to get a grip on reality.

"Here you go." She held a cup with a straw to my mouth.

I sucked greedily. So thirsty after everything that had happened.

"Don't rush. You can't have too much yet." She pulled the straw away.

"Ah," I muttered. "More."

"Maybe later. I'll get the doctor now that you're awake." She bustled out the door and my one good eye followed.

I reached up to touch my face, but all I felt was bandages. On my head. On my face. I touched my chest. No bandages there. I pulled my gown down. Oh, my bloody God! Look at those bruises. Bloody hell!

"Now, Jewels, no peeking." The doctor chuckled as he walked in.

"Ugh," I mumbled, and then lay there while he checked me over.

"How do you feel today?"

"Un oer I ate ain," I mumbled slowly.

"Ah." He seemed perturbed. "Didn't quite catch that. But you should be talking normally in a day or two." He put his penlight in his pocket. "I want you to sleep as much as possible. Don't stress, don't fuss, you're in good hands." He grinned.

"Ugh," I scoffed before drifting off.

*****

I heard whispering. Sounds from things rubbing on plastic. Chairs moving, machines beeping. I yawned. "Ugghh." My jaw made pain explode in my head.

"Jewels Jewels Linda get the nurse where are the painkillers get her some painkillers Jewels listen to me." I saw him hover next to the bed. "Don't worry about anything we're taking care of it all I called your mother and put out a press release to say you're okay the papers have gone nuts but you just rest." The nurse rushed in. "We'll take care of everything…you…just…rest…"

*****

"Ugh. Agh. Oh."

I was reliving everything. The car. The fall. The icy water. The pain. Death.

"Ugh." I lurched awake.

"Jewels." Callum rushed to my side. "It's okay." He leaned over me, stroking my head.

"Ugh." I reached for him.

"It's okay. Shh."

I gazed up into his big blue eyes and relaxed.

"It's okay." His voice calmed me.

My eye closed and the world went black.

*****

I breathed in and opened my eyes. Everything was clearer now. Or as clear as it could be with one eye working properly. I shifted and looked around for a clock. It read seven. I assumed in the morning since there was light coming through the window.

"Mmm." I tried to get up. "Ugh," I groaned. While I didn't feel sharp pain, I certainly felt muscle and bone ache. "Agh." I settled back.

A nurse came rushing in. "Now, now, don't rush. Take it easy. How do you feel?" She straightened the linen.

"Tired," I managed. "Worn out…exhausted…beaten up."

She smiled. "It's going to be like that was for some time. But in the meantime, are you hungry? I'll see what's for breakfast."

"Juice?" I asked hopefully as I was parched.

"I'll make sure it's icy cold," she said and walked out.

I sighed and nestled against the pillows she'd fluffed.

WHAT! THE! HELL!

Oh, God, what had happened?

I peered at my hands. Some of my nails were filed down. Who did that? Must've been Linda or Megan. There were scrapes and scratches on my palms, but they were already healing. My arms were the same. I reached for my left shoulder and tenderly poked it. "Argh." I felt some pain deep inside and gently moved my arm around. "Sssss, bloody hell."

Both of my hands searched my face and head. Bandages still in place. Swelling still prominent. I poked. "Ahh." Shouldn't have done that.

"Stop that," the nurse scolded, placing a tray on the table. She rolled it over to the bed. "Here's some toast, butter, jam, tea, coffee and juice. The doctor wants you eating simply for awhile."

"Juice," I pleaded.

She laughed and opened the container. "Here you go."

I took it and drank greedily, sucking down every last drop. "More?" I was like Oliver from the movie of the same name. He wanted soup, I wanted juice, and I wanted more.

"Tsk, tsk." She shook her head. "You eat, and I'll get you some more." She walked out the door, and I grabbed a piece of toast and shovelled it into my mouth, chewing as fast as possible.

Oh, my God, it was heaven!

I swallowed and picked up a second piece. It followed the first.

"Slow down." The nurse walked in with another juice, and a bottle of something I assumed was a drink of some sort. "Here. Slow down."

I took the juice and ripped it open, guzzling it down.

"You're going to give yourself indigestion if you keep doing that."

I sighed, licked my lips and then burped. "Oops." I covered my mouth, trying to suppress a giggle. "I'm hungry and thirsty, and I need a pee!" I exclaimed.

She laughed despite herself. "You can't have any more food just yet. But there's orange cordial." She pointed to the bottle. "As for a pee, I'll help you into the bathroom." She flung back the covers. "You'd better not let that good looking sergeant hear and see you act this way. It's un-ladylike."

"Sergeant?" I slowly swung my legs around.

"Yes. That nice man who was here last night between eight and ten. I know visiting hours end at eight, but he said he was on police business and needed to guard you."

I planted my feet on the floor and stood. "Ugh." I grabbed her. "Police business, huh?"

"Yes." She led me into the bathroom, and I saw the mirror had been covered. "He said he would be back tonight." She sat me on the toilet then stepped out so I could do my business in private.

He was here last night, eh? Police business, eh? Back tonight, eh? I washed my hands and opened the door to find her busily changing the bed. "That was quick."

"Figured I'd get it done now, so you can sleep some more."

I yawned. "God, what's the time? I'm buggered."

"Just on eight. Which means visiting hours are starting so your family will be here soon."

"My what?" I slowly climbed onto the bed.

"Your family." A slightly confused look came over

her face. "Aren't they your family?"

I thought about it. "I guess they are while I'm here," I replied just as they walked in.

"Jewels Jewels Jewels it's so good to see you up and awake how do you feel do you have enough painkillers have you had enough food is there anything you need?"

"Bob, be quiet," Linda interrupted and patted my hand. "How are you, dear? You gave us all quite a scare."

"Tired, sore, the usual."

"At least you're getting good care," she went on. "And don't worry about anything. I packed up your things at the hotel and took them back to our place. You'll be staying with us once you get out so we can look after you. And we've put your camcorder in the safe so no one can get their hands on the footage."

"Footage?"

"Of the accident, dear."

"Oh, right." I pouted my lips a little, thinking. "I'd forgotten about everything before." I looked up. "I'm tired, do you mind?"

"Of course not, dear. You just get some sleep, and we'll stand guard."

*****

When I woke, it was five p.m., and Bob and Linda were watching the small TV in between reading manuscripts or writing. "I'm hungry," I murmured. Yawning, I stretched and felt the stiffness in my muscles. "Oh, my God, I'm stiff." I groaned at the ache.

"Jewels you're awake how about something good to eat not this dreary slop they have here I can run out and get something."

His incessant droning got on my nerve. "Stop it," I snapped. They both looked at me in shock. "For the love of bloody God, Bob, slow down." I rubbed my head. It was pounding. "Just…slow…down." The pounding got louder, and my stomach joined in. "Oh, God. I'm gonna be sick…" And up came my morning toast all over the bedcovers. "Oh." I didn't know whether to move or stay.

"Nurse Nurse," Bob yelled. "Patient being sick in here."

She came running in. "Oh, dear. Don't move." She ran back out.

I slowly slid out from under the cover and Linda helped me into the bathroom to clean up. "I'm so sorry," I whined. "I'm sorry. I don't know what…I don't feel good and the pain." I washed my mouth out.

"Shh, it's okay." She wiped my face. "You've gone through hell, and we know it's going to get a lot worse before it gets better."

"I'm sorry." I looked at her. "But can't he just stop? Or slow down? I already have pain screaming through my head. I don't need him too."

She rubbed my back. "I'll talk to him. Tell him to calm down when he's talking to you."

"I don't mean to be a pain," I whined again.

"I know."

We walked into my room and saw the bed had been made for the second time that day.

"I'm sorry," I said to Bob. "I just…" I slowly shook my head. "I don't know. I'm sorry."

He looked from me to Linda then back to me. "That's okay, Jewels. You're under pressure," he said slow and calmly. "You're going to go through a lot, and need plenty of support." He glanced at Linda for reassurance, and she nodded. "Whatever is going on inside of you, you let it out on us. We're your support structure. Whatever we can do. Just ask."

I was surprised by his change of voice and was reassured by it. "Thanks. I will. But for now, I guess I won't be eating any fancy food."

"No. I guess not," he replied.

The nurse came in with a needle. "This will help with the nausea. And it might make you a bit sleepy, so get some rest." She injected it into my leg.

"Mmm, I am tired."

"We'll leave you to it then," Linda said. "Come on, Bob. Let's leave Jewels to rest." She ushered him out the door. "We'll see you tomorrow."

"Bye," I called and slid down in the bed.

I slept, but apparently quite restlessly; at least from what I could tell by the whispering.

"She ate her first solid meal today, but then brought it up a few hours ago. We gave her something, and she's been sleeping since. Although she's been quite restless."

"I'll see if I can calm her down," a deep voice rumbled.

I whimpered. "Callum. Callum." My right eye opened and I reached for him as he stepped toward me. "Ah, uh Callum."

He climbed onto the bed and gathered me in his manly arms. "Shh, sweetheart. I'm here. You go back to sleep. It's okay. I'm here."

"Callum," I whimpered, snuggling into the thick chocolate wool jumper covering his manly chest.

His arms enveloped me. "Shh, sweetie, you sleep. I'm here now."

I sighed and snuggled closer. Everything was okay now.

*****

Wednesday started a little better. I was able to sit and slowly eat my food. I had a shower by myself, and put on normal clothes…well, a tracksuit anyway. I was watching TV with Bob and Linda when the pain struck.

"Arggghhh," I cried, rubbing my head. "God, make it stop." I rocked back and forth, my head in my hands.

"Doctor Doctor," Bob yelled. "We need painkillers."

The jackhammer was pounding away, chipping bit by bit off my sanity until it was in a pile.

The doctor raced in and gave me an injection. "This should help. We are trying to ween you off so we can get you onto pills."

"What the fuck are you trying to ween me off for?" I yelled. "I'm in fucking pain here. Look what the fuck you did to me. Of course I'm in fucking pain." I gasped and burst into tears. "I'm sorry, oh, God I'm sorry. I don't know why I said that, I'm sorry." Linda rubbed my back.

"Jewels. You're going through major trauma. Your heart stopped twice, we cut your head open, and that was after hitting it on concrete. You drowned. You've gone through hell, and your emotions are going to be as well. You are going to be all over the place for some time because it's going to take some time to heal," the doctor told me.

I looked up at him, tears rolling down my face. "Can't you do something?"

"Except to give you pills to take every day and suggest a grief counsellor, there's nothing else we *can* do. It's a storm you're going to have to ride out, and everyone around you is going to have to deal with it."

"Oh, God," I sobbed, burying my face in my hands. "Oh, God."

The doctor walked out and Bob, not knowing what to do, left as well when Linda indicated to him to go.

"It's okay, Jewels. We're here. Let's talk things through."

So that's what we did.

Linda told me about their house, how I'd have a huge room and wing to myself, so if I needed to scream in pain, I could do so without disturbing anyone. They would also hire a nurse if I needed it. Their property was huge, and behind high locked gates, so I would have privacy while I recovered.

"Sounds great," I murmured. "I'm tired."

"Let's get you into bed." She tucked me in. "I'll go and let you rest. We'll see you tomorrow."

"Okay."

I relived the accident. The car hitting me. Me hitting

the concrete. Going underwater. The pain in my head. The pain in my head…the pain in my head…what?

I woke to that damn incessant pounding that wouldn't stop.

"Argh," I cried. "Make it stop, make it stop."

The nurse came running in with a needle. "It's okay, this will work quickly. It's okay."

I walked around the room waiting for the pain to stop.

Five minutes.

The pounding got louder.

Ten minutes.

There were two jackhammers going.

Fifteen minutes.

"Make it stop," I screamed, grabbing my head. "Make it stop. Arggghhh." I started throwing things around the room. Bits and pieces I could get my hands on.

"Stop it," yelled the nurse, running in. "Stop it this instant."

"I can't and I won't," I yelled back.

When I'm in pain, and it doesn't stop, I get frustrated. And that frustration leads me to cry. That's what I was doing now.

"Make it stop," I cried, clutching my head. "Make it stop." I grabbed the bed covers as I slid down to the floor.

"Jewels."

I cried harder.

"Maybe you can stop her," the nurse said impatiently. "You seemed to calm her down last night."

"Jewels." Callum walked around the bed and bent

down. "What is it, sweetheart? Come here." His arms slid around me.

I wrapped my arms around his neck. "Make it stop," I cried. "Make it stop." I buried my face in his neck.

"Shh, sweetheart. It's okay. I'll make it stop." He gathered me up and in one fluid movement, lifted me, and climbed onto the bed. Wrapping himself around me, he pulled me close. "There, there." He stroked the right side of my face. "It's okay. It's okay."

I gazed into his eyes, still crying, but feeling much calmer. "The pain won't stop," I whimpered. "It won't stop."

"I know." His deep voice was soothing and his finger gentle. "I know. Come here; let me take care of you." He rocked me gently, his words easing the pain.

I felt safe in his arms. Safe and secure. And I knew he would always be there when I needed him.

*****

"Okay. These will be your pills from now on," the doctor told me the next morning. "Anti-inflammatories. Painkillers. Antibiotics. Blood thinners. You won't be having injections anymore."

"I'll take the painkillers, but what do I need the rest for?" I dubiously looked at all the pills on the table.

"You swallowed river water, you need antibiotics. Blood thinners so your blood won't clot, and anti-inflammatories to help the swelling."

"How many do I take at one time?"

"Fifteen."

"What?"

"Fifteen," he repeated. "Three times a day with meals."

"What?" I repeated. "Are you fucking kidding me? You want me to take forty-five fucking pills a day." I shook my head in disbelief.

"For awhile," he said. "Then we'll start cutting back."

"Fuck that!" I exclaimed. "Forty-five fucking pills a day. No fucking way, José." I threw myself off the bed and stormed around the small room.

"They are going to make you better, you know that. And you'll have to take the full course."

I turned to him. "How long's that?"

"Ten to twelve weeks for some."

"What! I'm not taking them that long. I want to go home next week and can't take forty-five pills with me."

He looked at me strangely. "You *do know* you won't be going home just yet?"

I stared back. "What do you mean, *just yet?*"

"Well, it's going to be some time before you can fly."

"How long?" I demanded.

"With your injuries and pain issues, you can't fly for a good ten to twelve weeks."

"What?" My jaw hit the floor. "What the fuck do you mean I can't go home? I can't fly? What do you mean I can't fly home? I need to go home. I want to go home," I stuttered, tears flowing.

"Jewels." He stood in front of me. "You arrested. Twice. And have a serious head injury. You *cannot* fly."

"Get out," I said. When he didn't move, I screamed, "Get out."

He collected the pills and left me to my screaming and tears.

And I told Bob and Linda all about it when they brought lunch. "What the hell am I going to do? I, I, I need to go home," I stuttered through my tears.

"Everything is planned," Bob said. "We have a room ready for you at home. Frances is dealing with legal concerns, and I'm dealing with the publicity and hospital bills."

I looked at him. "How am I supposed to repay you for that?"

"Never mind," he said. "Just sell lots of books."

They stayed until six and then Callum turned up at eight.

"Hi." He stood in the doorway looking all gorgeous and shy in a royal blue wool jumper which brought out his eyes.

"Hi." I smiled, and my heart did a little dance. "Come in."

He took a few steps into the room. "I, um, don't want to bother you if you want to rest."

"Mmm. That hasn't stopped you coming here every night," I said.

He blushed then slid his leather jacket off.

"Take a seat."

He pulled the chair up to the bed, and for the next two hours, we talked. About his family, his work, my book, my life. We laughed and joked, and it was good.

No pain. No problems. It was good.

Really good!

And over way too soon.

"Sergeant." The nurse stuck her head in the door. "It's ten p.m."

"Oh, right." He looked at me, disappointment raining over his face.

"Come back tomorrow," I invited with a smile, wanting to kiss those lush, thick lips.

His lips smiled back. "Okay." He stood. "Um… goodnight then."

"Night." I bit my smiling lips.

Then he was gone.

*****

I was feeling good and couldn't wait for Callum's visit the next day. Until then, I had to have scans and tests to see how I was doing.

Bah! Bugger that!

Once they were over, and Bob and Linda had been and left, I showered and put on nice clothes. I know, I know. We weren't on a date. But I wanted to look nice, and my pain was tolerable. I was lying on the bed when he arrived. "Hi. Come sit." I patted the spot on the bed beside me.

He smiled shyly, took off his coat, and climbed up beside me.

"How are you?" I asked.

"Good." He nodded. "And you?"

"I had some tests today. I'm doing good. The doctor

said I might be able to go home in the next day or two."

"That's good," he enthused, his big blue eyes gazing into mine.

I couldn't stop smiling. The whole time we talked I realised I was smiling. I couldn't help it. The guy was gorgeous and everything I wanted in a man. He made me tingly and happy and calm and peaceful. He was everything.

My everything.

Listening to him talk I knew I was in love.

And wondered if he was.

*****

I was talking to Bob and Linda the next morning when the doctor walked in.

"Good news, Jewels. You can go home today."

"What?"

"You can go home," he repeated. "I have your pills here. The next two weeks' worth anyway. Your prescriptions will need to be refilled. Your tests yesterday were good. You can leave once you sign your release form."

"Fantastic!" I exclaimed. "Give them here, and I'll be on my way." He handed them to me, and I signed my name.

"I'll just get you a wheelchair, and you can go."

"Woohoo!"

"I'll run down and get the car," Bob said, running out the door.

"Let's get your things," Linda said.

The nurse came in with a wheelchair, and we rolled downstairs to the lobby. When I saw the cafeteria sign, I remembered what I'd been told. "Wait."

"What is it?" Linda asked.

"Take me to the cafeteria."

"Why?"

"Please." I looked at her. "Just take me."

The nurse wheeled me into the café, and I asked for a lotto ticket with the numbers I'd been told. Giving it a kiss for good luck, I finally left the hospital.

Chapter 6

Bob drove us through very nice neighbourhoods toward their home. I saw large two storey houses with big front yards, lush green trees overhanging the streets, and expensive cars in driveways. Stopping at a large wooden gate, Bob flicked a switch on the dashboard. The gates opened to reveal an enormous two storey large white brick mansion with healthy lawns, a circular driveway, and two white pillars out the front. We pulled to a stop at the front of the wrought iron screen doors.

"Here we are." Linda stepped out and opened my door.

I popped my buckle and slid out. "This is gorgeous," I breathed.

She shut the door behind me, and Bob planted my bag on the path. "Thank you, thank you," he gushed. "We like it don't we, Linda."

"Yes, we do," she said, taking my arm. "Let's get you inside and settled, and then we'll have some lunch."

Bob unlocked the doors, and we entered a spacious alcove with marble floors and white walls decorated with prints. A large carpeted staircase climbed up the wall on my right to the balcony above. A door on my left led to a spacious lounge area with fireplace, and beyond that the kitchen which you could also get to by the hallway in front of me. To my right was another cosy looking room with plush sofas and thick carpeting. A small chandelier hung from the white ceiling.

"This is so nice," I said.

"And we hope you enjoy staying here," Linda said as Bob took our coats and scarves. "We want you to feel as welcome and safe as possible so you can relax and recuperate."

"Well, that's going to be some time," I replied, glancing at her. "I've been told ten to twelve weeks. Think you can put up with my crap for that long?"

Linda laughed softly and held my hand. "Sweetie. We know it's going to get worse and much darker before it gets better. But we are here for you, don't worry about it. Anything you need. Isn't that right, Bob?"

He nodded in agreement. "Anything you need you just ask."

I smiled softly. "Thanks. That means a lot."

"Good. Now, let's get you settled upstairs. Wait until you see your room."

Linda led me upstairs, and Bob followed with my bag. We walked down the hallway to the right and stopped at the door at the end. She opened it and stepped through.

"Oh, wow." I followed her in. "This is nice too."

A massive four-poster bed sat against the wall on my left, with an ornate wood trunk at the end, and matching bedside tables. A crystal lamp with a blue shade sat on each one, and silky soft curtains hung from the railing around the bed. To my right sat a sofa, two lounge chairs, and a small coffee table between them on a blue rug. Against the wall in front of me was an old-fashioned roller door desk with a lamp.

"You can set up your computer on the desk, and there's a huge wardrobe next to the bathroom."

I turned around. Against the wall to the left of the door was a huge built-in robe and the bathroom door was beside it.

Bob put my bag on the bed. "Linda, why don't you help Jewels unpack and settle in, and I'll see about some lunch." He left us to it.

In no time, we'd unpacked both of my cases, put my toiletries in the bathroom, which had the mirror covered, and set my laptop on the desk with my other electrical gadgets beside it. I wanted everything within arm's reach. Plugging each one into the outlet, I let them charge up while we went downstairs.

The kitchen was very modern and had an adjoining dining room. French doors and windows ran the length of both rooms, and I saw a back porch and a green lawn with trees.

"I'm not hungry," I said when Bob placed a plate of sandwiches on the counter. I looked at the bag in my hand. "But, I guess I'll need to eat something to take these." I shook my bag, and the pills rattled.

"Just eat what you can," Linda said, settling me at the table.

I rubbed my head through my bandages. The pounding was still going strong, and while the morphine in the hospital for the first few days had all but stopped it, the pills weren't doing the job. I'd also been told I could have headaches for up to a year or more since my face was fractured and my head split open.

I divided up my pills. Five before eating. Five during eating. Five after eating.

Ugh!

I drank some of the juice Bob poured me. Down, down, down. One pill, two pill, three pill, four pill, five pill. Down, down, down they went.

Ugh! My head shook in disgust.

We sat and talked while the pills kicked in and I slowly munched on half a sandwich.

Five more pills. Down, down, down. I ate another half.

Five more pills. Down, down, down.

Red one. Green one. Blue one. White one. There was even a pink one.

Fifteen pills. Down, down, down.

"Oh, gawd I feel sick," I mumbled. "I hate taking pills. And what's the point, this damn pounding won't stop." I rubbed my head again. I was going to have to get those bandages off. Today! "I'm tired. Do you mind if I go lie down?" I glanced at them through a bleary right eye.

"Of course not, dear." Linda patted my hand. "You

just do what you need to. Don't worry about us. If you need to sleep. If you need to eat or get some air. You just do it. Whatever it takes for you to get better."

I gave her a tired grin. "Thanks." I trudged upstairs into my room. I wanted to sleep. I really did. I also wanted to get online and tell everyone I was okay. But I knew I needed to rest by the fact my eyelid was nearly closed, and my brain was turning to fuzz. So I kicked off my shoes and climbed onto the bed. Pulling a crochet blanket over me, I tried my best to snuggle down into the pillow and sleep.

And sleep…

And sleep…

And…oh, God…never mind.

The pounding in my head never subsided, and I wondered if the doctor had given me real painkillers or bloody sugar pills. They didn't work, and hadn't since during the week when he'd told me it was the pills or nothing.

Nothing my arse! There was no way I was going to suffer the full effects of that pain pounding in my head.

I rolled over, punched the pillow and sighed. No, not comfy. I rolled onto my back and stared at the pale blue ceiling. I rolled back onto my left and looked out the window at the fading sun.

Nope! Not working at all!

Throwing off the blanket, I plonked down in front of my laptop and turned it on. Waiting for it to boot up, I flicked through my folder, checking that my papers were there. I typed in my password, checked my phone, yep, recharged, and online I went. Clicking onto Blogger, I tapped on new post.

My Adventures in Merry Old England: November 19th, 2011

Should I load a pic? I wondered. *It wouldn't look good, but people would know I'm still here.* Pulling up the webcam, I freaked.

"Ogh, oog, argh." Hands flew up to cover my eyes, and I jumped back. My heart pounded in my chest, and I took a deep breath. Looking at the screen, I saw myself for the first time. My head was wrapped, and the left side of my face was bandaged.

"Ugh! Bloody hell!"

Quickly taking a snap, I uploaded it into my post.

Yes, peeps, as you can see by the photo of my hideously deformed self, I am still alive, and this is how bad I look. Don't believe any of the stories out there. There are only two people you can believe when it comes to me. That's my publisher and me. If anyone else dares post or talk about me and what they know, punch them in the head for me.

Now, I've been told I can't fly home for awhile, so I'll be stuck here in dreary old England recuperating. Well, more like hiding out since I'm uglier than Frankenstein's monster at the moment. But I will try to post occasionally, letting you know what I'm doing. Right now, I'm typing this, and I'm tired, and my head is killing me, and clearly, I'm going to need something to keep me busy. Who knows, maybe I'll write another book. But if typing this is making me tired, then God knows what a book will do to me. Can't do that no more, peeps, so I'm signing off.

See you all later.

Jewels xxoo

I hit the publish button and checked my emails. There were thousands. THOUS. ANDS!

My Twitter and Facebook pages were loaded with messages and emails. Most said get well. A few said die in hell.

Pfft. Been dead, done that! Besides, hell didn't agree with me.

I rubbed my eyes. "Ow." My left one hurt, still swollen almost shut, and my right one ached. I'd had enough, and the pounding hadn't subsided. I got up and strolled around the room, willing the pain to go away. I straightened some books on the coffee table, fluffed the couch cushions, and tucked the lamp out of the way. I folded the blanket, put the pillows back, and picked up my chapstick from the bedside table. Rubbing it on my lips, I noticed it was almost six.

"Oh, God." I sighed and walked over to the wardrobe. I pushed the doors open and started straightening my clothes. "Put that there, those here, jewellery together," I muttered.

There was a knock at the door. "Yes."

Linda popped her head in. "Would you like something to eat now? Bob and I normally eat at eight, but if you'd like to, you can pick your own time."

I glanced at my travel clock. Six-thirty. "I do eat

around this time back home. I don't really like eating late."

"That's fine. Why don't you grab your pills and we'll pop downstairs."

I grabbed the bag, and we headed for the kitchen. "I'm not hungry," I said. But that seemed to be normal these days.

"That's okay, as long as you have something so you can take your pills," Linda replied. "Would you like some soup?"

"Sure."

We chatted while she heated soup and I swallowed the first five pills with some juice. "Blech." I shivered. I hated swallowing pills. A few spoonfuls of soup and I swallowed five more. Finishing off the soup, I took the last five.

Bob came barrelling in with a huge armful of newspapers and documents. "Whoo. You're still in the news, Jewels." He dumped everything on the table. "Tabloids, papers, we've even gotten letters, emails and phone calls from people wanting to know about you." He pushed a few in front of me. "We're trying to get the book published as fast as possible to capitalise on your accident." He glanced at me in case he'd said something wrong.

"Well," I said. "Capitalising is good. We should do all we can to help push the book faster." I tried to read one of the papers, but it's kind of hard with one eye.

"Good, good. That's good. And, of course, you'll get final approval on everything."

I glanced up at him. "Thanks for everything you're

doing," I said and pointed at the pile of papers. "Are you buying everyone I'm in? I'd like to collect them and take them home."

"Yes, we are, and we'll keep doing that for you," he said, gathering them up.

A scream tore through the night!

I jumped and my brow furrowed. *"What was that?"*

"Probably the next door neighbour," Linda said. "While we do have space around us, the neighbourhood is so quiet at times you can hear people if they yell or scream. Cars racing down the street, tyres squealing if they brake."

"So, like any other neighbourhood then," I said.

"Like any other neighbourhood," Bob replied.

"I'm going upstairs." I stood up. "Pills aren't kicking in yet, but maybe a shower will help, and I'd love to wash my face and hair."

"Oh, I could help with that," Linda said, trying not to look alarmed.

I saw the look anyway. "No. That's okay." I wondered why they both looked worried. "I have to see my head sometime. The doctor said it was okay to wash now." That seemed to calm them a little.

"Well, if you need help, let me know," Linda said and linked her arm through mine. "I'll come and see if you've got enough towels."

"Uh. Okay."

There were enough towels, and I had plenty of shampoo and conditioner, so with a bit of a nudging, I got her out of there.

"God." I sighed, leaning against the door after I

locked it. Now, about that mirror. I stood at the cabinet and ran my hands over the huge wall mirror. It was there. I could see the light reflecting off it through the material they'd hung over it.

My hands explored, looking for a way to get the fabric off, and found it had been tightly tucked around the corners. I started tugging and managed to pull the black material free, leaving a few shards stuck underneath the corners.

God, my head! It pounded, and I saw my hand reach up and rub it. I hadn't seen my reflection in awhile. Since the day of the accident. My head was swathed in a bandage. My face had gauze stuck on it.

I fingered the zip of my jacket and pulled it down, wanting to see how badly my chest was still bruised. I already knew it was bad. Did I really want to see it again? I had to, didn't I? I needed to see it all. To see the whole picture. I needed to see. Against my better judgement, I unbuttoned my shirt and pushed it open. I gasped and quickly covered my chest, wrapping my shirt around me and closing my eyes against the sight of those ugly black bruises.

Come on, girl. You need to get tough. You need to see this. You need to see what happened to you so you can move forth and heal.

I opened my eye, took a huge breath and opened my shirt again. The sight was *so* ugly. Of course it was. My whole chest was full of black and blue bruises. I looked at my head and grabbed the bandage, pushing it off. There was gauze over the scar, but I saw the shaved strip.

I started tugging at the face gauze, plucking from the bottom and pulling it up. Up, up, up. Over my cheek. Over my eye. Over my head scar. I touched it. Not looking in the mirror. I gazed at the gauze in my hands. Slightly bloody. Slightly pussy.

Do I really want to do this? Do I really want to see what I have become?

I glanced around the bathroom, trying to find the strength. The mental strength. The emotional strength. I cried a few tears. I couldn't help it. It was emotional.

Get yourself together. You have to do this.

I took a deep breath…and looked.

And screamed…

"Arggghhh." The sound tore through my lips like a million mile an hour freight train, compounding the pain in my head, making it feel like it was actually exploding.

The sight before me was horrifying.

"Arggghhh. Arggghhh."

The swelling. The black. The yellow. The stitches. The ugliness. The animal.

"Arggghhh. Arggghhh."

I looked around for something to stop the image. To make it go away. I stared again. I was the most hideous, ugly, revolting, repulsive person I'd ever seen.

My head. My face. My chest.

All black, blue and yellow. Swollen and ugly.

"Jewels Jewels let us in," Bob yelled and banged on the door. The knob rattled. "Let us in."

"Arggghhh," I screamed again, sickened by the sight. The mirror shattered into a huge spider web.

Instead of one of me looking back, there were millions.

Bob kicked through the door, and he and Linda stood horrified at the sight of my arm extended toward the mirror. My fist was still in the middle of the web of shatterings.

I saw my hand. Saw the blood dripping down the mirror and into the cracks. Spreading red evil through veins of death.

"Oh, no," Linda gasped, grabbing a towel and reaching for my hand.

"I'll call an ambulance." Bob turned to leave.

"No." Linda quickly wrapped my hand. "Not yet, let's just see how bad it is first. Jewels won't want to go back to the hospital so soon." She ran the tap, and after removing the towel from my hand, held it under the cold water.

Blood thinned and ran in rivulets down the stark white porcelain and into the drain.

It was mesmerising. And I had stopped screaming. Everything was hazy. Everything was fuzzy. It's like I was underwater and could only just hear them. Could only just make out the words.

The cuts on my hand weren't too bad, so Linda stuck Band-Aids on them. Bob just hovered in the doorway.

I gazed up at the mirror. Millions of me stared back. Ugly, horrible, horrifying, revolting, repulsive, and any other word there was to use that I can't think of right now, me. The Elephant Man looked better than me. Frankenstein's monster looked better than me. The ugliest dog on earth looked better than me. I vomited into the sink. It wasn't much, but I kept dry retching.

Linda rubbed my back. "It's okay. Take deep breaths. You'll be fine."

I washed my mouth out and looked in the mirror. I was ugly. So ugly no man would ever love me looking like this.

Callum!

No. No. He won't love me. How could he love me looking like this?

That invisible woman I spoke to when I was dead said nothing about this.

Callum…

I sobbed.

Callum…

"Arggghhh," I cried, sobbing so hard my body shook. "Arggghhh." I pushed Linda away and ran into the bedroom, throwing myself onto the bed. "Arggghhh." I couldn't stop. The pain. The pounding. The emotional and mental strain of it all. The physical exhaustion, lack of sleep, and the thought of losing the one thing that right now was meaning more to me than anything else was too much.

"Someone's at the gate," Bob said.

"Argh." I crumpled the bed covers as I slid to the floor.

"Shh, Jewels. It's okay. It will get better."

"Arggghhh." I clutched my head as nuclear bombs blasted through it.

"Jewels," a deep voice rumbled into the room. "Jewels." Callum burst through the doorway in full uniform.

"No," I screamed. "No, go away, don't look at me." I cowered against the bed, trying to hide my head. Callum hadn't seen my scars, let alone my real hair. I'd worn one of those hat things the whole time in the hospital to keep my appearance secret.

He kneeled beside me. "Jewels," he commanded, grabbing both of my arms.

"No," I screamed again. "Don't look at me. Leave me alone." He turned me around to face him, and I thrashed around, pushing him away with my hand, aiming for his face. I didn't want him seeing me. He couldn't see me. "No," I cried through my tears. "Don't look at me. Don't look at me."

"Jewels." He shook me slightly. "Look at me."

I faced him square in the eye and saw the horrified look come over his face.

His eyes scanned my scars. My bruises. My chest.

"No," I screamed again and managed to get away from him, running out of my room, into the hallway, and into the room on my left. Locking the door, I slid down against it to the floor, racked with sobs.

"Jewels." He banged on the door. "Jewels. Let me in. Or come out. I want to see you. Jewels."

"Go away," I cried through tears. "Go away. I don't want you seeing me like this, it's not fair. I'm so ugly. You won't be able to love me looking like this." I grabbed my head. "You won't love me like this."

"What's she saying? What does she mean?" whispered through the door.

"I don't know," whispered back. "She's not doing well after seeing her scars. She just needs time."

"Why didn't I know you'd brought her home? I went to the hospital to see her, and they told me she'd gone home."

"It didn't occur to us to let you know."

"I could've been here to help her. Jewels." He knocked.

I cried harder.

"Look, sweetie. They're only scars. They *will* fade. It may take awhile, but things will get better. Why don't you come out so we can clean them up and everything will be all right."

"Go away. How can you love me looking like this? I can't let you see me. Just leave me alone and don't come back. Don't ever come back. I never want to see you again. Just go. Arggghhh."

There was more whispering…then silence.

I don't know how long I sat there. I had no idea of time or space. It didn't occur to me to find out or even move, but my legs were cramping, and I slowly stretched one then the other. I used my shirt to wipe my face, and slowly stood up then opened the door, and walked into the hallway. It was empty, and the house was quiet. I walked into my bedroom and saw Linda on one of the chairs reading a book.

She saw me, closed it, and stood. "You're out. How are you?" She came over to me.

"Empty."

Would you like to have that shower now?"

"Yes."

"Come on, I'll help you wash your hair."

Chapter 7

I sat on the side of the bed.

Thinking.

The tears had stopped. The pounding continued. I felt empty. It was morning, and I'd sat there all night. After Linda had helped me wash. After I'd cleaned my face and brushed my teeth. After I'd stopped crying.

The pain continued. That jackhammer pounding that didn't let up. Not for one second. Not even after taking painkillers.

I sat on the side of the bed.

A square hand mirror was trapped by my fingers which didn't want to let go. A mirror I'd been staring at myself in. The bruises. The colour. The ugly. A mirror I'd asked Linda for, because I could no longer see myself in the bathroom mirror, and my travel one was too small.

Too small to see the ugly for all it was.

The ugly black stitches zigzagging around the side of my ugly head. The ugly swollen cheek all fat and lumpy and hard to touch. The ugly swollen eye, and the ugly swollen lips, and the ugly swollen jaw, and the ugly swollen ear, and the ugly swollen head.

And then there was my chest. A torso covered in ugly.

Ugly! Ugly! Ugly!

I sat on the side of the bed.

Sorrow and self-pity. Anger and hatred. Despair and intolerance.

I sat on the side of the bed.

Night turned to day, and the sun shone its rays through the open curtained windows.

I sat on the side of the bed.

Staring into that mirror. Feeling my blood boil. Feeling the anger grow. Feeling the hatred roar.

I sat on the side of the bed.

I'd briefly seen a snippet in one of the tabloids yesterday that the woman I'd saved was going to sue me for saving her.

I sat on the side of the bed.

The bitch who'd tried to kill herself *and* her child by driving into the river. The bitch who'd wanted to take her child with her and kill him for nothing. The bitch that I should have let drown in her own vile anger and hatred.

I no longer sat on the side of the bed.

I am Jewels Diva, and *no one* sues me for saving their life. *No one* pisses me off.

Chapter 8

I went downstairs into the kitchen and handed Linda a piece of paper. "Here's a list of things I'm going to need." I sat opposite her. "Are you able to get them for me?" The list wasn't very long but had a few essentials I'd thought long and hard about. "And do you have a hair shaver? You know, one of those do it yourself hair cutters?"

She looked up from reading the list. "Bob has one."

I looked at Bob.

He nodded. "It's upstairs."

"Good. I want to deal with some business this week."

They were both staring at my head. Finally uncovered after a week.

"Yes," I said. "It's all going to hang out from now on. I think I'm back to my old self. In fact." My finger touched my lip. "I'm better than I was. No shit taking from now on. Jewels is out for herself." I looked at Bob. "Bobby boy, let's do business. I want to know what's been happening, what's going to happen, and who wants to know about it. Who wants Jewels and does Jewels want them." They sat dumbfounded by my newfound self. I clapped my hands. "Chop, chop. Let's get moving people."

We went to work. Bob laid out all the papers he'd bought, and we put them in order as I read them. I read all the letters and emails, and we filed them into a folder. He told me about all the phone calls the publishing house had gotten. So many they had to put the answering machine on, and it had run red hot. They had received invitations for me to attend parties and functions, and because I'd been branded the "wounded heroine", every newspaper, TV show, talk show, and host wanted an interview. Even overseas countries like America, Canada, my home country of Australia, and other European countries wanted me.

"All in due time," I stated, putting my hand out. "Are the invites in order? Let me see them." I questioned Bob about each one. Most didn't seem good enough to go to, but I put a few aside. "Keep these in mind. I might need them."

We stopped long enough for me to have my lunch of pills and then kept going. I dictated a few responses to emails, and we put together a publicity packet that reporters and papers would get before stopping around six.

"God, I'm buggered." I yawned, rubbing my eyes. "I might go to bed after I eat. Is there anything else?"

"Um." Bob looked uncomfortable and shifted in his seat. "There is… Some…thing."

"What?"

"Would you consider writing a book about your experience?" His hands fidgeted on the table.

I shook my head. "I don't have time. I'm too tired. I don't sleep."

"Exactly!" He got excited. "If you need to get it out talk about it deal with it in some way then write it out or type it on your computer I can get some recorders if you'd rather talk and then Megan could type it up." I started protesting, but he put his hand up to stop me. "Just think about it. It might help you to get it all out."

I sat looking at him, feeling my body sag with exhaustion. "I'll think about it."

"That's all I'm asking," he said. "Let me get you something to eat."

So, between mouthfuls of pills, I gulped down a small bowl of soup. "Oh." I rubbed my head and yawned. "I'm going upstairs." I trudged up into my room and threw myself on the bed. Trying to block out the pain, I buried my head under the pillow…

Gurgle, gurgle, gurgle.

I struggled for air. I couldn't breathe.

Gurgle, gurgle, gurgle.

I didn't want to open my mouth. I'd drink half of the river.

My lungs burned…

My head ached…

I couldn't breathe…

I couldn't breathe…

I couldn't breathe…

My body threw itself into a sitting position gasping for air. "Ah, huh, ah, huh, ah, huh."

My hands grabbed my throat. "Can't breathe. I can't breathe. Ah, huh, ah, huh, ah, huh."

My head pounded. My heart raced. "Ugh." I clutched my chest. "Ugh."

I took a few deep breaths. The pain in my chest subsided. My pulse calmed down.

The pounding in my head didn't.

I grabbed my travel clock. Eleven p.m. Ugh, at least I'd gotten a few hours sleep. I went into the bathroom and washed my face. Bob had removed the mirror, so now there was only an outline of where it had once hung. I brushed my teeth and changed into a pair of bed pants and a tank top. Wandering back into the bedroom, I lay on top of the bed and thought about things.

But then I realised I didn't want to think about things and tried to go back to sleep.

Which was *not* forthcoming!

As usual, the pain in my head kept up with its ever-present pounding. Tossing and turning through the rest of the night, I kept waking. And every time I checked the clock. Ugh. I was sleeping in ten minute increments.

When I slept, I dreamed. When I was awake, I thought. The images didn't stop pounding away in my head, almost as hard as that damn jackhammer.

I rolled out of bed, hot, sweaty and bloody exhausted. I managed to stand in the shower without falling, and collapsed on the chair Linda had put at the sink for me. My breathing was laboured, and I felt sick. Like when you get a head cold, and every time you breathe, you can taste the crap in your nose. It was that kind of sick feeling. Like I had germs in my body I could taste and smell. And it was making me sick.

I put my head in my hand, leant on the cabinet, and took a few deep breaths. They cleared my head, so I carefully walked into the bedroom and got dressed. I walked down the hall, reached the stairs, and nearly fell down, clinging to the bannister. Dizziness overtook me, and I sat on a step. "Ugh. Breathe, just breathe."

"Jewels let me help you." Bob pounded down the stairs behind me, helped me up, and into the kitchen. "Sit I'll get you some food."

Fifteen pills and three slices of bread later, I felt better.

Almost!

The dizziness was gone, but the pounding persisted.

"You going to work today?" I felt drained.

"I am, but Linda's home all day."

I saw her putting food away. "Mmm. Did you get me the things on the list yet?" I asked her.

"Yesterday, while you were sleeping," she said. "I put them in your wardrobe."

"Thanks. I'll go have a look." I stood slowly, so the dizziness didn't come back.

"Are you…" she started.

"I'm fine," I said. "I'll just go slow." When I reached my room, I checked the things she'd bought. Yep. Yep. Yep. It was all there. I headed for the laptop and went to Blogger.

My Adventures in Merry Old England: November 21st, 2011

It's Monday, and I'm still alive. Not doing well. Barely sleeping. 45 pill a day popping. Can barely stand sometimes. Head's always pounding, and I can't see out of my left eye still.

All in all, it's a fucking horrible day.

Jewels xxoo

I hit publish and stood, and opening a window, I breathed deeply. The air smelt good. Clean, crisp, and nice. I heard the message bell ding on the laptop and went to read it.

'*What happened to that hot cop who saved you? Have you married him yet?*' Cyn asked on Facebook.

Callum!

His name's Callum!

The other night came flooding through my brain. The way I looked. The look on his face. The fact he'd just turned up out of nowhere. I hadn't called him, and neither had Bob and Linda. But apparently, a neighbour had heard my screams and called the police. He attended, and upon seeing Bob at the door, knew it was me and had come running.

I remembered the look. The look that came down over his face when he saw my scars. My bruises. My ugliness. It was horrible. And so devastating. I started crying.

After a few minutes, I walked around the room. That woman, whoever she was, had told me we were meant for each other. But I was ugly, and he'd seen it. We were supposedly destined for each other in this lifetime, but after seeing the look on his face, in his eyes. I shook my head. I didn't see how it could happen. Unless he was able to look past the ugliness and open his heart to me, there was just no way.

I decided to put my thoughts into words and sat down at the computer. I was tired, but hoped setting my mind a task would work. Three hours later when I looked up, everything I'd written was garbled. None of it made sense. Not one word.

"Arggghhh." I angrily deleted it all and whimpered. "Make it stop. Please make it stop."

*****

"No, no, let me go. I want to die." The woman scratched and clawed at me viciously. *"Where's my baby. I want to die. Let me die."*

"Stop it," I yelled, sawing at the seatbelt.

The car went down…

I couldn't breathe…

Water filled the vehicle…

I couldn't breathe…

Water filled my lungs.

I couldn't breathe…

I couldn't breathe…

I couldn't breathe…

I sat up with a start, gasping for air. The only thing my nightmares did was relive them every time I slept. I looked at the clock. My head pounded. It was ten p.m. My head pounded. My stomach churned. My head pounded. I took deep breaths and grabbed the bottle of water from the bedside table. "Mmm, yuck, warm."

I got up and walked around, willing the pain to stop. I sat on the sofa. The pain didn't stop. I opened the window and breathed the cold night air. The pain didn't stop. I sat down at my computer. The pain didn't stop.

It drove me…

To write.

What is pain? Pain is what I'm feeling. The doctors said it would go away in time. I don't have time. I need it to go away now. Now, so I can have my sanity back. So I can sleep. So I can eat. So I can stand for longer than five minutes without feeling sick and wanting to vomit. I want the pain to go. Go away and never come back. Go visit someone else and terrorise them. Yes, that's right, pain, you are a terrorist, and I need to kill you. Kill you so you'll go away and never come back.

Are you living? Because I am. Does pain live? It's living in my head. I didn't invite it to move in. It invited itself, and it's settled in for the long haul. How do I get rid of you? How do I make you go away? To pack your bags, get in your car, and go far away. I hate you, pain. I hate you so much I feel like killing you. But how do I do that? How do I kill you? Can you tell me? Can you tell me how to kill you? Or would that be too easy? Too easy to kill pain. Can pain be killed? In order to kill pain, what must one do? Do they kill pain alone or do they kill themselves? Is killing yourself the answer? Will it stop the pain?

Physical pain maybe. Mental pain maybe. Emotional pain maybe. But what about soul pain? Will my soul still feel pain when I die? It didn't. When

I died, I didn't feel pain at all. Did you die then too, pain? The pain in my head from hitting it was gone. Did the pain die when I died? Is that what one must do to stop soul pain? Heart pain. Brain pain. My brain hurts. My eye hurts. My cheek hurts. My chest hurts. Everything hurts. Every fucking thing hurts. My shoulder hurts from hitting it on the wall corner. My brain hurts from where the doctors drilled it. My face hurts from the swelling. It's not going down you know. The swelling. It's still big and ugly and bruised and horrible, and my eye is still swollen, and I can't see out of it, and it won't get better.

None of it will get better. I'm on 45 pills a fucking day, and none of it's getting better. Why won't it get better? Why? Because pain is living in my head and my chest. Pain is beating on my head every fucking minute of every fucking hour of every fucking day of every fucking week. Day after day. Day after fucking day. Hour after hour. Hour after fucking hour. Minute after minute. Minute after every fucking bloody God fearing fucking minute. It hurts. It fucking hurts and nothing helps it. Nothing stops it. Nothing makes it go away. Not pills. Not sleeping. Not breathing. Not time helps the fucking pain go away, and that's why pain needs to be killed because it's hurting me and I want it to stop.

Stop terrorising me with its pain and the fucking anger and hatred. Pain needs to go away and leave me alone. Terrorise someone else with your fucking horrible bad self and leave me the fuck alone. Leave me alone to suffer in peace. Peace and quiet and calm.

That's what I need. Peace and quiet. Quiet from the pounding jackhammer going 24 fucking 7 in my head. Pounding, pounding, pounding. Chipping away at each and every little bit of my soul. My psyche. My brain. It's making my eyes pop out of my head. That's right. My eyes are popping out of my fucking head. They may not actually be doing it, but it fucking feels like it. Like I'm going to wake up, and my eyes will be sitting on the pillow beside me, watching me because you, you fucking pain, pushed them out during the night.

Oh, wait, that's right, I'm awake at night because I can't fucking sleep. You keep me awake with your incessant pounding. The jibes and insults that come with each chip, each bit of my brain that was sane once. Once, but no more. No, no more. It hasn't been sane for days. Now I sit all alone on this tiny little island called Insanity. Insanity is driving me insane. You're driving me insane, and I don't want to be alone on Insanity. You can join me when you're done. When you're done chipping away at my brain till there's nothing left. Nothing left of my body. My brain. My conscience. My thoughts. I have very blurred thoughts. Sometimes they make sense. Most times they don't. Not anymore.

Not since the accident. Although you can't really call it an accident. The first part was. Or was it? That bitch was determined to drive into the river and kill herself and her kid and to hell with anyone who got in her way. No one else mattered. It didn't matter if she killed anyone else. It didn't matter to her. So it really wasn't an accident, was it? More like an "incident". Yes, that's it. "The incident". The incident that changed my life and brought you into mine. Brought you forever until the end of time. Either my time or yours, and I don't know when that will be, but I suppose I must be the one to end it. I will end the pain. Pain, you stop with me, and it's up to me to stop you. It's up to me to stop the pain.

Chapter 9

I blearily gazed at the screen. The words and pictures were fuzzy and bleeding into each other. Bleeding like my head had been last Friday.

I stared at my Twitter page for what seemed like forever, and then my fingers reached for the keys. *It fucking hurts peeps. My head. My chest. My face. My heart. It fucking hurts, and I want it to stop. I need it to stop.'*

I vaguely remember hitting the tweet button before dragging myself into a standing position. Light was flaring through the window on the left, so I stumbled my way to it and pressed my face against the glass. Sun poured in. I opened it. Crystal cool air poured in. I greedily sucked it in. Breath after breath after breath.

Nothing eased the pain in my head. Sitting at my laptop all night didn't help. But then I'd had a need to write, or in this case, type. Type and get it all out into words on the screen, so maybe I could understand them. I rubbed my eyes. My head. My chest. The pain had eased there, only aching from time to time. My ribs felt bent and buckled. My back ached. Even my hands were sore from the hours spent typing away.

I slowly walked around the bed and picked up my clock. Seven a.m. I picked up my bag of pills and shuffled to the door. I shuffled down the hall and had just reached the staircase when Linda came out of her room, and upon seeing me, rushed to my side.

"Here, let me help you." She gently guided me down the stairs and into the kitchen. "I'll get you some breakfast." She put some food together while Bob just stared at me.

"Whuh?" I mumbled, barely able to speak.

"You, oh." He shifted uncomfortably. "Look awful. Did you get any sleep?"

"No," came my reply. "I was on the puter from leven ta seven," I gurgled.

"Your eyes are bloodshot, I mean your eye is blood, I mean, you don't look good," he stuttered, quickly drinking his coffee.

"Yeah, well, you'd look like shit if you did this," I mumbled with next to no strength. I looked at the plate Linda put in front of me. Marmite on toast. Downing the pills and food, I sat at the table cradling my head, willing the pain to go away. I didn't realise Bob had left until Linda prodded me.

"It's eight-thirty. Why don't I get you upstairs? You can have a nice hot shower, and then I'll tuck you into bed."

"Ugh." She led me upstairs, and while the shower helped clean my body, it didn't clean my soul. Or the pain.

Lying on my side in bed, the curtains now closed,

my laptop off, I tried to keep calm and quiet. Tried to make my mind go blank. It didn't work…

I pulled the woman through the window, the seatbelt having finally broken. Strong hands grabbed her and took her up toward the surface. I swam after them but didn't move. I swam harder but stayed where I was. I thrashed my arms and legs, willing myself to move, to go towards the surface, to follow the person who'd taken the woman. I didn't move. No, no this can't be happening. No. No, let me go, let me go, I need to go, I need to get to the surface, I need to breathe.

I can't breathe…

I can't breathe…

I can't breathe…

I sat up choking for air, and throwing back the cover ran into the bathroom and splashed cold water on my face. "Ugh," I gasped. "Ah." I was hot and dry and stripped off my jacket trying to cool down. I thrust my hand under the tap and gathered water, greedily drinking, the coolness calming the fire in my throat. "Ugh." I turned the tap off and dried my face, then, taking a few deep breaths, I walked into the bedroom, sat down on the sofa and stayed there for the rest of the day.

I sat in bed that night, my computer on my lap. I knew sleep wasn't coming, but I didn't write either. Images and sounds, colours and tones went through my head. Sirens. Screaming. Yelling. Callum running at me like I wanted him to. Tears rolled down my cheeks. I wiped them away and began to type.

I fell asleep, for what it was worth, sometime during the night. More like the wee hours of the morning, I suspected, but time seemed kinda irrelevant now.

After breakfast, I reminded Bob and Linda of one of the invitations I'd received. "There's a party tonight. I'm going."

They looked at me in shock. "But but but," Bob stuttered.

"Jewels," Linda said. "Are you sure? It's so soon, and you're not sleeping. You haven't eaten much. You're not well enough to go anywhere, let alone a party."

"Not well enough," Bob added. "What if you collapse and need to be rushed to hospital again?"

"Then I'll be rushed to hospital again," I snapped. "I'm sick of being sick. I want to go out. I want to make an impact. I want people to know Jewels Diva is not dead, but still alive, and regardless of how I look, if you don't like it then fuck off." I waved my finger. "*Nothing* stops Jewels Diva. Not even death. I am going out and showing the world I'm still here." I leaned back in my seat. "But I want someone to go with me. What about Megan? She can film the whole thing."

They looked at each other, unsure of what to say or do. I wasn't their daughter, only their temporary dependant. And since I was an adult, they couldn't really do anything. And they knew it. "I'll call Megan," Bob said, resignation in his voice.

"Great. And can you tell her to pick up this outfit for me." I handed over a magazine layout. "I want it for tonight." They both stared at the picture. "Is that okay?"

"Um," Bob murmured. "Sure."

"Great. Oh, Linda. Can you help me with my hair?"

"Sure."

She helped me upstairs and into the bathroom while Bob called Megan. I sat on the chair and Linda wrapped an old towel around me.

"What do you want first?"

"I want you to shave the other side of my head," I said.

"You what?" She was stunned.

"Shave my head on the right side to match the left. That way it's even." She stood staring at me. "And make sure it starts at the same spot." She didn't move. "Come on," I urged.

With a sigh, she went and found Bob's hair trimmer and got to work on my head. Half hour later I had matching stripes.

"Nice," I said, looking in the handheld mirror. "Now, the dye." It was one of the things she'd gotten for me a few days ago.

Linda pulled on the plastic gloves and poured on the hair dye, carefully rubbing it in around my scar. We left it on for half an hour before she carefully rinsed it out.

I looked in the mirror. "Bloody hell." It was the same colour as my wig which had been washed and placed in the wardrobe. There was a knock at the door.

"Come in," Linda called.

Megan walked in with several shopping bags. "Whoa," she said, her eyes widening. She dropped the bags on the floor. "I, oh, I." Her hand flew to her mouth.

"Don't worry, Megs, it feels worse than it looks," I

said, picking up the bags. Laying out the clothes on the bed, I smiled. "Nice. I'm going to look fucking awesome." I turned to Megan. "Got an outfit for tonight, Megs? You'll need to carry the camcorder as well. Film my first big adventure after the "incident"." I made the quotation marks with my fingers.

Megan's eyes were still wide, her hand still over her mouth.

I picked up the invite from the bedside table. "Let's see. It starts at eight." I turned around. "We'll get there at nine to make sure everyone's arrived. Want to drive, or will we have a car?" I looked at Linda.

"Well," she started uncertainly. "We could get you one."

"Fantastic." I glanced back to Megan. "Megsie, be here at eight-thirty. Now go. There's a few things I need to do before tonight." I turned back to the bed and held up my new outfit.

After lunch, I tried watching TV. I didn't want to sleep yet as I'd be too tired tonight. I flicked through the channels. Rubbish. Rubbish. Rubbish. I walked around the house. I sat on the back porch and tried to meditate. I sat on the computer and typed page upon page upon page. After eating, I threw myself down on the bed for a rest…

I tried to open my eyes. I wanted to open my mouth. I wanted to breathe, but I couldn't.

"One, two, three, four, five. Breathe two, three, four, five. Push two, three, four, five. Breathe, two, three, four, five." I watched Callum trying to resuscitate me. I wanted to open my eyes. I wanted to

open my mouth.

I wanted to breathe…

I wanted to breathe…

I wanted to breathe…

I sat up, gasping. After getting myself under control, I looked at the clock. Seven-thirty. Ugh, only one hour. I jumped in the shower and towelled off, and had just pulled up my underwear when Linda walked in.

"Oh, you've showered. Ready for your hair?"

"Yeah, let's do it." I wrapped a robe around me and sat while she gelled, brushed, blow dried and teased my hair. I now had a Mohawk thanks to the two shaved strips. Picking up the long red hair extensions she'd bought for me the other day, she clipped and wound them through my hair. After half an hour the effect made me look like a punk rocker. I moved the mirror around, trying for a better view. "Nice! Okay. I'll get dressed."

Sitting on the edge of the bed, I pulled on socks and the cobalt blue faux leather pants. The four inch studded and chained leather boots came next. Zipping them up, I stood. "Whoa."

Linda reached out and grabbed me. "You okay?"

I sighed and looked down. "Yeah, I'm fine. Just have to get used to these boots is all."

She picked up the matching corseted jacket and carefully slid it on my left arm then the right. Adjusting my breasts, I pulled up the zip which ended under my bra, so the chest lay open. It was part corset, part jacket with studs and chains. I pulled on black studded fingerless leather gloves and straightened my clothes. "How do I look?" I asked as Megan walked in the door.

"Like you want trouble," Linda replied, crossing her arms.

"Good." I grinned. "'Cause I do." I threw on earrings, some necklaces and my small digital recorder, which was on a chain, around my neck. Might come in handy for recording dirty conversations. Grabbing my phone, I held it up and took a picture of my head scar. Loading it into Twitter, I wrote, *Going out tonight and looking for trouble peeps. Think this will help?'*

With a click of the submit button, and grabbing the camcorder, Megan and I were on our way to a night we would never forget.

Chapter 10

We barged through the door like we owned the place.

Well, I did anyway. Megan shuffled behind, quickly showing the bouncer we had an invite. I strode across the carpet path in front of me. There was a long bar on the wall to my right, stairs ahead of me, and a stage between them and the three storey floor-to-ceiling windows on my left which faced the huge crowded area full of celebs. I stopped to listen to the man on stage.

"Who's that?" I whispered to Megan who held the camcorder up.

"Don't know," she whispered back.

"Mmm." I gazed around at all of the celebrities. TV, movie, reality stars all getting pissed on free alcohol. None of them had noticed me.

Yet!

"Let's go upstairs," I said and moved toward them. One, two, three, four, five, six, seven, eight. Eight steps to the landing before we had to turn around for the next flight.

"Oh, my God! Jewels Diva!"

I stopped in my tracks, not sure whether to turn around or keep going.

"Jewels Diva. That is you?"

The room had gone silent, and I slowly looked over my right shoulder, catching Megan's eye on the way. I saw the man on stage staring at me.

"You are Jewels Diva, right?"

I turned to face him and walked over to the bannister. A low 'ah' went through the room. Clearly, they'd seen my head and face. I leaned on the railing. "Who the fuck are you?"

"I'm Peter Fifer. I…"

"Who?"

A few laughs went through the room.

"Peter Fifer." He seemed uncertain.

*Mmm. Peter…*I gazed up at the ceiling, trying to remember if I knew him or not. Then it hit me. "Oh, right. The *fuckwit* who axed *The Bill, Heartbeat,* and a few other things."

Shock thundered over his face, and I heard a rumble around the crowd.

I leaned forward. "Now, Petey boy. Either you have an aversion to cops or just really good drama. And what was it you wasted the money on? Old farts like Simon Cowell and trumped up trollopy tarts…"

"Hey!"

I looked for the source of annoyance. "Ah! Katie Price. It's good to know you know what you are!" I turned back to Peter. "What a waste." I shook my head and swivelled to walk up the stairs.

"Ms Diva. I was going to offer you millions for

your own reality show."

I stopped again. Interesting! I turned back.

He smirked. "I knew that would interest you. Money always does that." He was so cocksure of himself.

I leaned on the bannister. "Let me tell you where you can put your money." I poked a finger at him. "*Exactly* where your head is. *Up your arse*," I yelled. Turning, I saw *The Bill* boys and everyone else applauding me below. I stormed up the stairs with Megan in tow.

"Jewels."

We reached the first floor, turned, and stormed up the stairs to the second.

"Jewels."

I stopped and peered down behind me. Christopher Fox was standing at the bottom of the stairs trying to get up. But since it was a women's only section, the bouncers stopped him.

"Jewels," he called.

I walked into the throng.

Five minutes later, I was bored and leaned on the bannister. Looking down, I saw Christopher and Dominic at the bar. Oh, Dominic. If only we had a chance. I looked at Megan then spoke into the camera. "Down there is Dominic Power. If I didn't look like the beast from hell, I might've actually had a chance with him." I looked down, and they were looking up.

"Why don't you come down and we can have a chat," Christopher yelled.

I noticed the other boys sitting at a table drinking and watching. "No, thanks. But Dominic can come up."

"No, thanks," his lips mouthed, and he walked away.

"Well," I said into the camera. "That's a man who looks just as good going as he does coming. In my bed that is," I joked. I glanced back at them and realised the weight of the situation.

He wasn't interested because of the way I looked.

And I looked ugly.

I spoke into the camera. "And there's no way in hell he'll ever be in my bed with me looking like this. Let's go." I headed for the stairs.

Christopher leapt at me. "Jewels, whoa, look at that head." He took a step back.

"Go away, Christopher." I started walking down the stairs to the ground floor.

"Jewels. Come back and show us your scars."

I turned so quickly he bumped into me. "Piss off. What part of that don't you understand?" I grabbed Megan, and we headed for the door. At the last minute, I veered off to the left before the coat check, pulling her with me down the hall and into the ladies on our right. Realising there was no one there, I let out a sigh. "Oh, God. *Why did I come here?*" I snapped, grabbing my head.

"Do you *really* want me to answer that?" Megan answered quietly.

"No, no," I said, looking at her. "It's *all* my fault. I just..." I rubbed my face. I hadn't put any make-up on so the bruises would be on full show. I sighed again, leaned against the sink, and gazed up at the ceiling. My head pounded, which wasn't new, and the longer the pain went on, the more frustrated I got.

A couple of women came in. I didn't know who they were, but they stared in horror at my head and face. "What are you looking at?" I snapped. They rushed into a couple of stalls, and I paced back and forth. I was a freak, and that's how everyone was looking at me. As a freak. And it was *pissing. Me. Off.* They rushed out and washed their hands, looking from each other to me to each other.

"Get out of here," I yelled, and they quickly scurried out. "Argh." I kicked a stall door. The sink. The wall. Even a pot plant. Dirt splayed across the floor in a mess. "Ugh. I need to pee." I stormed into a stall and tried to get out of my pants. I heard Megan in the stall beside me. She was also out before me. I stumbled through the door to see her washing her hands and a female cop barging in.

"Stop where you are. Put your hands up. Police."

We looked at each other in amazement.

"Say what?" I said.

"I said stop where you are and put your hands up. This is a raid."

I laughed. I couldn't help it. I hadn't laughed since before the incident, and for some reason found this scene to be incredibly funny. I didn't know why I just did. "Yeah right," I gasped, turning the tap on and washing my hands.

"I said put your hands up."

"Listen, girly," I snapped. "We just came out from taking a leak. I'm going to wash my bloody hands."

Megan cowered beside me. "I think she's serious," she whispered.

The blonde officer whipped out her asp and pepper spray. She looked young and a little unsure of herself and the situation, especially since she was staring at my head. "This is a raid. You're to raise your hands and do as I say."

"No," I disagreed, putting my left hand on my hip. "How do *we know* this is a raid? You could be an imposter, and you're trying to rob us."

"If you don't put your hands up and do what I say I'll spray you."

"Yeah, right. We don't even know if you're the real thing, and if you pepper spray me," I pointed to my head, "or *hurt* me, after what I've been through, you won't like what I do to you."

Megan whimpered and fiddled with my camcorder, which hung around her neck.

"Are you recording this? Stop touching that. Turn it off," the cop yelled.

Megan whimpered more.

"I said, turn it off," the officer yelled, and pepper sprayed Megan.

"Ahh," she screamed.

I swung my head away and threw my arm around it, crouching on the floor. I could not afford to be sprayed. I heard Megan screaming, and then pain tore through the left side of my back, dangerously close to my head. "What the fuck!"

Another beating.

I spun around to my right and lashed out with my leg. The kick took the cop to the floor and knocking her asp away, I jumped on her. Seeing the can of pepper spray nearby, I grabbed it and sprayed her in the face.

"Arggghhh," she screamed.

"Serves you right," I yelled back. Pulling her cuffs off her belt and rolling her over, I locked her hands behind her back, and stuffed a wad of toilet paper into her mouth. "See how you like *that,* bitch." I pushed her face to the floor and pulled Megan to her feet. "Here." I gave her some toilet paper. "Use this." I led her out through the door, down the hall and back into the club.

I stopped dead.

Cops were everywhere.

Celebs were gathered in a group, and everyone was complaining.

"What the fuck," I said, leading Megan to the bar. "Water and towels," I said. "Now!" The barman handed me a jug of cold water and several clean towels. Dipping one into the water I dabbed Megan's eyes. "Here, this should feel better." She held it to her face, and I looked around. The boys were at the front of the crowd and staring at me. I shrugged. Others were arguing with cops. Cops were running around. And I'd had enough!

I whistled. Sharp and piercing. "Who the fuck is in charge here?" I yelled loudly.

The noise stopped.

"Well," I yelled again. "Who's in charge of this fucking stupidity?"

"I am," a voice boomed.

The voice rattled my soul, and again, I stopped dead then slowly turned around.

Callum!

I whimpered.

He was seeing my face, head and chest for the first time since Saturday, and I was seeing him. His broad muscular shoulders underneath his coat. His chiselled jaw and big blue caring and concerned eyes underneath his hat. I gazed into those eyes.

"Jewels." His voice was tender. "What are you… how are you…I haven't seen you since…" His eyes scanned every inch of my face, my head, my chest.

For a moment I felt love. I felt concern. I felt real emotion out of him.

"How are you?" he repeated gently.

I couldn't breathe. I wanted him so desperately it made my heart hurt more than my head. Until I heard Megan crying behind me. Something snapped inside of me, and I hardened against the man I loved.

"What the fuck is going on?" I stormed. "Some bitch of a PC comes into the bathroom, and pepper sprays Megan, and then hits me with her asp all because we wanted to wash our hands after taking a piss." His gaze flitted to Megan then back to me, and he frowned. "Yeah," I continued. "Pepper sprayed her for no reason and then hit me while I was on the ground covering my head. My head." I pointed to it. "That if she'd hit me on I could very well be dead now. And you know I've been dead. Dead's not something I want to be again. What sort of sergeant are you if you can't keep your fucking PCs in line." That pissed him off.

"I'm sorry your friend got herself pepper sprayed, and yes…" Concern flooded his eyes, and his voice softened. "I'm sorry if you were hurt, that *never* should have happened." His fingers touched my cheek. I pulled away. He hardened. "But surely she had reason to?"

"Reason!" I cried. "She had *no* fucking reason, but the bitch paid for it anyway." I crossed my arms in defiance. "Gave her a taste of her own medicine. See how she likes it."

His eyes went cold. "What did you do?"

"Did to her what she did to us."

He stepped towards me, a furious hard look on his face. "What did you do and where is she?"

The look scared me, and I was reminded of the power within him. I gulped. "Sprayed her and cuffed her. She's in the ladies sucking it up," I said.

"Someone get in the ladies and get our PC out," he yelled over my head. "You'd better *hope* she's not hurt." His eyes flashed. "Or you could be up on serious charges." His face was level with mine.

I went from scared to angry in nought point zero five seconds. "Charges," I scoffed. "After what that bitch did to us." I pointed at Megan. " *We* have it all on camera. *We* didn't touch her."

His eyes flicked back and forth, doubt clear for all to see.

"We got her."

I turned around. Two officers had un-cuffed the PC and were leading her out the door.

"You'd better hope she's okay," Callum growled and stormed after her. "PC Knight, watch her."

An officer stood near me.

"Oh, that's fucking fantastic," I yelled. "You're

more concerned about your little bitch than me. I have a head wound. *I died,"* I screamed, and my head pounded. "Ah, fuck it!" I watched him go out the door then glanced at the PC watching me. "What are you looking at?" I sniped and turned back to Megan. I dabbed the towel in the water and touched it to her eyes. "Better?"

"Getting there," she said in a shaky voice.

I glanced around the room. Sniffer dogs were roaming the crowd, and none of the celebs looked happy. I had no idea what drugs they were looking for, I just hoped they didn't stop at me. I pulled a face at the PC babysitting me. "Do you do everything Sgt Stone tells you to?"

He shifted uneasily.

"Well?"

"Yes, ma'am."

"What? Speak up, I can't hear you. I'm deaf and blind on the left side of my head."

"Yes, ma'am." He seemed young, maybe early twenties. Certainly couldn't be all that experienced.

The sniffer dogs headed towards us. Cute little beagles they were. And since Megan, the PC, and I were the only ones at the bar, the beagle took one sniff of me and sat on his haunches.

"Hello, cutie. What's your name? Let me guess." I looked into his big brown eyes. "Fido? No. Rover? No. Rex?" I crouched down and mooshed his face. "Hello, cutie." He started playing.

"You're under arrest…"

I looked up to see the PC get his cuffs out. *"For*

*what?"*I sneered and went back to playing with the dog.

"For drugs and…"

"Stand down, PC Knight." Callum was belting toward us.

"But, Sarge. She's—"

"Not a drug user or seller."

"But the dog?"

"Is smelling the medication she's on," Callum continued.

I looked up from the dog to PC Knight and sneered. "Forty-five fucking pills a day. I'm a walking, talking, fucking pharmacy." I went back to the dog.

Callum waved the handler away. "It's all right, she's clean."

"Aw," I cried. "Bye, doggie." I waved at Fido, or Rover, or Rex or whatever his name was and stood. "Arggghhh." I grabbed my head.

"Jewels." Callum's hand shot out. "Are you okay?"

"Oh, I'm just *fucking* dandy," I snapped, pulling away.

He leaned in close. "Stop acting like a bloody idiot and grow up. I'm extremely sorry you were hit, but carrying on the way you are might get you arrested anyway." Cold blue eyes bored into mine.

"I hate you," I whispered.

He flinched, surprised by my declaration.

"I hate you for making me love you," I went on. "I hate you for coming into my life. I hate you for saving my life. I hate you for seeing my head and scars. I hate you for the way you reacted. I hate you for making me feel this way," I sobbed. "I hate you for making me love you and for not loving me in return."

A whole gamut of emotion swept over him as he digested my words.

A whole wave of hate, anger and guilt rolled over me. I had no idea why I'd just said all of that but then I hadn't been myself lately.

"Why would I love you?" he said softly. "Look at the way you're acting."

What!

I furiously seethed inside as I stared into his icy cold eyes. As much as I loved this man and knew I was going to spend the rest of my life with him, my anger was boiling over. No thanks to the drugs I was on, or the jackhammer pounding away on the left side of my head. I couldn't help what I did next. It just happened without me even thinking.

My right hand tore across his left cheek with ferocious speed and a very loud crack.

His head spun, and his hand flew to his lips. I'd drawn blood. The crowd went silent. We stood facing each other, a boiling sea of emotion making both of us sick.

I was trembling, panting. My nerves shot. I'd just slapped the man I loved.

"You're under arrest." His voice was low and deep.

I gathered my wits and put my hands out. "So, Sergeant. How do you want me?" I watched his face. "Missionary position from the front? Or doggy style from the back?"

He grabbed his cuffs, swung me around and pulled my hands behind my back.

"Oooo, typical. Wants to be the big man in control and take me from behind."

"Sergeant."

We spun around.

"I want a full report, now." Inspector Dale stood tall and commanding.

"Yes, sir," Callum said then turned to PC Knight. "Watch her." He started walking away.

I fiddled with my cuffs. I couldn't see them but somehow managed to get loose, popping one, then the other open. Oh, that was too easy! "Oh, Sergeant," I called. He turned, and I threw his cuffs at him. "You might want those back for when you catch *real* criminals." I planted my hands on my hips.

There were a few cheers and catcalls.

He was completely dumbfounded, looking from me to the cuffs back to me.

PC Knight whipped out his asp.

I cocked a brow at him. "Oh, no, little boy." I pointed to my head. "You're *not* going to use that on me, are you? I'd make sure you lose your job over it. Besides." I flicked an imaginary piece of fluff from his shoulder. "The asp is the penis extension of the pommy copper, and you don't look big enough to have a penis." I heard cheers and jibes and became a little nasty. "So, let me tell *you* something. You'd better learn how to *really* use that thing if you want to look like a man. So, here's what you do. Get on YouTube and look up old episodes of *The Bill,* because they *really* knew how to whip theirs out, and you'll definitely learn a thing or two." I glanced at the boys. My biggest fans were cheering me on.

"Put that away, Knight." Callum stood in front of us.

"Come on, baby," I crooned seductively at Callum. "Give it to me." He glared so hard he could've set me on fire. "Come on, you know you want to." I leaned in. "Give it to me." I could see decisions flitting through his eyes.

"You're nicked," he boomed, grabbing my left arm.

"And there you have it, ladies and gentlemen. The trifecta of the pommy copper. Got me some cuff action. Got me some asp action. Got me a 'you're nicked'." I did a little hand wave as he led me away. "It was nice not meeting you all. I wish I could stay." I looked back at the boys. "Can you take care of Megan, and get down to the station, and call Bob and Linda and the press," I yelled. "Jewels Diva is being arrested. Woohoo!"

Chapter 11

"Watch your head." Callum opened the back door of his squad car.

"Oh, sweetie," I mocked. "Watch yours." I gave him a saucy look. "The one in your pants, I mean."

He gave me a dirty look and shoved me into the back seat.

"It might want to come out to play," I called as he slammed my door and walked around to get into the driver's side.

"Put your seatbelt on," he growled and started the car.

I clicked the record button on the little gadget hanging around my neck. This was going to be good, and I wanted to catch every single second of it.

We stayed quiet on our way to the station, but I saw his eyes glance at me several times in the rear-view. I was calm. I don't know why. After the last week and a half not once had I been calm. But now I was. Like I wanted to play. I was feeling cheeky and saucy, and maybe I wanted to get into trouble. Maybe I had been looking for trouble wearing the outfit I was in.

Or maybe it was an emotional war I wanted to play

out with Callum. I had loved him. He had seen me. He had hated me. I had hated him. Well, I didn't really, but then my emotions were all over the place. One minute I was up, next I was down. Right now, I was madly in love with him, and aching *badly* for him.

Pulling to a stop in front of the station, he opened my door. "Come with me." He slammed the door and started walking.

"I'd love to *come* with you, sweetie, but not in the Police Station." He turned and stared. "I prefer to do it in a bed with some privacy, where no one can hear." I arched a brow and made a kissing gesture with my lips.

His fingers slid around my right arm, and he forcibly led me to the booking counter. "Jewels Diva. Assault on two police officers," he said. "Empty your pockets."

"I don't have any," I said and gave a saucy winked. "But feel free to search me."

"Do you have anything on you?" His steely gaze didn't waver.

"Mmm. Just my phone."

"Get it out."

"No." I wiggled my hips against his. "You get it out."

He had been holding my arm the whole time and now pulled me against him. "This is no game," he growled. "Whatever you have on you, put it on the bloody counter."

My good eye blinked a few times. Damn, he could be scary. I reluctantly pulled my phone out of my jacket and placed it in front of the officer.

"One diamante blue iPhone," he said.

Callum looked at another PC. "Put her in interview room one. I'll be in there soon." He thrust me toward the officer, and I whimpered then straightened my clothes. Standing tall, I followed the PC through the door.

Sitting down on the chair, I gathered myself. It was going to be a long night. I sighed. I hope the boys got Megan out of there, and that Bob and Linda are on their way. We need that footage to show we didn't do anything. And Callum. "Huh." I snorted. Dirty big headed pig he was. But damn, what a good looking one. And so take charge. I glanced at my watch. I'd been sitting there for fifteen minutes. I stood, stretched my weary muscles and walked around the room.

"Sit down," thundered behind me.

I jumped, freaking out. "God sake," I gasped. "You know better than to scare me." I tried to calm my racing heart.

He softened, and voice became gentle. "I'm sorry. Take a seat."

We sat opposite each other, and he clicked on the recorder. "This is Sergeant Callum Stone on Wednesday the twenty-third of November, two thousand and eleven. It's." He checked his watch. "Twenty-three fifteen, I am with the suspect, Jewels Diva, on assault charges." He shuffled his papers. "Ms Diva. Tell me in your own words what happened."

I gazed at him, trying to read his expression. It was neutral. "Megan Mortimer and I were in the ladies. Megan was at the basin, I was trying to get my pants up when I stumbled out of the stall and saw a female cop come in. She told us to stop where we were and put our hands up. She repeated herself and told us it was a raid." I crossed my arms. "I laughed at her, thinking it was a joke and not real. I washed my hands, she repeated herself, I told her I'd just finished taking a leak and was going to wash my hands. She whipped out her asp and pepper spray. She repeated herself again, and when Megan fiddled with the camcorder, she yelled to turn it off. When Megan didn't, the bitch pepper sprayed her. I spun around and covered my head, crouching on the floor, so I didn't get spray on my face. And the pain hit me on the back. Right here." I used my left hand to indicate the spot on my back. "*Way* too close to my head for my liking." I glared at Callum. "She hit me again, and that's when I kicked out at the bitch." I leaned on the table. "Jumped on her, sprayed her, cuffed her and shoved toilet paper in her mouth to make it harder for her." I shifted back in my seat and crossed my arms and legs. "Bitch deserved it. We did *nothing* to her. *Nothing,*" I spat. "But she could've killed *me* in one foul blow."

His expression softened, clearly concerned about that. "I'm sorry," he whispered. Clearing his throat, he went on. "I'm sorry you were in that position." He glanced down at his papers, uneasy as I glared at him. "I'll, uh, need to see your back."

Standing up, I unzipped my jacket and pulled it down. Making sure he got a full view to which his eyes widened. I turned around. "Has it left a mark? I can't see."

He stood behind me, his fingers gently touching my back. I shivered. "A red mark," he whispered. "But it might bruise later."

I pulled my coat back up. "Yeah, well. What else is new? Just another bruise." I looked into his face. Eyes I wanted to drown in. A cheek I wanted to stroke. Arms I wanted around me. Lips I wanted on mine. I swallowed.

He cleared his throat again. "Sit down." Taking his chair, he watched me.

I stared back, feeling sorry for myself. I was tired and wanted to go home. And my portable jackhammer was working away in my head.

"Jewels," he whispered. "Um, do you need to see the doctor?"

That stirred up the fire in me. I rubbed his leg with my foot. "Can't *you* be my doctor?" I leant against the table, making sure my breasts were in full view. "We can play hospital," I crooned seductively. "I'll be the patient, and you can be my doctor, and you can do a *thorough* examination." His eyes widened. "Don't worry about gloves, use your bare hands to caress and feel my hot velvety skin." He swallowed. "To explore every mountain, every crevice, every single inch of me." My foot rubbed higher. "Don't worry about your stethoscope, just lay your head upon my ample bosom and hear my heart race as your lush, thick lips enclose around my nipple, as your hands grab me, bringing me to your chest." His pupils dilated, his lips opened. "You know you want me, Callum. You know you want me. You want me so much you want to drink from my lips, my breasts, my body. You want to ravish me and eat me and never stop. Your hunger for me will never let you stop." My foot went higher. "You want to grab me with those strong manly hands and plant me on your strong hard shaft…"

The inspector barged in. "Sergeant."

"Sir." Callum sped to his feet.

"Oh, hello!" My brows hit my hairline.

Callum followed my gaze and quickly grabbed his papers to cover the erection straining to get out of his pants.

"Wish I had a camera. Or at least my phone." My eyes greedily watched.

"Sergeant, why don't you go and take a moment. I'll finish dealing with this."

"Sir," he choked and strode out of the room.

I laughed, putting my legs up on the table and crossing them. *"That. Was. Hilarious."*

The Inspector stared at my feet on the table. They landed with a hard thud when he knocked them off.

I stared dirtily at him. "That wasn't nice."

"Here's how it is, Ms Diva. I've seen and heard the footage. I've heard Miss Mortimer's statement. I've also heard PC Roland's statement. It's a very unfortunate turn of events. Especially, since it was our very own Sgt Stone who rescued you last week. And as your lawyer so forcefully pointed out, if PC Roland *had* have hit you in the head, we would have a death on our hands now wouldn't we?" He'd stood over me the whole time which was quite intimidating. Leaning toward me, his voice lowered. "Since PC Roland struck first, we have no choice but to let you go." His steely grey eyes bored into mine. "Here's your phone, Ms Diva. Don't ever let me see you in here, or anywhere else, ever again."

I took my phone with a shaky hand.

"Do I make myself very clear?"

I swallowed and wavered. "Yes sir," came out as a tiny sound.

"Good. Now, get out," he thundered.

I ran through the door, and PC Knight warily escorted me to the front desk. I looked around for Callum and spied him behind a window.

"Jewels Jewels Jewels," Bob yelled, and I turned to see him, Linda, Megan, Frances and the boys.

"Well." I grinned. "Quite a welcoming committee. Boys, must be the first time you've been in a cop station for quite some time. Does it feel like home?" I was greeted with smirks. "Frances, whatever you did, whatever you said, can't thank you enough for it."

"It's all right, Jewels, just doing my job and protecting my people." She heartily shook my hand.

I extracted it and turned to Megan and touched her elbow. "Are you okay?"

She smiled. "I can see, not clearly, but it's getting better."

"That's good," I replied.

"There's going to be no charges against you or Megan, but we are considering charges against the PC who hit you." Bob pointed to my head. "After what you went through and are *still* going through she could've killed you isn't that right Frances no charges."

She shook her head.

"Speaking of heads," Christopher said. "That's one hell of an ugly one you've got there." Andrew and Chris chastised him.

"He's right," I said with a wave of my hand. "It's an ugly bastard, and I gotta live with it. At least when I finally get home, I'll have advice for all Aussies, though."

"What's that?"

"Don't go to England. Too much shit happens."

Guffaws were heard all round.

"But, in the meantime, I'm hungry and tired and in pain. Can we go?" With a glance at Callum who was lurking at the back of the room, I barged through the door and into the cold night air. In the dim light, I looked down, and a little red light caught my eye. "Oh, oh, oh," I said in amusement then laughed. "This little baby's still going. I forgot I had it on." The others stopped around me.

"What is it?" Chris asked, shoving his hands in his pockets.

"A mini recorder." I grinned. "I turned it on in the car, and it's taped everything that's happened since." My grin got bigger. "If only I'd had a camera. You would not *believe* what happened in there." I gazed at curious faces and laughed again. "Let's just say, when Sgt Stone was interviewing me it got a little…um." I gazed up at the sky for the right word. "*Hard* in there."

"What do you mean, hard?" Linda asked.

I chuckled. "Well, to diffuse the situation, I hit on him, and then the inspector barged in, and Callum stood up so fast he didn't realise he was in the middle of an erection. He got all embarrassed and covered it with some papers. Then the inspector told him to go."

The others shook their heads or chuckled.

"Pity," I went on. "I could've helped him get rid of it. And I really wish I'd had my camera. Or at least my phone."

"Ugh." Bob shivered. "I don't need to hear this conversation. I'm going to get the car." He strode away.

"And I have to go," Frances said. "As much as I'd love to know all the details, I'm sure you'll tell me some other time." She touched my arm. "And if you ever see that erection naked and in person, let me know what it's like. Toodles." She walked off.

I was shocked by her boldness and shook my head. "Well." I laughed. "I gotta see it myself first, and I doubt that'll ever happen." My hand absentmindedly rubbed my head.

"So, things aren't looking up for you and the sergeant then," Chris asked.

I shook my head wearily. "No."

Bob arrived with the car.

"Let's get you and Megan home then," Linda said and Chris stepped up to open the door.

"Thanks." I smiled and climbed in. We settled back and took off.

"It's been quite a night," Bob said, keeping an eye on the road.

"Yeah," I muttered. "And I can't wait for it to be over."

We dropped Megan off, and after making sure she was settled in, headed home. Slowly getting out of the car, Linda helped me up the stairs, into the shower, and into bed.

I sat there. The light off. My head pounding. But what was so different about that? Pounded twenty-four seven. I didn't know what time it was, but I reached for my recorder.

In the dark of the night, I played it.

Over and over and over and over.

Just to hear Callum's voice. The deep rumbling timbre. It filled my soul. I relived every moment of meeting him at the party. The way his eyes glared into mine. The movement of his lips as words poured through them. The muscles in his jaw. His soft, smooth skin. His short brown hair. His strong manly hands and broad muscular chest.

I listened to the recording again and again and again. Over and over. Imprinting his voice in my mind. My heart. My soul. Every fibre of my being loved him. And hated the fact he didn't love me.

I jumped up and plugged the recorder into the laptop, turning it into a file. I did the same with my camcorder and burned it to a disc. I sat and watched it. Entering the bar. My argument with Peter Fifer. Heading for the bathroom. After that, it was mostly floor or wall shots, but our voices were clearly heard. The fight. Back to the bar. Me being arrested. After that I heard the boys approach and comfort Megan, her ringing Bob, bringing her to the station, sobbing from the pain of the pepper spray. The camera had kept rolling until Frances took it to check the footage.

I leaned back in my seat, trying to put all the pieces

together from the beginning. The party. The fight. Slapping Callum. The car ride. The station. Now home. All the sights. All the sounds. All the expressions.

I sat up and began to type.

How do you do it? How do you love someone with all of your heart, your soul, your body? How do you love someone so much, and yet hate them at the same time? How do you hate someone you love? How do you hate them with every fibre of your being to the point your blood boils and your anger flares, and your tongue spits venom at them? How do you hate someone as much as you love them? How do you love them as much as you hate them?

How do you? How do you? Well? Do you have the answer? Because I don't. I don't have any answers to any questions I ask. I'm empty. Empty one minute, and full of love or hate the next. How do you love and hate them at the same time? I don't know, but I do. But how can I? One second I'm falling all over myself loving him, and the next I'm slapping him with hatred and anger. It's like I'm two people feeling two different things at the same time. But how can I? I want someone to explain it to me. I need someone to explain it to me because I don't understand it. I really don't. So, how do you do it? How do you separate those two parts of you? How do you separate those two emotions? Love and hate. Hate and love.

You can't work it out. You can't separate them, but you can't keep them together either. Two different emotions fighting and brawling inside of you, each vying for attention. Each one wanting to come out on top and be the victor. The winner. The sole owner of you and your body. Your heart. Your soul. How do you do it? Do you fight it? Do you fight back by never seeing that person again? By never hearing them again? Never talking to them? Never acknowledging their existence? How do you do it? You can't!

Because either way you suffer. Seeing them. Not seeing them. It's all the same. If you see them, you hurt from seeing them. The way they look. The way they smell. The way they talk and walk, and the way they look at you. If you don't see them, you miss them. The way they look. The way they smell. The way they talk and walk, and look at you. You can't win either way. You just can't! You suffer with them or without them. The pain doesn't go away because you try and will it to. It doesn't go away because you tell it to. It doesn't go away because you pray and yell and scream and fight it and demand it go away. It doesn't go away if they stay in your life. It doesn't go away if they're out of your life.

You have to decide. You have to make a choice. You either live with them or without them. You deal with it, or you don't. In which case, you become a big crying, screaming, yelling mess all bundled up on the floor. Never going out again. Never eating again. Never dating again. If you don't deal with it, will the pain go away? Will it all get better and magically disappear? To leave you with no memories whatsoever of them and your time together. Will it all be better if they just disappear? So, how do you do it? How do you love and hate someone at the same time? How do you do it 'cause I want to know?

I clicked on my Twitter page and typed. '*I slapped him. I love him and hate him at the same time. I slapped him. How do I make the pain stop? I need to stop the pain.*'

I sat there staring at the screen, willing the pain to stop. And not the pain in my head. The pain in my chest from loving a man who so clearly didn't love me. Yet! Or maybe it was all a lie. Maybe that invisible woman told me a lie just to get me to live. Maybe we're not meant to be together at all. Maybe it was all a dirty filthy lie.

I walked over to the wardrobe and pulled out my bag of pills. Going back to the desk, I laid them out one by one and counted them.

And counted them…

And counted them…

Chapter 12

I stood in a cold dark room filled with metal and sterilisation.

People were gathered around something.

That something was a table.

With me on it.

I looked at their faces. Callum, Bob, Linda, Megan and Frances, all gazed solemnly at my stiff white body.

I searched Callum's face for emotion, but was met with the same coldness of the room.

Linda and Megan dabbed their eyes, Bob stood stoically. Frances just stared. And Callum still showed no emotion.

I looked down at my sickly white self. The bruises, brilliant yellow and bold black, stood out against the paleness of my skin.

"Callum," I whispered. "Callum." My hand lay on his. "I love you so much." I stared into those big blue eyes. "Why didn't you love me? That was all you had to do." My lip quivered, but he didn't move. "All you had to do was love me."

I looked down at my body. "And none of this

would've happened," I spat viciously. I laid my head on his shoulder, tears wetting his jacket. "I love you so much," I sobbed. "Why didn't you love me? Why?" I gazed into his eyes again. They were unwavering. "I never did anything to you, well, okay, I slapped you, but that was nothing. You're big enough to deal with that, and after what I'd been through, you should've understood what was going on in my head. You're the one who rescued me." I grabbed his jacket. "You're the one who saw me get hit and fall into the water. The one who saw me drown and had to resuscitate me to bring me back." I shook him. "You know what I went through, you know I love you," I yelled.

I received no response.

Hanging my head and letting the tears fall, I sobbed.

"We should go," Bob said.

Linda nodded, and linking her arm through Megan's, they walked out the door. Callum breathed in and moved.

"No, no, Callum. Don't leave me. Don't leave me. I know you love me. I know you do. All you had to do was show me. Show me you love me. All you had to do was love me, Callum," I called. "All you had to do was love me," my voice trailed off as he walked out the door.

I stared at his retreating back and was left with the one thing I feared most.

Once again, I was on my own.

Chapter 13

I lay in bed on my back, staring at the roof of the four-poster. I didn't know what time it was, and it didn't matter. I could see sunlight creeping in around the window, peeking through the curtains.

My hands were together, my fingers crossed. My right forefinger started tapping to no beat in particular. Unless it was the beat in my head. Certainly not the beat of any song I knew, but it had its own melody.

My eye was hooded. Tired from long nights on the computer, and long days staying awake. I wanted to sleep so desperately, but every time I found myself falling asleep, I found myself waking up. I slept in small blocks of time. Never-ending time. Where day blurred into night, and night blurred into day.

The house was quiet. Not a word or whisper. Not a running tap or talking TV. No phone ringing off the hook. No steps coming down the hall to my door. No sounds. No ticking clocks. No, *you have email* dings. No laptop shutting off on its own.

Just dead silence.

Dead silence.

Dead.

Silence.

Dead. Dead. Dead.

I sighed and reached for my clock. Ten. *Ten what? A.m.? P.m.?*

My back started hurting, so I rolled over. It helped my back, but not my head. There was a knock at the door. "Yeah," I mumbled.

It opened, and Linda popped her head in. "I have some breakfast for you, so you can take your pills." She pushed through the door.

I sat up. So, it's morning! "Thanks," I murmured as she placed a tray of food on my lap.

"Are your pills still in the cupboard?" She turned towards it.

"Yeah," I mumbled around a mouthful of toast.

"Jewels! You were supposed to take these before eating," she admonished me, laying my pills on the bed.

I stared dolefully at her and spat the food into the napkin. "Who cares?" I mumbled. I took my five pills and ate again.

"How are you feeling this morning?" she asked, straightening the bed.

"Like I don't want to be here," I replied.

She looked up in surprise.

"It's not you or Bob," I said. "It's just me. I don't want to be in my head or my body." I ate more pills and toast.

"I understand that." She sat on the bed. "You've been through hell, and I can't even begin to understand the pain you're in, but it *will* get better."

I cast a suspicious glance her way, my slice of toast stopping mid-air.

"It will," she insisted, patting my leg.

I finished the toast and pills. "I'm gonna stay in bed." She lifted the tray, and I shifted around.

"I'll be back at two-thirty with lunch," she said, closing the door behind her. I heard footsteps retreat down the hall.

Lunch! Bah! I could barely hold down food now, why would I want more? I lay on my left, willing the pain to go away. I was so sick of taking fifteen pills every meal time. Forty-five fucking pills a fucking day. And they weren't doing any good. The swelling was still prominent. The aches and pains were still there. And on some days, they reverberated around my body.

And do I even need to mention my head? Jack Hammer was there. *Hey, Jack! How are you today? Busy? Yeah, I hear ya! I'm busy too. Busy trying to get rid of you. Trying to come up with new ways of killing you. I've thought of a few. Want to hear them? No! Okay, here goes. 1 – Bashing my head in. 2 – Get someone else to bash my head in. 3 – Get another jackhammer to chip you out. 4 – Drugs!*

What's that? Drugs don't work. Oh, no, not these drugs. They don't work at all. But I know some drugs will. Just you wait, Jack. You and pain will soon be gone, and I'll celebrate your farewell. Just you wait!

Linda came in at two-thirty with my meal of soup and pills. I hadn't slept a wink and was exhausted.

"I'm staying in bed," I mumbled, sliding back

down. I heard her leave. *Hey, Jack! Did you enjoy lunch? Yeah, soup. What's that? Yeah, it was good. A nice change from bread. Yeah, it was. Normally I don't eat a lot of carbs 'cause it makes me fat, but since I haven't been eating much of anything, I think I'm wasting away. What's that? I look thinner! Why thank you, Jack! That's a nice thing to say. I feel thinner. I've noticed my tracksuits are bigger than they were before. No, I haven't weighed myself. As long as my clothes fit, no need to. I'm tired. Are you going to have a break now, Jack? No! No, I didn't think so. Thought I should ask anyway. Oh, well.*

More soup and pills followed at seven, and this time I decided to get out of bed and shower. The hot water felt good, and I scrubbed my body with citrus wash and loofah mitts. I carefully washed my hair, then dried off, and dressed in sleep pants and a long-sleeved top. Trudging into the bedroom, I saw new sheets and pillowcases. "Nice," I said, touching the new multi blue bedspread.

There was a knock at the door. "Jewels," Linda called.

I opened it. "Yeah?"

"Um." She was nervous. "Callum's here. He wants to talk to you."

My heart raced in my chest.

"Do you want to see him? You don't have to."

"I, I, I don't…know." I was confused. After last night I didn't know if I wanted to see him or why he wanted to see me.

"Jewels?" She was so concerned.

I took a deep breath. "Send him up."

"Are you sure?" She frowned.

"No! But send him up anyway." I quickly tidied the room while she went downstairs. I was fluffing a sofa cushion when he walked in. I stopped. All I could do was stare. Stare at the man I loved in the gorgeous blue jumper and black leather jacket.

He closed the door and took a few steps toward me. I hadn't moved. "How are you?" he asked gently.

I swallowed, trying to clear my throat which was dry all of a sudden. I took a breath. "Okay," I whispered, my heart racing.

"Good," he breathed. "How's your back?" Concern was all over his face.

"Sore."

He shook his head. "I'm sorry. I'm so sorry that happened to you."

"It's not your fault."

"It is, as you pointed out last night. *I* was in charge. Those PCs were under *my* orders. *My* control." He seemed so upset, his face crumpling with emotion.

I softened. "She acted like a moron, and even after seeing my head still beat me." I shook my head. "She severely needs to be reprimanded for attacking someone with a very clear head injury."

He nodded in agreement. "Absolutely, and she has been. The inspector has set up a training course making sure we are all informed about people with obvious brain, head, and physical injuries. We're being trained."

"That's good," I said.

We fell silent.

"How's the rest of you?" His voice was so soft and gentle it made my heart ache.

"In pain." A tear rolled down my cheek. "But then what else is new." I wiped it away, looking everywhere but at him. He only stared at me.

"About…last night," he started nervously.

"Don't worry about it," I interjected. "Forget everything that got said."

"I can't."

"You have to," I whispered, more tears coming.

"Jewels." He took a few steps toward me. I stepped back. "Why did you say…why did you say you hate me?" He took another step. "Why did you say what you said? I, I don't understand."

"You don't love me," I blurted and wiped my face. "So it doesn't matter. It's okay that you don't love me. I'm ugly. I'm hideous. I'm not from here. I'm not your type, certainly not someone you want to be with, so it's okay. It's okay." I moved away from him. "I, I shouldn't have slapped you, so I apologise for that, but just forget everything I said." He didn't love me, and that was obvious, so carrying on about it was not going to be beneficial for my health.

"Jewels." He stood behind me and gently turned me around. "I have no idea why you said all of that. But I hope it's not true. I don't know why you hate me. What have I *done* for you to hate me?"

Oh, God! I'd already said enough last night, I didn't want to have to repeat it, and he wasn't saying anything about it.

"I thought we could be friends but…clearly you don't want to be."

Friends!

I stared up at him and scoffed. *"Friends,"* I spat. "You want to be *friends!*" I couldn't believe what I was hearing.

He nodded eagerly.

"Why didn't I see it before," I cried to the heavens. "Clearly the only person you love is yourself. I don't want to be *friends. I* want to be lovers. *I* want to be your *wife.* The mother of your children."

Shock rolled over his face.

"I want to feel your hot naked flesh against mine. I want to moosh my breasts into your chest hair. I want your lips to devour me, and your hands to cover every single inch of me. I want you to love me and want me and need me the way I do you. I want to spend the rest of my life with you, and you want to be *friends.*" I raised my hands and shook my head. "Clearly you have no idea." I took a shaky breath.

His jaw worked up and down, trying to find the right words to say.

"I mean sure," I added. "I didn't come here to fall in love or lust or find a husband either, but I sure as hell didn't come here to die." I stopped pacing. "But hey! This is England. Shit happens." I went back to pacing.

All I heard was silence.

He stood there, seriously conflicted.

"You were clear last night," I said, and he looked at me. "When you said 'why would I love you? Look at the way you're acting'." He seemed shocked that I had remembered. "Oh, yeah, I got it word for word. Clearly, you don't like women who act like me. Clearly, I'm not *your* type."

"Jewels," he croaked.

"What," I sneered. "*Go on*, tell me why you don't love me. Tell me that you're too much of a man to possibly love a freak like me."

"Stop putting words in my mouth," he snapped. "You have no idea what you're talking about."

"Oh, please!" My voice rose. "I know *exactly* what I'm talking about. You think because you were in my hospital room every night it shows you *care*." I waved my arms around. "You *don't care*. You just wanted to make sure the poor pathetic tourist you saved didn't die, so you didn't look like a failure. So that you *stayed* a hero." I glared at him. "You haven't even come to see me since I've been home. So don't even *pretend* that you care," I yelled.

"Oh, you're right," he yelled back. "I should have let you drown in the river. Left you there deep down on the river bed trapped by that car. I should have left you there to drown, and not in your own vile crap because look at you." He thrust a finger at me. "*Look. At. You.* Look at yourself. Why would *any* man want you, let alone me? Why would *any* decent man look twice at you and your ugly face and your ugly scars and your ugly bruises? *Look at you.* Why would *any* man look at you or take a second look at you? Why would *any* man want you? *I* don't. *I* don't want you and your vile attitude. I'm too good for you. *Every* man's too good for you. *No* man wants you. *I* don't want you," he stormed, thrusting his finger again. "*And by the way.* My PC's not the only one who acted like a moron."

I stood shell-shocked. It was what I had guessed and not wanted. It was the complete opposite of what the invisible woman had said. We stood in the room, breathing hard, tears falling down my face. Hot rivers etching cracks and crevices into my sore swollen skin.

Callum wiped his mouth. "Jewels."

"Get out," I whispered.

"Jewels."

"Get out," I yelled. "I hate you. Get out. Get out, and never come back. I *never* want to see you again. I will *never* see you again. Get out," I sobbed, great wracks of pain wrenching my body.

He took a few steps backwards. "Goodbye, Jewels," he rasped and strode out the door, closing it behind him.

Closing it on me. Our future. Our life together.

I fell to the floor. "Arggghhh," I screamed. "Arggghhh."

Linda raced in. "Jewels, oh, Jewels." She ran to me and pulled me into her arms, rubbed my back gently. "I'm so sorry. I'm so sorry. Shhhh, it's okay. Shhhh."

All I did was scream.

Chapter 14

So…how do I stop the pain?

How do I recover from death?

Someone tell me, because…I still don't know.

How do I stop the pain of death?

How do I survive death?

Badly at this stage.

Death is unsurvivable. Unrecoverable. The pain. The fear. The nightmares. Jack Hammer going off in my head twenty-four seven. I've become insane. Living on that island called Insanity. Is there a manual on how to survive death? Does it tell you how to be happy after it? How to ignore the pain and heartache? I wish someone would tell me 'cause I *still* don't know how to survive death. There's no book. No brochure. No manual.

No. No fucking manual on how to deal with surviving death.

No. No fucking manual at all.

Chapter 15

I was a zombie. The one horror flick monster I feared most. Not vampires or werewolves, but zombies. Mainly because the possibility of becoming one was all too real with all of the diseases the government worked on in secret. And I *was* in the land of TV show *Dead Set*, and the movie, *28 Days Later.*

Linda had left me to myself, so I sat on the couch. Like a zombie. Rocking back and forth, staring at the floor, drooling, reliving every little detail of my visit from Callum. The anger in his face. The pain in my heart. The venom in his voice. He didn't love me. He didn't love me. *He…didn't…love…me…*

Jack was pounding away in my head. My face ached. My right eye was now as swollen as the left from crying. My nose was blocked. I was numb. Well, technically I wasn't since I felt Jack, but I was emotionally.

The man I loved didn't love me. Why *would* he love me? *Jack, how can you ask that? I know it's true, but you didn't need to say it out loud. What's that? It wasn't out loud, it was in my head. Yeah. It's in my head, and that's where you are, Jack. And I need to get you out.*

I climbed to my feet and just stood. *What am I doing? I'm standing here. Why? I don't know! Neither do I.* Thoughts raced through my mind. I tried to snatch one and hang onto it. I finally had something to do.

I shuffled over to the computer and sat heavily. My zombie eyes stared at the screen. My zombie hand turned it on and flicked to my blog dashboard. My zombie finger clicked on new post, and my other zombie fingers joined it.

My Adventures in Merry Old England: November 24th, 2011

I'm going away, peeps. I don't know where, but I'll be gone awhile. Your messages, tweets, and emails have meant a lot, but I need to go away. I can't cope anymore. I need to stop the pain. I need to make it go away. I need to go away. I need to make the pain go away.

Bye, peeps,

Jewels xxoo

I hit publish and watched it go out to the zombie world. I logged off and closed the laptop lid. I straightened the desk. The iPad beside the computer. The camcorder beside the iPad. The camera beside the camcorder. The phone beside the camera. The iPod beside the phone. The Nintendo beside the iPod. The digital recorder beside the Nintendo. All lined up like little zombie soldiers.

I pushed the chair under the desk and shuffled to the door. I listened with my zombie ear. I opened it. I listened. No sound. I shuffled along the hall and down the stairs with my zombie feet. I listened. No sound.

The mantel clock quietly chimed two a.m. I shuffled toward Bob's office down the hall and opened his door. I shuffled over to the small bar fridge and opened it. Removing a bottle of vodka, I tucked it into my jacket.

I shuffled back to the stairs, along the hall, and into my room. I locked the door. I shuffled to my wardrobe and retrieved my bag of pills. I shuffled to the bed and climbed on. I placed the vodka beside me and laid out all of the pills I had left.

A week and a half's worth.

I laid them out and counted. Lay them like little zombie soldiers. Antibiotics. Anti-inflammatories. Painkillers. Blood thinners. Little coloured zombie soldiers all lined up in little zombie lines on the multi blue bedspread.

"Let's see," I slurred. "Which one's first?" I grabbed the vodka and opened it. "Mmm…white first." I picked up the handful, threw them in, and took a great gulp of vodka. I sputtered, choking on the pills, and since I'd never had vodka before, that as well. I managed to get them down then reached for the rest of the white ones.

Down, down, down they went.

I reached for the pink ones.

Down, down, down.

I almost vomited and could taste the bile in my throat. I swallowed that too.

Big handful of red ones.

Down, down, down.

Then the green ones.

Down, down, down went the little zombie soldiers.

And last, but definitely not least, my favourite colour. Blue! All the blue zombies went down, down, down. The vodka was nearly gone, so I finished it off. All my little zombies were gone. Down my throat and into my stomach.

I felt sick.

But that was normal.

I felt weird.

But that was normal.

I felt dizzy again.

But that too was normal.

I thought about Callum, and my heart ached. A sob escaped my throat. "Callum," I whined. "Callum." I hauled myself off the bed and toward the desk. Grabbing my phone, I flicked through the phone book, and flopping back on the bed, I thought about dialling.

What would I say? What should I say? I felt drowsy, like I was ready for sleep. "It's coming," I slurred and pressed the number. I got his message bank. "Callum... it's Jewels...I'm going away from you...away from the pain...the pain's going to stop...it's finally going to stop...just want you to know...before I go...I love you... I do... I meant everything I said... It doesn't matter if you don't love me... I just want you to know I love you…the pain's finally stopping…" I smiled. "I can feel it going…it's finally leaving…I can sleep now…pain's going…a…way…" My eyes closed and my hand dropped.

"Jewels…Jewels…it's Callum. Can you hear me? Jewels. Jewels. Are you there? Say something, damn it. Jewels. Jewels. Wake up, Jewels…shit…"

Chapter 16

"Jewels. Wake up!" Callum yelled. "Call an ambulance."

"Jewels. Open your eyes we're almost at the hospital."

"Jewels. We're here. The doctor's going to purge your stomach."

"Jewels. They're putting a tube down your throat. They're going to pour charcoal down into your stomach."

I rolled over and vomited.

Vomited up all the little zombie soldiers that had not so long ago taken an alcoholic trip of a waterslide down into my stomach.

"Jewels. Let them out, sweetheart. Let them out."

I groaned. Gasped. Vomited some more. *What was that taste? I don't remember tasting that.* Up came some more little zombie soldiers. *What is that down my throat? Did I swallow something? Did the little zombies grow and get bigger?*

My mouth was rinsed out, and I was rolled onto my back. I tried to open my eye. Bright light blinded me. "Ugh." My eyes rolled back into my head.

"Jewels. Open your eyes for me. I want to check them," a new voice said.

My eyelids were lifted, and a light flicked back and forth. "Ugh," I repeated, moving my head, moving my legs. I wanted to move. I wanted to leave.

"Do you know how many pills she took?"

"Everything she had left."

Was that Linda?

"That's…shit four hundred and fifty pills."

"Will she be okay?"

"I don't know. They shouldn't react to each other. At least not in *small* doses. God knows what all of them will do."

"Will she die?"

"I don't…she shouldn't."

"When can we take her home?"

There was a huff. "*If* she gets better, not until the weekend. *If* she's lucky. It looks like we've gotten most of the pills, and taking them with a bottle of alcohol was bloody dangerous. We don't know what lasting effects that will have either. Do you know why she did it?"

"No."

"Has she talked about suicide?"

"No. At least…not with us."

"With anyone?"

"We don't know."

A heavy sigh. "We'll get plenty of fluids into her and keep a close eye for the next couple of days. You can have a couple of minutes with her."

"Ugh." I don't know how loud I'd been as I had no energy.

"Jewels, it's Bob and Linda, we…don't know why…but we…just get better Jewels…get better, and then we'll get you some help…get some sleep."

"Ugh."

"Jewels."

Callum?

"Jewels. I'm here for you. I don't know either, but when you're okay, we are definitely going to talk about it. I…I love you, too. And I'm not going anywhere. I'm staying right here. I'm never leaving you. Never."

*****

"Ugh," I murmured, half waking from a nice peaceful sleep. Finally! It worked! The pain has stopped. Oh, hallelujah! The pain has stopped. I tried to open my eye, but couldn't. I tried to move my hand, but couldn't. "Ugh." I was still too buggered.

"Jewels." Callum's voice drifted into my ears.

"Ugh."

"Jewels. I'm here, and I'm not going anywhere, my love."

I felt his hand on my head, fingers stroking my face. "Ugh." I tried to move toward him. He'd said, my love. *My love.* Why was he calling me that?

"Shh, you rest. You need to get better." His voice was soft and gentle.

"Ugh." I felt the bed shift, and a weight lie beside me. Strong muscular arms slid around me, enveloping me into their strength. "Ugh."

"Shh, my love. I'm here, and I'm not going

anywhere." He stroked my cheek. "I feel so responsible for this," he whispered. "It's *my* fault. My own stubborn fault. I've built a brick wall around myself. Buried myself in work, and when a woman comes along I might be interested in, I, I screw it up." He kissed my forehead.

"Ugh," I whimpered.

"I'm so sorry. I'm so sorry. This is *all* my fault. When you came and introduced yourself in the pub, I was taken aback. When I saw you again at the river, I wondered if you were right. And seeing you hit by that car, oh, I can still see it, the sickening thud as you landed on the concrete. But you had guts. You had the guts to help out a woman and child with no thought of your own safety. It was bloody stupid but incredibly brave. And when I saw you go down in the car, it scared me. When you didn't come up, it scared me. When I had to drag you out and resuscitate you, it scared me. Oh, Jewels."

He kissed my cheek and sighed heavily. "I didn't realise that I was going to fall in love with you. I didn't even realise it when I spent every evening at the hospital watching over you, helping you, talking to you. When I went to see you on Saturday, the nurse told me you'd been taken home, and I…I wondered why you hadn't told me. Or let me know where you were staying. I was so disappointed. I…I was hurt. Silly isn't it. That I could be hurt by not knowing where you were. And that night, when I was called to the house. The minute Bob appeared at the door I knew it was you. He pointed upstairs, and I followed your screams."

He held me tighter. "To see you like that. To hear the wildness of your voice. I know. I know that what I saw freaked me out. But the pain in your eyes was worse. When you ran away from me. Told me I would never love you. It hurt. It hurt a lot. And all I did was think about you and how I felt. I wanted to deny you made me feel something. Something I hadn't felt in many, many years. Something I wasn't sure I'd ever feel or find."

His lips pressed into my hair. "And then I saw you at the party, and I didn't know what the hell to think or say. You were there with it all hanging out, completely opposite to what you'd said and how you'd reacted a few days before. And you were hit, and I was hurt when you told me you hated me, and then you hit on me at the station. And, oh, my God, I had an erection, and the inspector walked in. And then the other night happened. Oh, Jewels."

His arms tightened. "I've been avoiding love, and at the very least not expecting it for so long I've forgotten how it feels. My heart was hardened to it. But you started melting it. You started melting my heart, and I have to admit to myself that I love you. I just have to tell you. Convince you that it's true. I want to be with you." He chuckled. "You'll think this is funny. I even started doing some research on Australia, and for some reason found myself on a page about immigration. Now, finally letting myself free of the wall, I can admit to loving you. And in order to be with you, either you have to move here, or I have to move there." He shrugged. "Since the weather's better there, I decided me moving would be beneficial for both of us." He kissed me again. "I just hope you wake up and live long enough for me to fill out the form and go home with you. I love you, Jewels. And I don't want you to die."

I snuggled against his chest. *Oh, Callum. I love you, too. Wait…what's that about dying?*

*****

I struggled to open my eye. My lids felt like sandpaper against my pupils, and I reached up to rub them. "Ow!" I'd forgotten my left one was swollen shut. Jack popped in to say hello. *Oh, God, not you again. Piss off!*

"Jewels." I saw a blurred version of Callum lean over me. I took a deep breath and smiled. "Jewels, sweetheart, you're back."

I slowly moved my arms and legs. They still worked.

"Let me sit you up." Callum pressed a button behind me, and the back of the bed rose into an upright position.

"Mmm, that's better," I muttered and smiled at him.

"I love you." He grinned a big sappy grin.

I smiled wider and harder.

"Is she awake?" A blurry Bob and Linda came through the door.

"Just woke up," Callum replied.

"Oh, Jewels." Linda came to the bed. "We're so glad you're awake. I brought you some fresh clothes. Maybe the doctor will let you up for a shower."

"Mmm." I ran my tongue around the inside of my mouth. Sandpaper was in there too. "Dry," I croaked.

"I'll get you some juice and the doctor," Bob said and ran out. Five minutes later, he ran back in. "Here's your juice. The doctor will be here soon."

I greedily drank it. I was so parched it felt like I'd swallowed a whole desert. Don't know which one, but a big one.

"So...Ms Diva. Here we are again." The doctor who'd treated me after the incident walked in and stood at the end of the bed. "Tell me. Why did you try to kill yourself?"

What?!

I wanted to laugh, but couldn't. I glanced at every face, and they all showed concern.

"Well?"

"I didn't," I croaked, an amused look on my face. Well, at least I tried to look amused since I didn't exactly know what expressions I could pull.

"You drank a whole bottle of vodka and downed over four hundred and fifty pills. That generally smacks of suicide. So, why did you do it? Do you need to see a counsellor? I know you went through a lot, but there's no need to kill yourself."

"I didn't." My voice was stronger, and I was angry. "*I didn't* try and kill myself smart arse, I was trying to stop the fucking pain. The pain that *your* fucking painkillers weren't getting rid of." He looked dubious. "Considering I have a fucking jackhammer going in my head *twenty-four seven*, I wanted it to stop, so I could get some sleep and peace and quiet. I wanted, the pain, to stop," I yelled. "Don't you *fucking* get that? Look at my head. I'm in *fucking* pain."

"All right, Jewels," Linda soothed. "We get it."

The doctor appeared unimpressed and unconcerned.

"No," I told Linda. "I don't think you do. Why don't you try giving me some decent fucking pills," I spat, "and *maybe then* the pain will stop."

"Well, clearly you're better. You can go home later this afternoon." He wrote on my chart before walking out the door.

"Ugh." I grabbed my head. "The pain's back. I want it to stop. I want it to stop."

"We know," Linda said, rubbing my arm. The three of them stood watching me.

"What's today?" I asked with a sigh.

"Saturday," Bob said.

"I'm tired." I put my head back, adjusting the pillow underneath it.

"We'll let you rest," Linda said. "We'll take you home later."

"Mmm," I mumbled and started talking to Jack.

I awoke about five and saw Callum sitting beside the bed. He was sleeping, and I watched him, remembering what I'd heard and wondered if it had all been a dream. But since he was there, it must have been real.

Bob and Linda walked in. "We can take you home now," Linda said. "Would you like to shower here?"

Callum woke and rubbed his eyes.

"Sure. Can you help?" She helped me wash and dress, and then Callum wheeled me downstairs to the car. He followed us home and stayed for dinner.

We lounged on the couch in my room afterwards, discussing the whole drama of our lives and coming to a sweet understanding of our feelings. We were in love. Or at the very least, the brand-new beginnings of it, and knew we wanted to be together to explore the boundaries of that love. Knowing we never wanted to be apart. Never again. It was forever, and we knew it. We both knew that this love of ours was the only one we'd ever feel or need.

"Are you working tomorrow?" I asked.

"No. In fact, I…I've taken two weeks leave."

"What?" I looked at him in surprise. "Why?"

He laughed. "To be with you."

"Why? You don't need to take time off work for that."

He shook his head. "You don't get it, do you?" he asked, smiling.

I grew warm at that smile. "Clearly not."

He took both of my hands. "I took two weeks off work so I can spend time with you. To get to know you. To help you recover." He shrugged slightly. "Maybe we can…I don't know…get away and take time out from all of this craziness."

I suddenly felt weird and pulling my hands away, looked around the room.

"What is it?"

I couldn't look at him.

"Jewels."

"There's a lot you don't know about me. Only Bob and Linda know because of work. But you don't." I took a deep breath. "I'm. I'm not…"

"Called Jewels Diva."

I looked at him in surprise.

He smiled. "Did you seriously think *I wasn't* going to check up on you after what had happened?"

I blinked and swallowed.

"I happen to know that no one by the name of Jewels Diva entered the UK in the last couple of months, let alone years." He grinned. "It's like a work name right? For your book?"

I took another breath. At least this was going to be easy. I smiled. "Yeah." I got up and walked around, every muscle was stiff as I stretched my arms above my head.

"It's okay," he said. "I *do* get it. It's work. Plenty of authors use pen names."

My breath came out in a whoosh, and I turned and looked at him. "My name's…" I faltered and cleared my throat. "My real name's Tamara. Tamara Cainer."

"C.A.I.N.E.R," Callum said with a grin. "I know. I figured it out when searching for visitors from Australia. I matched the name to you."

"Ha!" I half snapped, half scoffed. "No point *me* telling you anything, is there?"

"Come on." He walked over to me. "Don't be like that. I was curious. I went looking."

"Oh, you certainly did," I half-jokingly chastised.

He chuckled. "Go on."

I thought a few things through and then led him to the closet. Opening one of the cases, I pulled out my red wig. "When I wear this, I'm Jewels." I ran my fingers through it. "I'm working as Jewels. Author, blogger, social and media commentator. But when I'm not Jewels." I laid the wig down and picked up a shoulder length golden-brown one. "I'm Tamara. The real me. The real me who does other things and lives a real life." I looked up at him.

"Why brown?" He shoved his hands in his pockets.

"It's my real hair."

Surprise rolled over his face. "What do you mean?"

"I got sick of having long hair, so I decided to get it cut off. But since I still wanted the option, I had it turned into a wig. It will be good for a disguise." I laid it back in the case.

"What about your face?"

"What do you mean?" Now it was my turn to ask.

"Well, you can cover your head with your wig, but what about your face? It's very noticeable and still very swollen." His hand gently touched my cheek.

I touched it. "Yeah, I know. Linda saw a dermatologist and got some sort of spray on skin. It's part make-up part latex or something." I picked up the bottle. "You spray it on, and it covers moles, birthmarks, scars and what not."

Callum took my hand. "That's good. You can use it when we go away."

"Go where?" I asked, intrigued.

"Wherever you want." He pulled me into his arms, and I slid mine around him, resting my head on his chest. I listened to his heart beat slowly, and he kissed the top of my head. "We can go wherever you want. Do whatever you want. Countryside. Seaside."

"Seaside," I murmured. "I do like the sea. It's calming." I straightened and rubbed my head. "Maybe it will get rid of the damn pain."

Taking my face in his hands, he gently kissed my forehead. "We can go wherever you want. It's not like people will bother you when they think you're dead."

"What?" My brow furrowed. "What do you mean?"

"Ah," he said, not realising I didn't know.

"What?" I prodded.

"Someone at the hospital took a picture of you and sold it to a tabloid. Told them you'd died from an overdose."

"What?" I shrieked, unbelieving.

"It's okay," he said quickly, trying to calm me. "Bob threatened to sue them if they didn't rectify the story."

"And did they?"

"Well…"

"What?"

"There's a small," he held his thumb and forefinger about an inch apart, "paragraph on the tenth page."

"What?" I stormed around the room and spied my laptop. "Did Bob get a copy of the paper?"

"Yes, I think so."

"Go and get it."

"What?"

"Go and get it." I set up the webcam and brought up my YouTube page. Callum handed me the paper. I snorted in disgust after reading it. "Sit on the bed," I told him and clicked on the record tab.

"Well, peeps. It seems the unfortunate news of my untimely demise was wrong. But then what else is new. People lie to the tabloids for money, and tabloids print lies and hope they don't get sued for it. As you can see by the headlines…" I held the paper in the camera's view. "I apparently died of an overdose after committing suicide. Now, while I would down a load of pills if I ever *did* commit suicide, that's *not* what this was. I wanted Jack to stop. That's right. There's a jackhammer in my head, and I wanted him to stop. The pills I was on weren't working, and I thought if I took a few more it would. Unfortunately, it didn't. But the doctor has now reduced the amount of pills I'm on from forty-five to fifteen every day. *Whoop.ie*," I said sarcastically. "They seem to be working a little better, but the pain's still there. *So. I. Repeat.* I did *not* die. I am *not* dead. These are *not* special effects or a video of me from the afterlife. I. AM. NOT. DEAD! But *I am* going on holiday. I need to get out of London to try and finish recuperating from the original incident. So, I don't know how long I'll be gone, and may not bother coming online. But don't worry about me. I'll be in good hands. Very strong, manly hands." I winked and glanced at Callum who grinned. "Until then peeps, stay safe, and yes, I *AM.* JEWELS DIVA. *AND I AM.* ALIVE!"

I clicked stop, uploaded it to YouTube, and posted it to my blog. Fifteen minutes later, I shut everything off and turned to Callum. "You know you should decide exactly who you want to be with. You can't have both of us. It will make things awkward."

"How do you mean?" He gazed at me.

"Well, if you're with Jewels, then every time we go

out, and I'm not wearing red hair they'll know it's me and what I really look like. But, if you choose Tamara, then we'll have some sort of privacy."

He thought about it. "You're right. You're absolutely right." He came over and pulled me into his arms. "And since I want us to have privacy, then I'd better choose Tamara."

I smiled. "Nice! So, where are we going?"

"Wherever you want, my love."

My smile got even bigger. "Well, I have something in mind."

"Are you going to tell me?"

"No. Can we leave tomorrow?"

He kissed me. "Anything you want."

"Yay!" I did a little dance. "Then you'd better get home and pack a bag if we're leaving tomorrow." I stopped and thought about what I needed to take.

"Um." He shoved his hands into his pockets with an impish grin. "I already did."

"What? What do you mean, you already did?" I was intrigued.

"While you were asleep in the hospital, I ran home, took my leave, and packed a bag. I knew I wanted to get you out of London, so I got ready. It's down in the car."

"Okaayy," I said. "You'd better get it then." He moved to the door. "Send Bob and Linda up on your way down." I started pulling clothes, shoes, a case, and other things out of the closet.

Bob and Linda ran in. "What is it?"

"Callum and I are going away. We might need a few things."

"Anything," Bob said.

"Um." I paced the room while Linda packed my case, pulling things out she thought I'd need. "Paper. Lots of paper. White, um, a pack of printing paper maybe, so I can write or draw. Ah, my electricals, maybe a road map, a basket of food, um, I don't know, whatever."

He nodded. "I've got paper downstairs, and I'll dig out some maps."

Callum came back with his case and watched me pull out my list and start marking things off as I packed everything I'd need.

Linda finished my case as Bob came back. "I'm lending you my portable printer just in case. It's got new cartridges and a couple of extras."

"Thanks," I said and packed the paper and printer into my huge computer bag next to my laptop, camera, camcorder, cords and all other work and playthings.

Callum placed my suitcase next to the sofa alongside his. I sat my bag on top of it.

"Just need my toiletries, pills, and wig tomorrow," I said, clapping my hands. "I can't wait!"

<h1 style="text-align:center">Chapter 17</h1>

After spending the night together – *no* nothing happened except we slept in each other's arms – we were up early, sitting around the table at breakfast deciding the best way to go, and how long it would take. With a few clicks of the computer keys, Linda found us a nice quiet hotel to stay in and made arrangements. Taking the picnic hamper she'd packed for us, and a road map folder Bob put together, we stopped for petrol before speeding down the highway toward Dartmoor around ten.

Callum finally learned why we were going that way and why we would stop in Penzance.

"Nancy Drew!" I said matter-of-factly.

"Nancy…" He frowned. *"The book character?"*

I scoffed. "Not *just* the book character, thank you very much. The book *icon*. The old girl's been around for over eighty years."

"Wow." His eyes widened. "She is old."

"Pfft!" I playfully punched him in the arm. "She's an eternally youthful eighteen," I said. "Although in the early books she was sixteen, but after updating, the owner made her legal to drive in all fifty states of America."

"Must be nice being eighteen forever." Callum glanced in the rear-view.

I flung a strand of golden-brown hair over my shoulder. I'd managed to get my wig on that morning, and under a beanie, it looked all right. I'd also sprayed some of that latex make-up on, and it covered the bruising well. "Yeah, well. Would you want to be eighteen forever?"

He thought about it. "Nah! Maybe forty. It's a nice round figure. I know more now than I did then, and I'm smarter, bigger, stronger."

"Why forty?" I stared out at the passing scenery.

"Because I *am* forty."

"Really?" I swung my head around to look at him and touched his cheek. "Mmm. You've held up well for an old man."

He guffawed. "Old man! Nice! Real nice!"

I giggled and heard the blinker click on. "Where are we going?"

"Going to stop at a rest area so we can have some food, and you can take your pills. Plus we need to stretch our legs."

Getting out of his black Jeep Cherokee, I glanced at the lush green surroundings, rolling pastures, hills and trees. It was nice, and the air was fresh and clean.

Callum took some sandwiches out of the hamper, then handed me two of my pills. "Take these and then eat." Bob and Linda had put him in charge of my medication, so I didn't "overdose" again.

Munching on delicious chicken, cheese and tomato sandwiches with some sort of amazing dressing, we stood gazing at the countryside.

"This is nice," I mumbled around my food. "How long to Penzance?"

He glanced at his watch. "Three to four hours. Should get there before it gets too dark."

"Can't wait." I finished off my food and swallowed my painkillers. *There you go, Jack. Suck on that!*

Having cleaned up, we climbed back into the car and headed off. For awhile, we drove past steep green hills and high granite outcrops. Dartmoor was the largest national park in Devonshire. It was wild and seemed to match my sometimes moodiness. Rolling toward Penzance, I'd never seen countryside so green.

Callum told me about the area, pointing out the places in between talking about himself. He got to know me as well, and we found we had a lot in common.

Around four-thirty we slowed down, and I noticed we were approaching Penzance. After stopping to check the map, we slowly drove through. It was a gorgeous old market town, with the occasional cobbled street and quaint store. We kept on going, back into lush green countryside on our left and the ocean on our right.

I stared out the window at the whitecaps as Callum drove, and didn't even realise we were now approaching an old style castle. "Wow," I said. "Look at that."

I saw two storeys of grey brick. The old-fashioned

kind, since it was an old castle. A tower stood at each corner, there was a circular drive, and white crisscross window panes.

Callum pulled to a stop in front of two massive wood doors with mistletoe rings and huge concrete steps.

"God, look at this," I said, getting out. All I could do was stare.

Callum deposited our bags beside me and pulled the hamper from the back. Grinning, he looked up. "Well, we did want it to be an experience for you. Let's go."

Rolling our cases and bags up the stairs, I noticed a small porch ran along either side of the door. It blended into the brick wall and gardens, looking more like a path running each length of the house. The doors opened, and we were ushered in.

The lobby was huge. Red rugs, suits of armour, family shields, and ornate mirrors adorned the room. A huge staircase covered in rich red carpet started at the desk and extended up. To our right was a huge room with fireplace, sofas, and more royal artefacts. Through the archway to our left, was a long wooden dining table. Tinsel, baubles, fairy lights, and a huge tree decorated each room.

"Your name, sir?"

I nonchalantly covered my swollen cheek and turned away.

"Mr and Mrs Stone."

I suppressed a giggle. Linda had booked us in as a married couple.

"Of course. Sign here, and here's your key. If there's anything, you need?"

"Thank you," Callum said.

A porter carried our cases up the stairs, and I slung my computer bag over my shoulder as we followed. Down a hallway to the right, we stopped at the end, and the porter opened the door and placed our cases inside.

"Sir. Ma'am."

"Thank you," Callum repeated and closed the door on him.

"Wow," I breathed. "Look at this, it's kinda like my room at Bob and Linda's except with a fireplace."

There was a huge four-poster bed to our left. A huge fireplace was in front of us with a curtained window on either side. A small couch and matching chairs were to our right, a huge window faced the rolling sea, and there was an old-fashioned roller desk under the window next to the fireplace. Everything was covered in sparkly Christmas decorations.

I sat my bag on the desk and unpacked, laying everything out, so it was within reach, then stowed my bag under the desk and turned to Callum. He'd disappeared. "Callum," I called.

"In here," came the muffled reply.

I walked toward the sound, through the door I thought led to the bathroom, and found a small walk-in robe. "Nice!" He'd unpacked his bag and helped me with mine.

"Do you want to go for a walk before dinner? It's getting dark, but we could step outside," he suggested.

"I guess," I replied, tucking away my underwear. We still had our coats on, so we locked the door, strolled hand in hand back down the stairs and out the front door, seeing our car had been put in the hotel car park, so we didn't need to worry about it. We walked toward the bluff then stood and watched the sunset. The roar of the waves on rocks, and the gorgeous hues of red and pink in the sunset made the end of a perfect day. Once the colours disappeared, we went back inside.

"Do you want to eat in the dining room or upstairs?" Callum asked.

"Upstairs. I want to get my…" another couple passed us and I cleared my throat. "Accessories off."

Callum smiled his understanding, and we went to our room.

I stood in the bathroom and pulled my wig off while Callum set out the rest of the hamper.

"You okay?" he called.

I stared at my head. "Ugh, yeah." I laid my hair in a drawer and went to eat. I was feeling hungry, which was a surprise, and ate several sandwiches. A fire had been lit, and we sat watching it for awhile before getting ready for bed. It was going to be our second night together, and while we'd just held each other the night before, I wanted something to happen now. I just wasn't sure how far I wanted to go or *could* go, with my injuries. And what about Callum? Would he be ready? I straightened my silky nightgown and walked into the bedroom.

Callum was in front of the fire, making sure the

guard was in place as it would be going all night. I stood behind him, sliding my fingers through the dark blue velvet of his robe as my arms wrapped around him.

"Hey." He turned and kissed the top of my head.

"Hey," I replied, smiling softly at my lover-to-be.

"You ready for some sleep?" He took me in his arms.

I didn't reply for a few moments, trying to find the courage to say what I wanted. "It's not *sleep* I'm interested in," I finally said.

His eyes bored into mine. "We haven't discussed that yet."

"I know," I whispered and took a deep breath. "I… want it to happen, but with all my scarring and…"

"Shh." He touched his finger to my lips. "We won't rush. It's in your hands. Whenever *you* want. I will wait."

"Um." I didn't know how to broach the subject.

"What?"

"Did you…um…" I cleared my throat. "Bring um…" I coughed. "Protection?"

He chuckled. "Yes. But as I said, I will not rush you. It's all up to you."

"Yeeeaaahhh," I breathed. "Do you have a problem with my…my bruises and scars?"

"No." His voice was so gentle that I looked up to see tenderness and love.

I felt my face crumple, and I buried my face in his chest, feeling the softness of his hair. I rushed on. "I have rules. 1 – Always wear a condom. Always! 2 – No oral, no anal, not interested. 3 – No biting, no scratching." I looked up and grinned slyly. "Well, *you* that is, I'll scratch and bite you all I like. 4 – No electricals, no phones, no nothing. It's all about taking our time and not rushing."

He nodded his agreement. "Absolutely. You set the rules."

I took a deep breath and tried to stop myself from shaking. I held his hand and led him to the bed. Pulling back the covers, I climbed on and started letting down the bed's curtains. When finished, I faced Callum who'd turned the light off and was right there on the bed with me.

I slowly unpulled his belt, and sliding my hands up his chest pushed his robe off his shoulders. "Oh," I breathed, staring at his well-toned body. "Hello," I squeaked.

He grinned and threw his robe to the end of the bed before tugging on the tie around my waist. My heart thundered in my chest. My breasts ached for his hands, and my hands went to his waist as my robe followed his.

Fingers traced along my arm. My neck. My face. I was breathing heavily. Lips moved toward mine and planted themselves, tongue delving deep inside. Touching. Tasting. Wanting more.

Mine responded. My hands greedily slid all over him. Our mouths mashed together. His arms held me tight. Mooshing my body to his, he lowered me to the bed, our mouths never stopping their rhythmic pace.

"Mmm," I groaned, muffled against his mouth before it tore itself away and moved along my neck, my chest, my breast. It latched onto my nipple and sucked. "Ahh," I gasped, digging my nails into his shoulder. His hand slid up my thigh and between my legs, rubbing against my pelvis.

"Ohhh." It slid up further, finding the nipple he'd hardened. Rubbing it between his fingers, his mouth turned to the other.

"Oh," I cried, shaking to my core. His hands thrust up under my nightie, pushing it up and over my head. He pinned my hands there, his mouth claiming mine again. I felt his body against mine, setting it on fire.

"Ah," I moaned, matching his tongue movement for movement. I arched up against him, wanting to imprint his body on mine. His hand slid down, groped my breast and moved on to my crotch, thrusting between my legs it lifted one and hooked it on his elbow.

"Argh." I moved with him.

His leg planted itself between mine, and his manhood hardened. He thrust his other leg in between, and I wrapped myself around him.

My hands broke free and madly dashed all over him, wanting to feel every manly inch. I was so ready for him my vagina ached for him, wanting him inside of me. "Now," I gasped, tearing my mouth away from his. "Now."

Royal blue eyes stared into mine. "Are you sure? Are you ready?"

"Yes, yes," I rasped, gulping air.

His hands thrust down into my panties and tore them off.

"Ahh." My pelvis was throbbing as his fingers gently touched. I grabbed his hand and held it against my pubic bone. "Feel me," I gasped. "Feel me."

His fingers probed.

"Ahh." Deeper. Deeper. Deeper. "Ah, uh." I was going over the edge. "Now," I cried, pushing his hand away.

He turned to the bedside table, ripped something open, and rolled on top of me. My legs locked around his waist, my arms around his torso. Callum lay still, panting slightly.

I gazed into his eyes. "Now," I whispered. "I want you now."

He reached down and guided himself inside of me.

I almost fainted. The world had disappeared before, but now it went completely. We were floating in a black night surrounded by millions of dazzling white stars. I groaned. "Stay there. Let me feel you," I whispered. "Let me adjust to you." I held him close not wanting to let go.

"When you're ready," he whispered in my ear.

I breathed heavily. My face nuzzled his neck and shoulder. He shifted to change his weight. The movement stirred me deep inside. "Now," I cried. "Now."

He pulled out and then thrust. And again. And again. And again. Over and over and over. Pulled out and thrust. Pulled out and thrust.

I didn't realise we'd stopped. The light from the stars around us blinded me. I gazed into his eyes. "More," I whispered, and he started again.

Pulled out then thrust. I went over the edge, crying and gasping as he filled me. Filled my heart. My body. My soul.

"Ah, huh." Over and over and over. I felt myself peak, and I arched, quivering as my body shuddered.

He stopped. His mouth gently kissing me. His hand gently stroking me, my breast, my side, my leg.

I throbbed inside, feeling his fullness. He filled me completely, and I could swear he was throbbing too. "I love you," I rasped, my fingers digging into his back.

"I love you," his lips murmured against my neck.

The throbbing didn't subside. It was made more powerful by the rubbing of my nipple. My hands slid over him. This was everything I'd wanted. Everything I'd waited for. And I'd finally found the man I wanted it with. The stars shone around us, pulsating in sync with my body.

He stopped moving. His hand. His mouth.

I licked my lips and swallowed, gazing at him through a sex filled haze. The sexual heat between us was burning me up, and this man deliberately produced a lot of it. He was pure sexual heat. He placed an arm either side of me, pulled his legs up and got a grip.

My eyes widened. My whole body throbbed and pulsated. I knew what he was going to do. He was in control and taking charge, and he hadn't finished.

"Hang on," he growled and thrust with ferocious strength.

I cried out, not sure if I was screaming. The stars blurred into one big bright light. Callum thrust for all his worth, bringing me to the edge over and over. Throbbing like I would burst. Screaming like I would tear my throat out. I hung on and rode the wave. The never-ending wave of sexual heat.

Chapter 18

My eyes slowly opened. There was a sound. I blinked. I heard it again. I froze. It was a growl. Callum was asleep beside me, so it wasn't him. My heart raced in my chest, and not one part of my body wanted to move.

"Gahhhhh." It was soft and low.

Every muscle tightened, hurting me in all manner of ways.

"Gahhhhh."

It was a little louder, and coming around the bed toward me. I don't even know how my left hand managed to creep from under the covers and slowly move up toward the bedside cupboard, up toward the bedside light.

"Gahhhhh." Louder still.

My fingers reached the button, and with a deep gulp I turned it on.

"Gahhhhh." The zombie concierge screamed as he shook his head and jumped at me.

I screamed.

I woke up.

Panting and gasping, blackness all around me. I switched the light on and looked around. No zombie concierge.

"Tam," Callum mumbled, shifting beside me.

"Ah," I screamed.

"S'okay." His eyes opened sleepily. "Waz wrong?"

I looked at him to make sure he wasn't a zombie. He wasn't. "Oh," I breathed. "Just a bad dream. I'm okay, go back to sleep."

"Mmm, kay." He drifted back off.

I looked around the room, even standing on the bed so I could see around the furniture. Seeing no one, and no *thing,* I settled back in and listened for every little sound.

"Gahhhhh." The sounds were faint, like they were outside.

I froze, not wanting to believe it was happening again.

"Gahhhhh." Louder now and in multiples.

I tried to unfreeze myself, willing myself to move.

"Gahhhhh." The sound screamed outside. Right outside our window.

I couldn't move. I willed myself to move. I couldn't move.

Smashing glass flew into the room and hordes of zombies fell through the window. Bleeding, limbless, screaming zombies. Bleeding, limbless, screaming zombies that were spreading through the room like the plague they were. Spreading out like the virus they had, bleeding everywhere, running toward me, Callum, the bed. Bleeding and gah-ing and bleeding and baring their fangs ready to lay them into our soft white flesh to eat and tear apart and devour like the animals they were. Ready to annihilate and be rid of. Starving and screaming and bleeding and coming toward us at a very fast pace. Bloody saliva dripping from their very sharp teeth. Very sharp teeth that were coming toward us.

I screamed.

I woke up.

Panting and gasping, blackness all around me. I switched the light on and looked around. No zombies falling through the windows.

"Tam," Callum mumbled, shifting beside me.

"Ah," I screamed.

"S'okay." His eyes opened sleepily. "Waz wrong?"

I looked at him to make sure he wasn't a zombie. He wasn't. "Oh," I breathed. "Just a bad dream. Go make sure the windows are locked."

"Wah?" he slurred.

I pushed him. "Go make sure the windows are locked."

He leaned up on his elbow, wiping the sleep from his eyes. "They're locked."

I pushed him again. "Go check the windows."

"Oh, God, all right," he groaned and climbed out of bed. He checked all of the windows and the bathroom then slid back under the covers. "They're all locked. Are you right now?" He settled in with a sigh.

I gulped. "Yeah." I lay back down and pulled the covers to my chin. Callum gently snored beside me.

Bang…bang…bang…bang…bang…bang…

"Callum," I whispered.

Bang…bang…bang…bang…bang…bang…

"Callum." I pushed him. "Callum."

Bang…bang…bang…bang…bang…bang…

"What now?"

Bang…bang…bang…bang…bang…bang…

"There's someone at the door."

Bang…bang…bang…bang…bang…bang…

"Arghhh."

Bang…bang…bang…bang…bang…bang…

He rolled out of bed and walked over to the door. "What?" he demanded, flinging it open.

"Gahhhhh," Zombies screamed and poured in, jumping on him, devouring him. Bleeding and baring their teeth and screaming and jumping all over him knocking him to the ground.

"Arggghhh," he cried, blood spurting everywhere.

"Gahhhhh." Some of the zombies turned to me. Ice blue eyes with their pinpoint pupils stared at me. They growled.

I screamed.

I woke up.

Panting and gasping, blackness all around me. I switched the light on and looked around. No zombies devouring Callum. I turned to him. "Callum," I whispered, prodding him.

He growled and opened his eyes. Ice blue eyes with their pinpoint pupils stared at me. His teeth long and sharp. "Gahhhhh."

I screamed.

I woke up.

Panting and gasping, light all around me.

"Tam."

"Ahh," I screamed, scrambling away.

"It's okay, sweetheart. It's me." His hand reached for me.

We were in our big four-poster bed in our big castle bedroom, the light filtering in around the curtains. The fire was out, the air had chilled.

"Oh, God," I gasped. "Oh, God." My head pounded, my body shook.

"Sweetheart." The love and concern in his eyes calmed me, and I collapsed into his arms in a heap. "It's okay. Shh. It's okay."

We lay facing each other as he stroked my hair and held me tight.

"What time is it?" Jack pounded away in my head.

"Seven-thirty," he mumbled. "Bad dream I take it."

I snorted. "Yeah."

"Wanna talk about it?"

"No." We lay in silence, which was nice, except for Jack. I breathed in Callum's manly scent. It was sexual heat from the night before. It was hot. It was sexy. And it made me want him. I slid my arms around his body and pulled him against me. "Mmm." I slid my left leg over his and pushed his between mine. I arched my pelvis into his and felt his manhood harden. I rubbed my face on the soft furry nest on his strong manly chest.

"Do you want to?" His voice was gentle.

"I want to feel you. Your body against mine." My left hand snaked down and pulled him between my legs. He stiffened more. "I want to feel you. Feel every inch of you against every inch of me." I held him tight, and we lay there. I thought about last night and felt myself blush. My nipples hardened, and he sensed it. His fingers slid over my left one. I groaned, but his mouth caught it, crushing itself onto mine, his tongue delving gently. I was so ready for him again, and I let him know it by rolling him on top of me and wrapping myself around him.

He pulled away and grabbed a condom, ripping it open and sliding it down. He slowly entered me, and for awhile, we became lost in that black starry sky, where the world and Jack didn't exist.

We lay together, softly panting, gazing into each other's eyes, then, without words, we knew it was time to move. Callum carried me into the bathroom and ran the shower. Holding me in his arms, he soaped my body and washed my hair. When we finished, he dried it, then slid the towel over the rest of my body, bringing waves of arousal all over again.

We ordered room service and dressed. Finishing off our omelettes and juice, Callum asked what I wanted to do.

I gazed out the window over the sea. "Go for a walk," I replied then looked at him. "Maybe we should have…" I shook my head. "I don't know. Some sort of schedule."

He frowned. "We're on holiday. Why would we need a schedule?"

I stared at my computer then turned back to him. "Because, I've had erratic sleep hours, *when* I slept that is. Working all night. Pain." The sea caught my eye again, and I walked over to the window. "I think spending time outside will be very beneficial, and might help me get my pain under control. Maybe it will help me sleep." I turned back to him. "And the fresh sea air will do me good."

He placed his cup on the coffee table. "Any particular time you'd like to put this outing into the schedule?"

"Well." Thinking about it, I sat beside him. "How about morning? After breakfast?"

He smiled. "Anytime you want, sweetheart."

"Mmm, morning sounds good. After something to eat, we can get out in the fresh air for an hour or so, and it will help set me up for the rest of the day, when I'll *try* to work." I balefully glared at my laptop.

"You want to go now?"

"Mmm?" I looked at him.

"Do you want to go outside now?"

"Ah, yeah, why not." I headed for the bathroom and freshened up, staring at my head in the mirror. I pulled out the drawer with my wig and picked up the protective tape I wore over my scar underneath it. I looked at myself, then the tape, and put it back in the drawer. In the closet, I grabbed a woollen beanie cap and slid it over my head. I pulled on a thick jacket and popped the hood over my head, then grabbed a pair of big black sunnies. Walking into the bedroom, I saw Callum waiting.

"You ready?"

"Ah." My eyes wandered to the desk, and I walked over, picking up my digital recorder and popping it into my pocket. "Ready." I put on my glasses, and we headed down the hall to the outside world.

Oh, and *no* zombies!

Walking hand in hand to the bluff, we stood staring at the big blue ocean. I could see Penzance just down the coast with its surrounding towns around Mount Bay. The hotel overlooking it all. From its majestic clifftop, it oversaw rocky coves, pristine sandy beaches, and crystal clear seas.

I turned around and looked at our hotel. It was definitely an old castle with its grey stones and turrets, but only two storeys tall which I thought slightly strange. Its backdrop was rugged trees, vast moors, and the occasional stone mound. I wondered if we were able to explore them. "Let's walk."

Along the bluff and around the castle we found well-worn paths leading in all directions. Every now and then we came across a blaze of colour from late autumn flowers, or a craggy moor with the odd tree here and there, walking until we found a stone circle and mounds. I let go of Callum's hand, and after making sure there were no bugs or spiders or any other creature I should be wary of, I sat down facing the ocean.

I breathed deeply. "In and out. In and out," I murmured, eyes closed against the warm sun.

"I should have brought a book."

I gave him a dirty look. "Seriously?" I chastised. "Seriously?"

He gave me a goofy grin. "Well? What am I going to do while you're here meditating or whatever it is you'll be doing?"

"Ah," I paused, "fair enough." I sucked in the salty air. "How long have we been?"

"Half hour." He pulled his sleeve back over his watch.

"Let's keep walking." We spent another half hour discovering our holiday landscape before making our way back to the castle. I headed upstairs while Callum grabbed some snacks, then we sat on the couch munching away, my elbow leaning on the back of the couch, my head in my hand.

"Do you feel better?"

"Mmm?"

"Did our walk make you feel better?"

I sighed. "Yeah, a bit. Jack's still in there, though."

"Well, tell him to bugger off then. I'm the only man in your life."

I burst out laughing and kept on laughing. "That's the funniest thing I've heard," I gasped, wiping away tears.

His lips widened into his gorgeous grin. "I thought that would make you laugh."

I laughed again then leaned over and kissed him. "It did."

"So..." He got serious. "How do you want to do things while we're here?"

"Oh, I don't know." I sighed again. "I don't really want to bare my head or my face here, 'cause putting my wig and that make-up on is arduous." I scratched my head. "I'd prefer to stay in, have our meals sent up, try and..." I scratched again. "Try and sort out what's going on."

"How are you going to do that?"

I looked at him. "I have no idea."

That night, we lay in front of the fire, hot, naked, wet, and wrapped in each other. I had a smile on my face from ear to ear and snuggled into his chest. His arms tightened around me.

"Why are you smiling?" he murmured against my forehead.

"Because that was fantastic and I have absolutely no pain."

He pulled his head back to look at me. "Really?"

I gazed back. "Really."

"Wow." He pulled me tight. "The pills are working then?"

I grinned. "I don't think it's the pills."

He grinned back. "Well then, if we're going to get rid of your pain, we'd better do that again."

And we did.

*****

I was drowning. I knew it but didn't want to admit it. I couldn't release myself from whatever was holding me. I furiously thrashed my arms and legs trying to get to the surface. But it didn't work. My lungs were burning. My mouth wanted to open and gasp for air. I couldn't let that happen. If it did, I'd swallow foul river water and drown. But I was drowning anyway. I struggled, reaching down to push away the object that had a hold. I found nothing. I struggled and struggled and struggled… then stopped. I had no strength. I had no power. I drowned and felt myself falling…

Falling…

Falling…

Thud!

I woke up gasping for air, clutching at my throat. "Ahh, can't breathe, need air…" I rasped.

"Tamara. Tamara. What is it, baby? What's wrong?" He turned the light on and rolled off the bed to pull me into his arms.

"Can't breathe," I gasped. "Can't breathe, drowning, drowning…"

"Shh," he stroked my hair. "Shh. It was just a bad dream. Just a bad dream."

Chapter 19

I was pacing back and forth the next morning after our walk.

Callum watched from the sofa, all snuggly in the blue woolly jumper that brought out his eyes. "What's going on?"

I kept pacing, my finger on my lip, my eyes down. Several thoughts had run through my head during breakfast and continued through our walk, and now, they were finally coming together. "The drugs don't work," I said on the move. "But then I knew that. Even the new ones don't work. But there's one thing that seems to, and I noticed it last night." I stopped and stared at him, waiting for his expression.

"Okay. What is it?"

"Sex!"

His brows shot up in amusement. "What?"

"Sex."

"Ah." He shook his head and tried to hide a grin. "Are you sure?"

"Think about it," I said. "Jack's been in my head since the accident, and except for my little zombie pill party, the only time the pain has stopped is when we've had sex. I noticed it last night."

"O…kay…I guess that might make sense, since the endorphins or something are supposed the get rid of headaches." A cheeky look flitted through his eyes. "So, what does that mean? And what do you want to do about it?"

I caught the cheeky look and matched it with a grin. "It means, mister," I kneeled on the couch facing him, "we're going to have lots of sex."

He pulled me to him, and I met his lips with mine. "Are those doctors' orders?"

"Hell, no!" I exclaimed. "They're *my* orders." I eagerly shoved my tongue down his throat and played a game of tonsil hockey with him. Which, in thinking, would be difficult since I don't have tonsils.

After an hour or so we surfaced. "Okay," I gasped. "Where was I?"

"You were here." Callum pulled me back to his lips.

I pushed him away. "No, no, no." I went back to pacing and tried to remember what my other point was. "Ah, right." I sighed and rubbed my head. "Okay, there has to be some way I can deal with what happened. There has to be some way I can get it out of my head?"

"Are you writing it down on your laptop?"

"Mmm? Ah, yeah sort of. I've typed stuff up, but it's not really anything yet." I huffed and looked at him. "Bob wants me to write a book about it. Figured if writing was going to help me, he might as well get a book out of it." I paced my way over to my computer and turned it on. "Let's see what I've got." It took me fifteen minutes to find the word documents. All five of them were in different folders and not labelled clearly.

After moving them into a well labelled folder, I opened the smallest one. "Mmm, something about pain." I opened another. "Mmm, something about love and hate." And another. "Something about… don't have any idea. Argh." I rubbed my eyes and went back to pacing. "What do I do? What do I do?" I scratched my head. I rubbed my eyes. I gazed out the window. "Compartments." I snapped my fingers as the light bulb went off.

Callum looked at me. "What?"

"Boxes, containers, compartments," I said excitedly, pacing even faster. "I need to…I need to…" I was trying to latch onto the idea. "Separate everything into boxes and deal with them one at a time."

"You don't have boxes, although we could ask for some."

"No, no, I don't need actual boxes." I stopped and stared at the desk. Paper, sharpie, computer, files. Computer files. Boxes. Little yellow boxes. "Paper!" I exclaimed. "I'll write each thing down on the paper and…and…" I tried to think, but Jack was getting faster. "Stick them up on the wall. Yes, I'll stick each part up on the wall, and deal with each problem separately, one by one, and hopefully, things will be clearer and much easier to talk or write about and… and…" I turned to Callum excitedly. "It should work. Right?"

In one movement he was on his feet and pulling

me into his arms. "It *will* work," he said. "Have faith that you've found the answer you need to help you deal with this."

I hugged him back. "I hope so!" But I paced back and forth for the rest of the afternoon, throwing in meals, and the occasional moment in front of the computer. I was having trouble deciding how and where to start, and soon began wondering if I even knew how to decompress the situation long enough to find out.

I stared down at the printer paper on the coffee table. I'd opened it and pulled out a small pile, all ready to be written on. Different coloured sharpies lay next to it. Masking tape and scissors sat next to the sharpies.

I kept pacing. I had to get the order right in my head, so I could break it down properly. Otherwise, the plan might not work at all, and I'd keep having nightmares.

Lightning flashed, thunder roared through the window, and I jumped ten feet in the air. We looked out over the bay and saw rolling waves, black clouds, and rain heading our way.

"Mmm, we're in for a storm." Callum stood behind me at the window.

I shivered and rubbed the side of my head. "I love storms, but don't know how my head's going to cope with this."

His arms slid around me, and I leaned against his chest, resting my head under his chin. "Don't worry. I'll take care of you."

I smiled and felt safe and secure.

We watched as the sky darkened and the town's lights disappeared beneath the fog and cloud. Rain pelted outside the window and hissed into the fireplace. Feeling the chill, we closed the curtains and ordered dinner.

Later, I changed into my robe and brushed my hair, although, with what was left, I couldn't even cover my scar. And why the hell had I told Linda to shave the other side? I shook my head at my reflection. *You idiot!* Sighing, I flicked the light off and walked into the bedroom. Callum was lying in front of the fireplace on some cushions in his velvet robe. "Doors and windows shut and locked?" I asked, standing over him.

"Shut and locked," he murmured, watching me.

The storm raged outside as I knelt over him and pushed off my robe. I undid his, my hands making their way over his sexy chest, tight abs and sizeable manhood. I stroked him, and he rose. I thrust gently against him, holding it to my abdomen. My fingers slowly moved. His eyes closed, and my hands worked their magic, rolling a condom down to his base.

"Argh," the deep growl tore through his lips.

My fingers moved upward, sliding his robe from his shoulders as he lifted himself and pulled his arms out. His manly hands grabbed my hips and lifted me onto his thick hard shaft.

Slowly. Slowly. Slowly. I descended to the depths of pure passion, dirty lust and sexual heat. His hands roamed my body, and I flung my head back as they moulded to my breasts. "Argh," I groaned, my hands on his, guiding them. I moved his hands down and pushed his thumb onto my clitoris as I slowly rotated. "Ugh."

The storm raged outside, but we kept the same slow sensual pace. Darkness lit with brilliant stars was all around us. Hands did their work, making me rise into the heavens.

Callum sat up, and I gasped at the movement inside of me. His lips found mine and our tongues moved with the same rhythm of our sexual connection.

"Ugh," we moaned. Fingers traced. Hands caressed. Mouths kissed. The storm grew louder, harder, even more powerful, matching our physical movements, and the pulsating melody stormed around the room as it came to its stunning climatic crescendo.

Gurgle, gurgle, gurgle.

My head pounded and I couldn't breathe.

Gurgle, gurgle, gurgle.

My lungs burned and burst into flames.

I screamed and took a mouthful of water instead of air.

Gurgle, gurgle, gurgle.

"Ahh."

"Tam," Callum said softly. "S'okay, shh, just a nightmare."

I looked around the room. We were still in front of the fire with soft morning light drifting around the curtains. Rain fell lightly, sending the occasional drop hissing into the dying fire. As I breathed deeply, I sorted through my thoughts and realised what I needed to do.

Leaving Callum to sleep, I got up and showered, and after throwing on a tracksuit, I planted myself on the floor in front of the coffee table. I picked up a sharpie and piece of paper and began to write.

Meeting Callum.

Another sheet.

Seeing the car screaming toward me.

Another sheet.

Being hit by the car.

Another sheet.

Hitting my head on the corner and falling into the water.

Another sheet.

Saving the mother and child.

Another sheet.

Going under and pulling the woman out.

Another sheet.

Getting stuck and not being able to get out.

Another sheet.

Drowning.

Another sheet.

Watching Callum resuscitate me.

Another sheet.

Being dead and seeing things.

Another sheet.

Coming back and dying again in the hospital.

Another sheet.

Dealing with pain and seeing my head and face.

Another sheet.

Taking the pills and vodka.

Another sheet.

Callum!

"What are those?

I stuck the last sheet of paper on the wall. They spread around the grey brick walls, starting from above the desk and going to the window facing the ocean. I turned and saw him standing there, naked, and watching me. I grinned at the sight of his body. "My boxes," I said, pointing to the papers. "Each one is a small section of the story. If I break it down enough, I should be able to deal with each part on its own and come out the other end okay."

He smiled. "I hope it works for you, I really do. But, in the meantime, how about you order breakfast? I'll take a shower, and then we'll have our walk. Who knows, the fresh air might clear your mind."

Well, the air didn't exactly do that. We stood in the entrance watching the rain pour down.

"No walk today then," Callum said.

I looked along the castle walls. "We could sit on the porch. It's covered and has a bench at the end." I pointed to our left.

Walking along, we found ourselves around the side of the building. There was more room, and it was more private. We sat and breathed the cold icy air.

"In and out. In and out." I relaxed on the bench, but Jack kept hammering away. "In and out." The rain softened and the fog cleared. I saw the waves bouncing across the sea, and it reminded me of the river. "Ugh."

"You okay?"

"Yeah."

"Want to go back inside?"

"Not yet." Callum pulled me close, and I rested my head on his shoulder. "And in and out."

Five hours later, I was pacing again, stopping every now and then to watch the rain pour down.

I love the rain. I do. I could sit and watch it rain all day, and lie awake and listen to it pour all night. It made me feel good. It made me feel happy. *Usually.* But *not* today.

"Maybe you should just let it come instead of trying to force it," Callum suggested from the spot on the couch he'd made his own.

I kept pacing, willing the thoughts to come, and berating them when they didn't.

"Tamara."

I stopped and looked.

"Don't force them, sweetie, they won't come."

I felt his concern from across the room and sighed. "Yeah. I know." I plonked down beside him and into his waiting arms. "I know."

Late that night, I lay awake in Callum's arms, not knowing what time it was. The rain fell softly, the fire crackled gently, and I snuggled deeper into his embrace. I thought about everything on the papers stuck to the wall. It had felt good to get them all out. To put a name or label on them. Each problem that needed to be dealt with.

Jack softly hammered away, the effects of sex still lasting. He wasn't full force at the moment, so I was able to drift off to sleep.

I opened my eyes. I rolled out of bed. I walked over to the coffee table. I knelt down. I picked up a pen. I placed a piece of paper in front of me. I began to write.

I hadn't realised what was happening. When *it was happening. Sure, I was watching Callum at the time, and then saw Megan's expression turn to horror. My eyes followed the direction of her arm and hand and lay upon the car. The blue sedan that was barrelling full bore toward me. I wondered why it was coming for me, and wondered if it was going to stop. It didn't look like it was going to stop.*

Her face. *Her face was a mixture of many things. Emotions, I mean. She looked so determined. Like no thing and no one was going to stop her. Stop her from doing what she was hell-bent on doing. And that poor child. That child was screaming. Its face contorted and screwed up like it was in pain. But then I guess it would have been. Crying and screaming 'Mummy' and not stopping. Mummy yelling and screaming back. That child wouldn't have understood any of what was going on. Nothing at all. I feel sorry for that child. Sure, it survived. I pulled it out. Hopefully, it will never know or be told what Mummy did when they were two. Only two! Way too young to do anything to stop Mummy aiming for the river.*

Why *was she was aiming for the river? Was it a split second decision? Did she have any other way of suicide in mind? Suicide, yeah, I know about that, and I can see how people might think I tried it. But I didn't. But* that *woman.* She *did. But it wasn't just suicide on her part, it was homicide as well. She tried to kill her child. That look on her face sent chills down my spine. All I was doing was minding my own business, standing there playing the fool for the video, when* she *decided to take that street and come barrelling my way.*

Why *didn't I move?* Why *didn't I scream?* Why *didn't I do anything? Is* that *what this is about?* I didn't do anything. *I didn't run, move, twist, leap, nothing. I did* nothing. *And I suffered for it. I stood there, got run over by a bitch on a mission, and ended up paying for it.* I did nothing. Nothing is not okay. *Nothing is wrong and useless and stupid. I did nothing. And that's the problem. I did nothing while she drove over me, and tried to kill all three of us. I did nothing.* Could do nothing. *There was nothing I could do. Nothing I could do to stop her.* I did nothing…*and that's okay.*

I pulled down the paper from the wall labelled *seeing the car come screaming toward me.* I stuck the papers together and laid them on the desk. I went back to bed and fell asleep.

*****

I sat on the stone mound the next morning, breathing deeply, trying to meditate.

Callum was reading a book he'd borrowed from the hotel's small library room, and was awkwardly lounging on another rock.

In and out. In and out. The cold breeze filtered through my beanie. I wasn't wearing my wig, so I felt the cold more. But it didn't matter. It was refreshing. If I became too hot, I felt sick, so the cold helped blow the cobwebs away. I took a deep breath and opened my eyes, scanning the horizon, studying rocky outlets, barren trees, the odd palm tree, small bursts of colour, and rough stone ground. It was part moon surface, part bomb site.

Callum noticed me watching him and closed his book. "Feeling better?"

I smiled. "Yeah. Somewhat."

"I noticed one of your boxes had come down off the wall during the night. Did it fall, or did you deal with it?"

"I dealt with it." I calmly watched him, a small smile playing on my lips.

"That's good," he said, catching my smile, and a grin slid from ear to ear. "Are you having dirty thoughts?"

I drank him in. Short brown hair. Big blue eyes. High cheekbones. Full, lush lips to suck on. And they tasted good too. He was all snuggly in his chocolate brown jumper and black leather jacket. An image of him naked crept into my mind. *Oh, yes, Mr Stone, you are quite a man. What were those terms I used that first day? Hot, stunning, sexable, nuzzable and my favourite, extremely fuckable. Oh, he's certainly that!* I gazed deeply into his eyes and raised a jaunty eyebrow.

"You *are* having dirty thoughts, you dirty girl," he said, quickly coming over to me. He grabbed my hand and started leading me back to the hotel. "And I'm about to make those dirty thoughts happen."

He certainly did that all right. We lay snuggled under a blanket in front of the fire, lunch had been and gone, and we'd stayed there the whole time.

Fingers gently stroked my shoulder, and I breathed him in. My ear was right above his heart, and I listened to every single beat. Slow…rhythmic…calm. My head didn't hurt much, and I was beginning to relish those times. Every time Callum and I made love nothing, and no one existed. Not even Jack. Sex seemed to be the only drug that worked, and I was finding myself becoming addicted. Addicted to the drug. Addicted to the man. Addicted to the lack of pain. Hello, sex! Goodbye, Jack! It was peaceful without him there, pounding away in my head like a bloody Duracell bunny. He just kept going and going and going. Although for many years I thought it was the Energizer bunny, but apparently not. I stroked Callum's abdomen, my fingers trailing back and forth, up and down, and oh, hello, Mr Stone. Or do I call you, Mr Stone junior? Although you're not that junior are you? You're big and strong and manly like your owner and hello, Mr Stone senior, rolling on top of me like I'm your sex toy and oh…oh…I…ah…

*****

I stared out the window. Not the one facing the ocean, but the one closest to the bed, facing the moors and craggy cliff that dropped off at the ocean's horizon. The sun was setting, and I was watching the colours change. Grabbing my camera, I took several photos, hoping they'd turn out as good as the real thing.

"It's wild isn't it?" Callum placed his chin on my head.

"Yeah, it is."

We stayed that way until the sky went dark, and then after dinner, I sat on the desk chair in front of the wall, staring at my boxes. Only one had come down, and I was desperate for more. It was almost three weeks since the incident, and while Jack was still a fixture, the swelling had gone down a little. Even my eye was now half open instead of a slit. I read each paper over and over, trying to put it in some sort of order, trying to get it all to make sense. But I only caught glimpses and snatches. I couldn't even grasp onto them, or hold them long enough to figure out what they were.

"Blast it," I snapped, storming off the chair and into the bathroom, changing into my nightie and robe. I stared at my head trying to sort out how I felt. Still confused. Still sickened by the sight. Still swollen. Still angry. Still depressed. Still aching. Still ugly.

Still ugly. Still ugly. Still ugly.

I slammed out the door.

Chapter 20

Three weeks today. Three weeks today. Three weeks today that it happened. Three weeks today that I was hit by the car. Three weeks today that I had my face smashed in. Three weeks today that I saved a woman and child. Three weeks today that I drowned. Three weeks today. Three weeks today. Three weeks today that I died.

Twice!

I stared at myself in the bathroom mirror. Two shaved slices on my head. The ugly discoloured scar on my scalp going all the way from the front to the back. The stitches had disappeared, leaving me a hard, lumpy, fleshy war zone to deal with. I touched it.

"Ugh." I shivered. My fingers quickly pulled away and softly trailed across my face. Hard, sore, lumpy. The black was changing to yellow. *Big arse ugly yellow.* Yellow across the left side of my face. Yellow across my cheekbone. Yellow around my eye and into its socket. Yellow, black, yellow, black. Like a bee. Buzz, I'm a bee. I'm a bee that goes buzz. Pity I couldn't fly away and leave all of this behind. Bzzz fly away bee, fly away. Fly away.

I walked to the coffee table and began to write.

The pain in my head is no longer twenty-four seven. It's only eighteen-seven. The six hours a day respite I get from the pain is welcome relief. Jack disappears, and I'm cruising on a sexual high. It makes it better. It makes life more manageable to deal with. Those first few minutes that it slips away, and then the hours of sexual enjoyment that follows. That is a shield and barrier from Jack and his hammering pain. He goes away. I don't know where, but he goes away and leaves me alone for awhile. For a few hours a day, he goes away. Goes away to leave my head and face free of pain, but not free of scars and swelling.

The ugly swelling. The ugly bruising. Ugly. Ugly. Ugly. Lumpy, black, yellow, hard. Ugly. Ugly. Ugly. I don't know how long it will take to go away. I don't know. But those first days, that first week, lying in the hospital drugged out of my head. At least I had pain relief. Lying there out of it. Sweet, sweet pain relief. But the weeks that have come since have been hell. The constant thumping, aching, hammering that constantly took me to tears. Great racking sobs of pain and anger, hatred and fear. Fear of not understanding. Fear of never getting better. Fear of being like that for the rest of my life. The hatred and anger toward the woman who did this. Who caused my head and face to look like this. Who caused me to feel like this. Who didn't give a shit in the world for anyone she might hurt in the process. Now, I have to suffer through hatred and anger, although I don't really feel it anymore.

Maybe it's because I'm tired. Tired of feeling like shit when I did, that is. Being with Callum has made it better. He's willing to stand with me and help me on my way. He can. But that's now. It wasn't then. Then when I was lying in that hospital bed hooked up to all sorts of equipment and tubes, bandages around my head and on my face. The morphine helped with that. The pills after didn't. I'm not angry. I'm not full of hatred. Not anymore. And now I have Callum. Although we got off to a shaky start, and that last argument didn't help. Did I try to kill myself? I don't know. Maybe a small part of me unconsciously or subconsciously wanted to stay dead, so I didn't have to deal with the pain. The pain that burdened me so. But it wasn't what I was trying to do. I just wanted the pain to stop. If I was trying to kill myself, I would have packed all of my stuff up and laid it out so Linda wouldn't have to do it. And wouldn't I have left a note telling Bob and Linda that I was killing myself and to send my body and belongings home? So then, I wasn't trying to kill myself. I just wanted the pain to stop. For the ache and grind and constant hammering to stop so I could get some sleep, some peace, some quiet.

The pain frustrated me. It always does. Staring and sitting and walking like a zombie. Shuffling and lying and talking to the jackhammer in my head like he's a person, like a zombie. That's what I was, after. After Callum's visit. The pain from loving him, and not being loved by him, was too much as well. The pain from the look in his eyes and all I could think about was stopping the pain. The pain that racked my body. Making it shake and rattle with sobs of inhuman ferocity. I don't know why I swallowed them down with vodka. I'd never had vodka before, and the thought of it being dangerous never entered my head. I don't drink alcohol in general, so I don't know why or how I knew Bob had one in the bar fridge in his office. I don't know how. I don't know why. I just knew I wanted and needed the pain to stop. The pain had to stop for the sake of my sanity because I did not want to live on that island called Insanity. So, the pain had to stop, and I needed to make it stop.

I lifted my head and stretched. Walking over to the wall I pulled down the two boxes that read *dealing with pain and seeing my head and face*, and, *taking the pills and vodka*. I put the papers together and laid them with the others on the desk. "Three down, too many to go."

We sat on the couch cosying up after dinner. The sky had gone dark, the fire crackled merrily, and I was warm and snuggly in Callum's arms.

"So," he murmured into my hair. "What do you want to do tomorrow? It's Saturday. Do you want to stay in? Go for a drive? Go to town?"

I breathed in and snuggled closer. "I guess we could go to town. It would be nice to see it before we go. Maybe get some shopping done."

He hugged me tighter. "Sounds like a plan."

*****

I woke early and quickly showered and dressed. Callum had his turn in the shower as I applied the tape to my scar. Pulling on my brown wig, I adjusted it, fluffing out the fringe, a little bit of teasing. After a quick breakfast, I sprayed on my make-up. It took a few minutes, but I needed to make sure the yellow bruising was covered. A warm coat and boots, plus a pair of big oversized sunnies, and I was ready to go.

We drove into town and found a park in a shopping centre, then managed to walk the length of two of the major shopping streets before stopping for a delicious lunch. Strolling down our fourth street of the day, we made our way down to the promenade and stood gazing out at the ocean, finishing off the day in the local shopping centre, and dining in one of the local inns for dinner.

Back at the hotel, I surveyed my goodies. A gorgeous silk blouse. Retro jacket from a vintage store. Bits and pieces of jewellery from a vintage *buy it or make it yourself* shop. A funky pair of boots for half price, some books, and a few knick-knacks.

"Happy?" Callum asked, coming over to me and rubbing my back. His gaze flitted across my purchases laid out on the bed.

"Yes." I leaned in and hugged him.

"Good." He kissed me. "How do you feel?"

"Tired, but good, excited." I smiled to myself and nodded.

"So," he said. "What do you want to do tomorrow?"

"This." I nodded at my goodies.

He frowned. "What do you mean?"

"I mean," I said with a cheeky grin. "I want to go shopping again."

He laughed. "Sweetie, if that's what you want."

"It is."

"Then that's what we'll do."

*****

Monday morning, I laid my purchases out on the bed again and sighed. I had no idea I'd bought so much, and knew I wasn't getting it home in my case, so it was just as well I'd bought a huge funky pink and blue snakeskin overnight bag to pack it all in. Sunday's goodies had consisted of more clothes, shoes, jewellery, knick-knacks, hats, belts and scarves, either brand new or retro. The shops I'd found were amazing, and with it being December, everyone was on sale.

I held up the bright blue knee-length leather boots I'd found for one hundred and fifty pounds and tried them on. Nice! I slipped on a silky blue and pink long-sleeved low-necked top and threw on the multi blue snakeskin jacket then paraded in front of Callum. "How do you like?"

He looked up from the book he'd bought in town, and his eyes widened in appreciation. "You do love blue and pink don't you?"

"Yep. They're my best colours I think." I modelled back and forth.

He grinned. "I agree."

I went back to the bed and started organising everything into bags. Tops and blouses, belts, hats, and boots. After trying several ways of packing, I finally managed to get everything into my new overnight bag. Nice!

That night, I sat on the sofa staring at my boxes. Callum was beside me still reading the book he'd bought. We didn't have a radio or TV in the room as we wanted to get away from it all, and I wasn't going online, so we were pretty much electricals-free.

"Would you like to go downstairs?"

"Mmm?"

"Would you like to go downstairs? Interact with the other guests. Watch TV. Have a change of scenery."

"Mmm. No." I turned my head from the wall to him. "Are you feeling left out? You can go downstairs."

His gorgeous smile brightened the room. "I'm okay. Just thought getting out of here would help instead of staring at those." He nodded toward the wall.

"I don't know, maybe. Isn't there something on Wednesday night? Some Christmas celebration or something?"

"Yeah, I think so. Let me check." He walked over to the small table beside the door, and after leafing through some brochures, he came and sat down, scanning one, finding what he was looking for. "Here." His finger pointed. "Mid-week Christmas celebrations. Feast on succulent roasts, delicious puddings, and munch on Christmas biscuits handmade here at the castle." He read something else. "There's a class on Wednesday to make your own biscuits. You make, bake and decorate them yourself."

"Well." I grinned. "You can show off your culinary

skills and show me what you can do. I wouldn't mind seeing you barefoot and tied to the kitchen."

He snorted. "Like that's something *I* plan on being. That's *your* job."

"Oh, no, no, no," I admonished. "There is *no way* I plan on being barefoot and pregnant tied to the kitchen. No way at all, mister."

"Aw," he whined with pouting lips. "But I want to see you barefoot and pregnant."

I gave him a sidelong glance. "You dirty dog. You just want to get me knocked up."

He grinned, and his face became serious. "One day. I want to see you pregnant with our child growing inside of you." A big manly hand spread over my stomach.

I covered his hand with mine. "It will happen one day," I said. "I've seen it."

He looked up in surprise. "What do you mean, *you've seen it?*"

I shifted and took a breath. "The first time I died, I was floating over the water watching you resuscitate me. I don't know how," I said quickly before he could cut in, "I just was. And this woman popped up around me. I couldn't see her, or feel her, or anything, but I heard her, and she told me that you and I are meant for each other in this lifetime. That we've had other lifetimes, but they didn't work out. But in this one, we are meant to be together and have two kids." I stopped and tried to picture the scene. "Well, at least one with one on the way. I didn't get to see past that."

He was deeply moved and intrigued. "So," he said,

licking his lips. "What do we have? Boy or girl?"

"A daughter. With one of whatever on the way, I think it's a boy."

"How do you know?"

I shrugged. "Just do."

We sat thinking about it for awhile, and every now and then Callum asked a question. I tried giving him answers, but I didn't always have one. We went to bed, and after making love, I lay awake, thinking about when I'd died. I rolled out of bed and over to the coffee table. Taking pen to paper, I wrote.

Dying is strange. Dying is painful. Unless you're on pills, or it's instantaneous, in which case, you may be lucky enough to not feel pain at all. But if you are in pain, it hurts. And it's strange. Do you know you're dying? Maybe. Can you do anything about it? Maybe not. In my case, I couldn't do anything about it. I was in the water, and I was stuck. What on? I don't know. I had felt around for the object holding me there and never found one. I don't know what, or even who, held me there while I drowned.

Drowning is strange. It's unlike anything I'd ever done before. It makes your lungs burn inside out. It makes you want to gasp for air. It makes you panic. You try not to, but you do. How could you not panic? You're trapped underwater by God knows what. You're thrashing around trying to get disentangled. You're desperately trying to keep your shit together, and not lose your head and keep your cool, that you don't realise you're drowning. You're dying. Dying by drowning. Death by water. Your life flashes before your eyes. You relive everything of importance up until your existence is about to be extinguished, and then there's peace. There's calm. You stop struggling. You stop moving. You just stop. You stop thinking. You stop feeling. You just stop. And you die. You die. You're dead. Death by drowning. Death by water. You're calm. You float. You let go. You die. But then, in my case, someone decided it wasn't my time. Not my time to die.

Not today. Not that day. Callum swam down and pulled me out of the water, hauling me to the surface and onto that dock. His strong hands pressing into my chest doing reps. His mouth trying to breathe life back into my dead, lifeless body. I was there, watching him. Not even realising at first I was dead. I was just watching him trying to resuscitate me. Yelling at me to breathe, to live, to come back. And then I realised I was watching it from above the river. That hit me like a tonne of bricks. The fact that I was floating and not falling. That I was watching Callum try to resuscitate me. Watching my body. I wasn't in my body.

That *freaked the absolute shit out of me, that did. I freaked. Even when that female voice spoke to me, I freaked. I saw no one. There was no one there. But I heard her. I...felt her. Then she said she had things to show me, and then bang, we were there. Wherever there was? Watching me and Callum and our daughter.* That *was freaky. I just, I just don't know how to feel about it. I don't know what to do about it. Maybe I'm not meant to do anything since I came back, and I'm here. And I was there, floating above the water one moment, and then bang I was back in my body the next. That was freaky too. And all of a sudden I went from peace and calm and pain-free, to Jack hammering away in my head and everything feeling all achy and sore. Ugh! I can't believe I managed to get up and walk. Walk up the stairs. Walk to the ambulance. Hell, I even managed to record a video on the way to the hospital.*

God, I felt sick. I don't remember if I've ever felt sicker in my life. And then the hospital. Lying on that table feeling sick to my stomach. My head pounding. My heart racing. All those people around me. I suppose they were doctors and nurses. I barely managed to keep myself together, and then something happened, and I was standing in the hallway watching them work on my body. What the hell was that? I don't even know how I managed to die a second time, let alone how I was still there watching it all. And what was that she showed me? Ugh! I don't know, but I did see the pain on Callum's gorgeous face. And while I believed I was going to be all right the first time, and we would spend the rest of our lives together, dying a second time was freaking me out even more. And what was that deal I made? Something about singing? God, I don't even know, and I certainly haven't tried it. Singing that is. Maybe I should see if there's a radio somewhere and try it. Wait, I have my iPod, maybe that will help. I don't know.

All I do know is that I never wanted to die alone. Lonely. Single. Childless. I regret that. Floating there above Callum, I regretted all of those things. I never wanted to die alone, and I sure as hell never wanted to die single. Although, I suppose, if there was no one, then no one had to suffer. Makes sense, but it doesn't make it better. I died with regrets, and now maybe I should fix those regrets. Live my life never having regrets ever again. Always try and do what makes me happy, and have no regrets for the rest of my life. I regret dying. But there's nothing I can do to fix or change that. I regret the fights with Callum, but at least we've sorted those out and are together now. I don't want to regret things. Not anymore.

I took a deep breath and rubbed my hand. Damn, writing made it sore. I pulled down five boxes from the wall, put everything away, and went back to bed.

*****

After our morning walk, I sat at the desk staring at the computer, my eyes occasionally flicking up to the wall to see what boxes were left. Six. There were six boxes left. I looked at the pile of papers I'd written. It was almost one inch thick. I didn't feel like typing them up as it would take me hours, if not days. I glanced up and reached for a soft square case about fifteen centimetres in diameter. I slowly pulled the zip and opened it. Inside were two discs labelled *the incident* and *the party.*

I reached for one and slid it into my laptop. I needed to see it. See the accident from everyone else's perspective. I needed to see what I hadn't seen at the time.

"Okay, how's my hair? Have I enough lipstick on? Should I wear sunglasses?"

"Stop fussing," Megan chastised.

I watched my pink shirted, red-wigged self fuss around and knew what was coming. "Oh, you poor idiot. You have no idea," I murmured.

"Is it too cloudy? Should we do it here or move? Is the picture good?"

"Will you stop! Everything is oops."

I turned to see Callum walking toward us. "Ladies. Do you have a permit to film?"

Strong fingers grasped my shoulders, and I jumped. He was standing behind me with a concerned expression.

"I have to," I said simply, and he nodded his understanding.

I gushed over him as he handed the permit back and walked on. "Oh, my God! Oh, my God! Oh, my God," I'd squealed, acting like a lovesick teenager.

I giggled. "See, I knew then we'd be together." I squeezed his hand.

"Yes, you did."

Megan got me into position, and I did my spiel, then acted up for the camera. I stopped, staring at something in the distance.

"I was staring at you," I told Callum. "You were walking back toward us."

I turned from Callum to Megan with a frown, then to my right. Megan was screaming, car brakes were squealing, and I saw the blue sedan run straight into me. Hitting me just above the knees. I heard the sickening crunch and felt it again as I remembered. I went flying into the air over the car. The car tore into the river and landed with an almighty splash. Water flew in all directions as I landed on the corner of the river wall, my face cracking into smithereens as it connected to the corner. I fell into the water.

I ran for the bathroom, throwing up breakfast.

"Tam." Callum ran in after me. "You okay?"

I hadn't thrown up like that since the hospital when I'd drunk my little zombies, and the doctors poured charcoal down my throat. I rinsed my mouth and the sink. "Okay," I gasped and then brushed, flossed and gargled before we went back to the video.

Callum had paused it. "Don't do this," he begged.

"I need to. I need to see what happened from the other side. Not just my point of view."

He kissed my head and gave me a quick squeeze. "Okay. Let's continue."

The camera stayed there for a few moments and then surged toward the river, watching the water for any sign of life. Callum's voice was off to the side. I broke the surface and sucked in air. My hair was slicked to my head, blood poured from the left side of my face. I heard women screaming. I gazed off to the river then up at the shaking camera. I pointed and tried to move toward where I was aiming for. Callum jumped into the water toward me, scooping me into his arms, he touched my head, and I pushed him away, swimming for the car.

The camera followed me around to the right of the car, Callum by my side. He started swimming back, but I yelled something and pulled my knife out from under the water, smashing the window and scraping it around the edges. Leaning in, I pulled out a screaming child and handed him to Callum who headed for the dock. I smashed the driver's window and leaned in. Callum yelled to me, I yelled back, the car groaned, filled with water, and with the woman screaming, it went down and disappeared from view.

I hit the pause button. Wiping my mouth, I walked over to the window. While I had lived it, seeing it gave me chills. A sickening feeling took hold of my stomach, and I breathed slowly trying to stop it.

"Tam, you don't have to do this. Just stop now."

Tears poured down my face, and Callum took me into his arms. I sobbed for awhile. Sobbed for the way it had been. Sobbed for what I knew was to come. Sobbed for the pain and anguish I'd gone through. Sobbed for the pain and anguish I still felt now. I don't know how long we stayed that way, but I knew I had to finish watching the video. I pulled away from Callum and wiped my face. "I need to see it," I stuttered. "I need to see it." I sat down and pressed play.

Callum swam out and dived again. Bubbles broke the surface in quick succession. He came up with the woman and was pulled into the dock by the rope around his waist. I didn't come up with him. I remembered that time and didn't want to remember it again. I clicked ahead and saw Callum pulling me up and being dragged toward the dock. Being hauled up and laid flat. Callum doing CPR.

I stopped it again and leaned in. "Mmm, where was

I? Nope, can't tell." I hit play.

The whole scene took five minutes. I'd been dead for longer than five minutes. Then I rolled over and vomited. Up the stairs toward the ambulance. Blood pouring from my head. Onto the bed and into the vehicle. I spoke to the camera on the way. I slurred a little, looking pale and sick. Recited the lotto numbers, pulled off my wig. I was rolled into the hospital and surrounded by medicos. Megan's voice came through; she was calling Bob. I was screamed at, and pulled at, and Bob and Linda arrived asking questions. And then the PC, and my death, and Callum. My death. My second death in half an hour. They electrocuted me for what seemed like an eternity. And then I was fine. My heartbeat was back. They were taking me somewhere, and the screen went black.

I heaved a deep sigh and moved into Callum's arms. He was quiet as he led me to the bed where we lay wrapped in each other. Crying, sniffing, talking. We were silent for the rest of the day, lost in our own thoughts, our mind's full of pain and torture and remembrance.

Especially mine since I lived it.

That night, I sat in bed thinking. That was pretty much all I'd been doing all day anyway, and I realised I needed to watch the video again if I was to get any of it dealt with. I pulled on my robe, went to the desk, and plugged my iPod headphones into the computer. I watched the footage again. And again. And again. Every time I heard something new. Every time I saw something else. Every time there was something I hadn't caught the time before. With Jack banging away, I shut off the laptop and sat on the couch trying to put it all together. I looked at my boxes on the wall and started with number three.

I was hit by a car. Yes, that's right, you heard me correctly. I was hit by a fucking car. I've never been hit by a car before, so I didn't know what to expect. Was it going to be painful? Of course it fucking was! If I'd thought it would be anything other than painful, then I'd be a fucking moron with no fucking brain in my head. So, what is it like? Like a freight train is hitting you. Your brain goes bonkers and overloads so you can't think. You can't move. You can't do anything. You just watch it come toward you and expect the worst. And the worst happens. You get hit by it. And it hurts. It really fucking hurts. I'm surprised my knees didn't break. That car smashed into me so hard I was waiting for them to. But they didn't. And I flew into the air. That was kinda cool in a weird sort of way.

And seeing that car flying beneath me was like watching some movie in slow-mo. My brain didn't think. It didn't have time to think. How could it? It was in shock. Its body, its owner, had just been hit by a fucking car. Of course, it wasn't thinking and then seeing. The concrete corner racing for the side of my face was distressful. If you think hearing legs crack is bad, try getting your face smashed in. It's really bad. I can't really explain it. But I'll give it a go. Your brain sees this thing coming at its body at a million miles an hour, but it doesn't think. It doesn't have time to. Sure, life is in slow motion, but it's only a perception, not reality. The reality is, you know. That thing coming for you, your face, is going to smash into you and do some serious damage. And it did. I heard that sickening thud reverberate around in my head. The pain that went searing through was just as bad.

So was the screaming from my own bloody brain. It hurt. It really fucking hurt. Not to mention banging my shoulder into the ground as well, before tumbling into the water. Being hit by that car was nothing. Nothing *all that important.* Nothing *all that serious.* Nothing *all that much to worry about. People survive being hit by cars. People survive being hit in the head, but it's bloody horrible when you are. And all the ramifications that come with a head injury. Swelling, bruising, fractures, bleeding bits and bobs swelling up in your head that you don't know about, and then bang, it explodes in there, and you have your head shaved and your skull drilled, and it sucks. It sucks big time, and you're left with the ugliness that is left behind. Having to deal with pain and sadness, depression, anger and hatred.*

Hitting your head on something is not a good thing, and it's going to take quite some time to deal with it. But deal with it you must. Otherwise, you don't get over it. You don't move on, and you have to do that. You have to move on. Otherwise, you have no life. You have nothing. Nothing *at all.* Nothing *to be seen.* Nothing *to be heard.* Nothing *to grab hold of and hang onto.* Nothing. Nothing. Nothing. You have to have something. *Something to hold close and cling to with your life because your life is worth it. It's worth dealing with so you can move on to all the good things coming your way. Sure, there will be some bad shit too, but once you deal with the anger and pain, it's all worth it. For what you get out of it, is better than what you had before. And before I had nothing. And now I have almost everything. Almost, but that will come in time. Just like my love for Callum.*

Chapter 21

After breakfast the next morning, I stood adjusting my hair in the mirror while Callum tried convincing me to take the biscuit class. "I'll only do it if you come exploring with me this morning," I said.

"Exploring what?" He leaned against the door frame in a green wool jumper.

"Hullo!" I spread my hands. "*The castle.* There's no point being here if we're not going to explore for all sorts of nooks and crannies." I walked over to the desk. "Besides, I can't let Nancy be the only one to have some fun."

"Nancy?" He frowned quizzically.

"*Drew!*" I replied, grabbing a small bag from the desk and placing my penlight, digital recorder, Swiss Army knife, and a few other things into it.

"You want to get all Nancy Drew on me and go looking for mysteries," he said with a grin, sitting on the arm of the couch.

I pretended to look hurt and slung my bag over my head. "Yes, I do. And we're starting in this room." I tapped on the wall, moving around the room while

Callum looked on. I tried the bed, grabbing the posters, twisting, turning, looking behind and underneath it. I scoured the fireplace, looking for loose bricks and innocent designs that might mean something. I checked every drawer and nook in the desk and moved into the walk-in closet and bathroom. "Nothing." I sighed and walked back into the room.

"Well, what did you expect?" Callum stood and opened the door.

"What I *expected*," I retorted, "was that being an old castle there would be secret doors and passageways everywhere." I scanned the walls of the hallway, tapping here, spying through my magnifying glass there.

"Okay, look," he said. "I get that there *may* be, being an old castle. But it still doesn't mean you'll be able to find them or check them out. They could be dangerous now," he added as we walked down the stairs to the lobby.

"If I didn't know you were a cop, I'd say you're a party pooper," I scolded and headed off to the front desk where the concierge was waiting. "Hello," I said. "I was wondering if there are any old trap doors, secret passageways, or some sort of spooky thing going on in this old castle." I glanced at his name tag. "Bradley."

He smiled a big toothy grin. "There sure is, ma'am. It's part of the charm." He handed me a brochure. "This is a little tour we put together of the secret hidey-holes we have here at the castle. They have been secured for guests to explore, and are very safe. You won't get lost, but you will have fun."

I matched his toothy grin. "Thank you, Bradley." I

glanced at Callum who was still smarting over my earlier comment. "I'm sure we'll enjoy ourselves." I wandered over to Callum reading the brochure. "Ooh, look. There's a hidden door in the library, a passageway between the library and the lounge, and a staircase that leads from a turret through the castle to the basement and down to one of the caves. "Oooh." I looked up in glee. "Must be about the pirates." I did a little happy dance.

Callum softened, how could he not at the sight of me being happy. "Okay," he groaned. "Let's go exploring."

We walked into the lounge, and under the eye of two guests, we started tapping, knocking, and exploring toward where the passageway was situated. I pressed my fingers against the wood panelling and heard a tiny click. A huge panel creaked open, and with excited grins at each other, I pulled my penlight out of my bag. Stepping into the passageway, we noticed wall sconces, but they didn't really light up much, so I was glad for my torch.

We walked a few steps and heard the panel click shut behind us. I jumped a little, and giggled when I saw Callum's 'I told you so' expression. Walking along, we saw small pictures, handmade drawings etched into the dirt, and plaques on the wall giving tidbits of information on the Pirates of Penzance. Making our way along until we came to the end, I moved the flashlight over the wall and saw an outline of a door. With some prodding, it popped it open.

"Oh," a woman stuttered.

"Hi, there," I said with a smile.

The woman laughed and put her hand on her chest. "Goodness. I thought you were a ghost. So you found the hidden door and passageway then?" she asked eagerly.

"We did," I said, brushing down my clothes. "It's got all sorts of interesting info on the walls. You should have a look."

"Actually," she said, standing up. "I might just do that." She walked into the passageway, and the door closed behind her.

I looked around the library. Wall-to-wall and floor-to-ceiling bookcases full of books, a huge window framed by rich blue curtains overlooked the moors, thick carpet, comfy sofas and Christmas decorations finished it off. I glanced at the sofa, saw the book she was reading, and picked it up. "*The Ghosts, Goblins and Pirates of Penzance.* No wonder she jumped," I said with a grin.

Callum looked at his watch. "We have time before lunch. Do you want to do the tower now or leave it?"

"Mmm? Now. I want to see the view."

Walking hand in hand down winding zigzagging hallways, we came across a door and knew it was the one leading to the tower because there was a small sign that said *the tower staircase that leads to the basement*.

I giggled, and Callum opened the door. A chill hit me, and I shivered. "Oooh, that's cold." Rubbing my arms, I stepped inside the tower.

"Don't worry, sweetie, I'll keep you warm. Up you

go." He gave me a nudge.

"Oh, nice," I said and crossed my arms. "Too scared to go first?"

"Nooo," he said with a sheepish grin. "By going first, if you fall I can catch you. I can't catch you if you're behind me."

I harrumphed and stomped up the stairs. Two flights of circular stone steps later, I emerged into the turret of the back tower. "Wow!" I stepped over to one of the window gaps and gazed out at the view. "Wow!" We walked around in a circle taking photos and gaping at the view. "Wow!" I said for the third time. "This is…"

"Amazing," Callum finished.

We spent some time there before walking back down and finding ourselves on the ground floor again. I noticed the stairs kept going. So did we. Down, down, down. Small lights lit the walls, and I used my penlight to find my way. Big sook Callum was still behind me. So much for catching me if I fell. I was in front.

The basement was a stone floor room mainly used for storage by the look of it, and there was a small plaque on the wall leading down the stairs past the basement.

'This is the way to Mount's Bay, where the pirates came to smuggle their gain.'

"Oh, dear," I muttered, and we kept on going.

I don't know how far down we were, but eventually, we came to an iron gate. Behind the gate in a small room were mannequins dressed as pirates, standing and sitting around a table counting all their gold and jewels which was spread all over the place.

"Interesting," was all Callum could say as we looked at each other and burst out laughing at the corny scene before us.

There were signs pointing out the pirates, and what they stole and who they stole it from. And very faintly in the distance, we could hear waves crash on the rocks.

I shivered, and Callum wrapped his arms around me. "Let's go," I urged, heading for the ground floor where we smelt delicious aromas wafting through the hotel. My stomach growled, and we walked to the dining room. Other guests were already there digging into the amazing looking food.

We found a quiet spot down at the end away from them, and after receiving drinks, Callum inconspicuously slipped me two pills without anyone seeing.

Lunch was slow cooked roast chicken with roast potatoes, carrots, peas, beans, and corn with a thick creamy gravy drizzled on top. Callum slipped me two more pills and dessert of Christmas pudding followed.

After my painkiller, I pushed back in my chair. "God, I'm stuffed," I groaned.

"Ah, don't worry about it." He took a sip of wine. "You need to put some weight back on. You lost a lot over the last few weeks. Besides, that's the most I've seen you eat."

"I feel sick," I moaned and buried my face in my hands and leaned my elbows on the table. "I want to go rest."

"We have that biscuit class later."

"What time?" I mumbled.

"Four till five."

"What's the time now?"

"Two."

"Well, then." I put my hands down and slid my chair back. "We've got time for a rest."

Callum drank the last of his wine, and we headed upstairs. But come four, we were standing in a room off the kitchen. It looked like a preparation area with benches and cookware, and we were joined by five other couples and eight singles. All of us were wearing Christmas aprons and dividing up ingredients.

Pouring our dry ingredients into the one bowl, I added the wet, and Callum got mixing. After rolling out the dough, we used the cookie cutters I'd chosen to cut out trees, reindeer, candy canes, and baubles. I handed the cutters onto the next person as there weren't enough to go around. We placed the shapes on a tray, the staff popped them into the oven, and we used the time to sip drinks and nibble on munchies.

A half hour later, they were hot out of the oven, and we whipped up coloured icing while they cooled. Green went on the trees, red and white on the candy canes, chocolate for the reindeer, and a bit of everything for the baubles. A few spots and squiggles went on to decorate, a red nose for Rudolph, and they were put in the fridge to set. I had managed to write our names on the balls, so we knew which ones were ours.

After an hour out for dinner, the staff brought out our cookies in little decorated boxes so we could eat some now and take the rest to our rooms.

"Oh, look at that," I gushed over the red and green box with tissue paper and a red, green, and gold gingham ribbon bow. "That's so nice."

Callum grabbed a tree and shoved it into his mouth.

"You could wait for me," I grumbled.

He gave me a food filled grin, and after a couple of biscuits, we took the rest up to bed.

*****

The next day, I sat staring at the last four boxes on the wall. Since two of them were for Callum, I stuck them together. Now that made three.

"How come you made me into one?" he asked from his spot on the couch.

"Because you are one," I said.

"So, how come you don't know how you feel about me?"

My brow furrowed in slight confusion, and I turned around. "I *do* know how I feel about you, but everything needs to be dealt with separately, and at the moment you're all tied up in it. I need to separate you."

His expression was unreadable, and I worried slightly. Although, what did I have to worry about? Our love was on track and sex was fantastic.

"It's Thursday," he said, finally looking from the paper to me. "We head home Sunday, so any idea what you want to do for the next couple of days?" He looked back at the paper. "Or if you'll deal with *that* before you go?"

I followed his gaze. "There's really only two things left, and they should come soon. I thought we could spend tomorrow and Saturday in town again. Finish off any streets we didn't get to last weekend, maybe just drive around the peninsula and have a look at everything."

His lips finally turned into a huge grin. "We could do that."

That night, I sat in front of my laptop watching the video. Callum was snoring lightly in bed, the fire burned softly in the grate, and I sat staring at me flying into the air. Falling into the wall and water. Pulling that child out of the car. Going down trying to get that woman out. Why did she want to die? Why did she tell me to let her die?

I knelt down at the coffee table and began to write.

"No, no, no. Let me go. I want to die. Where's my baby? I want to die. Let me die."

Why did she say that? Why did she scratch and push me, trying to get me out of the car? Out of her way so she could die. Why did she want to die? I didn't get it. I still don't get it. I know some people think suicide is their only option, but to take your child with you. I didn't have to save her. After all, my head was smashed in. I couldn't see out of my left eye, and Callum was yelling at me to get out of the water. But I couldn't leave that child in the car.

I couldn't leave it there to die a slow horrible death by drowning, because that's what it would have been. Death by drowning. And I know how bad that is. But I couldn't let a child die like she wanted to. I just couldn't, and her, that woman, her eyes all wild and angry, her nails scratching and pushing. What was with her? *I don't know who she was or how bad a situation she was in, but it couldn't have been that bad that she had to try and kill her child too. Getting the kid out was the easy part. Getting her out was hard.*

Her seatbelt was stuck. I had to saw through it, and between her scratching me, me freaking out, and the car sinking, it was a precarious few moments. I certainly didn't expect to go down with it, let alone drown because of it. I can't believe I was still sawing through that belt when we went down. Trying to hold my breath, saw through that belt, and get her out is overwhelming to think about. Now. *But I didn't think at the time. Going under was scary, but I knew Callum was on his way, and when I was pulling the woman out, I felt him beside me. I knew it was okay. Until I couldn't move. But I've done that already.*

I don't know why she wanted to die. I don't know why she wanted to kill her kid. I don't even know why I was the one to save them, but I was, and it's because I was meant to, and that's okay. I saved a woman and her child, and regardless of her trying to sue me for saving her, which I think is bloody stupid, it's okay. Okay that it was me. Okay that it was here. Okay, that I did it. I'm alive, that child's alive, and even if she doesn't appreciate it, she's alive. And that's okay.

I pulled down two more papers and went to bed.

*****

After spending all day Friday in town, then coming home after an amazing meal at the local pub, we were fat, we were full, and we were loaded down with shopping. And it wasn't just me this time. Callum had found some woolly jumpers and an old battered brown leather bomber jacket from a vintage store. It looked good on him and was still in good condition, but we had it dry cleaned before coming home. He also had new jeans and a pair of black biker boots.

I hung a few things up in the wardrobe, knowing there was a party on Saturday night at the hotel, so I needed to leave an outfit out for that. The rest I packed away.

Lying in front of the fire in each other's arms, snuggled under a blanket after making love, I thought about the last week and a half. I'd changed a lot and was feeling better. Sleep was coming now, Jack only bothered me during the day, and I was finally letting everything go.

There was only one paper left on the wall, and I stared at it, letting the feelings come. I slipped out from under the blanket and pulled the paper off the wall. Sitting back next to Callum, I stared at him, lightly snoring, off in la-la land fast asleep. *What are you dreaming of? What fills your dreams at night?* I nudged him awake.

"Whuh? Oh, what Tam. What's wrong?" He struggled up.

"Nothing. Just, lean back against the couch and listen." He sat back and pulled the blanket up. "And don't interrupt. What I have to say is important. So concentrate."

He sleepily smiled. "I'm all ears and listening."

I held the paper up in front of me. "When I first saw you walk through the pub door back in November, the world stood still. It stopped, and all I heard was the song on the jukebox which was Elvis Presley's *Can't Help Falling in Love*." I smiled. "And that was what I did. I fell in love. My heart raced. I drowned in your eyes. You strode into that bar like you owned it, like you owned the world. I even labelled you the Son of God 'cause you're so bloody gorgeous."

"Tam," he said, all embarrassed.

"You are," I insisted, shaking my head. "I don't even know how I managed to walk over to you and introduce myself, and I know I came across all stalkerish and weird, but as you know," I grinned, "I'm not stalkerish."

He laughed. "But what? You're weird? Is *that* what you're saying?"

"Well, hey," I said. "Look at the way I've been. That day after meeting you, I never thought, never had any clue or inkling of an idea of what would happen next. Seeing you down by the river just concreted the idea in my mind that we were meant for each other. I felt it. Deep, deep inside I felt it. That you were for me." I closed my eyes and took a deep breath. "And then the incident where you came charging into my world, pulling me out of the river, resuscitating me, coming to the hospital. That was more than most people would have done. I…you came to the hospital and sat by my bed." I gazed into his soft, tender eyes. "*That* was beyond the call of duty. *That* was beyond *anything* and *everything. That* was outstanding. And you didn't *have* to do it," I whispered. "But you did, and I thank you for it." My eyes teared up, and he pulled me into his arms.

His eyes were teary too, and we laughed as he wiped mine away. "I'd do anything for you," he whispered, kissing me gently.

"*Now,* you would, but not back then." I sighed. "You saw my head, and I didn't want you to. I didn't even want to see it myself, and was repulsed and disgusted by it. I didn't want to see the look in your eyes when you saw me. But I did." I stroked his cheek. "I saw it." He opened his mouth to speak. "Shh." My finger against his lips stopped him. "I saw the look in your eyes, and I don't blame you. The whole bar thing. That was just *bad.* And as for the station, I was trying to prove a point which ended badly I guess." I stared into the fire for a moment before turning back to him. "Oh, God and that argument we had was horrendous. But all that time, from the moment I met you, I loved you. With every breath in my body. Every beat of my heart. Through all the pain and the tears and the pills, I loved you. And when you finally told me you love me too, I couldn't breathe. You told me you loved me and it made everything better." I kissed him and smiled. "*You* made everything better, and being with you, has made *everything* better. I love you, Callum Stone, and I want to spend the rest of my life with you."

Tears fell down his cheeks. "I love you, Tamara Cainer, and I want to spend the rest of my life with you."

We kissed, and the love flowed.

*****

Strolling hand in hand through town on Saturday, we finished up all the last minute things before leaving. After taking a drive around the headland, and going on a pirate tour, we arrived back at the castle late afternoon, and having a refreshing nap and shower, we dressed for that night's celebration.

I buttoned up a long-sleeved cherry red silk blouse and tucked it into forest green pants. I added mixed pieces of jewellery to blend the two colours together, while black leather ankle boots and belt finished off the ensemble.

Callum wore simple black pants and shoes, and a long-sleeved dark green shirt.

I touched up my make-up and fixed my wig, and then we went downstairs and joined everyone in the lounge. The massive Christmas tree sat front and centre, full of tinsel, baubles, and fairy lights. We mingled a little, as we hadn't gotten to know the other guests yet, and toasted the festive season with our wide array of drinks.

"Ah, there you are, young man. I do believe you're a police officer." A middle-aged man had come over to us.

"Ah, yes, sir. I am," Callum replied, giving me a quick glance.

"Well, then, maybe you can tell me why there's so much crime then. I'm a criminology professor, and crime is on the rise."

I studied him as Callum prepared his answer. He

was tall and stout with a receding hairline, a bushy moustache, and wore a three-piece suit. Kinda reminded me of someone. Colonel Mustard maybe? Callum was politely telling him his opinion, but I tuned out, and turning around, found myself face to face with the woman we'd come across in the library after coming out of the secret passageway.

"Hello, there. I've been eyeing off your necklace. It looks quite piratey, and I was wondering if you minded telling me where you got it." She thrust out her hand. "Oh, I'm Jo by the way."

I shook her hand. "I'm Tamara. And I got the necklace in that little jewellery shop in town, the one where you can buy it or make it yourself." I fingered the pendant, and the light hit the blood-red stone, sending out brilliant little rays. The stone was surrounded by smaller emerald ones, and it was set in a huge antique gold octagon. There were little carvings on each divided section, and it did look like a piece of old pirate treasure; something ancient and expensive.

"It's gorgeous," Jo breathed, dazzled by the little lights. "Was it the only one there?"

"In this style," I said. "But there were others in different sizes, shapes and details. I bought a few of them. Thread them on chains or beads, and there you have it."

"So you put it on that chain yourself then?"

I ran my fingers over the chain, which was antique gold to match the pendant, with red and green crystals mixing in every few centimetres. It was part chain, part bead, and it matched the pendant perfectly. "I did. Chose the beads as well. I did it for all of them. So, you'll be able to match it to whatever one you decide on."

"It's stunning," Jo said, playing with her own bead necklaces. "And I'm heading down there tomorrow."

The dinner bell rang, and we walked into the dining room. Callum made sure he sat on my left, and because he had given me my pills to put in my pocket, I was able to slip them out and swallow them without anyone noticing.

The hotel served roast chicken or turkey, with vegetables of our choice, and a matching gravy. Dessert was pudding or fruit with Christmas biscuits on the side.

After dinner we were back in the lounge, warming ourselves by the fire, listening to stories about ghosts, pirates and lost gold. Some of the guests sang carols, but I found myself hypnotised by the star at the top of the tree. I don't know how long I'd been staring, but I came back to hear Callum calling my name.

"Tam…Tam…Tamara!"

"Mmm?" I looked around, my right eye coming into focus.

"It's eleven," he said, standing between me and the tree. "You look out of it. Are you ready to head up to bed?"

"Mmm," I murmured sleepily.

We bade everyone goodnight and goodbye, since we'd be leaving the next morning, and went upstairs. Later, lying in bed, I wondered why I'd been so fascinated by the star on top of the tree. As far as I knew, it held no significance, and I didn't understand its mesmerising effect. Guess I'm just worn out. I curled into Callum's arms and fell asleep.

Gurgle, gurgle, gurgle.

The big white star shone its brightest.

Gurgle, gurgle, gurgle.

All of its spikes bright and white.

Gurgle, gurgle, gurgle.

The water was cold, making me shiver.

Gurgle, gurgle, gurgle.

I felt my lungs burn. I couldn't breathe. The water pulled me down. I couldn't breathe. The big bright white star shone in the sky.

I couldn't breathe…

I couldn't breathe…

I couldn't breathe…

I bolted upright, clawing at my throat. "Can't breathe," I gasped, gulping lungfuls of air.

"Tam?" Callum rolled over to turn the light on, then sat up and grabbed me. "Tam, what is it? Is it another bad dream? It's okay. I thought you'd stopped having them. You haven't had one for ages. It's okay. It's just a bad dream."

"It's nothing to do with this. It wasn't me drowning." I gasped and saw shock in his eyes. "It has nothing to do with what has happened. It's something new." I stared at him. "I think it's something that's *going* to happen."

Chapter 22

I stared out the window on the way home, trying to piece together what I'd seen. I didn't know what it was, or what it had to do with me. *If* at all. It worried me. Several times Callum questioned me about it, but I didn't want to talk, not even when he talked about something else. After stopping for lunch, we made it back to Bob and Linda's around three in the afternoon. They met us at the door.

"Jewels Jewels Jewels," Bob greeted me with a big bear hug then shook Callum's hand. "Glad to see her back in one piece."

"Not quite," Callum replied, watching me and Linda walk for the door.

"What do you mean?" Bob grabbed my bags. "Isn't she better?"

"I don't know," Callum said, following us in.

"Do you have any black cardboard and a white texta or crayon?" I asked when we were in the lounge.

"Uh?" Bob thought for a moment.

"I do," Linda said, going to get them.

I gazed around the room. It had been decorated

while we were gone, and was quite festive with its tinsel, baubles and lights. Linda came back with a pad of coloured cardboard and a box of crayons. I took them, and searched for a black piece of card, pulling it out of the pad. Kneeling in front of the coffee table, I pulled out the white crayon. I visualised what I'd seen, and began to make long strokes. Large ones on the top, bottom, left and right, smaller ones in between. By the time I'd finished, it looked like a round white spiky circle. "Does anyone know what this is?" I showed them.

"The sun," Bob offered.

"Sundial," Callum said.

"A clock," Linda chimed.

I looked at it. "Yes, a clock. I think it's a clock." Seeing the confused looks on their faces, I explained about last night's dream. How it was new. How I'd never dreamed it before, and that I didn't know what it meant.

"Other than that, how was the rest of your holiday?" Linda asked.

Taking it in turns, Callum and I told them. I pulled out the camera to show them pictures and gave them their gifts from Penzance.

"Have you dealt with things?" Linda asked sometime later.

"For the most part," I said. "And I feel good." They both smiled. "Still got the pain in my head, but we figured out a way of helping that." I gazed at Callum, and he blushed.

"Oh," Linda chortled. "So you two have cemented

your relationship then?"

I blushed, and she had her answer. "Can Callum stay?" I blurted out and watched their faces. "I mean here. For the rest of the time, I'm here."

"I don't need to," Callum piped up. "We can move into my place while I pack and sort my stuff out."

"Sort your stuff out?" Bob asked.

"Yes." Callum looked at me. "I'm moving to Australia to be with Tam. So I need to go through my stuff. Pack what I want, get rid of what I don't, and give up the lease."

"Oh, that's wonderful," Linda gushed, watching Callum run his fingers through my hair, and me smile back. "You're moving for love. Of course you can stay here. It's better for Jewels, uh, Tamara, to stay here. It's more private. And feel free to get your things tomorrow and start dealing with your flat."

"Thanks, both of you," I said, giving them both hugs, and after dinner, I asked for my papers, which Bob had placed in his safe while I was gone. Opening my passport, I pulled out the lottery ticket. "Do you have the numbers from that huge jackpot a couple of weeks ago? I think it went off the weekend we left?" We were sitting in the lounge room in front of the fire.

"I do," Linda said, hopping up to get them and coming back with a paper. "I kept it so you could see them for yourself."

The paper was opened and folded on the page with the results. I marked off each number then Callum and I looked at each other. Shock rolled over his face. "Well, Bobby boy," I said, waving my ticket. "Looks like we have another piece of publicity to use."

Bob took the ticket and the colour drained from his face. "Bloody hell Jewels you've won the jackpot first prize bloody hell!"

*****

Monday was quite a busy day. Callum went to give up his lease and start packing his things. He also set about retiring from the police force. Bob did a press release, letting everyone know that the wounded heroine, Jewels Diva, had won last fortnight's jackpot in lotto. Linda busied herself around the house, and I decided to work in the lounge room. I brought all of my things down and laid them on the coffee table. My laptop was going, and I was writing and uploading the pictures from my camera, and videos from my camcorder. I answered emails and made a call. A call that was a long time in coming.

"Hello."

"Hello, Chris. It's Jewels Diva."

"Jewels. Bloody hell! Hello. How are you?"

"I'm good. A lot better than I was the last time we saw each other. Listen, about your offer in the pub that day. I never got back to you, and I wanted to apologise for that."

"No, don't be silly. You have nothing to apologise for. I was there that day. I saw what happened. Do *not* apologise."

"That's nice of you to say."

"Don't be silly. Listen. I know we didn't get to do

anything, but what about an upcoming episode. We're filming one this week. You could do that."

I thought for a moment. "I don't know. My head's still ugly, and my face is yellow. I've spent most of the last two weeks hiding in a castle down in Penzance trying to recuperate."

"You've been on holiday? That's right. I saw your blog post. No wonder we haven't seen or heard from you. How was it? Feeling better?"

"You…read…my blog?" My left brow cocked, unsure of what I had just heard.

"Absolutely! We've been following you since we met. Blogs, vlogs, tweets. We've become addicted, especially in the days following the accident."

"Yeah…those days were…interesting."

"They certainly were. Listen, how about we get together and talk about it. Doing the show I mean. What about today?"

"Um." I looked around for Linda, but couldn't see her. "I guess. Don't expect much though."

"Okay, great. How about I meet you in town?"

"How about you come here? It will be more private."

"Okay, what's the address?"

Half an hour later he buzzed the gate and I let him in, opening the door and waiting while he got his bag out of the car. "Hi."

"Hello, darlin'." He hugged me. "How are you?"

"Uh." I was a bit freaked out by getting a hug. "Okay. Come in." I led him to the lounge and offered him a seat.

Linda popped her head in and asked if he wanted a

coffee. While she was getting it, we talked.

"So, this is Jewels Diva's blue laptop." He spied it on the table. "Where all the blogs and vlogs start from before they go out to the world." He peered at the screen.

"Oi. Don't be nosy." I closed the lid, and he grinned.

"Your face looks good," he said, staring at it.

I touched my cheek. "The swelling's gone down, but it's still ugly and yellow. And my eye is still blurry."

"But it's better right? And your head? The scar, how is it?"

"Ugly." I'd had enough brain to wear a bandana on my head so he couldn't see it.

"I see you're a natural brunette." He grabbed a few strands of hair poking out from under my headwear.

"Don't." I pulled away and straightened the bright blue material.

"Sorry. I didn't mean—"

"I know." My smile reassured him. "And yes, I'm a natural brunette. Well, the *real* me is anyway. Jewels is a redhead."

"The real you?" He seemed intrigued.

I saw his face and giggled softly. "Jewels is the redhead. Woman of mystery. Mystery author. Social and media commentator, columnist and blogger and… character. Pseudonym, nom de plume, pen name, alter ego. The real me is a brunette. Not at all outrageous, and quite ordinary and plain with business prospects ahead."

"Jewels is *also* a millionaire."

"Mmm, I told Bob to release that. It's all publicity, and all publicity helps doesn't it?"

"Yes, it does. Have you gotten it yet?"

"I have. We very sneakily managed to talk to the head of the lottery commission, and it was put into my bank account by electronic transfer. They kept all the details secret except for who won it."

"Must be nice then? Knowing you've got money now."

"With the amount of money I've spent, I need it. But back to Jewels."

"So what's your real name?"

"Ah, alas I cannot tell you—"

"Why? Would you have to kill me?"

I laughed. "I cannot tell you my real name because you are currently dealing with Jewels. But if you ever meet the real me, I'll be wearing long golden-brown hair. So come on over and introduce yourself, and you'll find out my real name. But, back to business. About that."

"Look." He accepted his coffee from Linda. "We wrote a skit a few weeks ago, and kept it on the back burner just in case." He took a sip and put his mug down to pull a binder from his bag. "Here, read it."

I read the skit. It was similar to what had happened in the bar that day when I'd backchatted Christopher Fox. And it was funny. "This is great."

"Will you do it?"

I sighed. "You do see how I look? My temper and moods have been all over the place. I can snap your head off one moment, and be nice as pie the next. And I have Jack Hammer going in my head." I rubbed it. "I just don't know how good I'll be."

He squeezed my hand. "You'll be great. We'll do

anything you want. Get you anything you need. Whatever. Just say you'll do it."

"You haven't heard my list of demands yet." I laughed.

"Tell me," he said ever so eagerly.

"I'd want someone there with me. Linda."

"Done."

"I still take pills, so I'd need food if it's around lunch or dinner time."

"Done."

"No audience."

"We've thought of that, and for your sketch, there will be no audience. But the boys would like to be there. They want to see you again."

I sucked on my lips. "No unauthorised photos or videos."

"Okay."

"What about if I flip out and throw a tantrum? I'm not myself you know."

"We will accept you with all your faults, and won't hold it against you."

"Mmm, you just want ratings," I scolded playfully.

He grinned in return.

"Linda," I yelled.

"Yes." She popped her head in.

"What are you doing on?" I turned to Chris. "What day?"

"This Wednesday."

"This Wednesday?" I repeated.

"Nothing. Why?"

"How would you feel about being on a TV set as

my assistant?"

"Love to."

I looked at Chris. "Give me the details, and we'll be there."

"Great. That's great." He wrote them down.

I looked at the coffee table and spied my black cardboard poking out of a pile of papers I was going through and pulled it out. "You don't happen to know what this might be, do you?"

He frowned. "Am I supposed to?"

"Huh. I don't know," I said, shaking my head. "All I know is that I had a bad dream about it, and it wasn't good." I stared at the white spiky circle. "Something bad is going to happen, and it has to do with whatever this is. I know it's bad. I just know. And I don't know what it is or what's going to happen. But it will." I looked at him. He was staring at the picture. "Sure you don't know?"

His blue eyes met my gaze, and he shook his head. "Nope. Nothing."

I sighed. "I just hope whatever it is, it makes itself clear before it's too late."

*****

Callum came home just before dinner, dragging two huge suitcases, and two bags with him.

I cocked a brow. "You have *that* many clothes. Didn't think you were the clothes horse type." I reached up and kissed him.

"Well." He slipped off his coat. "I'm not. It's just

that I kinda keep clothes for years until they're well-worn and I don't throw anything out. And now I've bought a few things in Penzance, I figured I may as well bring it all over and go through it here." He grinned. "You might be able to help me figure out what to keep and what to throw."

I slid my arms around his waist and kissed him. "I will, after dinner."

We stood in my bedroom an hour later, talking about Chris's visit and Callum's retirement plans in between sorting through his clothes.

"Oh, this has to go." I threw a hole-filled t-shirt on the floor like it was a dead rat.

"Hey." He picked it up. "I love this t-shirt."

"Sweetie, you may love it, and I get it, you love comfy clothes. But not with holes."

He looked forlorn. "But I *love* this t-shirt."

"Callum," I chastised lightly. "You're forty, and there's no need for holey clothes unless they're jeans and fashionable." I picked up a ratty old jumper then handed it to him. "Put them in the *to go* pile. You've got nice clothes now, so you need to come up in the world and wear good stuff."

"Mmm," he grumbled, folding the t-shirt and jumper.

By the time we finished, his good clothes were hanging or folded in the closet, and his gross stuff was bagged to go to the tip.

"So," I said as we snuggled on the couch. "You've got some good going out clothes, but you might need some more casual stuff. You only wore three jumpers on holiday."

"So, they're only jumpers." He ruffled my hair.

"Yes, but sweetie, I'm a fashionable up-and-coming businesswoman." He looked quizzically at me. "I plan on setting up a few businesses when we figure out where we're going to live. Anyhoo, I'm a clothes horse and am too good for hole-filled dirty clothes. Nice neat fashion is a good thing. You need to look good. There's nothing wrong with it."

"Aw," he said, making a face. "I'm just not that into clothes shopping. When I know what I want and where to get it, I go and buy it. I don't like wandering around shopping centres or streets looking for clothes."

"You didn't mind in Penzance."

"That was different. We were on holiday."

"So you only buy clothes when you're on holiday?"

"Yeah." He grinned. "Pretty much."

"Oh, God," I grumbled, getting off the couch. "What have I gotten myself into?" I sat in front of the laptop and went to my blog.

My Adventures in Merry Old England: December 13th, 2011

Hey peeps, just a quick note to let you all know I'm going to be on Chris Simmons' comedy show in the next couple of weeks. I'm filming a segment this Wednesday, so I'll let you know when it will be on.

Also, yes, it is true. I did win lotto and no you can't have any.

By the way, I am back from my holiday and feeling better, so thanks to all those who sent their good wishes, and can someone tell me what my picture represents. I have no idea what it is but need to find out. If any of you have any idea, let me know.

Jewels xxoo

I uploaded the scan of my white spiky thing into the post, and once it was all sorted hit publish. *Now, maybe I'll get an answer about that bloody thing.*

*****

"Today is the day," I breathed, staring at my reflection in the bathroom mirror. I placed my special make-up into a cosmetic purse, then put that into a bag with my red wig. After tying a bandana around my head, and with a final survey, I walked into the bedroom. I gathered my bags and walked downstairs.

"Ready?" Callum was coming with us as he didn't want me to be alone. Although Linda would be there, he wanted to make sure I was safe and okay at all times.

"Ready." We piled into his jeep and drove to the studio.

My face was covered with a scarf and big sunnies, and my hand flew up to cover it when we got to the guard house. Callum handed over the passes Chris had sent us, and we drove to Studio 2. Getting out and grabbing my bags, we walked through the door. I took my glasses off and looked around, finding Chris talking to someone.

He spotted us and walked over, hugging me when he got to us. "Hey, there darlin'. Glad you could make it. Linda, Sergeant." He gave him a strange look. "Come this way." He led us through the studio and backstage to a dressing room. "Right, now you've read your script, and you're fine with showing your head again?"

I grinned softly. "Well, if I can do it in front of every single celebrity in a club, then I can do it here."

"Great. I see you've brought your clothes. Why don't you get changed and do your hair, then we'll rehearse a few times and film it. You okay with that?"

I took a deep breath. "I'm fine."

"Great, I'll see you in a bit."

Linda helped me into my leather outfit and started teasing and fluffing my hair, clipping in the extensions. Every fifteen minutes Chris popped his head in to see if I was okay, and after an hour, he led me to the studio. It was empty except for his colleague.

"Jewels, this is Larry. Larry, Jewels."

"Hi." We shook hands.

"Hey, there, glad you could do this." He stared at my head.

"My pleasure." I tried not to feel like a prize pig on show.

We read through the scene several times, and Chris showed me my marker. I was a bar owning, pool playing, biker chick with a sharp tongue. I had my lines down with tone and sarcasm, but getting my mouth around them was a little harder than I thought.

Thankfully, they stuck my script to the bar out of sight of the camera. We walked through the scene three times, and Chris decided I was ready.

"Oh, God, are you sure?" I was sweating a little.

"You'll do fine, darlin'." He walked off to get the crew, and I saw the other *Bill* boys walk in and sit in the empty audience with Callum and Linda. Chris and Larry took their places.

"And we're rolling in five, four, three, two, one..."

Chris and Larry filmed their first scene standing and arguing outside the 'pub'. They barged through the door, and drunkenly staggered to the bar where I was leaning, reading a magazine.

"Tell me, darlin', will you marry me," Larry's character slurred.

Chris's character jumped in. "I'm so sorry about my friend. His girlfriend left him, and he's already been to five other pubs."

"Pubs? Is this a pub? It's empty," Larry said, glancing around.

"That's because everyone knew you were coming," I quipped.

"So why are *you* still here then?" Larry asked.

"I own the place." I reached for a glass.

"Great! So if I marry you then, I'll have free beer forever." Larry grinned.

"Sweetheart," I chastised. "If you married me you'd go the same way as every other husband I've had."

"Where's that?" Chris asked.

"Straight to AA with a pool cue up your arse."

"How come they had a pool cue up their arse?"

"'Cause I was trying to shoot some balls!"

The crew and very tiny audience laughed their heads off.

"What do you mean," slurred Larry. "Didn't your husbands have balls?"

"Not that I saw." I glanced toward the pool table and remembered the day at the bar with Christopher Fox. "The pool balls are harder than any of my husbands'."

"I've got balls," Larry said, falling onto the bar.

"Oh, sweetie," I purred. "No, you don't. Otherwise, your girlfriend wouldn't have left you."

"She didn't leave me because I have no balls."

"Then why did she?"

"She said I wasn't man enough."

"Same thing," I said, reaching down and pretending to remove two pool balls from my pants. "Here you go. Have these. You need them more than me, and at least you know they're real."

The scene ended with Chris and Larry disdainfully staring at the balls.

"And...cut!"

The small crowd clapped and cheered, and under the ugly yellow bruising I felt myself blush. I reached up and touched my cheek.

"Okay, let's just adjust the lighting and do a couple of more takes."

We took our places and started again. A half hour later we were finished.

"Thanks so much for that, darlin'." Chris led me back to my dressing room.

"You're welcome. It was fun."

"Hey, listen. If you want to stick around and watch a couple of other skits feel welcome."

"We might do that after…Argh!" I clutched my head and doubled over and then just as quickly straightened up.

"You okay?" He grabbed me.

"Jewels," Callum yelled.

"I'm okay. It's just time for painkillers. Jack's really banging away."

"Jack?" Chris frowned as Linda grabbed my pills and a sandwich.

"The jackhammer going in my head that's pounding away. He's been there since I smashed my head."

"Jack." Chris laughed. "That's right, you told me. Listen, you have something to eat and a rest, then come out when you're ready."

"Thanks." I smiled my gratitude.

He disappeared to keep working, and I swallowed my pills with food.

"You okay?" Callum asked, sliding his arms around me.

"Yeah. Just need awhile to rest. But if you guys want to go and watch, then don't let me stop you."

"No, we—" Callum started.

"Go," I said. "I need some quiet time. Go." I ushered them out the door, turned the lights down, got my iPod and stuck my headphones in. Sometimes the best way to beat Jack was to drown him out. I selected some Elvis songs, sat back, and closed my eyes.

My left earplug was pulled out. "Jewels."

I groggily opened my eye with a start. Chris was

sitting beside me. "What's wrong? What's the time? Did I sleep through everything?"

"No, no. We still have two scenes left. Listen, you were singing and you sounded great. I was wondering if you'd like to record something for the show."

"I was what?" Confusion rained down over my still groggy self.

"You were singing," he repeated.

"Yeah, badly." I pulled out the other plug.

"No. You were fantastic." He pulled out his phone and showed me some dark footage of me singing on the couch, my eyes closed, belting out a song.

"Shit!" The realisation hit me. I had been given the power of song for going through death. The invisible woman did it.

"You're good. I didn't know you could sing."

"I can't."

"But you can, here, listen." He played some more and damn I was good.

"Oh, God," I breathed. "It's happened. I never even tried…" my voice trailed off.

"Okay, what are you talking about?"

I sighed and looked at him. "I couldn't sing before coming to England, and then when I died, I asked what I was getting out of death. I was asked what I wanted, and I said the ability to sing. She said okay, but I haven't tried."

"Well, you have now, and I want you to sing something if you're up to it. And we'll play it at the end of the show."

I sat there thinking about it. I had sounded good,

but did I want to embarrass myself? "Look, I, don't want to make myself look like a dick."

"You won't," he encouraged. "Just give it a go and do the song you were singing."

I relented. "Okay. I'll give it a go. Just as well I brought extra outfits."

"Great. You get changed, and I'll be back for you." He left, closing the door behind him.

I stood and pulled out a red pantsuit from the garment bag. I changed, undid my hair extensions, pulled on my wig and sprayed make-up on my face. Simple earrings, a ring on each middle finger and I was ready. There was a knock on the door. "Yeah," I called out.

Chris came in. "Wow. You look great. Come on, let's go, we've got the studio set up, and the song ready to go."

"Oh, God, I'm nervous," I murmured as he led me back to the stage. Black curtains fell heavily around it, and a mic stand stood on a round platform. I stepped on it, spoke into the mic for a check, and looked at the floor while the lights were adjusted.

"You ready?" Chris asked.

"No, give me a minute to catch my nerves. I'll let you know when to play it."

"Okay."

I breathed deeply. In and out. In and out. I gazed ahead of me. Except for the lights, it was complete blackness. I saw no one. *Nothing.* I took one last long breath and let it out. One, two, three, four, five, six, seven, eight, nine, ten. I removed the mic from the stand and held it out. "Someone take this."

Chris came and grabbed it, then disappeared back into the darkness.

I closed my eyes again. "I'm ready." The music started, I breathed deeply. I opened my eyes and began to sing Elvis Presley's *If I Can Dream.*

Three minutes and eight seconds later the music and my voice stopped. There was silence. I stood gazing ahead of me, drained, overwhelmed, and emotional. There was thunderous applause and the lights flooded on.

I stood blinking as everyone rushed toward me. Callum, Linda, Chris, the boys.

"Oh, my God, you were fantastic," Chris said. "Better than before."

"Well, I…"

"Who knew that sound would come out of such a big mouth," Christopher Fox butted in, clearly not knowing what was coming next.

"Aw, sweetie. I have big everything. Especially balls. And they're real too."

More laughter ensued in between *'congratulations', 'you look great'* and *'give us a hug'.*

Linda took some photos of us, and with Chris's permission, Callum had filmed everything else.

After changing and saying goodbye to everyone, Chris walked us out to the car.

"The show's going to air next Wednesday on BBC1, but I'll send you a copy of the show to keep."

"That'd be great." We hugged.

"Thanks for doing this."

"You're welcome. I'd do anything for you lot." I paused. "Well, almost anything and only for you, not Chris Fox." We laughed, and I climbed into the car.

"Hey, before you go, do you have any more ideas on that white spiky thing you showed me?" He leaned on the door through the open window.

"I think it's about New Years. I had another dream, and something tells me it has to do with the end of the year."

He nodded. "It looked like a clock, so maybe it does. Let me know if you find out."

"I will." We waved and drove off home.

Chapter 23

Thursday and Friday I typed up my 'boxes'. I was feeling good about turning my experience into another book, and wore my fingers out hitting the keys for two days in a row. I also checked all of my websites in case someone had come up with the answer to my dilemma. What is that damn white spiky thing? No one knew. No one could give me any answers at all. I wondered if I was going mad, but crazily dismissed that thought and kept on typing.

Callum walked into the bedroom and came over to me. "Hello, there." He gently turned my head and planted a kiss on my lips.

"Mmm, hello there yourself. Finished your flat yet?"

"Just about." He sat heavily on the couch and rubbed his eyes.

"Surely you don't have that much to sort out?" I spun around in my chair and hauled myself up and over to him, sitting down in his lap.

"Oh." He wrapped his arms around me. "There's not a lot. But I had to be ruthless and sort everything into piles. Then pack the stuff I don't want into boxes and put them into piles ready to go tomorrow."

"So, we're getting rid of it tomorrow?" I murmured into his ear as I nibbled on it.

He groaned and slipped his hand under my jumper up to my breast.

"Naughty boy, save it for later." I pushed his hand away.

"Aw, no fair." He gently bit my lip.

"Did you get everything else done?"

He sighed. "Yeah. All of my paperwork is in order. All my legal documents are in my bag, and I've organised for a charity to come and pick up the stuff I'm donating tomorrow."

"Told your family yet?"

"Nope."

"Why not?"

"Why do I need to?"

"Callum, you have to tell them sometime. Besides, your dad still has friends in the force, he'll find out you've retired. And your mum will be devastated you haven't told them."

"So!" He shrugged. "It's my life. I don't need their permission to do it."

"Yeah, good point." I snuggled closer. "But when will you tell them?"

"When I'm ready."

I kissed his cheek. "Fair enough. Just don't wait till we're living in Australia for years before you do it."

"Oh, don't worry. I have the perfect time."

*****

Gurgle, gurgle, gurgle.

The big bright white star shone in the sky.

Gurgle, gurgle, gurgle.

I was drowning in freezing water. Screams echoing around me. Debris clawing at me.

Gurgle, gurgle, gurgle.

I saw the lights go off in the sky. Pretty, big, bright. All shapes and colours, looming large in the big black darkness above. I sank. Sank into the deep dark water. Those big bright lights fading away...

I sat bolt upright, gasping, sweating, gulping for air. Callum stirred beside me but didn't wake. I slipped out from under the covers and went over to the desk. The black cardboard with my drawing of the white spiky thing sat patiently, waiting for me to add to it. I sat down, picked up the crayons, and began to fill in some of the blanks. A half hour later, I got back into bed.

*****

"So, when's this charity supposed to be coming?" I asked the next day as we stood in Callum's lounge room surrounded by piles of boxes of all shapes and sizes. I picked through a box filled with knick-knacks.

"Eleven. Hey, I'm keeping those." He reached in and pulled out some sort of footy memorabilia.

I looked into the box and arched a brow. "You're keeping *that* stuff?"

"What?" he said, catching my eye. "I love this stuff, and it means a lot to me."

"It's footy stuff," I said sarcastically. "What are you going to do when you're in Australia? Who will you barrack for then?"

He pouted. "Well, I might pick an Aussie team and I might not." He put the footy item back in the box.

"Look, sweetie." I tried not to sound condescending. "The more you get rid of, the less you have to ship over. Besides, do you *really* need all of this?" I pointed to the pile he was keeping.

"Well, some of it is photos and school stuff. Academy things and honours that I've received; things I've done." He touched what looked to be a plaque.

"Okay, I get that you want all of that, and that's the important stuff you need and should keep." I picked up the footy thing he'd held before and still didn't know what it was. "But do you *really* need all of this?" I put it back down and sat on the couch watching his reaction.

By the time the workers from the charity arrived, the box had joined those that were going. An hour later we stood in an almost empty flat looking over the boxes we'd be taking to Bob and Linda's.

"Wow, this place is really looking spacious now." I glanced around and ended up looking out the second storey window that faced the street.

"Huh! You mean now that all of my junk's gone." He stood behind me, and I leaned against him, pulling his arms around me.

"It's not a bad flat actually," I said. "Are you sad to be leaving? And not *just* the flat?"

He was quiet while I waited for his reply. "A little,"

he said softly, resting his chin on my head. "I've had this flat for ten years. Been a cop for twenty. Studied law and passed the bar. Became a Sergeant. Won awards and plaques for my dedication to the service. I'm a little sad. I'll be leaving it all behind. Leaving London. Leaving England." He bent his head down and kissed me. "But I'm excited too. Excited to be living in another country. Excited to be doing new things and seeing new places. And doing all of it with the woman I love." His expression softened. "A woman I thought I would never meet." His lips met mine gently. "I love you."

"I love you, too."

He kissed my temple, and we stood there for awhile taking in the silence. Eventually, we moved, and making sure he'd packed everything, started carrying boxes down to his car. Once we were done, we took one last look around and closed the door on his past, and after packing the last box into the car, we got in and drove away.

That night, after hauling Callum's stuff inside and having dinner, I asked everyone what they thought of my drawing.

"You added to it," Linda said, taking it.

"Fireworks," I replied. "It definitely has to do with New Year's." I sat next to Callum on the couch in the lounge room.

"Well, it definitely looks like fireworks, so I can see how you'd think it was about New Year's."

She handed the card to Bob. "But do you have any idea when or where?"

I shook my head and sighed. "No, and that's part of the frustration. I'm in the water, that light was there, the fireworks were going off." My eyes narrowed as I remembered. "There was screaming."

"Male or female?" Callum asked.

"It was female. And I was in the water drowning."

"Uh, about that," Bob said nervously. "Are you sure you're not mixing up when you *did* drown with something else?" He handed me the card. "Maybe when you drowned you saw something that looked like the picture? You said you heard screaming. There were people screaming that day. The day of the accident." He laid his arm on the back of the couch.

"I've thought about that." I looked down at the card. "I've thought long and hard, and I don't think it has anything to do with me drowning weeks ago. This is something new. Something that *hasn't* happened yet. Something that's coming, and I don't think it's good." I rubbed my head. "If only I bloody knew what was going on. Ugh." Callum hugged me. I sighed again and looked into those big blue eyes. "Something bad is coming. I just know it."

*****

'Twas the week before Christmas and all through the house, not a creature was stirring not even a…okay, so there's no mouse in the house, that I know of anyway, but it was the week before Christmas, and Linda and I were spending the week shopping for last minute goodies.

"So, where are we going?" I asked as we left at eight-thirty Monday morning.

"Well, I thought we'd head for Oxford Street today, and maybe do a different street each day; that way we'll cover the most important ones before Christmas and hopefully," she grinned at me, "get loads of bargains."

"Let's go then," I said excitedly. I had no idea where we'd park, but Linda managed to find a car space, and we ran for the first shop.

Shop after shop, bargain after bargain. I used the direct debit card I'd set up on my account. I knew the money was in there, so I didn't have to worry about carrying too much cash. We struggled to find a place to eat and fell into the car around six.

"God, my feet hurt," I groaned as we drove home.

"My *everything* hurts," Linda added. "I don't think I've ever shopped like that before. *Especially* at Christmas."

"I certainly haven't." I looked at all the Christmas decorations hanging from street lights and signs. "*Especially* in stores like those. That's the first time I've been able to buy anything without worrying about the price tag. And how were all the Christmas bands and singers? I think I heard every carol in history. Every time we walked out of a store, there was another one."

Linda laughed and turned into our street. "That's December in London."

"Oh," I groaned. "Well, as long as I get bargains, I don't mind one bit." We pulled up to the door and got out as Callum and Bob came to help us. "Here, take these." I shoved about ten bags at Callum.

"What the hell?" he moaned. "Did you buy out the whole of London?"

I pulled more bags from the car. "No. Just the whole of Oxford Street!" Linda and I fell into giggles as we walked into the house.

"I've got dinner made and ready," Bob said. "If you're hungry we can eat now."

"Just let me put my bags upstairs and freshen up." We were back downstairs five minutes later, having a meal of Chinese.

"Bob," Linda chastised. "You didn't *make* this. You bought it from the local Chinese restaurant we always get it from."

He blushed. "Well, uh, no."

"Liar." Linda laughed.

I couldn't wait to get my painkiller into me as my body, not just my head, was pounding. Jack was quite loud, clearly not happy from his big day out.

"Oh, Jewels. I received a parcel from Chris today. I think it's the DVD of the show," Bob said.

I gazed at him through glassy eyes. "Mmm, I just wanna go to bed." I covered a yawn. "But I guess we could watch it before I go."

We all trooped into the den where the TV was, and Bob undid the package, popping the disc into the player. He handed me the letter that came with it and sat on the couch next to Linda.

The show went for about forty minutes, and I cringed when my skit came on. Bob laughed his head off and then stopped in awe as I sang. We all sat there staring, blown away by what had come out of my mouth. I was certainly astounded by the gift I'd been given. And it was the first time I was actually seeing the performance. The show came to an end, the DVD stopped, and we still sat there.

"Wow," Bob finally managed.

I nodded in agreement and took a breath. "Wow is definitely the word for it. Wow. I. Wow."

"You're definitely one hell of a singer," Callum said, looking at me in amazement. "Where did that voice come from?"

I shook my head. "A little gift for dying so much." I saw his confused expression. It matched Bob and Linda's. "When I died the second time I asked what was I getting out of everything I was going through. She asked me what I wanted. I said the ability to sing and didn't think anything of it until Chris took some footage of me in the dressing room at the studio. Apparently, I'm good." I shrugged. "But what I am *now* is tired. Let's go to bed. Night," I said to Bob and Linda and stood.

"Night."

Callum and I headed upstairs, and after a nice hot shower I threw my shopping bags on the couch and got into bed for some hot sex and sleep.

Gurgle, gurgle, gurgle.

The number twelve flashed before my eyes.

Gurgle, gurgle, gurgle.

The water flowed over me.

Gurgle, gurgle, gurgle.

Fireworks flashed before my eyes. The white spiky

thing burned amongst them.

12. 12. 12. Kept flashing, but the icy water pulled me down, down, down.

I saw nothing…

*****

On Tuesday, we hit both New and Old Bond Streets. Designer shop after designer shop dazzled us. Doormen opened doors, and the crowds weren't as smothering. I bought blouses in different colours, matching pants, leather boots, and all sorts of accessories. Linda matched me piece for piece. I think we spent about as much as each other, going home with basically a new wardrobe, and presents for others, to finally stumble in the door around six.

"What *is it* with you girls?" Bob said, shaking his head in disbelief.

"What?" I said in mock surprise. "What did you expect me to do after winning lotto? Just sit home and not spend any of it?"

He grinned. "You got me there."

"Besides," I cut in. "I'm gonna be here for another couple of months, so I need clothes."

"When do you see the doctor again?" Callum asked with a concerned look.

"*This* Friday. Can you *believe* it? *Two days* before Christmas I have my six week check-up. I wanted to shop that day. Bugger!"

*****

It was Wednesday, and Linda took me to Regent Street. Between the shops and eateries, we managed to get some time in at Hamleys, fully stocked with toys every child would dream of. I found some new Barbie dolls, and a couple of teddy bears, adding them to my never-ending shopping spree.

"I have no idea how I'm getting everything home," I said that night after dinner. "I'll have to pack it all up and send it home with your stuff," I told Callum. "By the way, have you bought your presents yet?"

He glanced up from the newspaper he was reading. "I have." That was all I got.

"I meant for your family." I sat beside him. "You *will* be seeing them for Christmas won't you?"

He folded the paper and looked at me. "They invited me around for Christmas lunch. I asked if I could bring someone. Mum said yes. I plan on telling them everything."

"On Christmas Day." I was somewhat shocked, and my eyebrows rose. "Is it appropriate to leave it until then? *And thanks for telling me!*"

He shrugged. "It's more than likely the only time I'll get to see them, so I have to tell them." His lips turned into a wry grin. "And sorry I didn't tell you."

"Will your brother and sister be there?"

"Mum said yes. So, you'll have the whole family to meet in one go."

"Aw," I groaned. "Fan-fucking-tastic."

"The show's about to start." Bob flicked on the TV just as the show's opener rolled.

Even though we'd watched it two days ago, it still

sent chills down my spine. It sounded like there'd been an audience for the other sketches, and I thanked God there wasn't one for mine. My song ended the show, and once again we sat stunned by my performance.

"I'll be getting calls about your performance tomorrow." Bob nodded.

"I'm sure you will," I said. "I'm sure you will."

And we were right. While Linda and I shopped all day in Harrods, Bob received call after call at the office, handing me a huge pile of paper after dinner.

"My secretary decided to just type up all the offers so you could read them, and decide if they're worthy of your attention. I read a few, and I'd say some are."

I read page after page of requests, putting a question mark next to ones I might be interested in. Invites for awards nights, Christmas parties, New Year's parties, TV appearances, carol singing. Everyone who wanted a celebrity who'd not only died saving a woman and her child, but then won lotto as well.

"I don't mind doing the Graham Norton show, but definitely *not* any shows on ITV. I also don't want to do any Christmas things, and as for New Year, I'll be too busy trying to find that white spiky thing."

"Any more visions about that?" Linda asked, sipping her chamomile tea.

"It has something to do with twelve. Twelve o'clock, twelve seconds past, twelve minutes past. I don't know. But the more I think about it, it's definitely New Year's Eve around twelve at night, since there's fireworks. I'm assuming it happens during the celebrations."

"What happens?" Callum played with my hair.

"Bad stuff," I replied.

*****

Friday morning, I sat in the doctor's office at the hospital. The clock clearly said nine, but he was running late. I paced back and forth, adjusted my beanie, and stared out the window. Linda sat patiently in her chair.

The doctor burst in. "Hello, there. Recovered from your suicide attempt?"

"It wasn't suicide," I snapped. "Let's get this over with so I can get the hell away from you and go shopping."

He gave me a dirty look and told me to get on the bed. He checked my scar, my face, my chest, asked how the pain was, and if I'd abused my pills again.

"I'll abuse you if you keep talking." I gave him a filthy look. He sent me off for x-rays, which took another half an hour, and then I had to wait half an hour to see him again.

"Mmm, your x-rays are good. Scans are good." He turned to me. "You still can't fly, but you can stop taking your pills. Except for the painkillers. No more than six a day if the pain gets too bad."

"Pfft," I spat. "If I'd been taking six pills a day after the accident the pain might've actually dulled to a loud roar."

"Ms Diva," he droned sarcastically. "Don't come back for another six to eight weeks. I'll see you then."

"God, let's get out of here."

Linda and I headed for Sloane Street, lunching at Peter Jones before tackling the rest of the road. I found antique trunks and books, knick-knacks, and a gorgeous chandelier made of multicoloured Swarovski crystals in multiple rows. It was to be wrapped and packaged before being sent to the house.

"So, where are we going tomorrow? It's Christmas Eve. Time for last minute shopping." I rubbed my hands together in glee.

Linda drove up to the house. "Nowhere. Tomorrow's the day of our Christmas Eve party, and I have the caterers coming to help set up."

"Oh." My face fell as I exited the car. "Maybe Callum will want to go somewhere?"

"Where will I want to go?" he asked, coming out to help.

I threw my arms around his neck and kissed him. "Shopping!"

"No, thanks. I've already done mine. Haven't you finished yet? Or do you just want to get all the bargains in London?"

"Pretty much." We piled through the door.

"Jewels, you've got more invitations today. Everybody wants you," Bob gushed.

"Of course, dah-lings," I said with an exaggerated lilt. "I am Jewels Deeva, ever-ay bud-ay wunts may!" I saw their faces and giggled. "Let's go through them after dinner," I said. This time Callum had cooked roast beef, mashed potatoes, and gravy. "Yum." I dug in till I was stuffed. "Okay, about those invites."

"Hang on." Callum stopped me on the way to the

lounge. "Your doctor's visit was today. How'd it go?"

"Ugh," I groaned as we sat on the couch. "*He* was a *pain* in the *arse*." I shook my head. "It took about three hours then we went to Sloane Street."

"But how are you?" he pushed.

"Good," I said. "Still can't fly, but good."

A huge grin sliced across his face. "That's great." He kissed me. "That's really great."

"Yeah, well." I comically rolled my eyes. "I had to expect it sometime."

"Here." Bob handed me another pile of paper.

We discussed the ones I was interested in. Opening Harrods for the after-Christmas sales, more parties, more functions. I eyed off the New Year's Eve invites. "How am I supposed to find out where this white spiky thing is?" I moaned, rubbing my eyes.

"Process of elimination," Callum piped up.

"Trust you to think of that." I threw him a dirty look and got a grin in return. "Okay, where will there be fireworks this year?" I continued.

"All along the Thames. The Eye features every year."

"What about the Thames? Have they showed anything about the fireworks yet? What they're planning? What's new?"

"No, not yet," Linda said. "But then they don't until after Christmas."

"Well, then, I can't find out can I?" We sat in silence for awhile before I turned to Callum. "So, what *are* we doing tomorrow?"

"I thought we'd spend the day together."

"Are you coming to the party tomorrow night?"

Linda asked.

"And be a sideshow freak," I sniped.

"No." She seemed hurt. "You're our guests. I thought you'd like to be there."

"I'd love to, but not if your *other* guests will be staring and whispering."

"Actually," Callum interrupted. "I have something special planned for tomorrow night." He glanced at me and wiggled his eyebrows. "Just you and me and a little privacy."

"I don't need to hear this." Bob covered his ears.

"What are you planning?" I pushed.

"Something special," he repeated.

"Could you at least come to my party beforehand?" Linda asked.

"Well," Callum said. "I *was* planning a night upstairs. We could."

"I'm not coming as Jewels," I said. "No way, no how."

"Well, then—" Linda started.

"I'll come as myself, wearing my hair and make-up, and you can say I'm a friend of Jewels who came over with her, and you've opened your house to. And if anyone mentions Callum, then we can say we got together after you met her. We met at the hospital and hit it off."

"We could," he agreed.

"Anything, as long as you stay awhile," Linda said.

*****

'Twas the day before Christmas and all through the house, no creature was stirring, only a...*Jack Hammer*?! Yes, that's right. Jack decided to get noisy, letting me know he's been busy making toys for Christmas. Callum and I were up early thanks to Jack, and were at the London Westfield Shopping Centre when it opened.

I bundled him up with last minute goodies, and he looked like a pack horse, trailing after me around the shops. He did find some inexpensive clothes for himself, and we managed to make it home around five-thirty.

"Oh, good, there you are. The party doesn't start till seven-thirty, so you have some time for dinner and a nap if you need it," Linda told us as she dashed past with a flower arrangement.

The house was already decorated, but the crew she'd hired added lots more, bringing elegance and fun to the rooms. Every room was decorated in a different colour theme. Tinsel ran up the stair bannister and along the hall. Even our room had been extra decorated. The bed had tinsel and fairy lights strung between the poles. There was a tree in the corner of the room. Lights twinkled in a rainbow of colours.

One of the caterers came in with a tray of food. We ate, and then wearily lay down on the bed. Callum set his alarm for an hour so we wouldn't be late getting downstairs.

I woke, feeling somewhat refreshed, and quickly showered and dressed in an elegant blouse and pants. I was ready when Callum emerged from the bathroom.

"Hurry up. The sooner we get down the sooner we can come back up."

"Okay, okay," he mumbled, grabbing his pants.

This was a night I really wasn't looking forward to.

Chapter 24

The first guests were arriving as we made our way downstairs, and quickly scurried into the kitchen.

"There you are," Bob called. "Eggnog?"

"No, thanks." I looked around. "This place looks nice."

"Thanks," Linda said, bringing her guests into the lounge. Everything was open plan, so it made for one big party room. "We do this every year. Will you hand out the eggnog, Bob?" She introduced us to the guests. Melissa and Aidan Hart. Michael and Michelle Barry, and Chisholm and Loretta Divine.

"Oh, dear," I murmured to Callum out of earshot. "Are they *really* called that?"

He suppressed a grin and accepted a glass of nog as more guests arrived.

"So, Linda, where's this special house guest of yours? I can't wait to see her head."

I blanched and turned away, hoping no one noticed.

"Jewels?" Linda asked. "She's off partying with people her own age." She laughed lightly and gave me a quick glance.

"Well, how rude's that," the woman continued. "You bring her over here, let her stay after the accident, and she runs off suiting herself. How unappreciative."

"Stop it, Veronica," Bob chastised. "Jewels is free to do what she wants. She's already thanked us for helping her."

"And how's that?" Veronica asked, taking a glass from a tray Linda offered.

"By letting us publish her next book." Bob laughed, and the others joined in.

Callum and I nibbled on the munchies laid out on the dining table, while the others mingled, but Veronica soon zeroed in on Callum.

"Aren't you the hot cop who saved the ungrateful wench?"

Blackness thundered over his face. "She's *hardly* ungrateful. But *you are* rude."

Shock rolled over her face, but then she hardened. "And who's this little thing?" She cast an evil eye over me.

"I'm not a thing," I spat. "And I agree. *You are rude.*"

She clearly didn't like people telling her the obvious. "And who are *you* to tell *me* I'm rude?" She placed a perfectly manicured right hand on her teeny tiny right hip. Her left was holding the glass of champagne.

"Bob and Linda's *other* houseguest," I hissed, and Callum and I walked away.

"Another one," Veronica wailed. "Linda what are you doing? Turning your home into a halfway house?"

"Veronica that's enough." Linda went to her side.

"I'll have who I want in my house. I don't need your permission. So be nice, or *go home.*"

I laughed under my breath and exchanged an amused grin with Callum. Veronica mumbled something, but we couldn't make it out. Chatting to the other guests, we ate a few more nibblies, and then sneakily snuck upstairs.

"Oh, God. I'm glad that's over," I groaned, taking off my shoes and slumping on the bed.

"I've locked the door, and we don't have to deal with it anymore." Callum pulled me to my feet. "Go and get changed for bed. I have that something special planned."

"Oooh," I murmured. "It had better be." I grabbed my own something special from the closet and walked into the bathroom. When I came out, Callum was in his robe on the couch which faced the tree. Plates of food and a chilled bottle of Pepsi Max sat on the coffee table. "Did someone just bring this up?" I draped myself over him.

"Oh, hello," he said, his voice deep and throaty. His fingers lightly slid over my red lace negligee and matching robe. "New?"

"New." I nuzzled his face, flicking my tongue against his cheek.

He groaned, and his hand groped up under my nightie. In moments we were making love under the tree, our bodies melting into one another's arms. We couldn't get enough, groaning loudly as we climaxed, and then we lay still, wrapped in each other.

"So," I murmured, gently biting his ear. "Was that

your something special?”

“No, that wasn't it.” He rolled away and poured us a drink. “Come, sit.”

Leaning against the couch with a blanket over us, we sipped our drinks and munched on Christmas biscuits, and M&Ms. Mmmmm…chocolate…

I snuggled my head on his chest and breathed deeply.

“Enjoying yourself?”

I smiled and rubbed my face on his furry chest. “Yes.”

“Good.” He moved as if he was reaching for something. “Tamara.”

“Mmm?”

“I love you.”

“I love you.”

“Will you marry me?”

My eyes opened. “What?” It took a moment for what he'd said to sink in, then my head shot up, and I saw the big sparkly ring in the velvet box in his hand. “Oh, my God, it's gorgeous.” Three big ruby hearts surrounded by tiny diamonds. “Oh, it's gorgeous.”

“Well?”

I looked up. “What?”

“Will you marry me?”

“Yes,” I gasped. “Yes, of course I will! Yes.” He placed the ring on my finger. It fitted perfectly. “A hundred thousand million billion trillion times yes!” I kissed him and sat on his lap, and a round of hot quick sex followed before we collapsed, totally exhausted.

“I love you so much.” I breathed hard. “So much.”

His fingers traced along my cheek, his eyes blazing into mine. "I love you, too." He let out a deep breath. "I'd do anything for you Tam. *Anything.*"

Thoughts passed through my mind, and I sat up.

"Tam." He reached for my chin and gently turned my head, so I was looking at him. "What is it? What's wrong?"

I wasn't sure how to broach the subject, although surely he must have thought about it. I took a deep breath. "Anything?"

"Anything."

"Would you sign a prenup?"

"Yes." He didn't blink.

"So, you've thought about it?"

"Of course. I don't have any right to any of your money. I understand that. I do have a law degree." He laughed lightly.

"I just don't…"

"Don't what?"

"Don't want to cause problems by," I waved my hands while trying to find the right words, "being a bitch. I have no problem with paying for you, and I'll possibly need to for awhile." He started to protest. "Let me finish. I don't like where I live, and when we get home, I'll be packing up so we can move. But since I don't know where I want to live, I thought we'd spend some time in three states to see where we'd want to set up base."

I remembered the house from my vision. "And since I have money, I might even buy a property in each state in case we travel with the businesses I want to set up." I took his hand in mine. "Now, I'm a bit of an old-fashioned kind of gal, and think the man should provide the house and support the family, but I also understand that in this day and age, it's the woman who does that just as much. And in our case," I touched his cheek, "that's the way it's going to be for awhile. I don't mind buying the house and decorating, and buying us cars and whatnot, I'd do that regardless of whether I was with you or not, but it also means you won't have much money to do stuff with, so I don't mind financially supporting you until you find something."

"Tam." He shifted uncomfortably.

"No, let me finish. I think there's two ways we can do this. Either I give you a set amount of money to call your own, which I really don't mind, or, I support you until you get a job. But don't feel that you have to rush anything. Take your time, adjust to a new life, do some courses, take some classes, and then do what you want. I don't mind either way."

"Tam, I've thought about it. I don't want your money. I have some of my own. My savings are quite healthy, and with the conversion rate it should be a nice little fallback cushion."

"Is it enough to buy and decorate a house?"

"No. And I've thought about that." He sighed. "You want me to be a man, and men support their wives, but in our case, I can't. So, I've thought some things through, and have, for the most part, accepted that." He grinned. "I'll try not to feel insecure because my wife's won millions."

"You won't go without," I said, stroking his cheek. "You'll benefit from living in the houses, and being surrounded by stuff. It's what I plan on doing anyway. Regardless of *who* I ended up with. I was always going to buy a house and car and decorate. It'll be you who gets to live a life of luxury."

"Tam." He seemed irritated. "I'm a man. It's my duty to protect and support this, our family. That's what I do. That's what my job is."

"I know, and I expect you to. But I also know you don't have the financial ability to do that, so what I need and want from you is to be a man. To physically, emotionally, and mentally support me. To be there when I get knocked into the river. To be there when I'm suffering pain. A house is a house; it means nothing. What *does* mean something is you standing beside me, supporting me in every way. That's all I want from you," I paused, "And really hot sex."

He grinned softly then his eyes saddened. "Doesn't make me feel like the man you want, though."

"You *are* the man I want." I kissed him. "As long as you support me in every way, shape, and form, and throw yourself into rivers to save me, and not be repulsed and disgusted by the wounds, then you are the man I want to be with. It's just money, and you will be well taken care of."

He pulled me into his arms. "I love you. And I will do anything for you."

I kissed him again. "I know."

"I'll even sign a prenup."

I smiled. "The answer will always be yes."

*****

"Rise and shine."

Something poked me. I groaned and rolled over.

"Rise and shine, Tam."

A hand lifted my leg, and a masculine one slipped through, bringing a very enjoyable toy with it.

"Ugh." I buried my head into the pillow as pleasure exploded through me. We'd never done it that way before, and it made it more enjoyable. I thrust back against him, meeting him, and matching his every move until it was over and we lay snuggling in the spoon position.

"Ugh," I whimpered.

"Merry Christmas," he whispered in my ear.

I curled into him, and we stayed that way until the damn alarm went off. Then, with distasteful annoyance at having to get up, we pulled apart, showered, and dressed. Once downstairs, I showed off my ring.

"Oh, my God, he asked you," Linda squealed. "And you obviously said yes. Oh, my God, look at the ring; it's gorgeous. Bob, look at the ring."

"I'm looking I'm looking," he gushed then turned to Callum. "You take good care of our Jewels." He shook Callum's hand heartily. "I don't want to hear that she's not happy or doing well."

Callum extracted his hand. "I'll be taking very good care of her. She's in good hands."

"Good. That's good."

"Let's have breakfast and talk more," Linda said, hugging Callum.

"What are you two doing today?" she asked over pancakes and hot maple syrup.

Callum grimaced. "I've been invited to my folks for lunch, and Tam's coming with me. They'll all get to meet her at once, and she'll get to meet all of them." He must have caught the disdain on my face because he laughed. "Yeah, don't worry. I feel the same."

"What about you two?" I asked Linda.

"Oh, we'll be heading off to Bob's parents for lunch, and then mine for dinner."

"Do you get along with either of them?" I stuffed pancake into my mouth.

They exchanged a glance.

"That bad?" I grinned.

Linda giggled. "Bob's parents are nice, but my dad thought I could do better."

"How much better than the CEO of a huge international publishing house could you get?" Bob puffed out his chest.

Linda kissed him on the cheek. "I didn't want to do better." She looked at me and took her plate and glass to the sink.

Bob looked confused for a moment before getting the joke, and we all laughed.

"What time are you going?" she asked.

I looked at Callum as I didn't know either.

"Get there about ten, leave about two or three." He pushed back from his seat.

"Same for us," Bob said, checking the kitchen clock. "It's nine now, better start getting ready."

We headed upstairs to finish dressing. I had my

forest green pants on with a tight red body top to keep me warm, and I slipped a soft red lightweight jumper over my head and pulled it down. It was a snug v neck and clung to my curves nicely. I pulled on dark green leather boots, and got a gorgeous red and green Christmas scarf and a thick red wool coat from the closet. After laying them on the bed, I went to put my wig and make-up on and saw Callum had all the presents for his family lined up when I came out. "So you did finish your shopping." I slipped on red stone and gold earrings which hung down to my shoulders.

"I did." He pulled on a boot.

I pushed several red, green and gold bracelets onto my right arm and reached for my watch.

"I have one for you."

"Uh-oh! Are we handing out presents now? I thought we were waiting for tonight?"

"We are, but I'd like to give you this one now."

I glanced in his direction and saw him holding a small gift wrapped box. "Well, I know it's not an engagement ring," I joked, accepting the box and lifting the lid, peeling back tissue paper to reveal a velvet box. "Okay, must be jewellery." I pulled out the box and dropped the wrapping on the bed. On opening it, I gasped. "Oh, Callum. It's gorgeous." I looked back and forth between him and the gorgeous gold heart-shaped locket with the big ruby heart surrounded by emeralds. It was quite large and hung from a solid chain.

"Look on the back," he said with glowing eyes.

"To my darling Tamara; I am yours always and

ever, love Callum xxoo," I read aloud. Hot tears rolled down my face. "I just put my make-up on," I joked, trying to catch my breath.

"Look inside."

"What?"

"Look inside."

I opened the locket. There was a picture of Callum inside, and I noticed it had a second hinge, so I pulled it open, revealing more picture spaces. "Oh, it's one of those," I said, closing it and kissing my fiancée. "I love it." The chain was big enough for me to slip it over my head, and the locket hung gently against my jumper. "I love it, I love it, I love it," I squealed, doing my little happy dance.

He pulled me into his embrace and met my lips with his. "I'm glad you love it."

"Wait." I pulled away. "I'd better give you one." I dug around in my luggage and pulled out a gift wrapped box which I presented to him. "For you, my husband-to-be."

Grinning, he opened it, pulling out a silver metal and black onyx watch. "Oh, my God, Tam." He shook his head. "You shouldn't…" Waves of emotion rolled over him. "I…love it. I love it."

"Put it on," I urged him.

He slid it on and shut the catch.

"It looks good." I took his arm. "It looks really good."

He stared down at me. "You're amazing."

"Me?" I frowned. "Please. I just gave you a watch, and you gave me a gorgeous locket and this amazing engagement ring." I stared happily at it.

"Well." He lifted my chin. "You *are* amazing." His lips were gentle before pulling away. "You ready?"

"Yes," I whispered.

"Let's go then." He gathered up the bags of presents. "I'll take these out to the car. Can you bring my coat?"

"Sure." I touched up my lipstick and pulled my coat on, popping a warm red beanie into the pocket. I wrapped my scarf around my neck, and grabbed my bag and Callum's coat, meeting him at the car just as Bob and Linda came out. I handed Callum his coat, and put my bag in the front seat.

"Will you come home after visiting your parents?" Linda asked as Bob set the alarm and closed the door.

"Can we drive around instead and maybe do something?" I asked before Callum could even open his mouth.

He grinned. "Sure we could."

"What about you guys?" I asked, buttoning up my coat.

"We may not be back until late," Linda said. "But you have the gate opener and the alarm code, so there's no need to wait for us."

Bob pulled up in their car. "Are you ready?" Linda jumped in.

Callum and I got in and buckled up, then followed Bob's sedan out the driveway. With a honk of the horn, we went our separate ways.

It took us half an hour to get to Callum's parents' house as they were on the other side of town, and we had to battle Christmas morning traffic.

I popped my belt as we pulled up out the front. "Ready?" I asked, gazing at the house.

Silence.

I turned and saw Callum sitting there looking very unsure about moving. "Things can't be *that* bad between you and your family. From what you've told me, it isn't." I watched his face. "Callum?"

He sighed. "It's not split us apart bad...it's just... Dad doesn't agree with me not applying to be an inspector. Although he is proud of my achievements, he thinks I need to apply myself enough to go to the next level of promotion. And Mum continually goes on about how I haven't produced any heirs yet, let alone not married and settled down."

I giggled. "Well, she'll love this then." I was nervous and felt the butterflies in my stomach.

He grinned. "Yeah. I've finally found a woman who'll put up with me and who has hips big enough to bear my children."

"Hey," I protested.

He put his hands up. "Hey, yourself. Mum's words, not mine."

"Mmm," I grumbled and got out of the car.

Getting the presents together, we walked up to the door. It flew open, and a tall, willowy blonde gushed. "Oh, Callum, you're here..." She trailed off when she saw me.

"Susannah," Callum greeted her. "I didn't know you would be here." He ushered me into the hallway and followed.

Susannah closed the door. "I...didn't know...you'd

be bringing someone," she faltered, glancing back and forth with a very desolate expression.

"Well, I did ask Mum if I could bring someone. We'll just pop upstairs and leave our coats then be back down. Good to see you." He indicated for me to go upstairs and then led me into a room being used for guests' coats.

"Who was that?" I set the bags down and pulled off my coat.

"Someone I've known for awhile, but never wanted to date." He lowered his voice. "Mum tried setting us up, but I wasn't interested."

"So your mother thinks she'll give it another shot then?" I smiled.

"Looks like it." He grinned back. "Don't worry, everyone's about to find out I'm taken."

After carrying the bags downstairs, we went down a hallway leading to the back of the house.

"Callum," a woman cried, running toward him and giving him a huge hug and kiss.

"Mel," he said. "Merry Christmas, here take these, presents for everyone."

"Fantastic, the kids can't wait to see you." She clearly hadn't seen me hidden behind Callum. We followed her along a short hall to the right and came into the kitchen. "Look who's here," she called.

I saw adults, but no kids, and my nerves were jumping all around.

"Callum, darling." An older woman hugged him. "I'm so glad you could come."

"Mum." He hugged back, lifting her off her feet.

She spied me over his shoulder. "And you must be Callum's guest. Welcome."

I got the feeling Susannah had already mentioned me. "Thank you," I murmured, taking a few silent breaths.

Callum put her down. "Mum, this is Tamara." His right arm slid around me. "Why don't I introduce her to everyone all together? It will be easier."

"Oh, all right, dear." She led us to the lounge off to the right. I saw several older men and women, and a younger man who looked like Callum. There was his sister, and another man and woman.

"Darling," his mum said to one of the men. "Callum's here and wants to introduce us to his guest."

"Ah, Callum, my boy. You finally made it," a tall grey-haired man said. "Go ahead. Introduce us to your lovely looking guest."

Callum's arm was still around me, my left hand hidden behind his back. I looked up at him in complete adoration, my right hand resting on his chest. He covered it with his and squeezed gently. "Okay, everyone. This is Tamara. My guest. Tam this is my mum and dad, my brother Liam and his wife, Leslie. My sister Melissa and her husband, Michael. My uncles and aunts, Bob and Sarah, and Desmond and Delilah. And my grandparents Edward and Sophie, and William and Denise."

Cripes!

Panic rose from my stomach to my throat. Bloody hell! All of these people to have to deal with. I took a silent deep breath. "Hello." I nodded, glancing around.

Callum looked down at me with a huge grin. "Tamara is my fiancée. We're getting married as soon as possible. I'm moving to Australia to live with her, and I've retired from the force to do it. We'll be leaving in a couple of months." He gave them a defiant stare.

I held my breath as silence landed around the room.

Everyone stared.

Everyone burst out at the same time.

"Oh, my God, that's fantastic," Melissa squealed.

"Congratulations, bro," Liam added.

"Oh, Callum why didn't you tell us?" his mother wailed.

"What the bloody hell do you think you're doing retiring from the force? You're only forty," his father bellowed.

"Oh, for God's sake, Dad, he's found the woman of his dreams and is finally going to get married and have kids," Melissa scolded.

"Ugh, I'm gonna be sick," came from behind us.

"About time, my boy," came from one of the grandpas.

"She's pregnant," one of the grandmas spitefully added.

"That's it isn't it?" his dad said. "She got herself pregnant, and is now a money grubbing whore of a gold digger."

"Dad," Callum yelled.

"Shut the hell up!" I exclaimed, stunning them all. Everyone looked at me. So did Callum, clearly not expecting that my potty mouth had hitched a ride with us to his family Christmas.

"How dare—" his dad started.

"No," I spat. "*How dare you!* I am a *guest* in your house, and you believe you have the right to *insult* me. I am your son's *fiancée* for God's sake, not some pregnant money grubbing whore." I shoved my finger in his face. "I'll have you know I have more money than your son, and I am *NOT pregnant*." I glared at the woman who'd claimed it.

"Dad…" Callum's voice was quiet amongst the silence. "I want you to apologise to Tamara. Or we leave now."

"Andrew," his wife fretted. "Apologise. I don't want Callum to leave."

"You should, Dad, that was *so* rude," Melissa added, staring angrily at him.

Andrew Stone softened. "I'm sorry, young lady. Callum's been single so—"

"No excuses," I said. "It's about apologising to me, it's not about Callum."

"You're right." He shifted uncomfortably. "I jumped to conclusions about you, and it was wrong of me. I'm very sorry." He held out his hand. "Welcome to the family, Tamara."

I waited a moment, glaring from his hand back to him, and then we shook. "Thanks."

"Callum, my boy, congratulations, finally you're going to produce an heir." He hugged his son while the women crowded around gaping at the ring. "She clearly knows how to stand up for herself," I heard.

"She certainly does," Callum replied.

"Beer?"

"Sure."

I caught Callum's eye and grinned before he walked into the kitchen.

"So when are you getting married?" Melissa asked.

"Don't know."

"Will it be here or in Australia?" Leslie asked.

"Don't know."

"Well, you have to get bride magazines and start making plans," Callum's mum said.

"No."

The women stopped. "What do you mean, no?" she asked.

"I don't need bride magazines or plans. I know what I want."

"Oh, well, why don't you tell us and we can help you with it," she continued.

"No, thank you. I have it all under control. Besides, we don't know whether we'll get married here or Australia. All depends on the legals. Either way, thanks for offering, but I know what I'm doing."

His mother's face didn't look good. She looked annoyed, angry, disgusted. But tough! My wedding. My plans.

"Well, you must be able to share something," Melissa asked, trying to calm a situation that I didn't think was out of control.

I shrugged. "We haven't discussed it yet. He only proposed last night. But I know what sort of dress I want, and I want the ceremony to be simple and easy."

Callum walked over and handed me a glass of juice.

"Talking about the wedding? We haven't made plans yet. Mum, Melissa, leave it alone. Tamara and I will decide. Ah, Mum," he cut her off when she tried to protest, "I know what you were like with Mel and Liam's weddings. You took over." Her face was indignant. "Don't pull that look with me. Tam and I will do this ourselves. Ah, no arguments. Be nice." He turned to his sisters as his mum stalked off. "Where are the kids?"

"Out the back," they answered together before giggling.

"Playing in the snow that's left from yesterday," Melissa added.

"So, when will we be opening presents?" he asked.

I looked over Callum's shoulder to see the elders huddling in the kitchen.

"If you want we can do it before lunch. I can call them in now," Leslie said.

We glanced at our watches. It was about an hour before lunch.

"May as well," he said.

Leslie walked off to get the kids, and we chatted with Melissa, Michael and Liam.

"Uncle Callum," came the chorus of voices. Three boys and two girls raced in and threw themselves at him.

"Hey, hey," he said, pulling all of them into his arms. "I've got some presents for you, but first I want you to meet someone very special."

"Who?" came the chorus.

He stood and put his arm around me. "Everyone,

this is Tamara. She's going to be your aunt because we're getting married. So you have to be nice and polite," he warned then looked at me. "Tam, this is Jason, Mitchell and Shaun, Mel and Michael's boys. And Jennifer and Michelle. Liam and Leslie's daughters."

"Hello." I smiled.

"Hello," they chorused. "Where are our presents?"

"Don't be rude," Melissa scolded.

Callum laughed. "That's all right. It's what Christmas is all about." He nodded toward the tree. "Over there." They ran over and scrambled around looking for their names on the bags. "Might as well open yours too." He handed Liam and Melissa theirs. "Mum, Dad, this is for the two of you."

"Thank you, darling," his mum said, taking the gift.

"Aunts Sarah and Delilah, grandmas Sophie and Denise."

"Cool."

"Look what I got."

"Teddy."

We turned. Callum had bought the latest toys for his nephews and nieces. Robots and spaceships for the boys. Dolls and teddy bears for the girls. Combinations of manly machines and girly goodies for everyone else.

"You certainly know how to shop," I whispered to him.

He grinned and whispered back. "Years of practice."

"So, what did you guys get each other?" Liam asked.

"This," we both said and laughed. Callum showed them his watch, and I held out the locket.

"Nice watch, bro." Liam inspected his brother's present.

"I was staring at that gorgeous thing before," Melissa said to me. "Lucky you."

"He inscribed it." I showed them the back.

"Aw, how sweet," Leslie crooned.

"Thanks for the E-Reader, my boy." Andrew patted Callum on the back. "Exactly what I was after."

"I know." He grinned. "Mum told me. And you've got the voucher to get you started, so that should keep you occupied in your retirement."

"Ha," he grumbled. "Retirement isn't that good. Just you wait."

"Oh, I won't be retired for long."

"Really? What are you planning?"

"I'll probably take six months off. Tam has to pack up her stuff, and we need to decide where to live. But once we do, we've got some ideas in mind for a business venture."

"Such as?"

"Private investigation business. I'd need to do the course and get qualifications. But it's similar to police work, so it should go well."

His dad nodded. "Sounds good. How long do you think that will take to get up and running?"

"Well, Tam said the course runs for about three months. We can get the name and business licences in that time, and employ other people from the course. Advertise, get some clients. Shouldn't take long."

"It sounds good. Let me know when you do, I'd love to see how it goes."

"Sure." Callum tried to hide his jubilation. He caught my eye, and I smiled.

"So do you know what sort of dress you want?" Melissa asked.

"I do."

"What about colour? White, cream, off-white?" Leslie asked.

"Red lace."

"What!" They were both stunned.

"Who wears a red lace dress at their wedding?" Sophie piped up from her place on the couch. I noticed she seemed a little straitlaced and old-fashioned.

"I will," I said firmly.

Denise was beside her. "Brides should wear white on their wedding day. It signifies purity."

"And virginity." Leslie grinned.

"Ha! Like that's relevant these days," I said. "Red is good feng shui. It's what I want, and I'm sticking to it."

"Paula Yates wore red and look what happened to her," Sophie said, running a rosary through her fingers.

Oh, God, she's one of those!

Delilah decided it was time to enter the conversation. She seemed quite nice and wore a long flowing velvet dress, a turban, and lots of jewellery. A little eccentric maybe, old-fashioned, but in a good way.

I hoped.

"Oh, for heaven's sake, Mother." Oh, she was Sophie's daughter. "This is two thousand and eleven. Not nineteen eleven. The world has changed, and clearly, Tamara knows how to change with it." She cast a critical eye over Sophie. "Maybe you should do the same?"

"Don't you speak to me that way, Delilah. I'm your mother—"

"Oh, here we go, she's getting all dramatic. Janice darling, is lunch ready yet? I need to get drunk." She headed for the kitchen.

Melissa, Leslie, and I exchanged glances and suppressed grins.

"If you'd all like to take a seat at the table, I'll start getting the food. Melissa, Leslie, can you help, please?"

The rest of us filed into the dining room which was off the other side of the kitchen, and along the back of the house overlooking the snowy and muddy backyard. The table was already set and decorated.

"Tamara, darling, sit next to me," Delilah said. "You can tell me what you want for your wedding."

"Del, she's sitting on my left. Callum, you're on my right." Janice placed bowls of steaming veggies on the table.

Delilah sat to my left and Callum opposite me, giving me a half-hidden thumbs up that made me smile.

Melissa and Leslie put more bowls on the table, and Janice placed the steaming turkey in front of Andrew then sat down. When we were settled, he cut the first slice and bowls were passed around.

"So, tell me, darling. A red lace dress. Sounds marvellous. Tell me *all* about it." Delilah swept a forkful of corn and potato into her mouth.

I swallowed and took a sip of juice. "It's—" I

shrugged. "Red lace, off the shoulder, bit of a fishtail thing. I don't have it yet. Haven't had it made."

"Sounds fantastic." She downed her drink and called out, "More wine."

"Why don't you have two weddings?" Melissa asked from next to Callum.

I shrugged again. "We might." I quickly shoved turkey into my mouth and saw him grin.

"So, Callum, when are you retiring from the force?" Janice asked.

"I've already set the ball rolling. I officially retire on the last day of the year."

"And will you be leaving after that?" Liam inquired from beside Delilah.

"Ah, no," Callum said. "We might spend some more time in Europe first. I'll show Tam some of the sights. Paris. Italy. Greece."

"Ha," Sophie piped up. "Why do you want to go there? England's the best place to be."

"Best place to be," Denise added with a nod of her head.

"Oh, I'm sure Tam would disagree with that," Callum said humorously. "I'm sure she'd say Australia is the best place to be."

I grinned.

"So, how many people will be attending?" Delilah asked in my ear.

"Don't know."

"Where will you be having it?"

"Don't know." I was becoming irritated and noticed Michael was busy looking after the kids, and the old boys chatted amongst themselves.

"So, Tamara, what do you do for a living?" Janice asked me.

Uh-oh, I hate being asked that question. It's so pissin' personal. I struggled for an answer then it popped into my head. "I work for a publishing house." I spied Callum's suppressed grin before he stuffed veggies into his mouth.

"Oh. Doing what?"

"Typing, editing, proofing etc."

"Have you been married before?" she continued.

Uh-oh, again! I gave Callum a look to say, I didn't like where this was going.

"So, when do you and Callum plan on having children?"

And there it was!

The one question that is *so* insanely no one's business and I had my future mother-in-law asking me that very question.

Oh, this was *sooo* not happening.

Chapter 25

The question all old-fashioned people ask their childless adult children. It doesn't matter *how* it's put, because it always means the same.

'*When are you having children?*' '*When will I be a grandmother?*' '*Have you found someone to marry yet so you can get pregnant?*' '*Why don't you have children yet?*'

All the same, no matter how they say it.

I silently sucked in a long deep breath and glared at Callum through narrowed eyes.

"Oh, for heaven's sake, Janice, leave the poor girl alone," Delilah slurred beside me. "When they want to have kids they will. And they'll have fun doing it." She gave us a big wink.

My expression to Callum was now, *you dirty bastard. You dragged me into this, now get me the hell out of here.*

"We certainly will," Callum said with a quick eyebrow wiggle at me. "So why would we be in any hurry?"

OH, MY GOD, I CAN'T BELIEVE HE SAID THAT!

I shook my head, took another deep breath, scraped up the last of my food, then wiped my mouth before taking a drink.

"Would you like more, Tamara?" Janice offered a bowl of corn.

"No, thank you."

"What about turkey and potatoes?"

"No, thank you." I took another sip and watched Callum finished his own food.

"You're such a skinny thing; you have to eat some more," Janice continued.

"I *said, no,* thank you," my voice was low as I gave her the evil eye.

"Mum," Callum warned. "We're leaving room for dessert."

"Can it, Janice," Delilah said. "The girl looks fabulous. You don't need to fatten her up." She nudged me. "That will happen when she has babies."

My jaw dropped slightly, and I stared at Callum, taking another deep breath and really hoping he saw how annoyed I was now that I was giving *him* the evil eye. My blood was boiling, and I was close to taking a knife and slicing them up the way Andrew had the turkey. Or jamming it into someone's throat. Or eye. Or head.

"I was just offering," Janice said. A few minutes later, she served dessert; mini steamed fruit puddings with ice cream. "Does anyone know where Susannah went?" she asked when we all pushed back from the table feeling bloated and full. We looked around. "Oh, she must have left," she said. "At least she could've told me."

"What did you expect, Mum?" Melissa asked. "You invited her here to set her up with Callum, and he arrived with a fiancée. I'd leave too." She grinned and started clearing plates.

"Melissa," she scolded. "I did not."

"Of course you did," Callum said with a grin. "You've tried to set us up before, and that failed too."

His mother turned bright red, but Callum and I looked at each other and laughed.

After lunch, she pulled us aside. "Darling here's your present." She handed him a brightly decorated box then looked at me. "I…well…we…"

"Didn't know I was coming, and so don't have anything for me. That's perfectly fine. I understand. Don't worry about it," I reassured her.

She smiled in relief.

Callum opened the box and pulled out a framed picture of him and his dad in their police uniforms.

Andrew came over and grasped his shoulder. "I haven't seen that picture in ages."

"Neither have I," Callum said. "Thanks, Mum." He kissed her.

We sat in the lounge and chatted for awhile, watching the children play with their toys. Callum joined in, his nephews falling all over him, his nieces convincing him to play dolls.

"He'll make a great father one day," Janice said in my ear.

She was sitting next to me on the couch drinking some sort of alcoholic beverage. I smiled and patted her hand. "I know. Don't worry, it will happen one day."

"Of course it will," Delilah said around her tenth glass of wine. Or was it twentieth? "Just look at those hips. She'll be popping out kids in no time."

"Aunt Delilah," Melissa chastised from the floor.

"What," she replied. "I said the same thing about you."

Shock crossed Melissa's face. "You said what?"

"I said you've got big hips and I was right. You popped three big male heads through those big wide loins of yours."

Bloody hell!

I tried to make myself as small as possible.

"Delilah, stop it," Sophie demanded. "You're making a fool of yourself."

"Hardly," she replied. "This is the way I am all the time."

I tried to hide a smile.

"What do *you* think, Tam? Doesn't Melissa have big hips?" Delilah asked.

"Don't bring me into this." I waved my hand in surrender.

"Well, it's true," she continued. "They run in the family."

"Delilah. I do not have big hips," Janice declared.

I extracted myself from between them on the couch and went over to play dolls with Jennifer and Michelle.

"Are you mar-ry-ig Uncle Callie?" Michelle managed to say.

"Michelle, Uncle Callum already told us they were getting married," Jennifer said.

I smiled at them. "Yes, I am."

"So, you will be our auntie. Like Auntie Melly. You will be Auntie Tammy."

Ugh, Auntie Tammy! I bit my tongue and smiled tightly. "That's right, sweetie."

Callum came over from playing with the boys, his hair all ruffled.

It brought a soft smile to my lips. "Hey."

"Hey." He returned the smile.

I began to tire and rubbed the side of my head and cheek.

"You okay?" Callum whispered in my ear.

I shook my head slightly. "Jack's really bad."

He checked his watch. "It's almost four."

"Can we go?" I whispered. "Head home and rest before going out again?"

"Sure." He planted a kiss on my cheek and helped me up. "We're going to go," he told everyone.

"Already," Janice panicked. "It's still early."

"It's almost four," Callum said. "Time for us to go."

"Four," Melissa yelped. "We have to get going too. We have to be at Michael's parents at four-thirty." She jumped up and started collecting the boys' toys.

"Mmm, same here," Liam said. "I mean Leslie's parents. Girls, get your stuff."

Janice looked depressed. "Can't you all stay a little while longer? Callum," she pleaded, "Tamara's parents aren't here are they? You can stay for dinner."

He shook his head. "Sorry, Mum, got plans for tonight."

We helped clean up so we weren't cutting and running on them, then those of us leaving piled upstairs to collect coats, hats, scarves, and bags before saying goodbye.

Janice handed me a container of food. "Take this. You can have it for leftovers, for dinner, or maybe lunch tomorrow."

I smiled and kissed her on the cheek. She was surprised. "Thank you," I said, taking the container and carefully placing it into my bag.

"Well, young lady, you certainly know how to stand up for yourself," Andrew said, shaking my hand. "Even if you were a tad rude in doing so."

Jeez, backhanded compliment much! "I try," I replied.

He gave me a hearty hug. "Look after my boy. Keep him well fed and in the police force somehow, even if it's the investigation section."

"I will. Don't worry. Your son is in good hands."

He turned to his son. "Callum."

"Dad." They hugged, then Callum swept his mum up into a big bear hug.

"Come and see us before you go," she said. "We don't see you enough."

"We will," he said, giving her a kiss.

We walked to the car, hugging and saying goodbye to Melissa and Michael, Liam and Leslie, and all of the kids before wearily hopping into the car. Heaving a big sigh, we looked at each other then buckled up and drove home.

After a two hour nap, we had a quick dinner and drove into town. It may have been Christmas, but the street was packed, with families and tourists, all wanting to see the lights and decorations adorning the city.

After managing to find a park, we started walking, and in no hurry, we made our way arm in arm up Oxford Street, taking our time, being dazzled by all of the window dressings, lights and carollers. Every part of the street that could be decorated was. It was a rainbow of colours that seemed to brighten the whole world.

Making our way toward Hyde Park, we crossed the road and entered, walking over to a huge group of people surrounding a rotunda. Singers sang carols, encouraging a mass of children to join in. They laughed and clapped and ran around screaming in excitement.

As I snuggled in Callum's arms, a man caught my eye. Standing in a group of adults, he was instantly recognisable, and seemed to be having a heated discussion with the others. He shook his head, waved his hands, and looked aggravated before walking to the side to make a phone call. Five minutes later, he snapped his cell phone shut, mumbled something, and turned in my direction. Once, twice, three times he looked.

I waved my fingers at him and smiled.

He stood staring, trying to figure out if he knew me, and upon noticing Callum, knew that he did and walked over with a huge grin on his face. "Hello, there."

"Hello." I grinned back.

"I'm Chris Simmons." We shook hands.

"Tamara Cainer."

"Tamara..." he said with a cocked brow, "look at you." He gave me the once-over. "You look great. How've you been?"

"Good. Doing a lot better than the last time you saw me." My head was nodding as I spoke.

"Well, that's good news. How's your Christmas in London been?"

"Ugh." Callum and I glanced at each other. "Good and bad..."

"Ah...like that is it?" Chris grinned.

"Yep."

"So, what's the good?"

I stuck out my hand.

He gaped. "Oh, my God, you're getting married," he said, giving me a big hug. "Congratulations, you two." He shook Callum's hand. "That's great. So, what's the bad then?" He frowned.

I breathed in deeply and let out a big sigh.

"It can't be that bad?" he said.

I nodded wearily. "I had Christmas lunch with the in-laws and they only just found out about me today."

"Aw, what." He laughed and looked at Callum. "Oh, my God, that's hilarious. So how'd it go?"

"A bit of a rocky start," Callum replied. "But things smoothed out, and it was okay."

"Aw," Chris looked at me. "They obviously didn't burn you at the stake or throw you out." His eyes flicked back and forth. "They didn't throw you out did they?"

"No, they didn't. It was..." I shook my head slowly. "An experience. And now we're down here just having some peace and quiet all to ourselves."

"You call this peace and quiet?" he said, looking at the crowd around us.

"Well, it's my first and probably *only* London Christmas. May as well take it all in."

"Absolutely," Chris agreed, shoving his hands into his pockets to keep them warm.

"So how come you guys are down here?" I asked.

"We donate our time for a charity that helps underprivileged kids and their families. We brought them down here to have some fun, and we were going to hand out teddy bears until the store we were getting them from decided to change their minds."

"Was that the heated discussion and phone call I saw?" I asked.

"Yeah," he said. "The bloody bastard pulled out at the last minute because he doesn't think they can afford to give away one hundred bears."

"Which store was it?" I asked.

"The one just back down Oxford. You'd think they'd want to do their bit for charity at Christmas and help out."

"It isn't easy for a small business to just give stuff away. Is there another store that might be able to help who wants to do good will at Christmas?" I glanced over my shoulder at the street behind us.

He scratched his head. "I don't know. Everyone's shut, and I don't know what to do. The kids will go without. It's just not bloody fair." He was pissed off.

I was angry too, looking at all the kids having fun who expected a teddy before heading home.

"How am I going to tell them?" His eyes followed my gaze.

"Where exactly was that shop?"

"Why?"

"Just tell me."

He pointed down the left side of Oxford, opposite the one we'd walked down.

"I saw a store on the other side. Quite large, had tonnes of teddies. Care for a quick walk?" I waited for his reply.

"What are you up to?" His eyes narrowed.

"Let's go." I linked my arm through his and pulled Callum along with the other. We walked back down the street to the toy store I'd seen earlier. "See." I pointed. "Tonnes of teddies."

"That's all well an' good though in'it." He indicated to the closed sign. "They're shut. It still doesn't work out for us. The kids still go without."

"Grumble bum," I muttered, reading the info on the door. "Mmm, I take it that's the number for the store, and there's no mobile. Callum." I turned and batted my eyes at him. "Can you do those hundred children a *really* huge favour?"

He caught on to where I was going and groaned. "Tam."

"Uncle Callie…" I drawled, batting my eyes faster.

"Uncle Callie?" Chris chuckled.

"It's what his nieces call him." I grinned.

Callum heaved a sigh. "What do you want?"

"Call one of the PCs you know, and get a private number for the owner so we can call and see if they'll come down and hand out teddies."

His expression was unreadable. "Are you kidding me?"

"No." My eyes batted.

"I can't do that."

"Why not?"

"It's not legal!"

I whispered something in his ear.

Ugh," he grunted and pulled out his phone.

"What did you say to him?" Chris inquired.

"Told him he wouldn't get any for the next month." I giggled.

"PC Knight, Sergeant Stone. I need you to do something for me. Check on the owner of Tacto's Toy Store in Oxford Street. I need their name and home number…mmm…that's right…just do it, PC Knight. Right, Jane and Alan Tacto…right…yes, that's right… thank you, PC Knight." He dialled the owner's number. "Hope you know what you're doing," he said.

I held out my hand for his phone. "Of course I do."

"Hello?"

"Hello, Mrs Tacto?"

"Yes."

"Merry Christmas. I'm standing out the front of your store in Oxford Street wondering how many of those gorgeous teddy bears you have."

"Excuse me?"

"I'm wondering how many of those gorgeous teddies you have, and if you'd like them to go to unfortunate children this Christmas night."

"Is this a crank call?"

"Not at all. I'm interested in your teddy bears, and quite a few other things I'd like, and want to know if you'd be willing to come down and open your store so those gorgeous teddies can make one hundred children's night."

"I'm sorry, but we can't afford to give them away to charity."

"Who said anything about giving them away?"

"You don't want us to give them away?"

"They're going to needy children, but I didn't say anything about giving them away." I saw Chris and Callum's faces as they caught on to what I was thinking. "I'm more than willing to pay if you're willing to come down and open your store for an hour or so. It will be well worth your while."

There were a few seconds of silence then, "Can you hold the line? I need to speak to my husband."

"Sure." I walked along the window staring at all the gorgeous toys.

"Are you there?"

"Yes."

"How do we know you're for real?"

"Well, I have Police Sergeant Stone and actor Chris Simmons with me. We'll all be here when you come."

Another silence.

"We'll be there in about fifteen minutes."

"We'll be waiting." I handed the phone back to Callum then asked Chris, "Can the kids wait another fifteen to thirty minutes?"

He glanced down the street toward the park then turned back. "If they know they're getting teddies they will. I'll run back and tell the other adults to hold them off a little longer." He started running for the park.

"Take your time," I yelled, "she said about fifteen minutes."

"You're really going to pay for all of those bears?" Callum asked, pulling me close.

"Of course." I snuggled under his chin.

"That's incredibly amazing of you." His arms tightened.

"Well, I died and won lotto. Not a problem giving back."

"I love you." He lifted my chin and kissed me.

"I love you." I kissed him back.

Chris arrived at the same time the owners did.

"You must be the woman I spoke to on the phone," Jane said, closing her car door.

"Yes." I grinned. "We want your teddies."

Alan Tacto unlocked the door. "This is highly unusual. Something we've never done before."

"First time for everything," I said, following him in. "And besides, it's for a good cause."

He locked the door behind us. "How many did you say you needed?"

"One hundred. Plus there's a few other things I've got my eye on."

"I'll go check the stock room." He walked out the back, and Jane asked what I was after.

I pointed to a large carousel and asked for three. "I'll take that massive carousel horse in the window. Does that go up and down?"

"Yes."

"Do you have another one?"

"Ah," she looked around. "There's one at the back of the store."

"I'll take them both. Plus those snow globes, that Christmas scene, all of those decorations, and this train set."

She gaped at me then ran around collecting it all.

"We have ninety out the back and…" Alan counted, "twenty on the shelf, so that's one hundred and ten."

"We'll take them all." I turned to Chris. "How do you want to do it? Bring all the kids down here, or carry the bears to the park?"

"I…" He shook his head. "Haven't even thought about it."

"Are the bears in bags, so we can carry them?" I asked Alan.

"Uh, the ones out the back are still in bags. There's about twenty in each. They're big bags."

"We can carry them," I told Chris. "Although you could get some of the boys down here. It will make it easier, then you can just put the bags in the rubbish bin."

"Great idea." He flipped his phone open.

Jane gathered all of the things I'd chosen, and while Alan tallied the bill, brought the bags of bears from the back.

"Do you have a bag for the twenty on the shelf," I asked. "We can start putting them in."

She got one, and we bagged the bears while Alan finished up on the register.

Sam and Alex arrived and knocked on the door.

"Cavalry's here," Chris called, and Jane opened the door for them.

"So, what's going on," Sam asked, seeing Callum and myself.

"We're getting bears," Chris said, pointing to the pile of bags. "Take two each, and we'll carry them back."

"Who's that?" Alex nodded in my direction. "She looks familiar."

"Oh, she's a very good friend of ours," Chris answered cryptically.

Sam and Alex exchanged confused glances.

"That's three carousels, two carousel horses, snow globes, train set, Christmas scene, decorations, and one hundred and ten bears…"

"Did you need any more bears? There's plenty out the back." Jane came into the store.

"There's more?" Alan and I asked simultaneously.

"I didn't see more," Alan added.

"They're hidden behind the big shelf. We didn't have anywhere else to put them, so they got stored there out of the way. There are loads of them, but they're smaller.

"Are they like those?" I pointed to the bagged bears.

"Yes, just half the size."

"How many?"

"Not sure, let me check." She searched the computer.

I glanced at Callum while we waited, and saw his huge grin. Chris had his own, and Sam and Alex still looked confused.

"Four hundred," Jane finally said.

"I'll take those too."

"What?" came the very shocked chorus.

I looked around at the astonished faces. "What? Surely you have a children's hospital full of children who'd like a teddy bear on Christmas night to snuggle up to?"

"Ahh," Callum said, catching on. "I know just the one."

"Can you get help to cart them over?" I asked.

"I can." He pulled out his phone while I paid for the goodies, then snapped it shut when he was done. "Help is on the way."

"Great." I put the receipt and my purse away. "Thank you very much," I told the Tactos. "We'll have to wait a few more minutes to load up the bears. Hope you don't mind?"

"Of course not. We'll get them for you."

"Great." I turned to Chris. "Can you big strong boys handle a few bags of teddies?"

Chris grinned from ear to ear and gave me a huge hug. "Of course we can. Thank you so much for this."

"Nah, don't worry about it. It's all for the kids." I opened the door, and they dragged the bags of bears out.

"Foxy's gonna be pissed that he missed you." Chris hauled a bag over his shoulder.

"Speaking of…" I grinned. "I never did find out if he took those balls I gave him. After all, they were a present."

Chris laughed heartily. "Nah, he didn't. Left 'em on the pool table."

"Pity, he so could've done with them." With a cheeky grin, I shut the door and watched as they walked away. From the looks on their faces, Sam and Alex finally realised who I was, and I was sure Chris would explain on the way.

Five minutes later, a police van pulled up outside, and Callum went out to greet the driver. "Tam, this is PC Davies. He runs the charitable section of the force, making sure everyone gets what they need, setting up fundraisers and toy runs."

"Nice to meet you." He shook my hand. "Callum, you've got something for me?"

"Yes." He pointed to the bags inside. "Four hundred teddies to go to the children's hospital."

He scratched his balding head. "That will take awhile, but I can get my reinforcements to meet me there and then we'll hand them out."

"Fantastic!" They shook hands. "Thanks for this."

We packed the bears into the van and watched it drive away.

"That's everything," I told Jane and Alan. "And my stuff will be delivered on the twenty-seventh."

"Absolutely," Alan said, setting the alarm and locking the door before we shook hands.

"Merry Christmas, and thank you," I said.

They drove off, and we walked back to the park to see one hundred kids with one hundred teddy bears.

Chris came over, carrying a half-full bag. "We've still got ten left; what do we do with them?"

The only kids who didn't have a bear seemed to belong to the boys. I nodded in their direction. "Hand them out amongst your own kids and partners."

He pulled a face. "Haven't got any, but I'll do that. Thanks again." He gave me a hug.

"Welcome," I called, watching him hand out bears to the kids.

"It's nine o'clock," Callum said. "What do you want to do now?"

"Go for a walk."

Arm in arm, we wandered through the park, marvelling at everything. It was good to be alive. Even if I had that incessant pounding in my head. I was alive and engaged to the most amazing man. Had money to do charitable things, and go shopping when I liked. It was bloody good to be alive.

<h1 style="text-align:center">Chapter 26</h1>

So, besides the fact Linda and I shopped till we dropped for two days *after* Christmas, New Year's Eve plans were also being talked about.

"New Year's Eve celebrations will once again centre on the London Eye and surrounding banks. We can expect the usual fireworks, but have found out that the Mayor plans on revealing something new this year. It won't be revealed, however, until New Year's Eve night, but we are told it will be very special."

Bob clicked off the TV. "Well, there's some news, so now you can narrow it down to the river bank around the Eye."

"Are they the only new gadgets for New Year's, do we know?" I asked as Callum massaged my calves, aching from two days of shopping.

"Sounds like it," Bob said, rummaging through the papers. "Yeah, it's all I can find."

"Well then, what's opposite the new surprise? Do we know exactly where it will be? Whatever's opposite will more than likely be it."

"Uh, from what I can remember of that area,

there's several restaurant's, function centres, and that club I arrested you in," Callum said.

"Where you arrested me," I remembered. "Those were the days." Everyone laughed. "Let's go through the pile of invites and whatnot and see if any are in the area." I looked at Bob. "Where *is* the pile anyway?"

"I think you have it."

"Oh." I dragged myself off the couch and ran upstairs to find the pile of papers. Spreading them on the coffee table downstairs, we started marking off everything that was irrelevant, leaving a rather thick pile of New Year's invites.

"What about…no…this one…no. Okay, it looks like every restaurant, bar, centre etc, on that street wants you for New Year's. I just don't know what's exactly opposite, though," Bob said as he sorted through them.

"Doesn't matter. Let's see what might interest me." I read a few papers and zeroed in on the one important one. "This is the club you arrested me in," I told Callum. "Apparently there's going to be every celebrity in London, and it's the biggest party in town. They want me to perform a concert for them."

"There's only four days to New Years," Linda said. "That's not enough time to get a concert together."

I thought about it. "Yes, it is. I can sing, only use a band occasionally for certain songs, same for dancers. I can whip together outfits from what I've bought, plenty of stuff. I've got my wigs, my swelling's gone down. There'd be just a few things I need. We can go see the manager tomorrow," I told Linda. "Hire dancers and a band. Get a song list and costume ideas together. Shouldn't be that hard, and we'll keep our eyes open for that bloody white spiky thing."

"Tam, are you sure?" Callum asked. "I know you've been better, but should you put yourself through the strain of getting a show together?"

"Do you think you can do it?" Linda added.

"We'll go see him tomorrow," I said, giving everyone a reassuring look.

*****

Linda and I turned up at the club at eight-thirty, and finding the place locked, we rang the number on the door. While Linda spoke to the manager, I walked over to the river bank and gazed out. To my left was the Eye and Big Ben, to my right I couldn't see as the glass function room of the club strut out over the water. I shivered, staring down into the murky depths of the Thames.

"He'll be here at nine." Linda stood beside me.

"Okay."

"Any more dreams?"

"Just the same."

"It will come to you."

I pulled my coat tighter against the cold wind. "I hope so." We waited in the car until the manager, Dick Dastard, arrived.

"Jewels, good to meet you. Glad you accepted my invitation. Doesn't leave you long to rehearse, though." He unlocked the huge double doors, and we went in.

Same coat check. Same bar along the wall on our

right. Same glass enclosed function room on our left. Same staircase in front of us.

"You were here that night, weren't you? You were arrested?" he asked, staring at the woman, so different to that night, before him.

I grinned wryly. "Yeah, that was me."

He led us over to the stage beside the stairs. "There's a backstage room for changing or waiting to go on. We also use it to move stage gear. There are change rooms as well, we have a great sound system, and I'm willing to pay for anything you want. Backup dancers, band, the works."

I walked up on stage and stood facing the empty room. "Who will be here?"

"Every TV, movie, music, reality star who's in town," he said, hands on hips.

I turned to my right and stared out of the floor-to-ceiling glass wall. It was three storeys high and showcased an impressive view. It also felt like the place I was meant to be. The stage wall stretched from the glass to the staircase so I couldn't see down the river to the right, but I could see the Eye and Ben.

"My talent co-ordinator deals with all our clients' needs. Anything you want, she'll get it for you."

"All right." I turned toward them. "Call her in. Call your sound engineer. I'll do a bit of a run through now, so I can get a feel for the stage, and when everyone's here, we'll talk details."

"Fantastic, Jewels." He shook my hand. "You won't regret this," he said, running off.

I turned back to the view. "I hope I don't," I

muttered, looking out at nothing. There was absolutely *nothing* opposite the club.

In the half hour it took for everyone to arrive, I'd written up a set list full of medleys, as there were so many songs I wanted to do, I wanted to try and fit them all in, and that seemed to be the only way to do it. I had ideas for lighting and staging and figured out some simple and easy dance steps that I would have the energy for.

"Hi, I'm Tina the talent co-ordinator." A redhead full of pep introduced herself.

"Hi," I said. "Let's get down to business."

She listened to my ideas, made a few suggestions, and walked me through backstage. We rejigged the plans a bit then she went off to hire dancers and a band while I spoke to the sound engineer. He gave me a microphone, and I sang a few songs. Hearing the backing track come up behind me, I got into the music. The stage was strong and non-slippery, and I was able to see all three levels of the club easily.

"You sound fantastic," Dick congratulated, coming out to see how we were going. "Would you like some lunch? It's twelve."

My stomach grumbled. I'd forgotten about eating and needed to take a pill. "Sure, something good I hope." I grinned.

"Only the best for my New Year's talent," he said, leading us to a table on the first floor where we enjoyed a meal of rib eye steak and thick chips covered in delicious gravy, and chatted about the show and ideas.

"Most of what you want will be easy to get," Tina

said. "Since you don't want a lot of sets, we can probably find them in a stage warehouse somewhere." She sipped her wine.

"That's good," I said. "I want things simple. Part me on my own, part dancers, part band. Everyone learns their parts, and we should be able to get it done in the next three days."

Four male and four female dancers arrived after lunch, along with a five piece band consisting of twenty-something looking guys.

I stood before them. "Okay, everyone. I'm Jewels Diva, I'm going to be singing, and you guys will be dancing or playing." I handed the set list to the band. "That's the order the songs you'll be playing are in." I handed a list to the dancers. "You guys will only be dancing for three and a half sets, and not every song. Now, are you just dancers or is one of you a choreographer?"

"I am." A tall Asian guy put his hand up.

"Your name?'

"Tim."

"Great, Tim, what I want is to copy the film clips for most parts, but we will also add our own steps. I want it simple and quick to learn." I turned to the band. "Can you guys set up on stage?" They lugged their instruments over, and I gathered the dancers. "Can any of you sing?" They did. "Great. You'll be doing backup vocals as well. Now, the sound engineer is getting the songs together, and this is the exact order I want them in. We'll dance just for the ones highlighted, and I have these ideas." I started pointing out spots on stage, suggesting coming down into the audience for some songs, showing them a few dance steps. By the time five p.m. rolled around, we had sung some vocals, and Tina had a costume shop turning up in the morning. We agreed to meet at nine sharp and then went our separate ways.

*****

"How'd it go?" Callum dished out his roast beef and mash meal as I sat at the table.

I shovelled some in my mouth. "Mmm, good." I took another spoonful of mash and gravy. "Dick is willing to do anything to have me and is paying for everything. Anything I want."

"Have you been paid?" Bob asked, slicing some beef.

"Half now, half later."

"Hope you did a deal. I read his offer. You could've gotten more."

"Oh, I did." I grinned. "Have you met Linda, my fantastic negotiator?"

Bob looked at his wife. "What do you mean?"

"Well," I drawled. "She mentioned how other venues wanted me, and what they were offering, and Linda the fantastic negotiator managed to get Dick Dastard to up his fee."

"So…how much?" Bob asked, his fork stopping in mid-air.

"Five hundred."

"Thousand?" he gasped. "Are you serious?" His jaw hit the floor.

"Are you serious?" Callum added, his own face full of shock.

"Yes," I said. "It can go to the children's hospital."

"Wh-what?" Bob stuttered.

"Well, I don't need it," I said simply, watching the stunned expression still on Bob's face. "Don't worry, Bobby, what you need to be doing is getting the publicity out that I'm doing the show and donating the money."

"Um, ah, yeah," he stuttered.

"So, besides all that," Callum interjected. "What about the spiky thing. Did you see anything that might reveal a few clues?"

"There was absolutely nothing across the river from the club. I couldn't see anything to the right; the view was blocked off, and there was nothing covered up to the left. So, unless there's something else we're not finding, then I have no idea."

*****

My Adventures in Merry Old England: December 28th, 2011

Well, peeps, Christmas went well, so did the shopping. I think I've shopped London out. Just letting you know I've decided to do a concert for New Year's Eve at the same club I was arrested in. That's right, going back to the scene of the crime, ha, ha. Well, one of them anyway. The money I'm getting for the show is going to the children's hospital, so don't listen to anything anyone else says.

IT WILL GO THERE.

Only two more days, plus New Years' eve itself, to rehearse, and no I haven't figured out what that white spiky thing is. We're going to record the show and might release it on DVD for all to buy. So, until then peeps, hope you are shopped out. I am.

Jewels xxoo

*****

Linda and I were at the club before nine, and watched the dancers and band roll in, and then we got to work. 'Cause it was going to be a long day.

Tim had scoured the film clips to the songs and come up with simpler versions of the dance routines. The sound engineer popped the music on, and we rehearsed, with me thanking God three hours later that they were not only good, but professional as well. We'd clicked, and that was good.

After lunch, Tina rolled in racks of costumes, and with some mixing and matching, we came up with the perfect outfits.

"These are fantastic," I said, looking at the dancers in their first set costumes. "How do they feel?"

"Good."

"Great."

"Snug."

"Think you can dance in them?"

"Only one way to find out," someone said.

With the backing track, we went through a set from beginning to end. We had the songs down pat, our vocals blended, and the steps were easy.

"That's great, guys. Put those outfits aside and make sure you have your name on them. I need to take a break." I struggled over to Linda.

"Are you okay? You look sick." She helped me sit on a bar stool.

"I feel sick," I whispered. "My head is pounding. Jack's splitting it in half. I need something to eat so I can take a painkiller." My hands were shaking.

The barman got me a burger, and I rested for half an hour. "Tina, let's get the other costumes sorted. Can you wheel the racks over?"

"Sure." She set them up in front of me.

"Okay, that leather thing with those feathers on you." I pointed to a blonde dancer named Rochelle. "That yellow outfit on you. Tim, take that one. You," I pointed to a guy, "take those pants and that top. That leather jacket on you." I pointed to another. We soon had it all figured out, and they tried them on. "Okay, great. Add those to your other costume. We just need one more." Mixing and matching, we came up with the third costume. "Make sure your name's on every item you'll be wearing, so there's no confusion on Saturday night. We can't have anything go missing." I turned to Tina. "Thanks for all of this."

"My pleasure," she said. "It's all rather exciting isn't it?"

I grinned tiredly at her enthusiasm. "It is. We won't need the rest of the clothes so you can send those back." The dancers came over. "Tim, can you lead everyone through the next set? I have to practise with the band. We'll go over our stuff tomorrow. Go down to the other end of the room if you want, or even up on the second floor, there's no carpet."

"Sure."

Linda helped me over to the stage, and I sat on the edge. "Okay, let's go over the first set." The band was good and had picked up the songs quickly, and with a few adjustments, the first set went well, and we stopped just before six. "Okay, guys. That was great," I called, gathering everyone. "Dick will let us stay until nine tomorrow night to get in some rehearsal time. Be here at eight-thirty tomorrow morning 'cause on Saturday we'll have to do a full dress rehearsal, okay? Everyone knows what they're doing?"

"Yes."

"Great, see you all tomorrow." Linda and I walked out and got in the car. "God, my head hurts," I whispered.

"Has it been this bad all the time or just today?" Linda asked, turning into traffic.

"It's been bearable." I frowned and rubbed my head. "But today's just a bitch." I sighed. "I hope tomorrow's better."

"I'll get you home, get you some dinner, and then you can have a nice hot shower and an early night," Linda said.

"Ha! I'll be lucky if it's early."

We pulled up outside the house and Callum came out to greet us. "How was it?"

"My head or the rehearsal." I fell out of the car and he caught me.

"Hey, you don't look good. Let's get you inside." He swung me into his arms and carried me into the kitchen. "We'll get you some food then I'll take you upstairs."

I sat in a zombie state while they prepared dinner. I sat in a zombie state while we ate. I was in a zombie state when Callum carried me upstairs and into the bathroom.

"Come on, snap out of it," he said standing me up and pulling off my clothes. "Get in the shower, then we'll get you into bed."

I managed to shower and not fall down. I managed to wash my face and brush my teeth and not fall down. Callum led me to bed and tucked me in.

He lay beside me and swept my hair out of my face. "You look awful. Should you be doing the show? It's wearing you out, and you've only just started."

I gazed up at him, not even hearing his voice. I just saw his mouth move and the loving, concerned look in his eyes. "Ugh," I mumbled. My eyes closed and I was a zombie…

Gurgle, gurgle, gurgle.
Terrified screams tore through the night.
Gurgle, gurgle, gurgle.
Shouting bounced off the river walls.
Gurgle, gurgle, gurgle.
The bright white spiky thing sat staring at me. Daring me to figure out what it was.
Gurgle, gurgle, gurgle.
Fireworks lit up the black sky as bright as day.
00:00:12

It blinked before my eyes.

00:12:12

It kept flashing, urgently trying to tell me something.

12:12:12

The bright white spiky thing was completely lit. All the little spikes all in a circle.

The screams died…

The shouting stopped…

We drowned…

Beep beep. Beep beep. Beep beep.

My eyes slowly opened on another day.

What day is it?

Don't know.

The beeping stopped.

What day is it? Am I supposed to know? I'm so tired, and Jack's pounding. Stop that, you little bastard! Stop it! Why are you worse? Why are you doing this to me when you've been good for the last couple of weeks? Why are you being an arsehole, Jack? Huh? What's that? It's not your time to go yet. What the fuck does that mean? What? You plan on hanging around for another six months to piss me off and be a pain in my arse? I know you're in my head, not my arse, I was making a point! But why are you worse, Jack? I've been able to manage you, to dull your aching roar to a tiny meow. But that's not happening now. No! Not happening at all. And now you're pounding away in the side of my head. Do you have enough yet? What I mean is, you've chipped away enough of my head you could build a new person. I'd like to be a new person. With no pain. No aches. No worries. Will I ever be a new person again? What? Not while you're in my head. Yes, you little bastard. I get that. So looks like I need to get you out again. But how am I going to do that?

"Tam."

You actually talk?!

"Tam."

Jack?!

"Wake up, Tam. You've got early rehearsals."

"Ugh," I groaned. "Go away."

Callum flung back the covers, and I tried to burrow deeper. "Get out of bed and have a shower. You've got rehearsals."

With a big fat complaining groan, I hauled myself off the bed, and into the bathroom, then dressed, and dragged my bag behind me down the stairs.

"Oh, you don't look good." Linda stopped short and stared.

"I feel like crap." I sat down at the table.

She placed a plate of food in front of me.

"Ugh. I feel sick." I grabbed my head with my hands.

"Tam." Callum rubbed my back. "If you have to pull out of this, then do it. Your health is worth more than a performance."

I took a few deep breaths and looked up. "No. I'm doing it. I don't know why I'm so sick, it's mainly Jack. He's twice as bad as he used to be. I need to do this." I saw his concern and swallowed two painkillers with my food. "I have to do this. Any more news on New Year's?"

"Just the usual, same as the other day. Won't reveal anything until the night," Bob said.

"Have you had the dream again?" Linda asked.

"Last night." I finished off my juice.

"Is that why you don't look good?" Callum asked.

"Meh!" I shrugged. "It's still the same, pretty much. White spikes, fireworks, screams, yelling, water, but twelve kept flashing before me. Twelve, twelve, twelve. Same as last time." I sighed deeply. "So, it definitely has something to do with New Year. It's something new, it will happen after midnight, and if that thing down the river is the only thing it could possibly be, then something's gonna happen down river on New Year's Eve. Something bad."

"Should I get someone to check it out?" Callum asked.

"I don't think that would reveal or solve anything." I shook my head.

*****

Linda and I met everyone at eight-thirty, and for the next four hours went over my sets with the band. It was only two, but they needed to be spot on. After lunch, and more painkillers, the dancers and I went through every step of our sets. By dinner, we had it down.

I stood staring out the glass wall at London lighting up, trying to figure out where and what. I knew the Eye would be prominent, but there was nothing around it on the river bank, or across from the club that was covered, or looked anything like my spiky circle.

"You *will* figure it out." Linda stood beside me and gave me a hug.

I sighed. "I know."

For the next two hours, we checked the lighting and sound system, the sound of the band, where the spotlights would be, and when to follow us into the audience. Everyone else cleared off the stage, and we set up for the last two songs. It would just be me and something very special, and Tina had managed to come through with the set. After I'd suggested changes, and they were fixed, we called it a night.

"Okay, everyone," I called. "Be here at nine. We'll do a full rehearsal in the morning and if needed, one in the afternoon. Then we'll have a rest before the show. And listen, get a good sleep tonight. Tomorrow's going to be a long day."

We said goodbye and headed home, where I fell into Callum's arms, and he carried me in.

"We're taking a holiday after this," he said, setting me down in the kitchen for a late snack.

"Just give me food and painkillers," I mumbled. "And some hot sex."

He grinned. "Here, drink this." He placed a mug of hot thick soup in front of me and massaged my shoulders while I drank. "One more day of this, and we'll be able to stop and go away again. Have some peace and quiet."

"Mmm," I murmured, draining my soup. "Drink?"

He poured me a Pepsi Max, and pulled a Cornetto ice cream from the freezer.

"Oooh, dessert."

"Should you be mixing hot with cold?"

I shrugged. "The soup will melt the ice cream. Mmm." The chocolatey goodness melted in my mouth, and I closed my eyes, savouring the cold molten lava flowing down my throat.

"You get that look on your face when we make love."

I opened my eyes. "Mmm?" My brows flew up, and I giggled. "Well, the experts do say chocolate is the next best thing to sex."

"Mmm," he grumbled. "Finish up and let's go."

Five minutes later, we were in the shower making love as Callum soaped my body and tried to prove the experts wrong about the whole chocolate thing. I clung to him, my back pressed against the wall as he thrust. My nails dug into his shoulders, my legs locked around his waist.

"Oh…ah…uh…"

Standing under the pouring water, he rinsed us off. He gently dried me, then himself, and carried me to the bed, where he pulled me into his arms and held me tight.

Chapter 27

"Okay, everyone, let's rehearse this from start to finish. Can you close the window please, we need darkness? Mack, got the soundtrack ready?" He gave the thumbs up. "Lights, dancers, stage. Let's do this," I called.

Backstage was a mess of sliding platforms for the band, sets for the dancers, and an area to change. God, it was bedlam.

"Jewels Diva, New Year's Eve concert in five… four…three…two…one…"

The music started, and I sung my heart out, ran backstage, and changed for the second set. It happened that way for the next two and a half hours then I finished off with my finale.

"And we're done," Mack said.

"Time for lunch. Let's go over the issues," I said, and we sat upstairs munching on protein and carbs trying to fuel up for the show.

"There was an issue with lighting, but that was fixed at the time."

"The music came off well, and we timed it right with the changes."

"Yeah." I nodded. "That was good." Turning to the dancers and band, I added, "Is everyone okay with the costume changes?"

"Yes," came the chorus.

"Do we need to rehearse again? I want it to be perfect," I said, glancing from face to face.

"Jewels, you don't want to wear yourself out," Linda said softly in my left ear.

"No," Mack said. "It looked perfect. Sounded perfect. Go home and get some rest. We've managed to pull this together in three days. That's quite a feat."

"Just want it to be perfect," I murmured, feeling more than weary.

"Let's get you home," Linda said.

"Everyone go home and rest." Tina motioned to the band. "Be back at six sharp."

Linda pulled me outside to the car, and when we got home and walked through the door, Bob and Callum met us.

"It's definitely happening tonight, and it's the one three doors down from the club. Apparently, it's going to play a big part in the celebrations," Bob said.

I stared glassily at them. "Right now, I really don't care. Just want to sleep." I bashed my head. "Stop it, you little bastard," I yelled.

"Tam." Callum pulled my hand away. "Let's get you to bed." He walked me upstairs, undressed me, and tucked me into bed, gently massaging my neck and shoulders, trying to help me fall asleep.

I don't know how long I lay there awake, but I finally drifted off…

Gurgle, gurgle, gurgle.
00:00:12
Gurgle, gurgle, gurgle.
00:12:12
Gurgle, gurgle, gurgle.
12:12:12
Gurgle, gurgle, gurgle.
12:12:12

I woke up drained and lay there trying to will myself to move. *Why is this happening? Will it stop tonight? Will it affect my performance? Why are you back, Jack? Get the fuck away.* I rubbed my head. *Why are you back? Go away.*

Glancing at the clock, I saw it was only five, and I had to be at the club at six. *Oh, God, do I really want to do this? Do I really* need *to do this?* I sighed. *I feel sick. Do you feel sick Jack? Or is it you making me sick?* I felt like vomiting. I rolled out of bed and over to my laptop.

My Adventures in Merry Old England: December 31st, 2011

Well, peeps. It's my show tonight. I've been told some of the names who'll be there. Big TV, music and movie stars. I plan on taking photos and posting them. My publisher and his wife will be there taking pics as well while I'm performing. I've been sick as a dog the last couple of days. Jack's back and wreaking havoc just like he was back then. I wish he'd piss off. Hope your New Year is good peeps, mine may not be.

Jewels xxoo

"What are you doing?"

I jumped, and Callum came up behind me. "Don't sneak up on me, you scared me."

"Sorry." He pulled me up and kissed me. "We need to get you ready."

I sighed and shook my head. "I don't feel ready."

We had a light dinner and then bundled my case into the car. I'd come up with my own outfits from bits and pieces I'd bought, and items from the costume shop. Bob and Linda were picking Megan up, so Callum drove me to the club. I kept my eyes closed on the way, trying to keep Jack down to a dull roar. The car stopped, and I opened my eyes to see we were in the club's car park facing the river. The Eye lit up the sky to our left. We got out and walked toward the door, but I stopped and stared across the murky water to the other side.

Nothing.

Absolutely nothing.

I glanced at Callum, and we went inside.

"Oh, there you are." Tina came running. "You were supposed to be here half an hour ago. Everyone's backstage ready to move. Let's get you back there now." She held out her arm, waiting to escort me.

I turned to Callum. "I think Megan's going to be filming stuff, and Bob and Linda's got my camera as well as their own. Can you stay with them at all times, just in case?" I smoothed down his royal blue shirt. He looked devastatingly gorgeous in his black suit and new Christmas watch.

"Sure." He hugged me. "Don't worry, everything will be okay. You'll remember, just have a good show."

I took a deep breath, let it out in a whoosh, and said, "I'll try," before I started to follow Tina. "Oh, and try and keep the boys together," I called over my shoulder. "We might need their help."

"Okay, you just go and have a good show." He waved, and the door closed.

"Let's get you to your room." Tina led me to the dressing room I'd have to myself. It was small, but spacious, with a couch on the wall to the left, and a mirror with light bulbs across the top and a vanity to the right.

"There's a toilet and shower in here." She opened the door at the back of the room.

"Great. I'll grab a shower afterwards." I sat my bag on the vanity and saw my reflection in the mirror. Ugh!

"I'll go and grab you a dress rack, and we'll get your costumes ready. Everyone else is doing the same." She walked off, and I stuck my head out the door. The dancers were sharing rooms down the hall to my right, and I popped in to say hello. "Girls."

Rochelle and Noelle looked up in surprise and smiled. "Hey."

"Are you right sharing in pairs?" I asked.

"Sure," they said.

I looked across the hall. The boys were two to a room as well. "Tina said you're getting your costumes ready."

Tim grinned. "Not that we get to wear much." The other dancers came into the hall.

I laughed softly. "Well, we needed to make you look good while baring a little skin, same with the girls. No need to flash everything, just the best bits. At least there's only three changes."

"That's right," said Rochelle. "You have seven outfits. You've got it harder than us."

I grinned. "Thankfully, the first isn't too detailed, and the last is pretty simple. So, if you feel like helping me into mine when you aren't getting into yours, feel free."

"Everyone, it's seven. We have one hour left. Start getting into your outfits, emptying your stomachs, and taking a leak," Tina called.

We all looked at each other and burst out laughing.

"You guys, make sure you have your costume list, and mark off every piece as it goes on and off. We don't want any missing bits," she added.

"Okay."

I headed back to my room, feeling the excitement build. Butterflies flew around in my stomach, and Jack merrily chipped away in my head. I unzipped my case and started setting out my costumes. "This one first," I murmured. "This second. Where are the boots?" There was a wire shelf on the bottom of the rack, and I laid out each pair of shoes under the costume. "Third, fourth, fifth, where's six, oh, there you are, and seven." I added the accessories, wigs and hairpieces, hats and other things I would need, then packed up my bag and case, making sure everything was easy to get to in my ten or twelve minute change time.

"Forty-five minutes," Tina fretted.

"Get out so I can change." I gently shoved her out the door. After quickly laying out my clothes, I slipped on the first costume, a long white flowing dress-style robe with wide sleeves. I pulled on a long gold red wig, and then grabbed my bottle of super-duper latex make-up, spraying it on, adding false eyelashes, mascara, and a little bit of blush, so I didn't look pale.

Tina barged in. "Twenty minutes, wow you look good."

"Everyone else ready?"

"Dancers dressed and warming up vocals. Band too."

I checked myself in the mirror, made some adjustments, took a last look over the costumes and walked out the door. Backstage, I climbed into a harness that was going to provide a very special effect in the last song of the first set, and slid on the headset with mic.

"Ten minutes," Tina yelled.

I could hear the crowd through the curtains, and suddenly my nerves quivered. I felt like I needed to pee, vomit, and have diarrhoea all at the same time.

"Jewels, my girl. The house is packed." Dick walked up to me. "Everyone who's anyone in London is here, and the idea of seeing you perform is exciting them."

"That's great," I muttered as he slapped me on the back. "The camera's in place to record it all?"

"Absolutely. Your publisher made sure his people were ready to get all the footage from every angle."

"Five minutes," Tina yelled. "Jewels get on stage."

"I'll let you go, Jewelsie baby, have a great one." Dick walked off, and Tina pushed me on stage.

I sat on a box style platform I'd be using for some of the set.

"Two minutes," Tina yelped, losing her voice.

"You're more nervous than I am," I said, noting my nerves had disappeared.

"Oh, oh, oh," she choked, running off stage as the workers put the set in place.

The stage went dark, and I was eerily calm. Mist wafted across in front of me, behind me, all around me.

"Ladies and gentlemen. Until last month, no one had heard of this woman," Dick said to the room full of people. "Until two weeks ago, we didn't know she could sing. And until just this very week, she didn't accept the invitation to play a New Year's Eve concert. So…I am very, very pleased that she accepted ours since about five and a half weeks ago she was arrested in this very club by the one and only Sgt Stone who is in our audience." I heard the cheers and tried to stop myself from laughing at the image of Callum blushing beet red. "So, not only has this young lady gotten quite a reputation since being in this country, but this club has gotten quite a reputation since having her here. So, without further ado, on this New Year's Eve night, I'm presenting to you. Jewels… Divaaa…"

The crowd went nuts, and the curtains slowly opened. The huge glass window was covered on the ground floor, making the room seem ominously dark. I sat calmly, spotting the sound engineer's lights at the back of the room. Mist swirled all around, and the first strings of *Iris* by the Goo Goo Dolls wafted along with it. It was just me and that song. I didn't really notice the audience since the room was mostly dark and still. I mixed it with *Chasing Cars* by Snow Patrol. The lyrics and melody blended smoothly.

The song ended, and there was minimal applause as I launched into a shortened version of *Power of Love* by Jennifer Rush, and that was mixed with *If You're Not the One* by Daniel Beddingfield. The whole point of the show was to tell a story from go to whoa, and I was starting off as an angel singing love songs. The soft white lights shone on me as I sang, making the whole performance ethereal and dramatic. I wanted it to be simple, elegant, understated because that wasn't how the show was going to end. I also knew I could turn people off, especially the guys.

Shania Twain's *From This Moment* mixed with Savage Garden's *I Knew I loved You* followed. Most of the songs were either about my feelings for Callum or about life in general. I had almost been an angel twice, and I thought I'd start the show on a note of memorandum.

I sang a mash-up of Bruno Mars' *Just the Way You Are,* and Lonestar's *Amazed,* Kelly Clarkson's *Breakaway* came next, which brought me to my feet after the song's bridge. The lights never faltered, and neither did my voice. Now and then tears fell. The emotion in the songs were hitting a nerve inside. Duran Duran's *Save a Prayer* followed, with Thirsty Merc's *All My Life,* and Josh Groban's *You Are Loved* and *February Song.*

I sat back down, and the stage crew quickly clicked something very special into place on my back, then I ended the set with Robbie Williams' *Angels* into Beyoncé's *Halo.* Only one spotlight stayed on me, illuminating my face and chest. I finished singing the words before the crescendo, and the big light went out, so only the music filtered all around. Little fairy lights twinkled from a sheer curtain hanging behind me, the notes rose, I stood, and my wings expanded, the whole stage was drenched in white lights, and I burst into the pre-chorus. The crowd cheered, I sang my heart out, and as the crescendo hit the final notes, I was lifted upwards. The harness I'd pulled on earlier was also attached to ropes that hauled me up. I floated above the stage singing the final words, and with the last beat of the music, the lights went out.

The curtains closed and I was yanked off stage. Off came the wings, off came the harness.

"Quick, go and change," Tina squealed.

I raced to my dressing room, and while I pulled on outfit number two, Tina packed away outfit number one. I changed wigs and ran back out to see the band already on stage. I walked on and stood at the front of the semicircle they'd formed. This set was to be a little intimate, close to the front of the stage and giving a similar feel to the performance we were paying tribute to.

The curtain opened, and the band played the first notes of *Viva Las Vegas* Elvis Presley style. I had the black leather suit and boots on. I had the slicked back black wig on. I thrust my hips through *Burning Love* and a short version of *Little Less Conversation*. The crowd bounced, the band played, and I strutted my stuff. I could see to the back of the room, pointed to the crowd upstairs, and gave it my all. We calmed down for *Can't Help Falling in Love*, which I sang to Callum, who blushed. He was standing near the front of the stage with Bob, Linda, and Megan. Some of the boys were there too, with Chris Simmons and Christopher Fox front and centre. For something a little different, we mixed in Bruno Mars' *Grenade* and *Runaway Baby,* and Darren Hayes' *Can't Ever Get Enough of You* and *Insatiable*. We finished off with Elvis again, with *Always On My Mind* and *You Don't Have to Say You Love Me.*

We rushed backstage, and I changed into my blue and pink pantsuit with matching silk shirt, high-heeled brogues and fedora. I rushed back, joined by the dancers in similar suits, and we stepped into our formation.

The curtain opened, and we went into Stan Walker's *Choose You*. The dancers were great singers and fell into harmonies perfectly. Kenny Loggins' *Footloose* came next, and they threw their hats into the audience halfway through. Toward the end, two male dancers grabbed my arms and legs and rocked me back and forth like a cradle. It was all very exciting and brought gasps from everyone.

Britney Spears' *Womaniser* and *If You Seek Amy* blended into Ke$ha's *Take It Off,* which had us ripping off pieces of clothing. Pants gave way to shorts; blazers gave way to corsets over see-through blouses. A mash-up of Pussycat Dolls' *When I Grow Up*, *I Will Survive* and *Flirt* came on, and at one point during the song I got down in front of the crowd and gyrated, giving Chris Fox an eyeful of breast and crotch, and we used the male dancers as fodder for the lyrical bitching. We launched into Gabriella Cilmi's *Don't Wanna Go to Bed Now* and *On a Mission*, and blasted everyone away with Aneiki's *Breathing Sin* and Noiseworks' *Just A Little Bit More*. We also got in a rock version of Bonnie Tyler's *I Need A Hero*, and ended with a mix of Kelly Clarkson's *My Life Would Suck Without You* and Katy Perry's *I Kissed a Girl*, which had all of us girls getting off on each other and getting very cosy.

A big gulp of drink and a costume change, and we were back on stage for the first notes of Adam Lambert's *For Your Entertainment*. I had the same outfit on that I'd worn the night I was arrested; blue leather pants, corset jacket, and stud and chain boots. My hair extensions were in, and I had a little top hat sitting jauntily on my head. We mashed the song up with Robbie Williams' *Let Me Entertain You*, and mashed it well.

There were plenty of breasts on show, to the delight of the many men in front of the stage. The dancers were dressed similarly, and during Adam's *Fever*, I was lifted into the audience so I could strut my stuff around the room. Stopping to sing to *Top Gear's* Richard Hammond I shook my booty against him and moved on, leaving Jeremy and James laughing their heads off, and Richard looking remarkably embarrassed.

I sang to a good looking guy down the back of the room before making my way up the other side. In between lyrics, I told Simon Cowell to get a new haircut, and ran into Adam Lambert himself. He joined me for a chorus and then my dancers lifted me back on stage where we launched into Powderfinger's *Burn Your Name.*

Adam's *Pick U Up* came next, and I surprised everyone with the way I belted it out in the key change. Even Adam was impressed. During the instrumental interlude, I spied David Tennant at the front of the stage and grabbed his hair. "Oh, David Tennant," I groaned.

"Darling."

"When are you going to park your Tardis in my bush? You're most welcome you know."

"I'd love to darling, but I'm gay."

"No, you're not!"

"Yes, I am."

"*Fuck you.*" I was surprised. "You *are* not!"

"I am."

"Well, fuck me," I said and ruffled his hair. "Don't worry. Plenty of others here will." I went back to the song and finished it off.

Adam's *If I had You*, my fave song, was just as eventful. Between the chorus and second verse, the male dancers parted the sea of guests before me and lifted me back down to the floor. We danced along to the song and made our way into the middle of the room. There was a camera on a wire above us, and we kept singing into it as it was able to change directions as we moved.

Slowing down for the bridge, Tim stood behind me so I could sing to him, and with a burst into the chorus, he bent down and lifted me above his head. I was on my back facing the roof, and he spun me around for sixteen beats. I cocked my left leg under my right, and around his right hip, and as he swung me down, we kept on spinning with my legs wrapped around his waist. I was still facing the ceiling as he lifted me up and I slid down his body. We stayed joined and danced wildly as we launched into Dead or Alive's *Spin Me Round*.

Through loud cheers, we heard Transvision Vamp's *I Want Your Love*. Making our way to the stage, I sang to whoever I came across. Simon Cowell was not impressed by me singing *I Don't Want Your Money*. I strutted past Piers Morgan, some guy I didn't know, the new and old Doctor Who, David and Matt Smith, and we ended the song on stage mixing it with Justin Bieber's *Somebody to Love*.

A medley of Aussie bands followed. Madison Avenue's *Who the Hell Are You*. Jet's *Are You Gonna Be My Girl?* and Savage Garden's *I Want You*. The last songs were Short Stack's *Planets* and *We Dance to a Different Disco*, and Invertigo's *Damage Control*, which seemed to suit the world I was looking at. Our hand movements started off all nice and polite at the beginning of the song, but in the last chorus, we were going full bore, imitating wanking ourselves, snorting coke, and grabbing our breasts. They all seemed so impressed.

"Only two more sets to go," Tina squeaked backstage.

I pulled on my hat as she packed the last outfit away. "Don't tell me, just let me get through it."

The girls and I took our spots on stage as the boys were having a rest in this set. "This set is a little special," I said into the mic. "I'm paying tribute to a force that needs thanks, and the boys from *The Bill* will get a kick out of it."

Strains of Aussie band Skyhook's *Women in Uniform* thundered out across the room, and there I was in my cop uniform. Baggy black pants, white shirt, tie, vest, belt and hat, I had another wig on, a dark red fringed long bob that came straight down to my shoulders. Sunglasses and police boots finished the outfit.

The boys cheered, standing at the front of the stage. I was the only cop as this was a special set. We had an Indian, a biker, an army and navy member in our midst. I swung my baton around and gave it all I had, gyrating against it, hitting my arse with it, doing very dirty things with it.

The lights went out, and I quickly ripped off my pants, vest and tie to reveal tight leather pants that came up under my breasts to a built-in corset. My boots came up to my knees, and I pulled my shirt undone and apart to reveal my red bra covered breasts.

We grabbed mic stands and lined up for the next three numbers. The music started. "Okay," I said. "I know most of you old farts will know this song, so I expect to see your geriatric arms do the motions." I got a few laughs out of that one. Village Peoples' *YMCA* belted out of the speakers. "Come on and do it," I yelled doing the arm movements myself.

I threw in a few choice words between the lyrics. 'It's a paedophile's paradise' 'or whoever you feel'. Those words didn't go down well at all, but dressing like a cop was putting me in a defiant mood, and I defied anyone to stop me. I saw Callum shake his head every time I said something. I shrugged and kept singing. *Macho Man* blended in, and we gyrated under soft backlights, so we appeared as shadows to the audience. We burst into the lyrics and kept gyrating. I walked to the left of the stage. I strutted to the right. I thrust my pelvis to the boys up front. Grabbing our mic stands we sang *You Can't Stop the Music,* mimicking the movie's choreography.

Pink's *U + R Hand* followed with insanely rude hand gestures. I flipped the bird, spanked my arse, danced around, and shoved my hand on my crotch. So did the other dancers. We mashed it with her song *Ave Mary A* where I belted it with every ounce of emotion I had. The Killers' *Somebody Told Me,* Darren Hayes' *Forgive You,* and Duran Duran's *Electric Barbarella* made the audience high on life. We ended the set with Indecent Obsession's *Kiss Me* and *My Reflection,* and Def Leppard's *Action.* I thrashed my head around. I got down on my knees. I was really feeling the music and throwing my whole self into it, and the whole crowd was too. Hands were in the air. I called out to those on the first floor, waved to those on the second, and threw all I had into the performance.

I left the stage dripping with sweat, and like I had a dry rag in my mouth. "Water," I gasped, pulling off my costume as I ran for the change room. I gulped down an energy drink as Tina packed the outfit and towelled me off. Slamming down the bottle, I pulled off the wig and dried my head, then grabbed the wig I owned. I valiantly yanked on my skin-tight short suit, slipped my arms in, and pulled the zip up to under my breasts. I zipped up the crotch high red leather boots and made sure my tail was attached, then I completed the outfit with bright red lipstick and a devil horn headband.

Backstage, the dancers helped me into a long funky cape and headpiece. They'd only be joining me for the first half, then the band would take over. We took our places, and Steps' version of *Chain Reaction* blasted through the sound system. Bursting into Lady GaGa's *Telephone,* we clapped, danced, and stomped our way through it and into *I Was Born This Way. Bad Romance* and *Paparazzi* followed in a mash-up. The lights changed with the songs blending together as if they were one. Singing the chorus of *Paparazzi,* we blended the lyrics with Take That's version of *Could It Be Magic.* If you listen carefully, you can hear that they sound very similar.

For several moments we mixed the songs, and then ripping off the cape and headpiece to reveal my red devil outfit, we drew huge grins from Take That themselves as we danced and sang. I stood in front of them singing, indicating for them to sing with me. They sang at the tops of their voices, and the audience cheered. I ended the song on a long note and then mixed in their hits *Satisfied* and *Give Good Feeling*. I hit the high notes with *Greatest Day*, and then the lights went dead.

The dancers left the stage and Color Me Badd's *Slow Motion* came on. I slithered and slinked my way back and forth across the stage, slowly gyrating and thrusting, turning every man in the room on. I swayed my hips from side to side, my left hand making come to me gestures, my eyes making come to bed suggestions. I gyrated down in front of the boys and could tell they were turned on as they had glassy eyes and dirty smiles. Chris Fox licked his lips, and I stared into his eyes as I slowly stood. With one last chorus, I walked slowly toward the back of the stage, ending the song with a flick of my tail.

There was silence.

"Do you like my boots?" I asked, facing the crowd.

There was thunderous applause and catcalls.

"I call them…crotch kissers…for the most obvious reason," I purred, watching all male eyes zoom in on my crotch.

The band came on, and I grabbed the mic stand. We launched into JC Chasez's *All Day Long I Dream About Sex*. It seemed to be the perfect song after *Slow Motion*. I held the mic in my right hand and used my left to thrust the stand between my legs, rubbing it against me, grinding into it as if it were a penis and I was getting off on it. Everyone just stared, and it made me want to fuck Callum right there and then.

Kelly Clarkson's *If I Can't Have You* started, and I bent over, singing into the mic on the stand. I looked up and into the light, covering my eyes in conjunction with the lyrics. I turned to face the ceiling, still in a half crouch. I bent forward, then walked to the right of the stage before singing the second verse. I slowly moved to the centre, singing to the men at the front. I took a few steps toward the band then spun back to the crowd, and whipped the mic from the stand and gyrated against it again, turning everyone on.

The lights went out, I set the stand to the right of the drum platform, and we gathered at the front of the drummer. Kelly's *Whyyawannabringmedown* belted out. I slid my hand up my body and over my head. I turned and burst into the lyrics, pointing at the audience making hand movements. The chorus had me thrusting, stomping my way forward in time with the beat. I stomped over to the right of the stage thrusting my crotch, breaking into the bridge I strutted to the left of the stage, and I hit the high note of 'Somebody'. The guitarist slipped his guitar neck between my legs, and I thrust and danced, making it look dirty. The lyrics started again, and I gave the crowd the finger then aimed my venom at Jett, the guitarist, as we thrust and strutted our way back to the centre of the stage. I faced the crowd, thrusting, stomping, touching myself, pointing at them. The song stopped on the beat, and I launched into Pink's *Raise Your Glass* and Katy Perry's *Fireworks* as it was New Year's and all.

I closed the set with ABBA's *Winner Takes It All*, belting out the high notes until the end of the song. I stopped. "Now that you've had your sixth orgasm of the night, I'll let you rest before I come back for my finale," I purred, strutting my way off stage.

The curtains closed. The crowd roared, and the band and I walked backstage. I was able to take a little longer getting changed, pulling off the red devil outfit and my wig. I towelled down and took a breath, drinking another energy drink, and watching Tina pack up the costumes belonging to the hire store, and those belonging to me in my case.

I stood in front of a small desk fan on the vanity to cool down, and then changed into my last outfit, a white pantsuit. I gave my hair a brush and blow dry, smeared on some more lipstick, then walked to the back of the stage.

There were big lighted letters spelling my name, and I stood between the W and the second E.

Elvis Presley's *My Way* came on, and I started singing. I wasn't going on stage yet as we'd set up a picture montage of my time in England to play over the first two verses.

I heard gasps as the photos moved by. Me before the accident. Me in the hospital. My head, my face, my scar, my chest. All documented by Linda or myself in photos and videos.

I walked out on stage into the darkness, and the light slowly highlighted me as I sang. With the last words of the song, I pointed to my head. *I Did it My Way.*

The stage went black, and I walked to the right as a screen was brought out on stage. The notes started, and Elvis Presley sang. We were doing a duet in matching suits. He was on the screen from the 1968 comeback special. I was from my only concert 2011.

Side by side we sang *If I Can Dream*, alternating verses until we sang the last chorus together, belting it out, swinging our arms. Everyone stood transfixed until I hit the last long note and threw myself into a bow.

"Thank you, thank you so much. Thank you for coming, happy New Year everyone." I waved and blew kisses then the curtain closed.

"Oh, my God, that was one hell of a performance," Tina squealed as we rushed to my room.

"Has everyone already gone?" I asked, panting for great gulps of air.

"Almost. All the costumes are packed."

All the dancers rushed me.

"Oh, my God, that was fabulous."

"How fantastic."

"I can't wait to see that on TV."

We hugged. "Thanks for coming and doing this," I said. "I know you may have already had plans, but if you go now, you might be able to still make them." We hugged again before I ushered them away and spoke to Tina. "Go, go to your plans. Send the band off and get the outfits in your car. I want everything cleared out. I'm gonna grab a shower and change." I closed the door on her and ran for the small bathroom.

In five minutes flat I showered, dried, and was

pulling on my underwear, socks, black jeans, and knee-length black sheepskin leather boots.

BANG. BANG. BANG.

I jumped.

"Jewels? It's Callum. Let me in."

I quickly pulled on my black turtleneck and flung open the door.

He pushed his way in, a half scared, half shocked look on his face.

"What is it?" I felt the fear and panic.

"Get dressed. You need to see what's across the river."

Every kind of emotion went through me. I tucked my top into my jeans, did up my belt, and zipped up my case. Standing it on the floor and packing my bag I said, "It may not be what I've been seeing. Try not to panic."

"Can't help it," he said, pacing. "It's exactly what you've been showing us for the last few weeks. And…" He stopped. "It wasn't supposed to be there. It was supposed to be down the river where we read, but they had to move it because there were some problems."

"How do you know?" I laid my black sheepskin aviator jacket on my case, and sat my bag on top, strapping it on.

"Because when you left the stage, the manager came on and said something about your show. The curtains opened, and there's this big thing across the river. He then told us it's the New Year's Eve clock built to count down the minutes between eleven and midnight." He looked at his watch. "It's eleven-thirty now. Let's go. Are you ready?"

"I don't know. Just stop." I put my hands up. "I need to think, and make sure I've got everything." I checked the bathroom and the floor, checking off my list. "Okay, got everything."

We rolled out the door and bumped into Tina.

"You've finished then?" she asked.

"Yes. Has everyone left? No one's backstage?"

She gave me a funny look. "The dancers and band have gone. I've packed up the costumes, and the crew are sorting out the stage gear."

"Make sure they're quick; they should get out of here by midnight."

Another strange look. "Okay."

"You should go, too," I said. "Go spend New Year with your family."

"Jewels," Callum warned, indicating the time.

"You go and have fun," I told Tina. "We're off now."

"Okay, happy New Year."

"Happy New Year." I rolled down the hall with Callum, and taking a left, I asked, "Are you sure it's what I've been seeing?"

"Definitely," he said beside me. "Even Chris Simmons is definite, and you only showed him once." He gave me a sideways glance. "*Which* you didn't tell me."

"I also posted a scan of it on my blog in case anyone knew what it was." We took a right. "But what's to say it's what I've been seeing? If it *is* a clock, it's not completely lit up yet." We walked into the club, the bar to our left, the stage and stairs to our right. "It may not be what I've been seeing."

We walked toward Bob, Linda, and Megan, standing with scared looks on their faces. Chris and the boys were with them. The others didn't know much except for following my blog, but Chris did. Standing in his black suit and open neck shirt, which he looked damn good in, he stared from me to point out the window.

I was suddenly walking in slow motion. *Seeing* everything in slow motion. Facial expressions, hand movements, words. My eyes followed the path to where he was pointing. Out the big glass wall, on the opposite river bank, sat a huge half white half spiky thing.

That was it!

My heart stopped.

The world stopped.

The crowd around me stopped.

My case fell from my hand.

I stopped dead and stared.

I heard nothing.

I saw nothing.

Except for that bloody big white spiky thing that had been plaguing me for the last three weeks.

I knew it was about to happen.

Doomsday was nigh.

Chapter 28

I was transported back to the time I died in the hospital, and the whirlwind trip the invisible lady had taken me on. I hadn't been able to remember it in any way, shape, or form.

Until now.

We stood in this room, the lady and I, watching myself and Callum count down the New Year. Standing by the window, staring out at the New Year's clock as each white spike lit up. It was almost twelve, just fifteen seconds to go. Callum and I gazed at each other as the crowd around us started the ten-second countdown.

The clock lit up and blurred into different formations. Everyone surged toward the big glass window to watch the fireworks and shout Happy New Year.

Callum and I kissed, holding each other tight. The glass panel in front of us cracked. We stopped and stared at it. Then the crack grew, and with no warning, the whole function room snapped, dropped, and fell straight into the river.

Women screamed, men yelled, glass stabbed to

death, and debris fell on top. People died quickly, from being dragged to the bottom of the river by bricks and building. Others bled from glass shards, dying slowly.

Callum was both. He yelled my name. I tried to hang on. Glass stuck out of his neck, and building dragged him away.

"Callum," I screamed. "Callum."

I saw myself flailing, slowly going under. The noise died down. The screaming stopped. The shouting stopped. Callum died and sank. I watched myself flounder amongst the dead bodies. Crying at losing Callum. Crying from the shock. Crying from not being able to do anything. I watched myself go under like so many others. I vanished from view. Drowned with Callum.

I looked up to see the fireworks bright in the sky. The big white spiky clock faltered, blinking on and off at twelve.

"This is what will happen if you don't stop it,' the lady said. "The building has structural damage from years of wear. If everyone surges toward the river, it will only make it happen faster. You can stop this. You have to get everyone out by midnight. The place needs to be evacuated, or everyone will die. You *must do this,* Jewels. You must."

I gazed over the river. It was like a holocaust. Dead bodies and debris. I turned and looked at the remaining building. The top floors collapsed into the river from an explosion caused by a ruptured gas line after the collapse. I looked for my body. It wasn't there. I knew I didn't want to die again.

"Ah," I gasped through pouring tears and fell straight down.

"Jewels, Jewels." Callum grabbed me, spinning me around and into his arms. He trapped me against his chest. "What is it? What did you see?"

I clung to him, trying desperately to calm my breathing and make sense of what I'd seen. "Drowning…building…die…"

"What, Jewels? Go slow. Tell me," he said in my ear.

I tried to stop crying. "We need…to get out… building…falls into river…we all die…must get out… get out now." I pulled away and looked into his eyes. "Get out now," I whispered between sobs. "Or we all die."

"We need to evacuate?" he asked.

I nodded.

"I'll find the manager and get everything in gear. Get your stuff and leave." He turned to Chris. "Look after her."

"Absolutely," he said, pulling me into his arms as Callum strode off in search of Dick.

Everyone gathered around.

"What did you see?" Linda asked.

"What is it, Jewels? Do you know now?" Bob asked.

I glanced up at the ceiling looking for cracks, then down at the floor. The ground felt uneven, like it had cracked in two and half had dropped. I rocked my foot back and forth knowing it had already started, and the worst was yet to come.

"Get out. Everyone needs to get out." I looked at

each one. "Get whoever you came with and say nothing. Get your coats and get out now." Clearly, my expression and what had just happened convinced them, and most of the boys went off to find their partners. Chris, Christopher and Dominic stayed.

I turned to Bob and Linda. "Let's get your coats now," I hissed, and we barrelled up to the coat room. It took only a minute for them to get their coats, but it seemed like a lifetime to me.

11:40

I was panicking as I opened the door and we piled out as the others came with their wives. "Bob, take Linda and Megan. Take my bags and go." I grabbed my coat, scarf and hat. "Take them and go. Get in the car and leave." I pulled my coat on. "Megan, I'll take my camera, you go home. Now." Without a word, they hurried to the car. I wrapped my scarf around my neck and pulled on my hat. The others came out, and I gave orders. "Sam, Alex, stand here and direct everyone down the path to the left and into the last row of the car park. Chris, you and Fox stand in the second row, so no one strays. Dom, Andrew, Ben, stand in the last row and direct flow. Once the row is three quarters full, send them into the second. I'll let Callum know what we're doing." I walked back in, seeing Callum and Dick walking toward me. We stopped to confer.

"I'll hit the alarm button, and we'll let everyone know what they need to do," Dick said.

"Direct everyone down the path to the left and into the last row of the car park. The boys are out there and will help to direct."

"Great," Callum said. "I've already put in a call to the station to get more help out here."

I looked out at the clock.

11:45

"You've got ten minutes," I said.

They ran for the stage, and Dick gave a signal. An alarm went off, and everyone stopped.

"Ladies and gentleman. I'm Dick Dastard, the manager, and this is Sgt Callum Stone. You need to listen to him."

The coat check doors shut, and the doorman opened both front doors. I saw Sam and Alex waiting impatiently, and listening intently.

"I am Sgt Callum Stone." He showed his warrant card. "We need to evacuate this building." There were a few grumbles and moans. "It is incredibly important we do it quickly, quietly, and smoothly. Do not stop at the coat check; the coats will be taken outside for you to collect later, and there will be staff handing out food and drink. So, let's get this moving. Will all of you on the ground floor please move toward the bar, and then to your right and out through the door. Staff will direct you. Stay calm, and move quickly. Now go."

I grabbed a chair and stood on it near the coat check. "Okay, everyone; move quickly, quietly, calmly. Don't push or I'll punch you in the head." I waved celebs past me. I heard Sam and Alex direct them outside.

"Keep moving people. Quickly now. This is not a fucking Sunday walk. Move it!" I yelled.

"Will everyone on the first floor please come down in two rows," Callum said, and I saw those people slowly join the queue.

I clapped my hands. "Come on, people, move it out the door, down to your left. Move, move, move!" I glanced out the window.

11:50

We had five minutes with a space of five in case of emergencies. Other police arrived and filed in through the hallway behind me.

Callum came over and grabbed a radio from one of them. "We're evacuating the building, tape off five and ten metre safety zones around the whole building. You four, go check every room, every floor. You have five minutes, stay in contact by radio."

The last of the stragglers slowly filed past me, and taking a quick look around, Callum and I followed.

11:55

"Are there any leftover guests?" Callum yelled into the radio.

"No. We've done the second floor, doing the first now."

"Knight, what about you?"

"Ground floor now, Sarge, everything's empty."

"All right, get out now. I want everyone out now."

We were standing in the second car park row watching staff hand out coats and drinks.

11:56

I was still panicking. I pulled out my camcorder and checked the battery, gearing it up as Chris came over to me

"Need a hand with that?" He saw my shaking hands.

I smiled gratefully. "You steady with a camera?"

"Give it here." I showed him how to work it, and he turned it on.

11:57

We stared at the clock.

"Everyone out of the building and away from it now," Callum yelled into the radio.

The air was full of electricity. The car park was full of celebrities. The river bank was full of people ready for the fireworks.

11:58

Chris kept the camera steady on the club.

Callum stood beside me. "Are you sure?"

"No." I was shaking all over.

11:59

I made a decision and stood between the clock and the club, indicating to Chris to zoom on me and the clock. He nodded, and I took a deep breath.

"Hey, peeps. Jewels Diva here in merry old London on New Year's Eve. As you can see by the clock over my shoulder, it's almost time." I paused. "Wherever you are, whatever you're doing, have a good New Year's. And *don't* take anything for granted."

I made a hand gesture for Chris to pan toward the clock and fireworks to come, and then stood beside Callum as the crowd counted down.

"Ten, nine, eight, seven, six, five, four, three, two, one, Happy New Year's."

The clock stopped at twelve, and the fireworks went off. The crowd oohed and aahed in between

Auld Lang Syne. I waited with bated breath.

Ten seconds. Eleven seconds. Twelve seconds. Thirteen seconds. Fourteen seconds.

Nothing happened.

Callum pulled me to him. "Exactly *when* was it supposed to happen?"

"Ugh? I..." My jaw fell. I looked up at him and spread my hands. "I saw it, it was twelve seconds. Isn't that what double zero, double zero, twelve means? Twelve seconds?" I stared at the building, questioning my sanity.

"Everyone stay clear," Callum radioed. "Wait for word from me." He stared at me. "Jewels?"

"I don't know," I cried. "All I know is it happens, and believe me, I don't want to drown again. So, it was better to get everyone out and be safe over sorry."

He sighed and looked away. Police rescue boats arrived on the river, and more cop cars parked out front. Those around me stood staring at me with questions in their eyes. I could only shake my head and cry.

"*What* is going on?" Dick demanded, striding up to us. "You told me you'd received a call about the building being unsafe, and that we needed to evacuate, and yet nothing's happened." He waved his hands around. "So, what do we do now, huh? What do we do?"

"Tell your staff to keep handing out food and drink so everyone's happy, and we'll have the professionals check the place out," Callum said as Dick huffed. "Do you want a billion-dollar lawsuit on your hands if you let everyone back in and they die?" Callum demanded. "The families will take a class action suit against you, and I'll be the one telling them to do it."

Clearly, Dick didn't like being told off, because he stormed toward a waiter. "More champagne," he yelled.

I wiped my face and glanced at the clock.

It was eight past midnight.

"So, what do we do?" Callum asked me, looking very disappointed.

"I don't know." I shook my head. "She said because we all surge forward it makes it happen faster." The light bulb went off in my head. "But we didn't surge forward 'cause we got out." I stared at the club. "So…maybe it wasn't twelve seconds 'cause we weren't in there. Maybe it's twelve minutes. But it *will* happen," I said to Callum.

"And what if it means twelve lunchtime, or twelve tonight?" he said.

I shook my head. "No fireworks then." I glanced at the building and saw a huge crack slowly snake down the wall. A brick fell, smashing onto the path. I grabbed Chris's coat. "It's happening," I whispered.

He nodded, having gotten it all on tape.

It was ten past midnight.

"Okay," Callum conceded. "Keep away from the building and keep everyone else away too," he radioed.

"Sergeant," a voice bellowed behind us. "What the hell is going on?" Inspector Dale bore down on us, shoving past to look at the club. He turned and eyeballed Callum. "You're officially retired now,

Sergeant Stone, so what is the meaning of this?"

"I evacuated the building due to structural damage," he said simply.

"And how do you know it has structural damage?"

"I was well informed…*Arthur!*"

I snorted at Callum's defiance. It was quite sexy.

Arthur gave me the evil eye. "And I might have known *you'd* have something to do with this. Just a load of rubbish, making up stories again, I bet."

There was a sound, not sure what, but with a groan that could easily rival the Titanic's splitting in half and sinking, the club wall cracked, glass shattered, and the whole function room seemed to snap off and collapse straight down into the river on an almighty wave of power.

The crowd screamed and shouted behind us. I just stared in wild shock.

It was twelve past midnight.

The water police made a run for it, churning up the river as they sped away. We still stared. Not even sure what to do.

I grabbed Chris's arm. "Hold steady, there's going to be an explosion."

And there was; racing out across the river from the wreckage, and out the back side door toward us. The metal staircase along the wall on the first floor groaned and shuddered, still attached to the wall that was still standing.

Inside, the second floor partially collapsed onto the first, and they both went tumbling into the river, taking the bar with them. The whole front of the building from the main door was ripped from its moorings. Bricks fell, debris burned. What was left was nothing but an ugly gaping hole.

Arthur turned to Callum looking white as a ghost. "Good job, my boy. You got everyone out safely." With a last look, he walked off to take over.

It was fifteen past midnight.

I took a couple of deep breaths and slowly released them, trying to calm myself.

"You were right." Callum stared dumbfounded at me.

"Well." I shrugged. "Not quite." I looked at Chris filming and wanted to say something. Gathering my thoughts, I went over the points I wanted to make. I glanced around. Everyone was staring, dumbfounded at the ruined building.

It was twenty past midnight.

I tapped Chris on the shoulder and stepped in front of the camera.

I sighed. "Well, peeps, as you can see by the building behind me, something has happened. Now, it's okay, we all got out safely, and we're okay. But I'm not." I winced. "When I died the second time in the hospital, I was shown what would happen tonight. But when I woke up, and in the weeks since, I haven't been able to remember it. I only had flashes and dreams. After my show, I saw the clock for the first time in real life, and I remembered like I was reliving it. So, peeps, this is going to be the only time I take credit for preventing mass murder and rescuing Britain's celebrities. Now, on to more important stuff."

I spread my hands and grinned. "It's New Year's Day. That's right; it's New Year's Day. A new day, a new week, a new month, a new year. It's time to stop regretting the past and make your future. Make as much as possible happen for you. Whatever comes your way this year, grab it with both hands and run with it."

I choked, but managed to swallow it back. "I died last year. Twice. And believe me, you don't want to unless you're in chronic pain and even then..." I shook my head slowly. "I died with regrets. Big fat massive regrets, and I've been trying to fix them ever since. You don't want to die with regrets, peeps. You just don't. It doesn't make you happy, it only makes you sad, and you end up worrying more about what you don't have or didn't do, that you forget you've been given the chance to continue life, and you get to live on. You have a chance to make it right. And you *need* to do that. You *need* to take your life in your hands and say *I'm* worth the risk. *I'm* worth the chance. *I* will do this. If you're being abused, stand up and say no more. If you're doing the abusing, then stop it. Stop hating. Stop hurting. Stop bullying. *Your* life is in *your* hands, and whatever is going on in your life, *you* can stop it if it's bad. *You* can emphasise it if it's good. *You* can shine down and illuminate your life like no one else can. Stop hating and start loving yourself. Love yourself and have no regrets. Stop what's bad and start what's good. Take a long hard look inside of you, and change it if you don't like it. Add to it and make it better. Only *you* have the power to stop hating and start loving. Only *you* can change yourself and your life. Only *you* can make your life better. Stop hating the world, and stop hating yourself, and start loving everyone and everything around you. It's magical. Life is a great thing of beauty, and I'm lucky to have another chance, and I'm going to take everything that comes my way and run with it. 'Cause I'm happy to be alive, and you should be too. Be happy, peeps. Be happy, and accept what the New Year brings. It's a new day, a new month, a new year. Open your heart, and your mind and your life, and all the good will flow into it."

I sighed. "Don't have regrets peeps. They're a burden." I spied Dominic over Chris's shoulder. "In fact, I know one regret I'm going to have if I don't fix it before I leave England." I took a step toward the camera. "There's a certain sexy, scruffy stud muffin whose throat I need to shove my tongue down."

I indicated for Chris to follow me, and I barged up to Dominic, grabbed his face in my hands, and slammed my lips onto his. It took only seconds for the shock to wear off, and he kissed me back.

And damn he has a very strong tongue!

"Now, why the hell can't I get one of those?" Christopher Fox said.

We stopped pashing and saw the camera aimed at us. Chris had a huge grin, and Callum was shaking his head in the background.

"So, peeps, don't have regrets. 'Cause you'll regret it. It's a new day, a new year, go out and enjoy it." I nuzzled Dominic. "I certainly will." With an eyebrow wiggle at the camera, Chris panned off us and over the crowd. "Thanks, gorgeous," I told Dominic.

"Oh, baby, *thank you*," he said, licking his lips.

"What the hell were you doing?" Callum whispered, pulling me aside.

"What?" I whispered back. "Technically, *Jewels* is *not* engaged to you."

His expression went from angry to defeat. He knew I was right.

It was thirty past midnight.

We stood watching the fire brigade try to put out the flames that roared, but since the building was still collapsing on itself and into the river, there wasn't much point.

I finally noticed Jack. He was still pounding away. *Why haven't you left yet? I did what I was supposed to. Why are you still here?* I rubbed my head, trying to move him to somewhere else then yawned, staring at the gaping hole where the club once stood.

Something moved.

What?

Probably just debris.

There it was again.

No, my eyes are deceiving me.

No, there it was.

Oh, for God's sake, stop it. Jack, is that you making me see things, or is it lack of sleep and working too hard?

There it was.

I wiped my eyes and saw something move. I frowned. I straightened. I stared really hard at what I was looking for.

No, wait, there it is.

What was it?

"Did you see…?" I started and motioned for Chris to slowly move to the first car park row so we could get a better view. The building was still falling. Bits of floor, roof, wall, glass and bottles from behind the bar.

There it was.

What was that?

It has to be my mind playing tricks. But what if it's not? I moved forward, toward the building. The police tape blocked my way. I stood staring into the gaping hole, trying to see what was moving, if anything was moving at all since stuff was falling and flapping in the breeze. Flammable insulation, prints and pictures, fires burning from the kitchen. The gorgeous jukebox was gone, the small light up dance floor dead in the water, and huge gaping holes in each floor. My dressing room was gone, and I thanked God I hadn't left anything in there.

It moved.

I stared, craning my neck around trying to get a clear view.

It moved.

What was it? I couldn't tell. Clearly, my eyes were deceiving me, and with Jack pounding away, I wanted to bash my head in.

It moved.

Is that a person?

I moved forward, wanting a better look.

"Jewels," someone called.

I went past the five metre police tape. I craned my neck to see what was moving, if it was a person or just debris.

"Jewels," came loudly out across the noise.

I stood staring, trying to see if there was a person.

BOOMMM!

Fire ripped through the back of the building and out the side door. The side wall splintered, and with another loud boom of a fireball, cracked and sent the metal staircase tumbling.

The biggest explosion tore through the back of the ruins, and in one fell swoop, sent that almighty metal staircase groaning.

The problem was, it sent it groaning toward me.

The bottom flew off the building, ripping out and sideways off the crumbling wall, as it tore from its bolts and screws in the wall that was no more. In one split second that great big hulking mass of metal caught me with such ferocity that all I could do was cling to it as it sped toward the river and out into the night.

Chapter 29

"Jewels," Callum screamed, and I saw him run toward the river as I went plummeting into it under the massive metal staircase.

Gurgle, gurgle, gurgle.

Down, down, down.

Gurgle, gurgle, gurgle.

I struggled, trying to get away from the weight that wore me down.

Gurgle, gurgle, gurgle.

I was suffocating, struggling, thrashing around. I couldn't see. I couldn't hear. I couldn't move. I couldn't do.

I stopped.

Stopped struggling. Stopped thrashing. Stopped drowning.

I. Just. Stopped.

Powerful hands grabbed me, hauling me upwards. My arms went around Callum's neck as he thrust us to the surface, taking great big gulps of air as we floated.

"Over here," he yelled.

I laid my head on his shoulder and closed my eyes.

"Here. Take her."

I felt myself being wrenched from his arms and onto something hard.

Callum came up after me. "Jewels." He gently slapped my face and shook me. "Jewels."

"Ugh," managed to escape from between my lips.

"Jewels." He pulled me into his embrace, trapping me there for the ride back to the river bank.

My eyes opened to slits. Men rushed onto the boat. Callum tried to pick me up to carry me onto the dock. He managed a half lift, half tug. We slid onto the dock against the wall and sat panting. The only lights I saw were the river lights. I closed my eyes against them.

"Jewels." He gently tapped my face again. "Wake up. Open your eyes."

"Ugh." They slid open to half-mast. "Ugh."

"That's my girl. Open your eyes. Come on."

I coughed and stared into his big concerned eyes.

"We need to get you back to the hospital, so they can check you out. You might have swallowed water."

"I didn't," I rasped, having another coughing fit.

He shook his head and let it drop. "How could you do something so stupid? How? The police tape was there for that very reason. To keep people away in case something happened. And it did." He gave me a sour look. "That was so stupid and foolish and idiotic."

"I thought I saw someone."

"What?" He became alert.

"I thought I saw someone." I shook my head. "Or *something.* I can't be sure. My mind could've been playing tricks. Jack was in my head…" My eyes narrowed, and I thought. I cocked my head, and I thought. I took my hat off, and I thought. I touched my head. "He's gone. Jack's gone." I looked up in surprise. "He's finally gone. No more pounding. No more chipping away. Jack's finally bloody gone." I laughed with joy.

"He's gone?" Callum was astonished. "Are you sure? Are you really sure?"

I rubbed my head. "He's gone. Oh, my God, he's really gone." I cried tears of happiness.

We hugged, holding each other tight, and with new found strength, got to our feet and slowly made our way up the stairs. Callum pulled the blanket tighter around me, trapping me under his right arm as we climbed. Step by step, we went up to the car park to find ourselves surrounded by cheering officers and members of the crowd.

"It's all right, we're okay, let us through," Callum yelled. We stopped in front of Chris, the camera still rolling.

"Well, ah, peeps," I managed. "From what you just saw, I'm still alive and *unfortunately* on my way *back* to the hospital. I don't want to, but this one here," I flicked my thumb at Callum, "is demanding that I go. So!" I sighed. "This will be the last time you hear from me for awhile 'cause after I get *out* of hospital, I'm taking a nice long holiday." I snorted. "Again. And I may be doing a few other things." I winked and then looked down at myself. "Not only do I look and smell like a wet sheep, I feel like one too. So, I will bid you adieu and leave you with some sage advice." I paused. "Don't come to England 'cause way too much shit happens. Okay, peeps, I'm off, and I'll blog or tweet or whatever you soon."

Callum and I walked past the camera, and then I turned and whispered in Chris's ear. "Pan over the club then shut it off. It's time to go."

He panned over and then switched off, turning to give me a huge hug. "You right, then, that was fucking amazing."

I sighed and grinned at the same time. "I'm fine, worry wart wants me to get checked out. I'll load the footage up online later."

"All right. You make sure you blog about your adventure. I'll be reading." He grinned.

I laughed. "I will don't worry." As I was hugging the boys, I noticed the crowd was half the size it was, and saw limos pulling up and taking passengers.

"They're leaving, we may as well." Callum opened my door, and I got in.

In record speed, we were at the hospital, but the two hour wait was atrocious. They wanted me to stay, but I managed to convince them I hadn't drunk the dirty filthy vile cesspool of a river. It was four a.m. when we got home, and Bob and Linda were up waiting.

"Oh, my God, it's all over the news!" Linda said. "But what happened to you?"

I grimaced. "Went for a little dip in the river."

"Oh, my God, that was you," she shrieked. "All the networks have crews down there, and they couldn't get too close, so they zoomed in. We saw someone fly into the river."

"I'm gonna get upstairs and have a shower," I said.

"And maybe get some sleep. You couldn't bring me up some soup could you?" I asked. "I wanna upload this video to the web."

"Of course, of course, you go." They scurried into the kitchen, and we scurried into the shower, coming out fifteen minutes later to find Bob and Linda planted on my couch, and the coffee table laden with food.

I grabbed a cup of soup and drank greedily as I hadn't eaten in almost twelve hours. Callum explained what happened, receiving oohs and aahs and stunned or shocked expressions from them, as I shovelled sandwiches and handfuls of M&Ms into my mouth.

I grabbed the camera and plugged it in, turning on my laptop, downloading the footage into one large file. I went to Blogger, clicked on new post, uploaded the video, and then wrote.

My Adventures in Merry Old England: January 1st, 2012

Hey peeps, this is the video of what really happened after my show tonight. This is not fake, not photoshopped, not anything except real. This did happen, and I'm okay. It's about an hour long, but worth watching, so take the time. I'm off for awhile, another holiday. I might or might not let you know where I am. I need some peace and quiet, and some hot sex to go with some hot men. But for now, go and live your life, peeps.

Jewels xxoo

I made sure the video had uploaded properly and hit

the publish tab. "Ugh," I groaned, turning everything off. "I need to get away." I yawned.

"Where do you want to go?" Callum asked.

"Somewhere warm." I got up and walked over to the closet.

"What do you want to do?"

I found what I was looking for and slid it on, then ran over to him and jumped on his lap, planting a big kiss on his lips. "I want to get married."

His lips turned into a grin. "Really?"

I nodded eagerly.

"So do I." We kissed so passionately it prompted Bob and Linda to cough, "Ahem," several times for us to notice.

"Sorry." I giggled, shifting to the side of the chair. "How soon can we get married?"

"Um, how about this week?" he suggested.

"How about today," I replied.

"What?" came the stunned chorus.

"Well, hasn't it been over a month now since you applied for all of your documents? Wasn't there some sort of month time frame or something we had to wait before getting married?"

"Uh, yeah." He frowned, remembering. "Once I'd filed the papers for immigration, we could get married here or Australia. I filed for both just in case." He grinned.

"So our month is up?" I snuggled into his lap.

"It is." He snuggled back.

"So, we can get married today, then?" I looked between all three of them. "Surely one of you must know a judge or something who can legally marry us in the registry office. Sign all the documents, and make it all nice and legal?"

They thought about it.

"I do," Callum finally said.

"Great. How would they feel about heading in to work today for a half hour while we say vows and sign papers? Then we can go somewhere special and maybe have a small ceremony just between us."

His smile was soft and his eyes full of love. "I'll give him a call later when the time is right. But right *now*, we need to get some sleep."

"It's five-thirty," Linda declared and started collecting the trays. "We'll take these downstairs then head to bed. Try and get some rest won't you; it might be another big day." They left, and we went to bed.

But not for sleep.

We were up at nine, with Callum making a call to a judge he knew, while Linda and I made plans of our own. A half hour later he put the phone down. "Judge Benedict will meet us in the registry office at eleven. We'll need witnesses, and he'll have one of the office workers there to get everything together. We just need our papers." He pulled me into his lap and we snuggled.

"Great. We can make it all legal at the office then get dressed, go somewhere nice, and have a ceremony."

"Is the registry office not enough for you?" he asked, running his fingers through my hair.

I kissed him. "Believe me, mister, after the last couple of months I've had, we're having a ceremony."

Callum gathered his papers, and Linda and I quickly had a whispered conversation before she went off to make some calls. I went upstairs and placed some jewellery in a quilted purse, got my red leather boots and my brown wig. I packed them in a bag, pulled on a hat and coat and ran downstairs. "Ready?"

"We going in my car?" Callum asked as Bob and Linda got their coats.

"God no!" I exclaimed. "I'm sure it smells of wet sheep after last night." I turned to Bob. "Mind taking us in your car?"

"Not at all. I'll drive."

We walked into the registry office at ten-fifty to see Judge Benedict and a woman already there waiting.

"Arnold," Callum greeted.

"Callum," he returned.

They shook hands, and Callum introduced me. "This is my fiancée Tamara, and our witnesses Bob and Linda."

"Hello, nice to meet you." I shook his hand.

"So, you two want to get married and not wait," he said. "Follow me." He led us down the hall and turned right, walking into the second room on the left. "Do you have your papers?" he asked, taking them when Callum handed them over. "Mmm, seems to be in order. Mmm. Okay, it's simple. I ask you, Callum, if you take this woman to be your wife and you say?"

"I do."

"And I ask you, Tamara, if you take this man to be your husband."

"I do." I grinned at Callum, squeezing his hand tight.

"By the power vested in me, I now declare you husband and wife. Sign here and here." We both did. "I sign here, and witnesses sign here." Bob and Linda did. "I now stamp each page. My colleague here will do her work, and you are now…" He looked at both of us. "Husband and wife."

I gaped. "Seriously?"

"Seriously," he said with a nod.

"Wait," Callum said, confused. "Is that it? We're now legally married?"

"Yes, my boy, congratulations." We shook hands, and once the paperwork was filed, were given a printout of our marriage certificate.

"Bloody hell," I said, staring at it. "That was quick." Callum and I looked at each other. "Hello, husband." I went all gooey inside.

"Hello, wife." His grin said he felt the same way.

"Okay, you two, let's go. We have something special planned for you," Linda gushed, ushering us out the door and back to the car.

We drove to a small function centre normally used for weddings, plays, theatre productions and such, and after Linda knocked on the door and it was opened, we walked into the spacious and still festively decorated lobby.

"Okay," she said. "Bob, you take Callum to get changed, and I'll work on Tamara. Take this." She handed over a dress bag, and hanging onto the one with my things in, led me to a dressing room down the hall. "Okay, let's get you beautified."

I changed into my red leather boots, pulled on my

wig, and sat while Linda tied it into a soft knot at the nape of my neck, clipping in several gold beaded chains in a crisscross fashion.

I sprayed on my make-up to hide the bruises that were yellow, but fading, and added blush, eyeshadow, mascara and lipstick. Linda helped me step into the gorgeous red lace gown I'd bought and had altered in the week before Christmas. The design hadn't been what I had in mind when I first laid eyes on it, but the store owner happily agreed to alter it.

It was off the shoulder, with a sweetheart neckline, snug body, and fishtail train. Gold accents highlighted the lace, and after adding the locket I'd received from Callum for Christmas, earrings, and wraparound gold and red bracelets, I was ready.

"Ah, Jewels. Tamara. You look gorgeous," Linda breathed.

I studied my reflection. "I hope Callum thinks so."

"Oh, he will." She quickly gathered my things but left my long dark red velvet cape over a chair. "Let's go get you two together." She rushed out the door only to collide with Bob.

"Ready."

"Ready."

She turned to me. "We'll leave you two now, and go plan your special night at home. Stay as long as you like. There's food and drink, and a limo will be waiting for you when you're ready to leave. Have a great night." They rushed off, leaving me alone in the room until Callum walked in from the hallway.

"Oh, my God…Tam…" He breathed hard, and

slowly walked toward me, holding out his hands. "You're gorgeous. Look at you…so beautiful."

I smiled shyly. "Look at you," I murmured. He was resplendent in a sharp black suit and red open neck shirt. A gold buckle belt, shiny shoes, and gold cufflinks finished off the look. His hands slid around me, pulling me close. I rested under his chin and breathed in his strong manly scent. "Mmm, spicy." I sighed.

His hand stroked my cheek, his lips caressed mine. We became lost in each other.

"Ahem."

We pulled apart in shock to find a man standing in the doorway.

"Hello. I'm Michael. I'll be here all day, seeing to whatever you want, so if you would please come this way." He held out his hand, and we followed him back to the lobby and into the most magical kingdom you'd ever seen.

The main room was a winter wonderland full of twinkling decorated Christmas trees, fake snow falling gently, and paths winding through the room taking us to the centre where a snow-covered platform turned slowly.

"It's beautiful," I gasped.

"Feel free to do whatever, there will be food and drink whenever you want it," Michael said, closing the doors behind him.

Hands flew to my mouth. "Oh, my, God. This is gorgeous." My eyes darted everywhere, and I spun around under the falling snow. "It's…" I shook my head in wonder. "Wow!"

"Bob and Linda did all of this?" Callum asked. Holding hands, we walked along the path, looking at all the dazzling lights and baubles.

"I suppose. I know she made some calls this morning." Reaching the platform in the middle of the room, Callum helped me step up then wrapped me in his arms. "It's like being in a snow globe." I laughed softly.

"It's beautiful," he said. "But not as beautiful as you." He glanced down at my dress. "Why do I get the feeling you already had that dress before we went to my parents' house for Christmas? You described it perfectly." His eyebrow rose in amusement.

I grinned. "I'd already found it while shopping and knew it would come in handy." I pulled him close. "I knew we were getting married sometime. Just didn't know when."

"Speaking of..." He pulled out a small velvet box and opened it. Two gold wedding rings nestled inside. He gave me his, kept mine, and put the box back in his pocket. He took my hand. "Do you, Tamara, take Callum, to be your lawfully wedded husband? To have and to hold, for richer or poorer, in sickness and in health, till death do you part?"

I gazed into his eyes and saw the love he had for me. And melted. "I do."

He slid the ring on my finger and it joined the gorgeous engagement ring.

I held his hand. "Do you, Callum, take Tamara, to be your lawfully wedded wife? To have and to hold, for richer or poorer, in sickness and in health, till death do you part?"

"Damn straight I do." He grinned.

I slid the ring on his finger and he grabbed me and spun around. I laughed, and he stopped, pressing his lips to mine. We stayed that way for awhile, joined at the lips, the hips, the body, slowly rotating on that snow-covered platform, standing in each other's arms.

We danced. We floated. We ate the fluffiest chocolate sponge cake covered in strawberries and cream. We drank Pepsi, and flew around the room, flying high from the exhilaration of being married.

Mr and Mrs Callum Stone.

One year I was single and alone and bordering on depressed. The next I was married to the most amazing man on Earth and as happy as Larry. Whoever the hell Larry's supposed to be.

We lost track of time in our own little wonderland until Michael walked in.

"Ahem. Mr and Mrs Stone. It's eight p.m. Your limo is waiting to take you home, and we have a present for you; this lovely photo album and DVD of your time here."

Callum and I looked at each other and frowned at the intrusion.

"The company are very discreet. They stayed in the background taking photos and video. We did it in a little gift pack." He handed it to us. "I hope you enjoyed your stay. We have your coats."

A lady handed Callum my cape, and he put it over my shoulders then took his coat.

"Let me escort you to your car."

With another look at him, we followed him out to the front where he opened the car door.

"Congratulations. We hope you enjoyed your day."

"Thank you," Callum murmured.

We weren't sure what to think or say on the way home, we just kept looking at each other. Flicking through the album, we saw the photographer had taken the most amazing shots, capturing every personal and private moment.

Arriving home, Bob and Linda ushered us upstairs. "Just go. You don't need anything, don't come down for anything. Just go."

We saw why they wanted to get us upstairs so fast. They had redecorated the room. Gone were the Christmas decorations, instead, simple white fairy lights hung all the way around the bed with soft white curtains. The linen had been changed, there were rose petals all over the place, and a bottle of Pepsi chilled on the bedside table.

We grinned, and then passion overtook us.

Callum's jacket. My cape. His shirt. My jewellery. His pants. My dress.

I stood in my sexy red lace underwear and red leather crotch high boots.

"Oh, God." He groaned. "You have those on." Passion flared all over his face.

"If you don't like them, why don't you take them off," I purred, my crotch aching for him.

He saw the passion in my eyes and ripped off my bra. My hand thrust into his boxer briefs, unleashing the wild animal within. Our lips mashed. Our tongues delved. His hand dived into my panties and felt my readiness. Tearing the material, he threw it to the ground. He lifted me. I guided him. In one fell swoop, he entered. My leather covered thighs tightened around him. We landed on the bed already lost in the heights of steam, lust, desire and passion.

Chapter 30

I nestled into fur. My leather clad left leg hooked over a torso. My left hand slowly slid down until it found the wild animal it sought.

It stroked.

It caressed.

It teased.

He groaned.

His right hand slid over my leg and found what it was after. The secret cave that the wild animal called home.

I groaned.

I moved.

Flattening my body against his, I pushed myself up then slowly slid down, down, down.

The wild animal sought refuge in the secret cave.

Up and down.

In and out.

The wild animal couldn't make up its mind. The furry beast sat, making the wild animal move, his arms holding me in position, so the cave was easily accessible.

And it was.

Wide open for the animal to rest in.

To hibernate in.

My hands held on as the furry beast lifted me then brought me back down.

Lifted. Down.

Lifted. Down.

His hands held me captive as the wild animal did what it wanted.

Teased.

Tortured.

Tormented.

Driving me to dizzying heights.

The beast's mouth latched onto a mountaintop, the peak hardening under his expert tongue. He sucked, making the mountain high and round and firm. His mouth tore away, and his hands held me to his chest, my mountains trapped against the furry beast's torso teased by his wild nest.

The other mountain hardened.

Its peak stood tall and firm.

The wild animal thrust hard and fast then slow and soft. The beast's hands guiding my hips, so the animal had easy entrance to its secret cave.

My legs spread wider to accommodate the animal that was bringing so much joy. I took one of the beast's hands and led it down to the secret cave, guiding and showing it the pleasure mound that guarded the opening.

Fingers and thumb probed and pushed, rubbed and flicked the pleasure mound, its mouth moving in conjunction, latching onto the other mountain peak to claim the climb and fly the flag.

The beast blew all of my senses holding me tight while he attacked all three zones.

The mountaintop.

The pleasure mound.

The secret cave.

All three being probed and invaded.

The wild animal throbbed and plundered moving faster and faster.

Thrusting.

Poking.

Rampaging through the cave until it found the shelter it sought and came to a deafeningly loud roar!

Chapter 31

We collapsed onto the bed, exhausted. My head rested on his hairy chest, my hand nestled in his big head of hair.

His laugh was low and deep. "What a way to wake up in the morning." His hands lazily ran all over my back.

"Mmm," I murmured. "What a way."

There was a knock at the door.

"Argh," I mumbled. "Go way."

It became persistent.

"Just a minute," Callum yelled, rolling me off him despite my groans and protests. Giving me a dirty look, he threw on his robe and opened the door.

"Are you two up? Of course you are," Linda said, looking in at me. "It's nine o'clock."

"Ugh. Only nine o'clock," I moaned, not moving under the sheet.

"We have a wedding present for you. Can you come down when you're ready?"

"Sure," Callum said, closing the door after her.

I threw back the sheet and spread my legs wide.

"Yeah," I told Callum as he threw his robe off and jumped inside of me. "When we're ready."

An hour later, we trotted downstairs.

"In here," Linda called from the lounge room.

"What's so important you had to drag us from our marital bed?" I demanded.

"Your honeymoon," Linda squealed. Bob had a huge grin on his face.

"What?" Callum and I said simultaneously.

"We're giving you a honeymoon. Come sit, and we'll tell you all about it." We sat next to her on the couch. "We have it all planned." She opened a slimline portfolio. "We have your train tickets to Paris."

"Paris," I gasped.

"And your hotel accommodations for your two week honeymoon."

"Oh, my God!" I looked from her to Bob back to her. "I…we…"

"And then," she added excitedly, "a ride on the Orient Express to Rome."

"Oh, my God," I yelled, bouncing up and down on the couch.

"And then." She bounced with me. "A two week stay in Rome."

We screamed, bouncing even higher.

"Oh, my God! Oh, my God! Oh, my God!" I screamed. "Thank you so much." I hugged her. "When do we leave?"

"This afternoon," she said.

"What?" I stopped. *This afternoon?* I turned to Callum. "We'd better go pack."

"We'll come up and help you," Linda said, and Bob nodded in agreement.

They followed us up the stairs and told us all about the holiday package while we packed.

"You'll need mostly warm things obviously. And have anything you buy sent here, so you don't have to carry it around everywhere," she said.

I went over to my desk and grabbed my phone, camcorder, camera and digital recorder, popping them into their bags then into my cabin bag.

"I was wondering if you'd go on to Greece," Linda went on. "I know you want to go there."

"Yeah." I scratched my head. "But I can't fly, so unless there's a boat." I shrugged. "I don't know, we'll see how we go." I shut my suitcase. "And I'm done! When do we leave?"

"Not until one. But we can go have lunch somewhere, and then drop you off at the station. Once you get to Paris, a car will pick you up and take you to the hotel."

I hugged them both. "Thank you so much for this. We'll let you know what we decide along the way. But for now, let's do lunch." I pulled my brown wig on then grabbed a coat, and we piled downstairs and into Bob's car.

After lunching at a restaurant close to the station, we waved them goodbye just before one, sitting by a window and watching the world fly by until we hit the tunnel. A couple of hours later, we emerged back into the sunlight to find ourselves in France, travelling past green hills and quaint buildings into Paris itself, where we were met by a limo driver who took us to our hotel in the heart of the city. After booking in and unpacking, we stood staring at the view.

"My, God, it's amazing," I said, staring at the Eiffel Tower.

"It is." Callum's arms slid around my waist.

"Oh, my God, I can't wait. I want to go now. I want to shop twenty-four seven for the next two weeks and not sleep. Not eat. Not stop. Just shop."

He frowned. "What, not even stop for sex?"

I glanced back at him. "Well, I guess we could take five minutes out for that."

His snort turned into a laugh. "*Five minutes.* What's this *five minutes* business? I always go for at least an hour."

I laughed. "Yes, you certainly do."

"It's afternoon. How about we take a guided tour of the city, and then tonight, we can plan our trip and get an early night for an early start in the morning. I think I saw something about a hotel tour guide. They help you plan your stay," he said.

"Sounds good. Let's go."

Heading downstairs, we asked about the tour guide and only had to wait five minutes for a guide called Jan. She piled us into a limo and off we went, with her pointing out museums, theatres, shopping, the best eateries and restaurants, which is where we ended up for dinner chatting about our plans for the next two weeks.

"Okay, so where do you want to go?"

"Anywhere there are shops," I said with a grin.

She took notes and put together a plan before taking us back to the hotel. We wearily said goodbye and went to our room.

"I take it we are going to be doing nothing else but shopping for the next two weeks?" Callum fell onto the sofa.

"Not at all." I kicked my shoes off. "We can shop during the day, eat at a nice restaurant, and maybe see a show or go somewhere nice at night." I slipped into the bathroom and freshened up. Leaving my clothes on the floor, I slid on a see-through silk robe and walked back into the bedroom. "Unless you want to come back to the hotel at night and stay in?" I grabbed the armless desk chair and placed it in front of the window.

"What are you doing?" His eyes hungrily devoured my body.

"Come." I held out my hand, and he came over. I pulled off his jumper, his shirt, his jeans, his shorts. "Sit." I pushed him onto the chair and mounted him. We held each other close, kissing, caressing, licking and sucking. Our bodies ached for each other, and with the Eiffel Tower twinkling in the distance, we really didn't care if anyone could see us.

*****

The next two weeks were amazing. We went walking along the Seine, scouring the two small islands in the centre of Paris, Île Saint-Louis and Île de la Cité where Notre-Dame is. We saw the Garnier Opera House where the Phantom of the Opera lived and wreaked havoc. I bought out all of the high fashion houses on Rue du Faubourg SL-Honoré, and Avenue Montaigne, department stores Printemps and Galeries Lafayette, and the shops on the Champs Elysées.

We devoured the bookstalls in Quai Saint Michel and spent two days at Marche aux Puces, Paris's flea markets. We lunched in cafés and ate cheese and baguettes, and dined in posh restaurants with French celebrities, even seeing Johnny Depp and his partner at a table across from ours. Callum took a tour of the Eiffel Tower while I shopped, and we even caught a show or two.

After two blissful weeks of shopping and eating, we left on our Orient Express train journey that would take us to Rome, thanking God we'd sent everything we'd bought back to Bob and Linda's so we didn't have to carry it all with us. 'Cause after everything I bought, it wouldn't fit on the WHOLE train!

The journey took us on a four day, three night trip through snow-capped mountain ranges and beautiful countryside before arriving in Rome. Checking into our hotel, we were treated to another guided tour, and then made a plan for the next week.

Between shopping at Gucci, Dior, and Versace, we threw a coin in the Trevi Fountain, saw the Vatican, St Peters Square, the Spanish Steps, the Colosseum, and the Pantheon. Renting a Vespa, we scooted around town and bought gifts for everyone at home.

We decided to only spend eight days in Rome before hopping on a small plane to Greece. As much as I didn't want to fly, I took the risk to get to Athens, and everything went okay. Booking into the nicest hotel we could find and get into, we settled in for another eight days. The good thing about Europe in January and February is that the sales are non-stop.

We visited the Acropolis, and the Parthenon, dedicated to the goddess Athena, Plaka flea market which is located along Ifaistou Street for all sorts of goodies, and Kolonaki, a posh district located in central Athens known for its upmarket shopping locations. Hello, shopping! And we ate and drank our way through town.

On Saturday, we jumped on a small plane and headed for Santorini. I'd seen it on so many TV travel shows I really wanted to go and sunbake on the sandy beaches and have hot, heady sex with Callum, but being Feb, there was no way we would be doing that. So we spent the night, and shopped for the day and Sunday before heading to Mykonos Sunday afternoon.

"I wish it was summer. But then I'd probably complain about it being too hot," I grumbled, gazing out of our hotel room Sunday night.

"It would be nice to be here," he agreed, reading through a travel brochure. "But then would you want to come back in summer?"

"No. I'd love to, but no." I sat beside him on the bed. "We're only here for three days, so we'd better get an early night so we can shop, shop, shop tomorrow." I picked up a town brochure. "Anything you want to see?"

"There is, but not in the brochure." He threw them

on the floor and grabbed me, planting his lips firmly on mine.

*****

We did the touristy thing on Monday, and after a nice meal at the local restaurant decided to hit a club that night, showering and walking to the local bar that housed the town's best DJ. Sure, the music was too loud and the place too dark, but I wanted to dance, so pulling Callum into the throng I started gyrating. He wasn't much of a club dancer, but got his groove on long enough to enjoy himself.

"Ladies and gentlemen, we have a special guest in the club tonight. Actor and singer, Michaelangelo Telltorro…"

A dark-haired good looking young Latino guy walked up beside the DJ and waved.

"Bah, never heard of him," Callum mumbled.

I shrugged. "Neither have I."

"So, Michaelangelo, tell us, are you here with anyone special," the DJ went on.

Michaelangelo grinned shyly, waved a hand at the crowd and said, "I'm just here with a few friends."

"But Michaelangelo," the DJ riled the crowd, "surely you must know we've all heard of your wildly passionate affair. Jewels is a very popular author."

The crowd cheered.

"What!" I frowned.

"Well," Michaelangelo said quietly, "I prefer not to kiss and tell."

There were catcalls and wolf whistles.

"What's this not kissing and telling?" the DJ mocked. "You've been telling everyone you and Jewels Diva are having an affair. Surely she's here with you now. Come on, don't go quiet on us."

"Yeah," someone in the crowd yelled.

"What!" I spat as Callum and I looked at each other.

"I prefer to not talk about it tonight. I'm just here to lay down a few tracks."

"But surely—" the DJ started before Michaelangelo said something in his ear. The DJ relented, and Michaelangelo started playing a song.

"What the fuck?" I stuttered, wanting to kill the little bastard.

"Don't worry about it," Callum said, rubbing my back. "Just take a few breaths and let's keep dancing."

Callum and I danced awhile longer, and we watched Michaelangelo as he played a few more songs before walking off to party with friends. I decided to take that time to go freshen up. "I need to pee, back soon." I wandered off toward a hallway and found the ladies. After doing my business, I came back into the hall, and as I adjusted my clothes, I saw something from the corner of my eye. It was Michaelangelo at the other end with a hot young guy; they were laughing and talking and slipping down another hallway.

I stood there, my interest piqued. Part of me wanted to go back to Callum. The other wanted to follow. Suspicion won out, and I quickly trotted down the hall. Turning the corner, I walked along to the end and could only turn left. I sneaked along. It was darker, with the light barely penetrating. I heard moans and groans.

I tiptoed to the end and peeked through a half-open door.

OH, HELLOOOO!

Michaelangelo and his friend had their shirts undone, and their tongues down each other's throats.

I quickly whipped out my phone and hit the record video button. I was gonna get this baby for all it was worth.

"Oh, Michaelangelo," the guy against the wall groaned.

Their hands pushed down pants and pulled out penises, rubbing theirs against each other's, hands all over genitals.

"Suck me!" Michaelangelo demanded. "Get down on your knees and suck me!" He grabbed the young man's head and pushed him to the floor.

The man's mouth greedily sucked his idol's dick.

Michaelangelo held the man's head there, his left hand leaning on the wall. He groaned his pleasure.

The man's head bobbed faster and faster.

"Taste it, taste it," Michaelangelo hissed, thrusting his hips back and forth. He grunted in time with the bobs and thrusts, then wrenched the man up and spun him around, pushing him to the wall. The man's pants went down, and Michaelangelo went in.

The young man squealed.

Michaelangelo held onto the man's penis, hands, hips, everything going back and forth in quick successive motions.

With a few heaving grunts and thrusts, they were done.

Michaelangelo pulled his dick out and his pants up.

"Oh, no, let me do it to you," the young man said, quickly grabbing at them.

"No!" His hands were shoved away. "Michaelangelo does the fucking. Not the being fucked." He buttoned his shirt. "Easier not to catch AIDS that way."

"But Michael…" the young man pleaded.

"No! I am done!"

I ran for it, hearing heavy footsteps behind me, and made my way into the club to find Callum standing just inside the hallway.

"I was beginning to think you were sick…" I grabbed his hand and pulled him along. "Hey," he protested as we slipped outside.

"Let's go," I said and hailed a cab. Getting back to our hotel in record time, and after locking the door and closing the curtains tight, I showed him the footage.

His eyebrows hit his hairline. "Fuck!"

"Oh, they certainly did." I paced around the room.

He gave me my phone. "What are you going to do with it?"

I kept pacing, sending the video to several email addresses. I shrugged. "Don't know. Keep it. Use it. Who knows? But I have a very strong feeling this baby's going to come in very, very handy."

*****

We flew back to Greece and then Rome on Wednesday in preparation for taking the Orient Express back to Paris on Thursday, rolling into London late Sunday afternoon.

I'd phoned ahead, and Bob and Linda met us at the station.

"Oh, my God, you've been gone so long." Linda hugged us both. "You can tell us all about it on the way home."

So we did, and were still going when we walked into the house around eight.

"And then I whipped out my phone and filmed the whole thing." I sat on the couch in the lounge room.

Bob shook his head. "That little scuzzbag" – seems Bob had picked up some of my Aussie slang – "has been bleating on for the last few weeks that he's been having a hot steamy affair with you all over Europe. That you're hard and fast lovers who fell in love the moment you saw each other across a dance floor, and it's still going strong. Love at first sight and all that bloody crap."

"What?" Callum and I both exclaimed. It was worse than we'd thought.

"Well," he corrected. "With Jewels."

"But…" I frowned and looked at Callum. "That little bastard. I'm gonna kill him."

"No, you won't," he said, "because I am." His lips pursed in anger.

I sighed. "Well…no…" An evil thought came to mind. "I'm going to humiliate, embarrass, and annihilate the little turd." I rubbed my hands together.

"Bobby, let's plan revenge."

"Before we do that, there's some awards ceremony this week, and the producers want you there."

"What day?"

"Thursday."

"That's fine. Who else will be there?"

"Just about everyone that was there New Year's night. We've been collecting all the newspaper clippings and recorded TV shows that have mentioned what you did, and the amount of invites that have flooded in. Simon Cowell wants you to do a cd. Producers want you on their shows. TV hosts want interviews with you."

"Ah, bugger them," I said with a wave of my hand. "We'll go over it tomorrow, and then Callum and I will celebrate Valentine's Day by locking ourselves in our room, and then we'll get ready for Thursday." I rubbed my hands together again. "And revenge!"

*****

I went through everything the next morning, and then Linda led me to the spare room on the first floor.

"All of this is yours." Her arms swept out.

"Bloody hell." I stopped in shock. "I could *not* have bought all of this?"

"Oh, you did. As everything came in, I packed them into piles so they'd be easier for the movers when they came to pack and ship everything.

"Shit." I shook my head at the waist-high piles, boxes, bags of clothes, shoes, accessories, not to mention all the stuff I'd bought before Christmas. The couch, the coffee table, the side tables were all covered. "This is going to cost a lot to ship home. Bugger! And then there's Callum's stuff as well."

Later that day I got my dress ready for the TV awards, and downloaded the video to a small flash drive. I left a copy on my laptop just in case I wanted to upload it to my blog or YouTube.

*****

On Tuesday, Valentine's Day, Callum and I stayed locked in our bedroom, not even bothering to get out of bed. And you can guess what we did, so there's no need to tell you.

*****

On Wednesday, I did a lot of packing and then chatted with the producer of the TV awards.

"We want you to present best love scene in a TV show or movie with Michaelangelo Telltorro, since the two of you have been hot and heavy the last six weeks," Caitlin Ryan said.

My eyebrows flew up in amusement. "Really? Has it been six weeks?" I mused. "It still seems like it hasn't even started."

"Yes, well, it must be so exciting? You're a lotto winning wounded heroine lifesaver, and he's the up and coming hot, good looking actor singer."

"Mmm," I murmured. "You should see the footage

I've got of the up and comer. It would not only blow your mind but possibly get you the best ratings ever."

"Really?" She was so intrigued.

"Really," I replied. "You haven't let out that I'm going to be on the show, have you? We should keep it as a surprise for Michaelangelo. He doesn't know I'm going to be there, so don't tell him. Let's surprise him."

"Oh, good idea," she agreed. "We'll keep it to ourselves."

"You'd better. Or you don't get the footage, so you don't get the ratings."

Discussing the details, I demanded a privacy agreement. I was going to sneak in through a back door and hide somewhere before joining Michaelangelo on stage. We had it planned down to a T, and she was going to meet me and take me in. No one would know, especially the bastard I was seeking revenge on, and boy was he going to get it. He was going to get it so bad his career would end, and I'd make sure he paid. Paid for all the ugly revolting lies and rumours he'd spread. Spread about me. Oh, no. There was *no way* in hell he was going to get away with that!

Chapter 32

Our plans changed a little on Thursday because Callum collected his mail from the post office and found an invitation to the same function I was going to. It seems after saving me, when I saved the woman and child, and then helping to save all the celebs on New Year's Eve, he'd become a bit of a celebrity himself. As we talked it over, we realised we could do a little bit of a switcheroo on everyone, so called Megan to the house and filled her in on the plan. She agreed, as long as she wasn't caught out.

"Don't worry, you won't be," I assured her as I pulled my brown wig on. "Here, pull Jewels' wig on, and we'll see how you look." She pulled on my red wig, and I nodded. "Don't say much. Don't talk to many people and they won't know."

She sighed. "I suppose I could pull it off."

"Of course you can." I gave her a dress to wear. "Go change into this, and I'll get ready." She walked into the bathroom, and I pulled out the snug red glitter dress with a high neck, long sleeves and a soft train behind it.

"Nice," Callum said with a hungry look in his eyes as he buttoned his shirt.

I grinned and pinned my hair with a few clips, then slipped on some jewellery. I took red sparkly shoes from the wardrobe, grabbed the dress Jewels would wear on stage, and placed it in a garment bag with matching shoes and jewellery.

Megan came out of the bathroom. "Well?"

Linda walked in. "Stand side by side." We did. "Mmm, same height, slightly different build, but with the right make-up you could pass as each other."

"Right then, let's put our make-up on," I said, and we got to work. A half hour later, with shading and the right foundation, we could pass for the same person. "Okay." I picked up a cape. "Wear this." I put it around her shoulders. "Add this turban and those glasses, and don't take them off until I get to your dressing room."

"I won't," she said, taking Jewels' invitation.

"We'll try to get there as soon as you do, and after walking the carpet, we'll get inside and head for your room. I've already called ahead and stated that my assistants will be coming to help me." I clapped my hands. "Okay, let's get our things and be on our way."

Callum held out my red velvet, sleeveless, open floor-length jacket, and I slipped into it before giving Megan the dress bag.

After waving goodbye to "Jewels", we piled into a limo ourselves. Bob and Linda were also invited since they were the publishers.

Rolling into the centre of London, we joined the queue for the celebrity arrivals, taking fifteen minutes to stop at the red carpet and have our door opened.

Callum stepped out then helped me, and Bob and Linda came next. The crowd went wild.

They didn't know who we were, but then I had a feeling they went wild for everyone.

Flashlights popped. People screamed. We were ushered along slowly to each section on the carpet so photographers could get their happy snaps.

Callum sighed and looked irritated.

"Guess this isn't your thing then," I murmured with a sly grin.

He gave me a filthy look. "No," he said dryly. I giggled, and we kept moving. "Bet they're all wondering who *you* are," he said as we stood still again.

I snorted. "Yeah, and like they all know who *you* are."

Finally making it inside, we found ourselves in a sea of celebrities. The huge lobby was elegantly dressed in red and gold with crystal chandeliers and a huge staircase leading up to the theatre.

Slowly winding our way through the crowd, I saw Sam, Chris and Alex watching Michaelangelo Telltorro giving an interview surrounded by photographers and reporters. I walked up behind them as Christopher, Dominic and Andrew joined them.

"Michaelangelo, is it true you and our resident heroine, Jewels Diva, are an item? That you got hot and steamy on holiday recently?" one reporter called out.

He laughed softly and fingered his jacket button. "Well, Jewels and I, we…"

"Are having a hot affair on the beaches of Ibiza?" another said.

"Please, please, Jewels would not want me to say anything. She wanted to keep our hot steamy love affair a secret so no one would find us."

"But you were recently in Mykonos. Was Jewels with you? No one saw her."

"Yes. I was in Mykonos, and yes Jewels was with me. But she wanted to stay out of the spotlight, so we didn't have any extra attention."

"So, you and Jewels are having a full-blown affair? Are you an item? A couple? Will you be going to Australia with her, or will she move here for love?"

Michaelangelo laughed. "Ladies, gentlemen, please. What is between Jewels and me is purely a full-blown sexually lustful affair. Sex and nothing *but* sex. She is a wild animal in bed. Her sex drive is insatiable, and so is mine. I match her every move. I—" A man tapped him on the shoulder. "Please, I must go now. Thank you and goodbye."

"God that dog makes me sick," Chris said. "I'm gonna ring Jewels. She needs to know what he's been saying."

I grabbed his arm. "She already does," I said softly.

He recognised me in my natural state and noticed Callum, Bob, and Linda behind me. "I can't believe that fucking arsehole said those things," he went on as we watched Michaelangelo's retreating back.

"Don't worry," I said. "Revenge is planned, and it will be explosively hilarious. So don't go anywhere. It will happen about, ah, halfway through." A sly grin slid over my lips. "Make sure you've got your cameras rolling and check my blog for all the entertainment." I let his arm go. "Boys, see you all later." We walked off, heading backstage to the room Jewels was securely and secretively secluded away in.

After getting through countless security guards, we finally made it to the room. I knocked, and Jewels let us in.

"Oh, thank God, you're here," Megan said. "I've been panicking that something was going to happen and someone would find out I'm not really Jewels." She slipped out of the red dress and pulled off the wig.

I changed into the dress I would be wearing as Jewels, and Megan pulled on the one I was just wearing. I gave her my wig and pulled on my red one. With a few adjustments, I was now Jewels, and Megan was Tamara.

"Fantastic," Linda said, studying us both.

"Are you staying?" I asked Callum.

"I want to, for you. But I'm not interested in the ceremony."

"Well, you and your wife," I pointed at Megan, "Can leave. You can drop her off and go home. I'll call to let you know what's happening."

He nodded. "Okay."

"I'll go too," Bob said. "This isn't my cup of tea either."

"Bob, are you sure?" Linda asked. "That will be just Jewels and myself."

"Well," he whined. "There's no need for me to be here. You two girls go and enjoy yourselves, and I'll get Callum and his wife home."

"Hey," I snapped at Bob and then pointed at Megan.

"That don't mean you get the same privileges."

She giggled, and Callum rolled his eyes. They left, and five minutes later there was a knock at the door. It was Caitlin Ryan, the producer I'd spoken to on the phone.

"Okay, hey there. How are you doing? It will be some wait for the award presentation, and I was wondering what you've got for me?"

"Oh, I've got something explosive," I said. "Tell me how that award is going to go."

She detailed everything. Michaelangelo coming out on stage, reading the nominees, then presenting to the winners. "We did tell him if he felt like mentioning you he could since the two of you have been hot and steamy."

"After the nominees are announced he can say something," I said. "And then you can show a pre-recorded snippet of me talking about him and then the footage I have, and then when everyone's surprised, I'll come out on stage and see him. We'll need to pre-record something. Can we do that in utmost privacy without anyone knowing?"

"Um." She thought. "We could. I could get a Handycam down here and record something, then put it together with whatever footage you've got then play that."

"Great. Can you go arrange that for me?"

"Sure." She left, and Linda and I sat down and watched the beginning of the awards show. Half an hour later, Caitlin was back with a video camera.

"This is the exact thing you need to suggest to him

that he can say. It's nothing overboard, just mention it is the only appropriate thing he *can* say that won't get him cut out of the show. His ego will make him do it. The recording will be my reply," I told her.

She took the paper and glanced at it in surprise. "Oh. Okay." After setting up the camera, she gave me the signal. I began talking and lasted about thirty seconds. When I'd finished, Caitlin just stared. "What do you have on him?"

"I have two minutes of footage for you to show. The rest will be on my website the minute it airs. I need you to add the footage onto the end of what I recorded and play it after he says what you tell him to. When the footage ends, I'll walk out from backstage and take over presenting the award." I stood in front of her to drive the point home. "You *have* to do this *exactly* as I tell you, so the timing is perfect. Now, is there a production room we can go hide in while you cut it together?"

Shaking her head at the bizarre nature of it all, she said, "Um, yes. There is. Let's go." Linda and I followed her upstairs, through hallways, and into a small room full of computers. "Here. I can put it together here." Caitlin loaded the recording, and then I handed her the small flash drive. She plugged it in and watched it with wide eyes, and her jaw dropped. After it finished, she turned to me, the same look on her face. "*Oh. My. God.* This is explosive."

"It's what the little bastard deserves for lying about me," I said simply.

She added the footage together and burned it onto a

disc. "Fifteen minutes till he's on stage. He'll be backstage in five. Hang on to this till I get back." She took off, and we were able to watch the show on the monitors.

One camera scanned the crowd, and I saw Chris anxiously check his watch then pull his phone out and send a text.

Beep beep. Beep beep.

I checked my phone, and it was him. '*What the bloody hell is going on and when's it happening?*'

'*Soon, within fifteen minutes. P.S. I can see you,*' I texted.

The camera scanned back, and I saw him read it then look around trying to find me.

'*On camera,*' I texted.

He got it and waved at the camera with a huge grin.

Caitlin came back in. "I told him exactly what to say. Let's get you out of here." She led us to the control room hanging on tight to the disc. "Stacey, can you escort Jewels down to the backstage area? Make sure she doesn't run into Michaelangelo. It's a surprise for him."

"Uh." Stacey looked shocked at the sight of me and Caitlin's words. "Um, okay."

I followed her down hallways and stairs to an area at the side of backstage, narrowly missing running into Michaelangelo as he blew past me with several people. I hid behind a curtain, straining to keep an eye on him, so he didn't see me. The timing had to be perfect.

"Ladies and gentlemen, to present the next award for best love scene in a TV show or movie is the young, hot, up and coming actor and singer, Michaelangelo Telltorro."

I saw him strut out on the stage. "Thank you, thank you, ladies and gentlemen. I'm here to announce best love scene, and the nominees are…Michael and Zara for *Gateway*. Richard and Vanessa for *Breakthrough*. Montalban and Sarah for *Love Never Dies*. Gavin and Anna for *Murder in Daytime*. And Andreas and Bianca for *The Heights of Love*. The crowd cheered. "Personally…" He laughed. "I think there is one missing. Michaelangelo Telltorro and Jewels Diva for *A European Affair*." There was applause and cheering. "I know everyone has read about our steamy story. And yes, it is true."

"True my arse, you lying arsehole," I muttered behind the curtain.

"Is that so, Michaelangelo?" I heard myself say on the footage I recorded half an hour earlier. "We've had a steamy hot love affair all across Europe? Full of sex and more sex." I wagged my finger. "You lying little arsehole. Telling people all about my sex drive. Something you would know absolutely *nothing* about." I leaned toward the camera. "Especially since it wasn't *me* you were fucking all over Europe." I heard the footage.

"Suck me. Get down on your knees and suck me."

The crowd went dead silent.

I heard the grunts and groans of Michaelangelo in heat, then the young man say, *"Oh, no, let me do it."*

"No. Michaelangelo does the fucking, not the being fucked. Easier not to catch AIDS that way."

"What the hell is going on?" his manager yelled a few feet from my hiding place.

"Revenge," I spat at his shocked face, stepping past him and onto the stage. Floating over in my red velvet and jewel encrusted gown, I walked up to Michaelangelo. He just stared at me, totally humiliated.

"That's what you get for lying about me," I hissed. The crowd didn't move. "Lie about me, and I get my revenge." Tears rolled down his cheeks. "You'll be hearing from my lawyer about slander and defamation." I snatched the winner's envelope from his hand. "Get off stage. Get out of England, and *never.*" I stepped closer. "*Never* talk about me ever again. *Or, I, will, hurt you.*" My top lip sneered at him.

The manager ran out at the same time he ran backstage.

No one made a sound.

I took a deep breath and stepped up to the mic. "Ladies and gentlemen. Michaelangelo is a man fucker. And a lying one at that. Learn the lesson. You fuck with me and my reputation, and I cut your dick off." I glanced around. "And if you want to see the full video head to my website, Facebook, Tumblr or YouTube pages, and there's a link on Twitter." I brandished the envelope. "Now, the winner of the best love scene in a TV show or movie is…Gavin and Anna for *Murder in Daytime.*"

There was half-hearted applause from one end of the room. "Oh, for fuck's sake people, *clap!*" The sound grew louder, and Gavin and Anna came up to accept their award.

I went backstage and Stacey, in a very shocked state, led me back to the control room where Caitlin and Linda were waiting. "How'd it look?" I asked.

Linda shook her head. "You reduced that poor boy to tears."

"Poor boy, my arse," I snorted. "The bastard has been spreading stories about me for six weeks. Jumping on my stardom, using my name to get publicity. Fuck him," I spat. "Oh, wait. That guy already did."

An hour later we walked into the after party and found Chris. "Well?" I asked.

He exploded into laughter. "I can't believe you did that. Where did you get that footage?"

"A little present from Callum's wife," I said with a wink.

"So that footage was for real then?" Christopher asked.

"Oh, it certainly was. How could it not be with those last two lines he said?"

"He's been getting around Europe using you to help him get publicity. What did he expect you were going to do?" Sam asked.

"Exactly! Who the fuck was he kidding? If his manager told him to do it, then I'm suing that bastard too. All I called him was a man fucker and showed footage of him fucking some guy. Yet he completely lied about me. I'm suing both of them, and as for him crying on stage, oh, puh-leeze; he'd better not get a career out of this."

"You'll have the gays on your back for this," Linda said.

"Well, fuck them too," I said. "Oh, wait, they

already have been. He slandered me. I told and showed the truth about him. We'll soon see who's in the right."

Mingling for an hour or so we joked and laughed. A few people shunned me, but it didn't matter. I was going home on the weekend, and I'd never see those people ever again. I pulled Chris aside to say goodbye.

"We're heading home. I've got my last doctor's appointment tomorrow, I have to get everything I've bought packed and shipped over, and then we're leaving Sunday, so I better say thank you and goodbye now."

"Oh, you don't have to," he said, giving me a big hug.

"I do. Being on your show gave me other opportunities, and we know what they led to. Hello, New Year's."

He laughed. "Where you saved our lives and nearly lost yours. Again."

"Yeah." I laughed. "I really need to stop doing that, don't I?"

"What's this, you're leaving then?" Christopher came up with the others.

"Yes, we are. Leaving the party now, and England on Sunday."

"Well, I need a hug then," he said, grabbing me before I could complain.

I screwed my face up and looked at the others. "Really? Seriously? You can let go now," I said. "Let. Go." I pushed him away then hugged and kissed the others. "Oh, hello, my sexy scruffy stud muffin," I told Dom. "Now, if anyone had the right to start a rumour, it was you."

"Well, thanks to your impromptu New Year's kiss, I've had hundreds of people want to know what it was like."

"What! Only hundreds," I deadpanned, getting a laugh from everyone. "Well, gotta go. Bye." Linda and I headed for the door.

"Wait. I'll leave too and walk you out," Chris said.

"So will I."

"Same here."

"Yeah, it's time to leave."

We walked arm in arm out the door, and into the frenzied media pack waiting just for me and my story on Michaelangelo Telltorro.

Chapter 33

"Well, Ms Diva, you are now free to fly home to Australia," the doctor at the hospital said. He'd been a pain in my arse since day one of my accident, and then telling me I'd tried committing suicide was appalling, then there was my six week check-up, and now I had to put up with him again. But fortunately, for the last time.

"Yeah, well, I flew a week ago, so I already knew that."

He gave me a sour look.

"Can I go now? I'm done with you."

He ripped a certificate from a pad. "Here. Tell your doctors back home. And try not to OD on any more pills."

"Fuck off, arsehole." I gave him the finger and walked out the door.

It was Friday. And I had two days left. So, between finishing up my manuscript and printing it out, I directed the moving company to the room where our stuff was. Linda helped, and with a team of twenty people, the company got it all done in one day.

It was six o' five when I printed out the last page and placed it on top of the others in the box which I presented to Bob. "Here you go. An eight hundred and ninety-eight page manuscript."

He took it and stared. "Thank you so much, I'll get through it and let you know if it needs changes."

"It won't," I interjected.

He gently put it aside like it was a Willy Wonka golden ticket, then we chatted over dinner.

"We have to pack our own stuff tomorrow and get it ready for flying home," I said between mouthfuls of roast chicken.

"We can do it tonight," Callum suggested. "And do something special tomorrow."

"Actually." Bob and Linda glanced at each other. "We were going to take you out for lunch tomorrow," Linda said.

"How about one last tour of the city," Bob added. "We can go in a limo."

I shrugged. "Sounds good."

"A toast." Bob raised his glass. "To Jewels, Tamara and Callum. May your health be healthy. May your life stay happy. And may your book sell millions of copies."

We laughed and dinged glasses.

After dinner, Callum packed his stuff, and I made one last blog post.

My Adventures in Merry Old England: February 17th, 2012

Hey, peeps, it's Friday, and in two days I leave dreary old England.

FOR. EV. AH!!!!!

I don't plan on ever coming back. After the time I've had, why the hell would I? I've been hit by a car once. Flung into a river twice. Drowned twice. Died twice. Been rescued by Sergeant Stone twice, and attended his wedding to my good friend. I've been on two holidays. On a comedy show. Done a New Year's Eve concert, and a TV awards show where I outed a gay arsehole that spread lies and rumours about me. That was some footage, wasn't it? It's just sitting here next to all of the other footage. My New Year's show, the club arrest, even the original accident. My laptop is full peeps. Full of interesting, never to be seen again, footage. Tomorrow's a last tour of the city, and Sunday is a flight home. So, until next time, peeps, I'm off.

Jewels xxoo

I hit publish, turned off, unplugged, and packed up, then grabbed my list and checked off all the extras I'd bought before starting on my case. It took an hour, and I left a few things out for the next couple of days. After packing, Callum and I lay in bed in each other's arms.

"We go home day after tomorrow," I said, my fingers sliding through his chest hair.

"Yeah." A pause. "Home."

I sat up and looked at him. "You okay?"

He took a breath, and slowly shook his head at every thought. "No. I'm…moving to another country. I…I don't know what to think, what to say, what to feel."

"Feel excited. Happy. Floating on air." *I* was feeling concerned.

He grinned. "I am. I am it's just, new wife, new life, new country, and you don't know where you want to live. So, I just have to stick it out and enjoy the ride."

I matched his grin. "Don't worry. It's a ride you'll definitely enjoy."

*****

"Okay, so you guys go spend a couple of hours together, and then you can meet us at the restaurant at twelve. How's that?" Linda asked the next morning.

I sipped my juice. "Sounds good. That gives us three and a half hours," I told Callum.

"For what?" he asked.

"To do whatever." I ruffled his hair. "Show me *your* London. Then we'll meet up for lunch." I turned to Linda. "Which restaurant?"

"Bartelli's. On the river."

"Oh, God." I groaned. "*The bloody river!* I need to stay away from the bloody thing."

She laughed lightly. "It overlooks but isn't near. You'll be safe."

I grinned. "I'd better be." Tidying up, we grabbed our coats. "Okay, husband. Exactly *where* do you plan on taking me?"

Callum grabbed his car keys. "You'll see." After driving for half an hour, we pulled up outside a hospital.

"I really don't need to see another one of these," I said with a scowl.

He grinned. "This isn't for you. It's where I was born."

"Ohhh. You're taking me on a tour of your life."

"I certainly am." The grin widened, and he pointed. "Maternity ward, third floor. Nine pounds, eight ounces."

"Bighead. I feel sorry for your mother." I cast a glance at him and tried not to laugh.

"Nice," he said, driving off to another suburb and stopping in front of a house. "I was brought home from the hospital to this house. We lived here for ten years. I used to play in the street with my brother and the neighbourhood boys."

I gazed from the house to the street.

He drove on, pulling in front of the local school. "Primary school. Years one through five. I made friends, and I beat up kids. I was tall for my age, and liked to push the other kids around."

"Nothing's changed I see." I wiggled my eyebrows.

"Cute." He drove to another suburb. "Lived here from eleven to twenty-one. Went to the local high school and started at Uni. There's the high school there." I looked at the sprawling structures just down from the house. "Joined the force after a couple of years of University. Later went back and got my law degree."

"Smartarse," I mumbled.

He showed me the Uni, Police Academy, and several hotspots around town where he played the hero or arrested people in big stings.

"Speaking of playing the hero…there's someplace I want to go before we go home."

"Where?"

"Back to the river where it all began."

Shock rolled over his face. "You…want to…to where you were hit, and you drowned?"

I frowned. "I need to put the last of the demons to bed."

He sat staring thoughtfully at me before finally saying, "Okay." Driving to the road alongside the river, we got out and walked over to where I'd been hit.

I stood there, trying to calculate exactly where I'd been standing, and found a small blob of dried blood on the corner of the river wall. I knelt down and touched it. It was my blood. Where my face had smashed into. Where I'd fallen into the filthy vile cesspool called the Thames. I sat back and stared into the water where I'd landed. The water where the car had been. They'd managed to haul it out. I tried to pinpoint exactly where the car was, but couldn't. I saw the wall stairs and dock and ran down to find more blood. I looked across the water but still couldn't pinpoint the spot. I jumped. Callum had touched my shoulder.

"You okay?'

I nodded. "You?"

"It's weird," he said. "Everything that happened, it was all so quick. So obscenely bizarre. And now, a lifetime ago."

I nodded again. "Yeah. A lifetime ago." I touched my face. The swelling was gone, and the bruises were faded yellow. My hair was growing out, and I was feeling good. Now…it was all over. "Let's go."

We walked up the stairs and over to the car where I sat staring out the window.

"You okay?" Callum squeezed my hand.

I sighed. "Yeah. Can we drive to the club? I want to see what happened."

"You sure?"

I nodded. "Yeah."

Driving along the river and over a bridge till we came opposite the club, we saw that the debris had been cleared, and so had the rest of the building.

"They had to demolish the rest of it," Callum said. "It was just too bad to build again, so they pulled it down."

I stared at the big open space that had been the spot for my New Year's concert. Thank God we got the show on disc. Otherwise, there'd be nothing. Nothing at all of my work. I stared into the water. "Did they clear out the river as well? Beside the staircase and rubble, there would have been a lot of glass in the water. Would've wreaked havoc on boat motors."

"They did. Took them about two weeks." He looked at his watch. "It's almost twelve. We'd better get to lunch."

At the restaurant, we easily found a park, and I wandered over to the walking path that ran along the river and gazed out at the sights and sounds of London.

"It's our last day." Callum stood beside me. "Your last day after three months. My last day after forty years. Our last day as husband and wife."

I smiled and wrapped my arms around him. "How

about we just take a walk. Bob and Linda have a party planned, and unless you don't mind spending the rest of the day with your family, I say we sneak off now and leave them to it."

"Another one of your death visions?" He grinned.

"Nope." I pointed to the car park. "Your brothers', your sisters', Bob and Linda's, and I think that one's your parents."

He glanced at the plates. "So they are Miss Nancy Drew. Very observant of you."

"Mmm." I kissed him. "Make that Mrs Tamara Stone."

He grinned and kissed me back. "Mrs Stone. My wife. My life partner."

"For what life is, since men only average to their eighties, so already you only have half your lifetime left while I get at least another twenty years on top of that," I mused.

"O-kayyy." He laughed and shook his head. "Wherever that came from? Ready to spend our life together?"

"Ready to spend it in another country?"

"Ready to go wherever whenever for the love of my beautiful wife!"

My eyes teared. "Aw. I love you."

"I love you, too." His lips gently pressed to mine. "Ready to go inside and face the crowd?"

"God no!" I threw my head back in protest.

"Come on, stop whining." He led me back to the restaurant, up the ramp, and through the double glass doors.

"Here's to Tamara and Callum," Bob and Linda yelled, raising their glasses.

We stared in astonishment. Besides Callum's parents, brother, sister and their partners, there was Chris, Christopher, Sam, Alex, Andrew and Dominic.

A banner reading *Goodbye and Best Wishes Tamara and Callum* hung across the far wall. Streamers and balloons crisscrossed from the ceiling, and there were several tables pushed together to form a buffet.

Glancing at each other, we walked over and pulled off our coats.

"Hey," I stuttered, completely surprised by the people attending. Callum's family surrounded him, while Bob, Linda and the boys mobbed me. "Hey, hey, thanks for coming." I hugged each of the boys. "Hey," I said to Linda. "Could've told me."

"That would've ruined the surprise. Let's make a toast," she called.

Callum and I got glasses of Pepsi Max from a waiter and waited while everyone calmed down.

"Okay, everyone." She dinged her glass. "We are here to wish Tamara and Callum good luck and safe journey back to their new home in Australia. May your flight be safe, may your life together be happy, and may your future be filled with adventure."

"Hear, hear."

"How come you guys were late getting here?" Melissa asked. "We expected you right on the dot of twelve. It's not like you to be late, big brother."

"We…ah were driving around. I showed Tam our old houses and schools."

"Oh, God, you didn't?" Liam said. "You bored her with that? I didn't even do that to Leslie."

She grinned. "No, he didn't. Not that I would've minded."

I shrugged. "I didn't mind. It was nice to see, but we weren't late because of that. We, ah, stopped by the river where Jewels was hit." Everyone stared. "Her blood's still there you know." I slipped a glance at the boys.

"Why would you go there?" Janice asked.

"Her blood's still there?" Christopher said. The boys had strange expressions, for they knew what had happened.

"I know Jewels," I told Janice. "We came over together, and she's the reason I met Callum." I smiled up at him. "And yeah." I turned to Christopher. "Blood's still there on the corner of the wall." I paused. "Where she smashed her face in." Another pause. "There's blood on the dock too, where Callum pulled her out and resuscitated her."

"Oh, that's such a strange story," Melissa said. "The poor thing comes over here for an opportunity, and she gets hit by a car and drowns."

"Yeah, but big bro was there to save her." Liam pounded Callum on the shoulder. "The big superhero who's always around to save a damsel in distress."

"Not to mention she then won lotto," Leslie added. "Talk about lucky."

"We also drove past the club that collapsed," I butted in. "It's all gone now." I felt a bit sad that so much of my recent past was gone.

"Yeah, they demolished that end of January," Chris said. "The cops were quick to determine structural damage and condemned the building. The owner has been fined millions for lack of safety and not abiding by the law."

"He's just lucky we're not *all* suing," Alex added.

"Were you at the concert, Tamara?" Janice asked. "Callum and this Jewels girl were all over the news. Especially when he saved her again."

"Regular hero, our bro." Liam punched Callum again.

"Stop hitting me, or I'll punch you twice as hard," Callum growled.

"Boys," Andrew Stone injected authoritatively. His tone was enough to stop them, and they gave him sheepish looks of apology.

I laughed under my breath. "Um, yeah I was. Backstage, helping with costumes. I went home with Bob and Linda." I glanced at them with a neutral expression. "Told Callum to stay and play the Big Hero."

"That's my boy," Andrew said, clearly so proud of his son.

"Weren't you boys there as well at the New Year's Eve show?" Melissa asked.

"Yeah, we were," Chris replied. "Helped out a bit. I even took the footage that Jewels put on her blog."

"Oh, my, God. What was it like?" Leslie asked.

"Kinda scary," Andrew Lancel said. "We all got hustled out and stood around waiting, and then bang the building falls apart."

"Freaky is what it was," Christopher said, waving

his glass around. "Bloody freaky." He downed his drink. "Anyone for a refill?"

"So, you were filming the whole thing?" Liam asked Chris.

"Yeah. Jewels was a bit shaky, and I offered. Filmed the fireworks, the argument between Callum and Arthur, the club collapse, Jewels' New Year's monologue, her going into the river."

"Again," I said and burst out laughing, then noticed everyone staring.

"That wasn't funny," Callum said with a stern expression.

"No," I gasped and calmed down. "But I saw the footage." I turned to Dominic. "The look on your face when she kissed you! Bahahahaha! That was hilarious!" I bent over and slapped my knee.

"And all over the internet," he drawled.

"He was a bit shocked wan' 'e," Chris said with a grin on his face.

I kept laughing. "That ain't the word for it."

"Glad you think it's so amusing," Dom said, trying to suppress a grin.

"Hey, you enjoyed it," I pointed out.

He thought about it and grinned. "Yeah, I did. And she's a damn good kisser too."

Those of us who were there that night burst out laughing, much to the disappointment of those who didn't know, and Callum who didn't think it was funny.

"Okay, we have no idea what you're going on about," Liam said. "So tell us, when are you going to get your new home?"

"Don't know," Callum replied. "Will have to figure out where we want to live first."

"I just have to pack up all of my stuff back home first, then we can go on a big long holiday, and I will show this guy around *my* country until we find the house we're looking for." I leaned into him and slipped my arm around his waist.

"God, I hope you don't have too much after everything you've bought," Linda added.

I giggled. "I know I've bought a load of stuff, but it will be in storage until it's ready to be shipped to our new house. Wherever that may be."

"Well, wherever it is," Christopher said. "We'd better get an invite for a free two week vacation."

"Get out," Liam argued. "We'll be invited before you lot. We're family after all. We're going to come first, aren't we, bro?" He slapped Callum on the shoulder and got a furious look in return.

"Children," I placated. "If or when we get a house, *none* of you will be invited." I looked at Callum and we burst out laughing.

"Another toast," Linda said. "To Tamara and Callum."

"Tamara and Callum."

"And Jewels," Chris said.

"Wherever she may be," I added, and we laughed again.

About the Author

L.J. has been writing since 2006, when her first of many novels, ***The Road To Vegas,*** was born. In 2016 she created the ***Porn Star Brothers*** series about three sizzlingly hot Australian born Greek Island raised brothers who became the hottest porn stars in '70s America.

L.J. lives in Australia, loves '80s music, disaster movies, and collecting Jackie Collins books as Jackie is her inspiration and mentor.

L.J. Diva is the adult pen name for author Tiara King. You can find more about Tiara on her website; follow her on social media, or visit her publishing house, Royal Star Publishing.

Socials

tiaraking.com.au/ljdiva

royalstarpublishing.com.au

Sign up for *Tiara's* Newsletter...

Make sure you're always in the know and never miss free exclusives, the latest news, book updates, and so much more with newsletters from...

tiaraking.com.au

Or these?

NOVELS

Burning Desires
Anything for You
Falling for London
The Road to Vegas
Hollywood Dreams
The Billionaire's Dirty Little Secret

SHORT STORIES

The Body
The Perfect Plot
The Star of Your Own Crime Scene